# THE HOUSE THAT JACK BUILT

-«««•»»»-

## MURDER IN AMBER

# THE HOUSE THAT JACK BUILT

## MURDER IN AMBER

Colver Harris

**COACHWHIP PUBLICATIONS**
Greenville, Ohio

*The House that Jack Built / Murder in Amber*
© 2020 Coachwhip Publications
*Murder in Amber* © Estate of Colver Harris. Reprinted
    with permission.

*The House that Jack Built* first published 1935
*Murder in Amber* first published 1937 (*Maclean's* serial)

Polly Anne Colver (Harris) Graff (1908-1991)
No claims made on public domain material.
Cover image: Miguna Studio

CoachwhipBooks.com

ISBN 1-61646-497-6
ISBN-13 978-1-61646-497-4

# POLLY ANNE COLVER (HARRIS) GRAFF
## (1908-1991)

Anne Colver was born to William and Pauline Colver in Cleveland, Ohio. (William Byron Colver was chairman of the Federal Trade Commission, 1918-1919, and one of the founders of the Scripps-Howard newspaper chain.) Growing up in Cleveland, St. Paul, and Washington, D.C., she earned her bachelor's degree at Whitman College (Walla Walla, WA). She married, and moved to the northeast, where her husband, Mark Harris, taught English at Williams College (MA). She published her first mystery novel, *Hide and Go Seek,* in 1933. Several more mysteries followed (using the pseudonym Colver Harris) during the 1930s, before she started writing popular historical and biographical fiction, particularly for children, as Anne Colver. Her well-received *Mr. Lincoln's Wife* was the Literary Guild Selection for June 1943. Later titles were co-authored (usually as Polly Anne Graff) with her second husband, Stewart Graff.

# THE HOUSE THAT JACK BUILT

## (1935)

If I live to be a hundred years old, I shall never forget the awful moment when I first caught sight of the house that Jack built. There are a number of reasons why I remember the moment so distinctly. For one thing, it occurred on the second day of my honeymoon. For another thing, the sight of that house, looming huge and dark and lonely on the craggy hill, was such an amazing contrast to the snug white houses which made up the settlement of Witch Harbor.

We had come, Timothy and I, to this little village on the coast of Maine, for three weeks of what we fondly supposed would be a quiet, lazy and utterly unexciting vacation. It would be difficult to imagine a more isolated and peaceful retreat than Witch Harbor—twenty miles from the nearest railroad station—and a million miles, it seemed, from trouble and violence and murder. And yet, before we had even arrived at the little cottage by the shore which we had rented, I had seen the house that Jack built—the great empty house which was to cast its shadow of terror and mystery over our would-be placid days in Witch Harbor.

It was just at sunset when Amos Plunkett's ancient car, carrier of the mail and ourselves, swung off the main highway from Pineboro (the railroad junction) and turned sharp left into a narrow uphill road. The car had scarcely begun its laboring ascent of the steep grade when I, stowed in the back seat with luggage, mail sacks and Timothy, caught sight of the house—its rambling outline silhouetted against the glorious red sky, its windows reflecting the last rays of the dying sun.

I am not at all certain that I can convey the effect of that house. The effect of its brooding loneliness, set high on the hilltop—shut in on three sides by the heavy pine woods, cut off on the far side by a sheer drop of three hundred feet to the rocky shore below. Plainly the house was deserted. It had the unmistakable air of a place long empty and neglected—and yet, as I leaned out of the car to look, I had an instant impression that some nameless, brooding mystery still lived within the four dark walls. Something intangible—something sinister and fearful. Involuntarily I gasped and clutched at Timothy's hand.

"What is it, Skeesix?" Timothy's voice was reassuring as always.

"N-nothing," I managed a smile, "only that house up there. You don't suppose it's haunted, do you?"

Timothy craned over my shoulder. "It certainly looks it," he agreed cheerfully. "Shall I ask?"

Before I could say no, Amos Plunkett bellowed an answer above the roar of the motor. "That's what folks around here call the house that Jack built," he informed us. "But it ain't haunted." At the peril of our lives, Mr. Plunkett turned clear about to bestow a ponderous wink on Timothy. Then, with half an eye upon the twisting road, he continued to yell over his shoulder. "All this property belongs to Emily Cotton, but she ain't lived in the big house since old Dr. Jack died. She lives in a shore cottage right next to the one you've rented. See there—?" With a

wave of his hand, our guide indicated the group of summer houses which, from the brow of the hill, were now
visible. "Miss Emily owns all the land from the main road
clean out to the point there."

Timothy and I exchanged a glance of surprise. Our
only knowledge of Emily Cotton had been gained from
our correspondence concerning the cottage, but her prim
handwriting and frugal stationery had certainly not indicated that she was such a vast landholder.

"Old Jack left her the property," the Plunkett voice
went on, "along with the big house on the hill, and she
built the summer places the first year after he died."

"Who," I asked, *"was* this old Jack person?"

The effect of my question was alarming. For the second
time disregarding the safety of our lives and limbs, Amos
Plunkett swung around to regard me in astonishment.
"Y'don't *know?*" he demanded.

Meekly I shook my head. "Was he so very famous?"

"Guess he was," Mr. Plunkett faced front again. "We
thought he was just an old doctor fellow that come to live
up here, but the papers made a terrible fuss about him
when he died." Just then the car stopped, with a great
screech of brakes, before the enchanting two-room shack
which was to be ours. "There y'are, folks—just make yourselves at home. Door's unlocked, and Miss Emily'll likely
be over after supper to see that everything's all right."

And for the rest of that evening we were too busy unpacking and settling to give further thought to the subject
of old Dr. Jack and his house. The next morning we were
in the midst of a vast breakfast of scrambled eggs and ba-
con, when someone knocked at our door.

"That," said Timothy, through a bite of toast, "would
probably be Miss Emily Cotton, come to inspect her tenant
turtle-doves."

But it was not. I opened the door to a trio of tow-head-ed children. In the center stood a girl, perhaps fifteen or sixteen, dressed in a faded cotton frock which, scanty as it was, hung loosely over her slight body. She held out a pail of huckleberries for sale, and all three children grinned in an amiable if somewhat toothless way. "They're fifteen cents a quart," the girl said apologetically, "but they're fresh picked."

"Well, I guess we can stand that," Timothy grinned. "Suppose you kids come in and measure us a quart."

The transaction was executed in silence, save for a couple of brief but intense remarks exchanged in whispers by the two smaller boys. Then Timothy escorted the merchant trio to the door. "Come again," he said cordially.

"We will when we can git more berries," the girl glanced up shyly at his great height, "but the best patches are up by old Jack's house and we got to look out Miss Emily don't catch us pickin' 'em."

"Miss Emily wants them for herself, I suppose?" Timothy suggested.

"No she don't," the girl shook her head. "She just don't like anybody to go near the big house, and Ma says we got to mind her. Ma says Miss Emily's crazy, and you've always got to mind what a crazy person says. Ma says old Jack was crazy too, and since he died Miss Emily's afraid his ghost is gonna get her—and that's why she keeps everybody away from the big house."

"Does Miss Emily actually say she's afraid of a ghost?"

"Not her," another scornful shake of the girl's head. "Miss Emily never says anything. That's why she's crazy. Ma says any woman that don't talk is bound to get crazy sooner or later." She shifted the subject suddenly. "You folks are new around here, ain't you? What's your name?"

Timothy told her. "And what's yours?"

"Ruby Turner."

"Well, good-bye, Ruby—come again when you've got more berries." Timothy came back to the table, but after the three Turners had gone I observed that he did not continue his breakfast. He stirred his coffee in silence, and presently I saw him look out of the window toward the house on the hill with a curiously thoughtful expression. In answer to a question from me, Timothy explained. "I was just wondering," he said, "if the Jack person who built the spooky house yonder might've been Dr. Albert Jack of tabloid fame."

"Sorry, but I don't read the tabloids. You'll have to tell me more."

"I'm a little hazy on the details myself," Timothy admitted, "but it was a big case six or seven years ago. I was a mere stripling then, of course, but I remember that this Dr. Jack was a big bug in medicine or psychology—or both—who trekked off to the wilds somewhere to carry on some secret experiment, and when he died there was a big row. His family tried to claim his estate, and some medical society was after his scientific records—and neither of them got to first base. There was a woman mixed up in it, and Dr. Jack left everything to her—secret experiments and all—and she played clam. The whole case got nowhere, and died very dead. It probably has nothing to do with this place here—but I was just thinking of Miss Emily Cotton and wondering if maybe—" his speculations were cut short by a second knock at the door. "Speak of the devil," Timothy murmured.

A moment later I opened the door and found myself face to face with Miss Emily Cotton.

And here I pause, wondering how best to describe the effect of the woman—an effect as curious, as instantaneous, as intangible as had been the effect of the house

that Jack built. Outwardly, there was nothing remarkable
about Miss Cotton. She was a perfect type of New Eng-
land spinster, tall and spare, with a look of considerable
strength in the set of her angular shoulders. Her dress
was plain blue gingham, neat and freshly ironed, and she
wore flat white sneakers on her large feet. Iron gray hair,
brushed back in an uncompromising knot, enhanced the
severity of her features—features undistinguished save
for a broad forehead and clear gray eyes. Surely there was
nothing so strange about Miss Cotton's looks, nor her quiet greeting—and yet there was an air about her I can never
describe—nor quite forget. It was an air of coldness, of
indomitable will, of super-human control. It was as if I
had suddenly come face to face with a woman of iron.

She came in and stayed for a few moment's conventional conversation. "I hope," she observed presently, "that I
didn't disturb you by coming so early. I wanted to be sure
you were quite comfortable." Miss Cotton spoke with a
strong down-east accent which contrasted curiously with
the formal precision of her words—very unlike the casual,
rambling dialect of Amos Plunkett and little Ruby Turner.

"Not at all," I smiled. "We rather expected you last evening when Mr. Plunkett told you we had arrived."

Miss Cotton looked straight at me, but there was no
answering smile on her plain features. "Amos knows quite
well," she said distinctly, "that I never leave my cottage in
the evening. You may imagine that there is a good deal of
bookkeeping to be done in a place as large as this, and since
I am always at home after supper, that is my time to work."

"Yes," said Timothy easily, "I can imagine your evenings must be well occupied." He fetched a box of cigarettes and passed it to our caller in what I supposed to be
a perfunctory gesture, but to my surprise, she accepted

one. It was, somehow, strangely incongruous to see this severely prim country woman with a cigarette between her gnarled fingers.

When, after a few minutes more of casual conversation, Miss Emily took her leave, I turned to Timothy with a smile. "Well," I said, "do you think she was the mysterious Dr. Jack's rustic paramour—or do you think she's just plain crazy like Ruby's ma says?"

"She's certainly *not* crazy, with an eye like that," Timothy shook his head with decision. "She's smart as they make 'em. But beyond that, my pet, I refuse to speculate. This is, after all, a honeymoon—and not an expedition to dig up local mysteries."

"Personally," I said, "I'm darned interested in local lore. And when I married you, my dear Inspector Timothy Fowler of the New York Homicide Squad, I expected to be surrounded by mysteries and murders for the rest of my natural life. So don't swear off your snooping on my account."

"But," Timothy grinned, "there's nothing to snoop about—and there won't be, if we mind our business. So get into your suit, and we'll go for a swim."

"All right," I agreed with enthusiasm. "And from now on I don't care if Miss Cotton is as crazy as a bat, and if the woods are full of gory corpses, and if the old house up there is alive with spooks. *I'm* going to have a good time."

How terribly callous those words of mine seem as I record them now. But I couldn't, after all, foresee their prophetic meaning at the time. A few minutes later we were on our way down the rocky path to the beach—and we encountered neither corpses nor spooks on the way. Little Ruby Turner was the only person we saw—and she was very much alive.

"Listen, Mr. Fowler," she snatched at Timothy's arm with surprising suddenness. "You won't say nothin' about what I told you this morning, will ye? Cause if Ma finds out I been talkin' again, I'll get the dickens—and if Miss Emily knew about it, she'd skin me."

"I hardly think," Timothy's drawl was reassuring, "that you said anything as bad as all that, Ruby. But you needn't worry—I'll never breathe it to a soul."

"Honest?" the girl's tense expression relaxed in a beaming smile. "Gee—*thanks*. Y'see," she leaned forward confidentially, "I just seen Miss Emily, and she said somebody'd been talkin' to you folks. I told her it wan't me— but I don't think she believed me. She said if I told you any more tales, she'd skin me alive—and she would too."

"Forget it, Ruby," I slipped my arm across the child's thin shoulders, "you haven't done anything wrong—and Miss Cotton can't hurt you anyway."

"Ma says she could," her voice dropped to a whisper. "Do you think Miss Emily's a witch?" she demanded.

"Certainly not," Timothy spoke sternly. "Your ma didn't tell you anything as silly as that, did she?"

"Well—n—no," Ruby faltered. "Ma says she can't be a witch because there's no such thing—but she says if there *were* witches, Miss Emily'd surely *be* one."

Later that morning we stretched out on the sand after a swim in the shivery Maine water. Timothy lay on his back and squinted up at the blue sky, and suddenly he spoke out of a long silence.

"What *I'd* like to know," he said, "is what the hell gave Miss Emily Cotton the idea that someone had been talking to us."

$\longrightarrow$ 2 $\longleftarrow$

We had been at Witch Harbor nearly a week before Louise Benson had her scare. During that time Timothy and I had managed, without any particular difficulty, to keep our resolution about not snooping into the past history of the deserted house on the hill, or the present eccentricities of Miss Emily Cotton. Those days slipped by in a lazy and pleasant round of swimming, sunning, boating, eating and sleeping, which we discovered to be the usual routine of the little summer colony.

Miss Cotton's other tenants, the Benson family, Lila and Allen Gilbert, and young Tony Jackson, proved to be pleasant if unexciting neighbors, and we found ourselves drawn into their group activities by the comfortable friendliness with which they welcomed us. Nothing could have more effectively dispelled my early sense of some sinister undercurrent at Witch Harbor than the company of these casual, easy going people. Both the Gilberts and the Bensons had spent several summers in Miss Cotton's colony, and they were apparently unaware of the slightest disturbing element in the atmosphere of the place.

As for Miss Cotton herself, we saw very little of her after the initial call. Beyond a few chance encounters on the path, when she invariably inquired as to our comfort, we were scarcely aware of her presence in the cottage next to ours—and Mrs. Gilbert assured me that Miss Cotton's greatest virtue as a landlady was her ability in keeping out of sight.

"Really," said Lila Gilbert, in her carefully elegant clipped speech, "Miss Emily is a remarkable person. So quiet—such marvelous poise and reserve. I do admire a woman like that, don't you?"

I agreed, since I had learned in the first half hour of conversation with Lila Gilbert that the only possible way of answering any remark she might make was to agree.

"I've known Miss Emily," Lila went on, "for four summers—and yet I've never heard her make one personal remark. I know absolutely nothing more about her than I did the first time I saw her. Don't you think that's quite an ideal way to live, Mrs. Fowler? So utterly adjusted in one's private life that one need never intrude personalities upon other people?"

Again I agreed, but I couldn't help thinking, as I looked at her prettily fragile face, of Mrs. Benson's comment on this particular notion of Lila's.

"Lila's death on privacy," Mrs. Benson had said tartly. "Always talking about living alone with one's self, and rising above personalities. As a matter of fact, Lila Gilbert is the most thoroughly self-centered and selfish woman I know. All that twaddle about being alone is just her way of keeping people away from that precious husband of hers. She's so afraid he might look at another woman that she keeps him shut up in cotton wool, poor soul. And then," Mrs. Benson snorted, "she has the nerve to call it 'spiritual privacy'."

But however misguided might be Lila's opinion of the motive for her own or anyone else's desire for seclusion, the fact remained that Miss Cotton kept herself very effectively out of the picture during those first days in Witch Harbor, a fact upon which Timothy was commenting that Friday morning when Mrs. Benson came over to ask us if we would join the others in a clam-bake supper.

"Those two big boys of mine," she gurgled, "are simply longing for a bit of excitement, so we've engaged the Plunkett boat to take us all to the island for a good old clam-bake. Of course I know that newlyweds want to be alone—" this with a coy glance at Timothy, "but we *do* hope you'll share this one evening with us old fogies?"

"We'd be delighted, Mrs. Benson," Timothy managed a weak smile in response to the arch question. "Wouldn't we, Joanie?"

"Yes, indeed," I chimed in quickly.

"Oh, *lovely,*" Mrs. Benson clasped her hands with enthusiasm, "my boys will be just thrilled when I tell them you'll go. Now don't you give a *thought* to the food—we'll take care of that. Just meet us at the landing at five o'clock. Good-bye." With a final nod and a wave, Mrs. Benson turned away and trotted energetically down the path.

"I can just imagine," Timothy observed drily, "how thrilled her big boys will be to hear that we've accepted."

I smiled at the idea of Mrs. Benson's dour husband and her sulky, silent, young son being thrilled at anything at all. Even then, we knew the family quite well enough to be sure that the original idea of the clam-bake, and all the subsequent work and enthusiasm for it, would of necessity be supplied by Mrs. Benson herself.

"Did you really want to go?" I asked.

"Not particularly," Timothy stirred his coffee. "But why not give the gal a break? Anybody who works as hard as she does to have a good time ought to get a hand."

"I'd really like her," I said, "if only she weren't so *darned* coy."

Timothy nodded sympathetically.

"Still," he said, "you'd probably be coy yourself if you'd lived twenty odd years with that gathering storm of a husband she has. No wonder she even gets romantic about a bloke like me—you just watch her coo over me tonight."

But as it happened, Mrs. Benson was in no condition to coo over anyone that evening. When it was time to go we learned that she had been taken with a violent sick headache, and had given orders for the picnic to proceed without her. I offered, of course, to stay and keep her company, but from her cot in the darkened bedroom she waved away the suggestion indignantly.

"You go right along, dear child, and don't even think of me. Richard will stay, of course, he never *dreams* of leaving me when I have one of these miserable spells." With evident difficulty, Mrs. Benson raised her head from the pillow to gaze fondly at her husband who sat, engrossed in his usual gloom and a magazine, in the opposite corner of the room. "Dear Richard," she went on, "is *so* patient with me. But you children must go on and have a glorious time. I wouldn't have you miss the moonlight sail home for *anything*—you and that sweet husband of yours."

I left her, not without some reluctance, to the doubtful mercies of dear Richard, and went to join the others who were gathered on the landing. The party was in excellent spirits and thanks to the superlative food which had been prepared by Mrs. Benson (probably at the cost of her headache) we did have a splendid time. Even young

Jerry Benson emerged from his customary silence and, in the absence of his parents, played host very adequately. I found, considerably to my surprise, that he was really quite a charming lad when not oppressed by his father's excessive gloom and his mother's excessive cheer. As for Lila Gilbert, she found it impossible to maintain her manner of fragile and cultivated dignity while dismantling a broiled lobster and listening to the nonsensical remarks of Timothy and Tony Jackson—and she so far relaxed her vigilance as to allow her husband all of five minutes uninterrupted conversation with me.

By the time we sailed home across the moonlit bay, we were all in a state of pleasant torpor. Timothy and I, seated in the stern of the little launch, held hands and gazed out over the black water soul fully. Directly ahead of us rose the craggy hill above the shore line, and among the sharply silhouetted pines along the summit we could see the dim outlines of the big deserted house.

"You know," I whispered to Timothy, "that old place doesn't look spooky any more—it just seems sort of friendly."

Timothy nodded absently and seemed about to say something—when suddenly he jerked forward and peered through the darkness at the landing. I followed his glance and saw, to my astonishment, a vague white form which seemed to be poised upon the very edge of the dock. Before either of us could speak, there came a strange sound—a sort of a wail—which floated out over the water and reached our ears with a faint but distinct and chilling sound of distress.

Instantly everyone of us in the boat sat up straight, and every eye was strained upon that wavering white figure.

"Good God, who *is* that?" Tony Jackson was the first to speak.

Allen Gilbert, at the wheel, cupped his hands and shouted.

"Hello—who's there?"

For a moment there was no answer save the echo of Allen's words which resounded weirdly from the shore. Then, still very faint but this time distinguishable, came the wailing reply.

"Help me—hurry please."

"Timothy—who *is* it?" I could not yet identify the voice.

"Darned if I know," Timothy shook his head.

Suddenly young Jerry Benson spoke.

"It's mother," he said, and his quiet voice gave not the slightest evidence of either excitement or concern.

Allen Gilbert cupped his hands again.

"Is that you, Mrs. Benson?" he called.

Tremulously through the darkness came the reply. "Yes—oh, please hurry."

"We're right here—" Timothy scrambled up from his place beside me and made his way to the bow. "Take it easy, Mrs. Benson, everything's all right." His big voice boomed out across the narrowing stretch of water with comforting assurance.

Somehow the landing was negotiated, and Timothy, with two big bounds, was out of the boat and up the steps. I saw Mrs. Benson cross the dock and collapse with one shuddering sob in Timothy's arms.

"Oh—I've been so *frightened,*" her gasping voice sank to a whimper. "I—thought you'd *never* come."

"Easy now," I saw Timothy pat her shoulder. "What is it that frightened you so?"

"Something—in the woods up there—" a quivering finger indicated the blackness beyond the cottages. "It—it was right by my house—by my window. Oh, it was—*dread-ful*—" her voice trailed off into another quaking, shuddering sob.

"Where," Timothy asked quietly, "is Mr. Benson?"

All of us waited while the woman struggled to speak. Then slowly, as if with painful effort, came her words.

"I—I don't know," said Mrs. Benson.

## 3

One by one the rest of us climbed out of the launch and groped our way up the landing steps to the dock where Mrs. Benson stood. All of us, that is, except young Jerry Benson. He remained in the boat until we were ashore, and then, without a word, shoved off again and headed out toward the channel. I realized, of course, that he was returning the launch to the Plunkett dock on the other side of the point, but it struck me as odd that even this curiously silent lad should display such deliberate indifference to his mother's hysterical fear.

"Try to be calm, Louise. You must control your mind and remember exactly what happened." I recognized the voice of Lila Gilbert—likewise her favorite theory of "control."

"I—oh, it's all so confused. I was asleep, you see—and—" Mrs. Benson's words were still breathlessly disjointed.

"Wait a minute," one of the men spoke. "Let's go back a bit. When did all this happen, and where were you—and where was Mr. Benson?"

"I was in my room, on the bed," Mrs. Benson was making an effort to speak more steadily. "I can't tell you just

when it happened, because I had fallen asleep. I'd taken
some medicine, for my headache, you see, and it always
makes me drowsy. Suddenly I woke up—and even before
I opened my eyes I knew I heard something a funny sort
of scuffling noise just outside my bedroom window. I listened for a minute—and then I could hear it again, the
same scuffling—only it wasn't by the window any more. It
seemed to have moved around toward the back of the house
near the porch. I started into the living-room and called
to Richard. I never dreamed, of course, but what he was
there—reading. But he—didn't answer me—and the living-
room was empty. I called again at his bedroom door—still
there was no answer. And I knew then, that he—he was
*gone*—" Mrs. Benson's voice faltered and broke.

From where I stood, close by Allen Gilbert, I could
see the struggle Mrs. Benson was making to go on speaking. Her face, lifted toward Timothy, to whose arm she
still clung, showed ghastly pale in the moonlight. A folded towel, which had been bound around her aching head,
hung askew—adding a curiously rakish touch that only
emphasized the look of distress upon her round features.

"It was then," she said, "that I was really terrified. Being alone there, with those awful sounds—I—I'm afraid I
lost my head—"

"So I should imagine," Lila Gilbert's clipped words cut in.

"I went to the front door and screamed for Richard,"
Mrs. Benson hurried on, apparently unaware of the inter-
ruption. "Still he didn't answer me—and I ran out into
the path. I was terrified to leave the house, of course, but
I simply *had* to find Richard. I knew that all you people
were away—and then suddenly I remembered Miss Emily
—so I cut through the path toward her cottage and as
I came into the clearing I saw a light in her window. I

thought then that I was safe—but just as I got up onto her porch—*the light went out.* I pounded on her door—I called to Miss Emily to let me in—but—" her voice failed in a shuddering breath.

"What then?" Timothy asked sharply. "Didn't she answer you at all?

*"No—"* the word was almost a whisper. "Oh—it was awful—standing there alone in the dark—calling and calling—and not a sound from the dark cottage—and *knowing* that Miss Emily must be there when I'd seen the light go out with my own eyes.

"Well—after that I don't remember things very clearly. I know I must have run away from the cottage—and the next thing I realized was being down here on the dock. I—I've waited here ever since. It seemed hours until I finally saw the lights of your boat. And—that's all."

"Just one more thing," Timothy bent toward her. "After you got down here to the dock, did you see anyone or hear anything up by the cottages?"

Mrs. Benson shook her head.

"There wasn't," Timothy persisted, "any light?"

"None," said Mrs. Benson, "except in our house. You see, I left a light there when I—I ran out."

"I see," said Timothy very slowly.

We all turned to look toward the shore. Through the pines we could see a faint glimmer from the Benson windows. The other cottages were lost in the darkness of the heavy woods.

"Well—" Tony Jackson spoke suddenly, "there's no use standing here any longer. We ought to get up there and see what the devil is going on."

The rest of us nodded agreement. In silence we gathered up the picnic things. Allen Gilbert led the way with a flash-light, and the rest of us followed the flickering beam up along the twisting path. Mrs. Benson, still clinging to Timothy's arm, walked unsteadily.

Since our shack was the first one on the path, Timothy suggested that Lila Gilbert, Mrs. Benson and I wait there while the men proceeded to investigate the situation.

"The first thing," he said, "is to locate Mr. Benson—then we'll have a look around and see what the hell has been going on. You girls can wait in here—and we'll keep you posted if we find anything." To me he added privately, "Get Mrs. Benson to lie down and give her a drink. You and the Gilbert dame, between you, ought to be able to quiet her."

"Don't worry about us," I whispered back. "But for heaven's sake hurry and find out what happened to dear Richard—and *what* Miss Cotton was up to."

"If it's the last thing I do," Timothy promised grimly. But just as the men started away from the porch, Lila Gilbert decided to upset the plan.

"I think," said Lila, "that I should prefer to wait in my own cottage." Her manner, as she started toward the door, was her usual one of studied calm.

At the threshold, however, she found herself checked by Timothy's large presence.

"Sorry," he said, "but you'll have to stay here."

Lila raised her small head and studied his face for a long moment.

"Perhaps," her eyebrows were delicately lifted, "you do not understand. I am not in the least afraid of waiting alone."

Timothy's amiable drawl sounded suddenly harsh as he swiftly cut in on the heels of her clear, clipped speech.

"No one," he said, "cares whether you're afraid or not. But you're needed here to help Joan take care of

Mrs. Benson. So here you'll stay." With an abrupt gesture he shut the door and was gone.

Lila offered no further protest, nor did she make the slightest move to disobey. She simply remained.

I settled Mrs. Benson as best I could and went to fetch the drink that Timothy had prescribed. She accepted the glass which I held to her quivering lips, and swallowed the whiskey obediently. Then, eyes closed, she sank back upon the pillow. Only once did she look up at me and speak.

"Do you think, Joan dear," her white face registered anxious appeal, "that Richard is all right?"

"Of course he is," I did my best to sound heartily reassuring. "He probably only went out for a walk—and the men will find him in no time. You just wait and see."

Mrs. Benson nodded faintly, then her weary eyelids fluttered and closed once more.

I turned away and poured a second drink. It was intended for myself—but suddenly I remembered Lila.

"Here—" I swung around to offer her the glass. "Wouldn't you like to—" my words faded before the expression of amused contempt upon Lila's face.

"No thank you," she spoke with sweet sarcasm, "I really don't need a stimulant. Perhaps you'd better take it yourself."

I took it, and said nothing. Presently Lila went on.

"You see," she said, "these little spells of hysteria don't upset me in the least."

"Are they so frequent then?" I inquired.

Lila shrugged her shoulders delicately.

"The woods are full of noises," she said, "real or imaginary. And Louise is a nervous woman. You must see that she had absolutely no control."

I could feel my patience wearing thin.

"Real or imaginary," I said, "control or no control—the fact remains that Mrs. Benson had a nasty scare. It's certainly not pleasant to find yourself alone in a house with mysterious sounds outside—and to have your husband disappear and your only neighbor refuse to open her door."

Lila surveyed my indignation with a tolerant smile.

"Perhaps not," she said, "if that's what really happened."

"You don't mean," I stared, "that you think Mrs. Benson, feeling as wretched as she did, would deliberately invent that whole scare?"

Lila shrugged again.

"It's amazing," she said, "how much some people enjoy a scene."

I was on the point of saying, "You, for instance," when the sound of footsteps on the porch cut short rising temper. I hurried to the door and found Tony Jackson outside.

"Tell Mrs. Benson," he said hastily, "that her husband is all right." And before I could ask for details he turned and was gone again.

When I told Mrs. Benson the news a smile of touching relief spread over her pale face.

"Oh I'm so glad," she breathed. "Poor Richard."

Personally, I could think of a more appropriate adjective to describe him—but I held my tongue. Lila, of course, made no comment on the finding of Richard save for a look indicating that it was quite what she had expected. Fortunately for my peace of mind, Timothy came bursting into the shack a few minutes later in search of another flash-light—and I seized the opportunity for a word alone with him.

"Timothy—" I grabbed his arm. "*Where* did you find Mr. Benson?"

"In his own living-room," Timothy informed me in a whisper, "reading a magazine and looking as calm as a basket of apples." He turned to see my look of amazement, then hurried on. "I was just as surprised as you look," he said, "but there he was. Claimed he'd been there more than an hour and had seen no evil, thought no evil, and heard no evil."

"But—what about Mrs. Benson? Wasn't he worried about her being gone?"

"He said he thought she was in her room asleep," Timothy's expression indicated his opinion of this statement. "Said he'd gone out for a short walk earlier—and the whole business must have happened while he was gone. Then he came back, supposed his wife was still asleep, and sat down to read. And that was all."

"But—Timothy—couldn't he even come over here to see Mrs. Benson? Wasn't he the least bit concerned about her?"

Timothy gave me a long, significant look.

"You know as much about it as I do," he said. "But I can't stop at this moment to unravel the domestic affairs of the Benson family. The point is that something funny *has* been going on. There are traces of a prowler around the Benson cottage—and we're going to divide up and have a look in the woods."

"What—do you think it was, Timothy?"

"Damned if I know," he shook his head. "The popular theory is that a tramp or a drunk was moseying around for food in the Benson kitchen. But me—I'm not so sure. Well, anyway," Timothy shrugged himself into a heavy coat and caught up the flash-light, "we'll have a look. Tony Jackson is taking the shore path, Benson and Gilbert will do the

cottages, and little Timothy snagged off the hill assignment."

Instantly I thought of the big house.

"You—you won't go too far, will you?"

"Don't worry about me," Timothy grinned at my concern. "I'm having the time of my life. You'd better say
nothing to Mrs. Benson. Let her sleep where she is—and
you take my bed. And *don't* get the fidgets!"

"But what—" I had a sudden thought, "shall I do with
Lila? There's no place for her to sleep."

"Lila can go to hell," he said in a loud whisper. "Let her
sleep on the stove and see if it thaws some of the nonsense
out of her."

Even in the stress of the moment I had to giggle at the
picture of Lila curled up on our two-by-four stove—but I
managed to catch Timothy for one last question.

"You didn't tell me," I said, "what you found at Miss
Cotton's house. Was she there?"

"She was not," Timothy's voice was suddenly grim.
"And *that* is why I'm all aglow to do a bit of snooping on
that thar hill path. Good-night, my pet, and remember—
keep your shirt on."

With a final wave, Timothy was gone—and I was left
to compose myself, my patient, and my unwilling guest to
wait for the results of the searchers. I was, however, spared
the necessity of coping further with Lila Gilbert. For when
I returned to the living-room she was gone.

After a moment's indecision, I came to the conclusion
that there was nothing to be done about Lila—and I settled down on the cot next to Mrs. Benson to wonder and
wait—and wonder some more.

And that was how it happened that only Mrs. Benson
and I had an alibi that could be checked when it came

to proving our whereabouts from midnight until nearly two o'clock. And it was during that time that little Ruby Turner met her tragic death in the woods near the house that Jack built.

## 4

It was just half-past two when a loud knock at the door wakened me. I had been dozing for an hour or more, it seemed, for the last thing I could remember was glancing at the clock and observing that it was after one. My first thought, as I scrambled up from the cot, was that Timothy must have returned, and I paused only to glance at Mrs. Benson before hurrying to unbolt the door. She was, I saw with relief, sleeping soundly.

It was not Timothy but Allen Gilbert who stood on the threshold—and one look at his disheveled hair and wild eyes was sufficient to tell me that something had happened. Before I could ask a question, he pushed past me into the living-room.

"Where's Lila?" he demanded.

"She's not here," I spoke in a low tone, and indicated the bedroom door beyond which Mrs. Benson lay asleep.

But Allen Gilbert ignored my signal for quiet.

"Lila—not here?" his voice was high pitched with excitement. "My God—where is she then?"

"I suppose," I said, "that Lila went to her own cottage. She left here without speaking to me some two hours ago."

"Two hours ago?" the words were echoed blankly. Then, with sudden decision, Allen turned and started for the door.

"Wait a minute—" I caught at his sleeve. "You must tell me—*what* is the matter?"

For a moment he stared down at my hand, then his eyes traveled upward to my face—and for the first time he seemed to focus on me.

"There—has been an accident," Allen spoke more quietly. "I've got to find Lila."

Seeing that I had no chance of getting further information, I let go of Gilbert's arm—and instantly he was away. For a minute I stood, watching the glimmer of his flashlight move away through the pines as he plunged along the path toward his cottage, then I turned back into the room and slowly closed the door. I dared not leave Mrs. Benson long enough to go in search of the others—and I could only wait, in a fever of anxious and futile wondering, for someone else to bring me news of the "accident."

Luckily I was not left alone long. Scarcely ten minutes had passed before I heard another footstep on the porch and a light rap at the door. I flew to open it—and a moment later I was clinging to Timothy.

"Oh—*Timothy*. I'm so glad you're safe."

I felt a reassuring thump on my shoulder, but obviously there was no time to waste in mere rejoicing. Timothy crossed the room in two long steps, closed the bedroom door and turned to face me. Instantly I was aware of the gravity of his manner. The enthusiasm with which, a few hours earlier, he had set out to search the hill path was quite gone from his stern, set features.

He motioned toward the bedroom door.

"Is Mrs. Benson all right?"

I nodded.

"Asleep?"

"Yes."

"Good. Now listen, Joan," Timothy's voice was low and tense. "Something has happened—something very bad. I'm going to give it to you straight."

"Yes, Timothy."

"It's Ruby Turner, Joan. She's dead. I found her—in the woods about half-way up the hill—in a berry patch just off the path. She—was murdered, Joan."

"Oh—" I drew back, "how—dreadful." I had an instant and horrible picture of Ruby, in her faded cotton frock, lying dead in the woods. "Timothy—you found her?"

He nodded.

"There were no traces of the—the murderer?"

"None," he said slowly, "that I could see. I took a quick look around—force of habit, I suppose—and then I came back to tell the others. They were waiting for me at the Benson cottage. Tony Jackson volunteered to go down to the village and notify Amos Plunkett—it seems he's the local constable—and the rest of us went back to the hill. We stayed there until Plunkett appeared to take charge, then he sent us back here. We're all in for a grilling, of course, and the hell of it is that not one of us has a decent alibi—except you girls, of course. During the hour when Ruby was killed we were each alone—each searching the woods in a different direction."

"Timothy," I began doubtfully, "you don't think that one of them could have—have done it?"

He looked at me for a long moment.

"Hell—" his voice was suddenly harsh. "*I* don't know. The theory still is, of course, that it was a tramp or something like that—but I'm too much of a natural born cop

not to suspect everyone on general principles. Anyway—
it's going to be damned unpleasant for us all unless things
clear up a whole lot faster than I think they're going to."
Timothy walked over to a chair and sank down wearily.

"You've gone and married a jinx, Joanie," he shook his
head sadly. "We couldn't even have ourselves a honeymoon
without running square into a murder."

"Pooh," I said, "*I* don't care. But—oh, it is so awful
about poor Ruby. Whoever could have wanted to kill the
child." I paused. "Timothy—how was it done?"

For the first time Timothy did not look at me when he
spoke.

"I—I'm not quite sure," he said.

"You might as well tell me, Timothy. I'll know sooner
or later—and I'd rather hear it from you."

"As nearly as I could make out, Ruby was strangled.
Her throat—" Timothy paused. "It was pretty bad, Joan,"
his voice was very low.

"I—see." Again I closed my eyes upon a sickening
vision of Ruby Taylor—of her thin, scrawny little neck.

"I'm afraid—" Timothy shook his head, "that there's
more to this than meets the eye. Things worked out just
a bit too patly this evening to be pure coincidence. The
scare—the evidence of a prowler around the Benson cottage—the necessity for a search which meant that each of
us was out alone in the woods at the time of the murder—"
Timothy paused.

"You mean," I said slowly, "that you think the whole
thing was planned?"

"Well, if it wasn't, it was pretty damn lucky for the
murderer. And I'm not much inclined to believe in luck."

"But surely Mrs. Benson wasn't faking her story." I was
remembering her wide-eyed terror. "You can't make me
believe she's *that* good an actress."

"Maybe not," Timothy shrugged. "Personally, I think she's pretty good at dramatics. After watching her technique of trying to convince the world that her home-life with those two oysters she calls her 'big boys,' is just too jolly, I'd spot Louise Benson as the type who spends a large part of her life acting."

"But, Timothy, what motive would she have had for making up that story—unless you think she knew something about the murder—"

"Hold everything, my girl," Timothy cut in quickly. "It's too early yet to talk about motives. As a matter of fact, she could have had a number of reasons for faking the story—*if* she did fake it—but my only point at present is to convince you that you mustn't take what any of these people say for gospel. As for the rest of our dear neighbors, in whom you display such a touching faith, *I* think they're an elegant bunch of suspects. I've already indicated my impression that the Benson gents, dour father and sulky son, are a couple of volcanoes kept from erupting only by the constant efforts of Mrs. Benson—and as for Lila Gilbert, I wouldn't trust her any further than she trusts her handsome and spineless husband. Tony Jackson seems normal enough—which is probably an excellent reason for keeping an eye on him. And then, of course, we mustn't forget Miss Emily Cotton of the iron jaw and lurid past. In other words, my pet, it's a sweet set-up—and I'm willing to bet that Sheriff Plunkett will uncover some soiled and tangled linen in the course of the next few days—unless," Timothy finished gloomily, "he gets so wound up in the mess himself that it chokes him."

"Well—" I took a long breath, "if you've been trying to throw the fear of God into me, you've certainly succeeded. From now on I'll suspect everyone, and say nothing."

"Good," Timothy nodded approvingly. "It's the best technique in the world for working your way out of a hornet's nest. And now, if you think you could share that vacant cot with me, I think we could use some sleep. Something tells me that the old blood-hound Plunkett will be after us bright and early in the morning."

## 5

Timothy was quite right. It was scarcely seven o'clock when a knock at the front door wakened us. I opened my eyes and saw Mrs. Benson sitting up in her bed across the room.

"Oh, my goodness," she said, "is it *morning?* How dreadful of me to sleep here all night. Whatever will my boys think of me?"

I refrained from saying that her boys had evidently not thought enough about it to so much as stop in and inquire for her, but she was far too intent upon getting up and settling her rumpled dress to observe my silence. She didn't even pause to coo over the sight of Timothy and me curled up like a porpoise and a sardine on our cot.

When Timothy had ambled out of the room, I turned to the somewhat embarrassed Mrs. Benson.

"How do you feel this morning?"

"Oh—quite all right, really," the bright tone did not match the drawn pallor of her face.

"Hadn't you better stay quiet," I suggested, "until I can get you some coffee?"

"No, *no,* dear child. That's ever so sweet of you, but I really *must* get back to give my boys their breakfast." Mrs.

Benson hurriedly smoothed her hair, and started toward the back door. "I'll just slip out here—I'm such a *sight*."

For a minute after she had gone out I sat quite still on the edge of my cot, thinking. Then, at the sound of low voices from the living-room, I rose, drew on a negligee, and went to the door.

Amos Plunkett was deeply engrossed in conversation with Timothy, and both men turned at my approach.

"Come along, Joan. Nothing we have to say is so secret that you can't hear it." Timothy smiled at me, and then at the sheriff.

For a moment I thought Mr. Plunkett looked a bit doubtful on the proposition.

"You see," Timothy went on quickly, "my wife knows all about what happened last night—and she probably has more ideas on the subject than either of us."

"Well, now," Mr. Plunkett eyed me with a new interest, "is that so?"

"I'm afraid," I smiled, "that Timothy exaggerates. I haven't an idea in my head at this particular moment. But you go ahead with your conversation, and I'll get some breakfast for you both."

Whether it was my presence, or just natural reticence, that made Mr. Plunkett slow in coming to the point, I do not know. But it was not until the coffee was boiling and the eggs were nearly done, that he suddenly broached the purpose of his call.

"Say, Mr. Fowler," he cleared his throat, "I hear you're a detective."

I turned from the stove just in time to see Timothy's startled expression.

"So?" he said. "And where did you hear that?"

Mr. Plunkett shifted a bit uncomfortably.

"Well," he cleared his throat again, "as a matter of fact, 'twas Miss Emily that mentioned it."

"Did she?" Timothy leaned forward with sudden interest. "It's true, I'm on the New York force—but I wasn't aware that Miss Cotton knew it."

"She knows it, all right," said Mr. Plunkett with emphasis. "And she didn't seem none too pleased a couple of days ago. I dunno how she feels about it this mornin'. But I'll tell you, Mr. Fowler, I'm durned glad you're here. That is—" at last he achieved the question, "if you'll be willin' to help me out on this business."

"You mean," again I caught Timothy's look of surprise, "you came here to ask me to join forces on the case?"

"Sure," said Mr. Plunkett. "What else?"

"To be quite frank," Timothy smiled, "I rather imagined you came here first this morning because you were hot on my trail. After all, I *was* the one to find the body."

"Hell," said Mr. Plunkett scornfully. "I've more sense than to suspicion you. The trouble is," he scratched his head reflectively. "I dunno *who* to suspect. You see, Mr. Fowler, we ain't had a murder in Witch Harbor in the three years since I've been sheriff—and folks in the village are awful upset over this. I've just gotta find out who done away with Ruby, and I figured maybe you wouldn't mind givin' me a few tips. Course I know this is your vacation, and—" with a glance at me, "your honeymoon and all— but I thought maybe—" he paused hopefully.

I saw Timothy look at me. It didn't take any ability at mind reading to see that he was dying to say yes—honeymoon or no honeymoon.

"Of course he'll help, Mr. Plunkett," I spoke up quickly. "After all, the sooner we get this awful business settled, the better it will be for everyone—ourselves included.

Timothy came over and patted my shoulder.

"Good girl," he beamed at me approvingly. "Now then, let's tackle this breakfast and get down to business." He drew an extra chair up to our small table, and motioned for Mr. Plunkett to join us. "The first thing is for us to tell Mr. Plunkett exactly what happened last night, and then he can give us the low-down on the background of these dear neighbors of ours."

"I dunno," the Plunkett head was shaken doubtfully, "as I can tell you much. These summer folks keep pretty much to theirselves."

"Oh," said Timothy, "I didn't mean them so much. I was thinking of the big house on the hill, and old Dr. Jack, and—" he hesitated briefly, "and Miss Cotton."

Mr. Plunkett, on the point of attacking his scrambled eggs, paused with his fork in mid-air to look up in blank astonishment.

"Say—" the Plunkett voice was wondering, "you don't think what happened last night had anything to do with that old business, do you, Mr. Fowler?"

Timothy was a long time in answering.

"I don't quite know what I think," he stirred his coffee very slowly. "But this is a strange place, with a strange history—and Miss Emily Cotton is a strange woman. It's been my experience that one strange thing leads to another, and I have a hunch that plenty led up to poor Ruby Turner's fate last night. So I'd appreciate it, Mr. Plunkett, if you'd tell us what you know about the history of the house that Jack built. And please start at the beginning."

Slowly Mr. Plunkett's fork was lowered to his plate. He took a generous mouthful of egg, chewed it solemnly, swallowed—and then spoke with sudden decision.

"All right," he said, "I'll tell you as much of the story as we folks around here know—but it'll take some time."

"I don't doubt that," Timothy nodded, "but I can practically promise you that it won't be time wasted."

$\longrightarrow$ **6** $\longleftarrow$

Before Mr. Plunkett, between bites of breakfast, had more than launched himself upon the account that we were so eager to hear, Timothy had the bright idea of my taking stenographic notes of the account.

"I may put you to work anyway," he explained cheerfully, "when we come to questioning our little suspects. So you might as well get your hand in now and take down this story for future reference."

I fetched pencil and paper willingly enough. It was quite like old times to be taking notes for one of Timothy's murder cases—but Mr. Plunkett viewed the procedure with obvious skepticism.

"I don't see," he shook his head, "what you expect to find out about Ruby Turner's gettin' killed from somethin' that started more'n twenty years back."

But Timothy was firm, and I took down the Plunkett recital in full. I have the notes before me now, neatly typed out and edited as to grammar and vocabulary, just as they were submitted when the record of the case was complete. It will, perhaps, be best to quote from the transcription here.

During the summers of 1902 and 1903, a certain Dr. Albert Jack, accompanied by his wife and two small sons, came to vacation in Witch Harbor. Since there were, at that time, no cottages available for summer people, the Jack family boarded at the home of Miss Emily Cotton. Miss Cotton was then about twenty-five years old, and had been living alone since the death of her father, the Reverend Elmer Cotton, some years before.

Very little was known, in the village, about Mr. Cotton and his only daughter, despite the fact that he had been, for some ten years, in charge of the small local church. Father and daughter lived a very secluded life, and were regarded by their neighbors as extremely aloof and eccentric. They were, however, quiet, dignified, and well-behaved, and the village people were inclined, on the whole, to accept them with tolerance, and allow them the privacy which they so deliberately cultivated.

("After all," Mr. Plunkett explained, "we had enough sense to know that there wasn't no hope of keepin' a minister in Witch Harbor in them days unless he was a little mite queer. Nobody else would've stood for the peewee pay he got, and we figured we was pretty lucky to have such a good preacher as old Mr. Cotton. As long as he went on givin' us our Sunday sermons, we figured it was his own business what he done the rest of the week.")

It was known that Mr. Cotton was a man of considerable learning, and that he had, in his modest house, a really remarkable collection of books. Among his other eccentricities, was his insistence upon educating his daughter privately, teaching her himself with the aid of his library. As a result of the strict discipline of study imposed by her father, Miss

Emily was rarely seen outside of her home, and she was even less known to the village than the minister whose duties required at least a minimum of contact with his flock. The few people who were, from time to time, permitted a glimpse inside the Cotton home, reported always the same thing: that young Emily was invariably to be found in her father's study, surrounded by his books and apparently deep in scholastic work.

After the death of Mr. Cotton, his daughter continued to live in virtual seclusion, but it was generally supposed that she would, sooner or later, have to emerge from her solitude in order to earn some sort of living. The village was not surprised, therefore, when Miss Cotton accepted the Jack family as summer borders.

Of Dr. Albert Jack himself, the village people knew little, and apparently cared less. It was not until the time of his death, some twenty-seven years later, that they discovered how prominent and celebrated a person he had been before his retirement to the seclusion of Witch Harbor. That he was not only a brilliant physician, but a pioneer in the field of experimental psychology and psychiatry, whose work had gained him an international reputation in medical and scientific circles, was a fact of which his village neighbors were quite unaware.

When, in the Summer of 1903, Dr. Jack arrived for his third season in Witch Harbor and announced his intention of building himself a permanent home there, the village found nothing remarkable about his decision. The only point which aroused a certain amount of gossip and conjecture was the fact that his wife and sons, who had previously accompanied him as a most devoted family, did not arrive with him that third Summer. And as the season wore on, and plans for Dr. Jack's house progressed, they still did not come to join him.

Meanwhile Dr. Jack had purchased, after considerable negotiation, a point of land which was surrounded on three sides by water and to which the only approach was a narrow path branching off from the main road. Almost his first act, after taking possession of the property, was to put a substantial gate across this single entrance, and to post the boundaries liberally with "No Trespassing" signs.

Up to this point, the village had been no more than mildly concerned with the activities of its new resident. It was his procedure in actually building the big house which finally roused them to active curiosity. That—and the fact of Miss Emily Cotton's close connection with the doctor's plans. It soon became evident that she was his confidante and advisor in the entire project, and that no one else in the village was to be allowed so much as a look at the house which was under construction. Dr. Jack had, in fact, gone to almost unbelievable extremes in keeping his plans secret. Instead of employing carpenters and workmen from Witch Harbor and the surrounding villages, he had imported a crew of builders from a firm in Portland. These men lived in an improvised camp on Dr. Jack's property, and were, it appeared, kept virtually prisoners there during the period of building. As a result, no one in the village had any more knowledge of the house than could be gained from distant observations. And the site of the house, on the peak of a heavily wooded hill in the very center of the property, was so remote from both land and water that little could be seen by outsiders save the four great walls which loomed high above the village.

The house was completed sometime in September of that year, and immediately after the workmen had departed for Portland, Dr. Jack moved in. Still there was no sign of his family. To the few bolder souls in the village who dared question Dr. Jack on this point, he replied, blandly courteous as always, that Mrs. Jack and the boys were in Europe, and that they would join him later. But when the Summer wore on into Autumn, and still the doctor remained alone in his big house, two things became apparent. First, that Dr. Jack intended to stay on in Witch Harbor indefinitely; and second, that he had broken with his family.

It was early in October when Miss Cotton closed her house and moved up on the hill to share Dr. Jack's home. No explanation of this move was given by either of them, except to say that for reasons of health Dr. Jack had decided to retire from active practice in Baltimore and remain permanently in Witch Harbor—and that Miss Cotton had agreed to be his housekeeper. There was, of course, a great deal of agitated gossip following this announcement—gossip to which the doctor and Miss Cotton was apparently quite oblivious as they went about arranging their quiet and secluded existence.

Before that Winter was ended, the two inhabitants of the big house on the hill had settled themselves into a routine which was evidently to be permanent. Complete privacy was their one object, and with the only entrance to their property strictly barricaded, they were able to achieve it. Dr. Jack himself made regular trips into the village for supplies—but aside from these occasions he was rarely seen. Miss Cotton ventured out even less often—sometimes as much as several months would pass when no one got so much as a glimpse of her familiar, tall, spare figure.

And the village people, after the first flurry of excitement, accepted the queer state of affairs with much the same tolerance they had accorded to the eccentric existence of Miss Cotton and her father. It was generally supposed, in a vague way, that the two were more to each other than master and housekeeper—but the village was neither scandalized nor particularly interested in this supposition. Neither the plain and angular Emily Cotton nor the austere, middle-aged doctor, were, after all, types to suggest any very flaming attachment, and they sank so completely into the strange solitude they had chosen, that outsiders were inclined to dismiss them both as a pair of harmless lunatics. Even the sight of the big house gloomy and forlorn on the hill, ceased to arouse any curiosity on the part of the village. It was now referred to, as the house that Jack built, more as a commonplace landmark than as an object of mysterious interest.

The only revival of gossip concerning the affairs of Dr. Jack was occasioned by the sudden and unexpected arrival of Mrs. Jack in Witch Harbor. It was sometime during the second Winter of Dr. Jack's sojourn that Amos Plunkett, having gone to Pineboro to fetch the mail, was astonished to find Mrs. Jack waiting at the railroad station. She asked to be driven to the village store in Witch Harbor.

("I won't never," said Mr. Plunkett, "forget that ride. Not if I live to be a hundred. It must have taken a coupla hours or more to get down from Pineboro—in them days I had horses—and there was Mrs. Jack settin' beside me, never sayin' a word the whole time. I can see her now, with her face hid down in the big fur coat she was wearin'—only her eyes showin', and then lookin' straight out in front of her as if she didn't see nothin' at all. And me not darin' to speak. When we got to the store, Mrs. Jack turned around to look at me. 'Thank you, Amos,' she says, and she climbed down out of the sleigh. I asked did she want me to take some message to the doctor, sayin' she was here—but she just shook her head. 'That won't be necessary,' she says, 'I've already arranged to meet him here.' And with that she went into the store.")

By arrangement with the village storekeeper, Mrs. Jack was able to see her husband alone in a back room. No record exists of their brief interview, except for fragments of the conversation which were overheard, and duly retailed to the townspeople, by the storekeeper's curious wife. It seemed that, quite as would be expected, the purpose of Mrs. Jack's visit was to implore the doctor to return from his voluntary exile. The gist of her plea was based not on a personal appeal, but upon his folly in abandoning the work of his brilliant career. To which Dr. Jack replied that he was engaged in an experiment of far greater importance than anything he had previously undertaken—an experiment of such proportions that it would require the remainder of his lifetime to complete. But why, Mrs. Jack inquired, must the work be shrouded in such secrecy? Because, said the doctor, that was the most essential part of a project so daring, so revolutionary. Above all else he must be left absolutely alone in order to complete the great work—the work for which he had given up home, family, friends and fame, and to which he was prepared to sacrifice the rest of his life. He had, Dr. Jack said, already made adequate financial provision for his wife and children— and beyond that they must simply think of him as dead. Dead to everything in the world except this one great experiment which, if it succeeded, would far outweigh anything else he had done in its importance to the body of scientific knowledge. And this, so far as the storekeeper's wife could learn by eavesdropping, was the end of the interview. No mention had been made by either Doctor or Mrs. Jack of Emily Cotton.

When Amos Plunkett stopped at the store to collect the evening mail for his drive into town, he found Mrs. Jack ready to go with him. And from that time on she was never seen again in Witch Harbor. The brief flurry of excitement occasioned by her visit, and by the account of Dr. Jack's

strange explanation of his retirement, died down as the Winter wore on, and the solitary existence of the two eccentrics
continued quite as before. People were more than ever inclined to dismiss the whole situation as a problem which
would never be solved. And as months lengthened into years,
with no break in the inconspicuous monotony of their routine,
the topic of the big house and its inmates was relegated to the
position of a local institution which was no longer interesting
as a subject of conjecture.

Not until the year 1928 did the next event occur which
focused the attention of Witch Harbor upon its two mysterious residents. It was in January of that year, toward evening
of a stormy day, when Miss Cotton and Dr. Jack came into the
village store. The doctor, it appeared, was ill. Bundled in a
big overcoat, he leaned heavily upon the arm of his companion, and his drawn, gray face showed plainly the effort it had
been to make the journey down the hill into the village. It was
the first time, so far as anyone could remember, that the two
had been seen together in the twenty-odd years of their shared
exile. The doctor was by this time well on in years, and the
lines of age and care in his face were, that night, sharpened
by weakness and suffering. It was evident to the villagers
gathered in the store that Dr. Jack was a very sick man.

Miss Emily, however, was calm enough. She explained
briefly that her companion was in need of medical care, and
that she was taking him to the hospital in Pineboro. Amos
Plunkett, on his evening mail trip, drove them both into town,
and took Dr. Jack directly to the hospital. The local physician diagnosed his illness as double pneumonia. Within a few
hours the old man sank into a coma from which he never
revived. Before morning Dr. Albert Jack died.

That day Amos Plunkett stopped by the hospital, and found
Miss Cotton waiting to return to Witch Harbor. Beyond a

single sentence in which she informed Mr. Plunkett that the
doctor was dead, that she had arranged to have his body
returned to his family in Baltimore, and that all other details
had been attended to, she made no comment whatever on the
loss of her lifelong companion. She seemed, indeed, precisely as calm and poised as always, her only display of emotion
being an evident anxiety to return to the big house as quickly as possible. Mr. Plunkett took her to the gate, and, at her
direction, left her there to make her solitary way through the
snowy path up to the empty house.

The village was, of course, considerably agitated by the
news of Dr. Jack's death. And when, in the days that followed, Miss Cotton did not again appear, a gradual feeling
developed that something ought to be done. The apathy with
which people had tolerated the strange couple for more than
twenty years changed, almost overnight, into a feeling of
communal concern—and focused itself in a violent suspicion
and resentment against Miss Cotton. People said that she had
deliberately let the old man die without sending for medical
aid, that she had no right to live on in Dr. Jack's house now
that he was dead—and that they, the villagers, should go up
to the big house and turn her out.

But before any action could be agreed upon, the people
of Witch Harbor discovered that others besides themselves
were concerned over the death of Dr. Albert Jack. On the
morning of the third day after the old man died, Amos Plunkett had two passengers for Witch Harbor on his sleigh. They
were both distinguished looking gentlemen, and they were, it
seemed, both lawyers. One had been sent for by Miss Cotton
to protect her interests, and the other represented Mrs. Jack
and her two sons. There followed a heated legal battle between the men, out of which Miss Cotton's attorney emerged
victorious. He was able to prove that his client was not only

the rightful heiress of all Dr. Jack's worldly goods (which consisted chiefly of the house and the property upon which it stood) but that the doctor had also left specific orders that all of his records and documents were to be left entirely in her hands. Miss Cotton had, therefore, every legal right to remain unmolested in the big house, and she was not obliged to divulge anything concerning the great experiment upon which Dr. Jack had supposedly spent the last twenty-five years of his life.

But the victory for Miss Cotton's interests was not allowed to stand unchallenged. The lawyer for the Jack family retired from Witch Harbor only to bring suit against the doctor's will, on the ground that he was not of sound mind when he made it.

(The trial of this suit, and the attendant publicity, had been referred to by Timothy on our first evening in Witch Harbor.)

The result of the court battle, which attracted wide newspaper attention, was another vindication of Miss Cotton. It was during this time that the early and brilliant career of Dr. Jack was reviewed by the papers, and Witch Harbor discovered at last what a famous and prominent person it had sheltered for so many years. With this realization came a second change in the village's attitude toward Emily Cotton. They were inclined to view her with a certain grudging respect, now that she was legally established as the rightful heiress to Dr. Jack's property and works. The fact that certain tabloid papers had capitalized her taciturn and forbidding manner in the courtroom—had even gone so far as to hint darkly that she might be a witch—only increased the feeling of loyalty among the village people. Miss Emily was, after all, one of them—and they had no wish to foster the idea that their community was so backward as to harbor any witch traditions.

Miss Cotton was, therefore, allowed to resume her life of seclusion in the big house without interference from the Witch Harbor people. And when, in the Spring of 1930, she announced her intention of building a group of cottages and opening her property to summer tenants, the village considered that its faith in her had been vindicated. Miss Emily's further decision to close the big house on the hill and move down to one of the shore cottages seemed to clinch the matter. All save a carping few of the village people (Ruby Turner's mother was one of those few) admitted that Miss Cotton could surely be up to no mischief, or she would never have dared open her estate to strangers.

From the very first, Miss Cotton's modest summer colony was a success. The Bensons and the Gilberts had been her original tenants, and they returned year after year with unflagging enthusiasm. The other two cottages had been occupied by a series of tenants who were likewise delighted with the place. In the four summer seasons which had passed since the beginning of Miss Cotton's venture, not one disturbing element had intruded itself into her quiet little colony. Until the night of July twentieth, 1934, when Ruby Turner was found murdered in a blueberry patch, halfway down the hill from the house that Jack built.

## 7

"And that," said Amos Plunkett, "is the whole story—or leastways as much as I know of it. And how you figure it has anythin' to do with what happened last night, I really don't see."

I put down my pencil and looked at Timothy. There was a long pause before he answered.

"Well—" Timothy scratched his chin thoughtfully, "to tell you the truth, Mr. Plunkett, I don't quite see the connection myself—*yet*. But I'm still convinced that there is one. For instance—" he paused for a moment, as if to grope for an idea.

"Fer instance, *what?*" Mr. Plunkett's skeptical tone challenged him.

"I was just wondering," Timothy went on slowly, "if Ruby Turner, prompted by her mother's suspicions of Miss Cotton, might possibly have done a little too much snooping for her own good."

There was another pause, while the meaning of these words sank gradually into the Plunkett consciousness.

"Do you think," he leaned forward with sudden interest, "that Ruby might've been figurin' to butt into Miss Emily's business?"

"Maybe," Timothy sighed, "and maybe not. But I do know one thing. If the village and the summer people in general have forgotten about the strange past history of Miss Cotton—Ruby hadn't. She was full of the story—began babbling to us about it the very first time we saw her. It's likely, of course, that the child was simply repeating her mother's idle remarks—but at any rate it was plain that she'd been brought up with the idea that Miss Cotton was not only crazy but dangerous, and that there had been something queer about the big house up there. With a fixed notion like that, and a child's natural curiosity, it wouldn't be surprising if she'd managed to find out more about Miss Cotton than Miss Cotton wanted her to know."

"But you don't think Miss Emily'd go so far as to kill the girl, do you, Mr. Fowler?"

"That would depend," said Timothy calmly, "on what Ruby knew—or thought she knew. Even granting that Miss Cotton has led a blamelessly normal life in the four years since she started her summer colony, we all know that she still has her peculiarities—and among them is the old yen for minding her own business. From the little I've seen of Miss Emily, I'd say she had practically a mania for keeping people from finding out anything about her. Whether she really has any secrets to hide, or whether it's only the habit of years of solitude—I don't pretend to know. But either way, I'm pretty damn sure it's the dominating motive of her life. And if, by any chance, Ruby Turner stumbled on something that Miss Emily didn't want her to know—well—" Timothy shrugged expressively. "Miss Cotton doesn't have that iron jaw for nothing. And her actions last night were not what you'd call exactly open and above-board. Personally, I'd like a little conversation with the lady—now that I know more about her case-history."

"Sure, Mr. Fowler," Amos Plunkett pushed back his chair and rose from the table. "I figured you'd probably want to ask all the folks some questions."

"You mean," Timothy grinned, "that *you* want to question them. After all, Sheriff, I'm only a helping hand on this case."

"Gosh," Mr. Plunkett shook his head dismally, "I wouldn't know where to start. You better do the askin'—and I'll back you up with my badge." Proudly he displayed the polished emblem beneath his coat.

"O.K.," said Timothy. "It's a bit irregular—but I guess we can get away with it. You, Joan," he turned to me, "get yourself dressed while I post Mr. Plunkett on just what happened last night—and when you're ready we'll all make a formal call on our dear landlady."

I hurried to obey, and less than a quarter of an hour later we were on our way through the path that led to Miss Cotton's house. I had a moment of doubt as we stood on the front porch. What would Miss Emily think of us, her tenants, suddenly turning detective on her? But when she opened the door she accepted our presence without a flicker of surprise.

"Good-morning," said Miss Cotton. Her voice was quiet and natural. "Will you come in?"

The three of us entered the small living-room—a room as neat and austere as Miss Emily herself.

"Will you sit down?"

We ranged ourselves upon three straight chairs grouped about a center table.

"Do you care for a cigarette?" Miss Emily offered the box to each of us in turn, then took one herself, and sat down on the couch facing us. "I expect," she said quietly, "that you have come about this dreadful thing which has happened?" Miss Cotton did not actually smile, but her manner was as pleasantly undisturbed as if she had been discussing the state of the weather.

Mr. Plunkett nodded, a bit unhappily.

"I figured," he said, "that you might be able to tell us somethin' about what was goin' on last night."

Miss Emily regarded the tip of her cigarette for a moment, then spoke as calmly as before.

"I'm afraid," she said, "that I can't tell you very much. But I shall be glad to help in any way I can. Naturally, the fact that this terrible crime was committed on my property is most distressing to me, not only on my own account, but for the sake of my tenants—and you may be quite sure that no one is more anxious than I to discover who was responsible for it."

Miss Cotton paused for a moment, and I found myself staring with blank fascination at this curious woman. Seated before us, gaunt and plain in her gingham dress and white sneakers, she was speaking of the dreadful murder with a poise which was both inhuman and disarming.

"I understand," Miss Cotton turned toward Timothy, "that you are a detective, Mr. Fowler."

"I am."

"And I assume, from your presence here this morning, that you have consented to help Amos with the investigation?"

Timothy nodded.

"I'll do what I can," he said, "if my unofficial advice will be of any help."

"That," said Miss Cotton, "is very good of you indeed, and I appreciate your co-operation more than anyone. You understand, of course, that our local facilities for handling a thing of this sort are extremely limited. There has never been, in my memory, a murder in Witch Harbor—and without your help I'm afraid Amos would be very much at a loss. But you, I'm sure, will know exactly how to proceed." Miss Emily's voice was smooth as velvet, and her clear gray eyes looked into Timothy's face with an expression of the utmost candor.

"I hope," said Timothy, "that my suggestions will be of some help." His tone was as formally polite as Miss Cotton's had been.

"Just how," Miss Cotton inquired, "do you intend to begin the investigation? Or perhaps you would rather not say?"

"Not at all," said Timothy graciously. "I should like to begin by asking you some questions."

"Of course," Miss Emily nodded. "I expected that."

"The first question," said Timothy, "is this. Were you here in your house last night between half-past eight and ten o'clock?"

"I was."

"And did you," Timothy proceeded politely, "hear any disturbance during that time, either outdoors or from one of the other cottages?"

Miss Cotton paused to reflect.

"No," she said slowly, "I am quite certain that I didn't."

"And you saw nothing unusual?"

This time Miss Emily did not hesitate.

"Nothing whatever," she said positively.

"I see," Timothy nodded thoughtfully. He gave no sign of doubting the two statements, nor did he seem inclined to pursue the questioning further. Instead, he rose and made a little bow in the direction of Miss Cotton.

"Thank you very much," Timothy spoke with the utmost graciousness. "And now I think," he turned to Mr. Plunkett and me, "that we'd better be about our business."

It was evident from Mr. Plunkett's expression, as he struggled to his feet, that he was as baffled as I by this sudden change in tactics. But the two of us followed Timothy in obedient silence.

Miss Emily, still calm, still poised, still unsmiling, stood in the doorway as we left the porch.

"If I can do anything further," she said, "please call on me. I shall be right here, of course."

"Of course," Timothy executed another small bow, and then turned to lead us up the path.

I could scarcely wait to get out of earshot before pouncing my question.

"Timothy—what *is* the idea of letting her get away with that?" I demanded breathlessly. "You know perfectly well Miss Cotton must have heard Mrs. Benson making all that fuss last night. And you didn't even try to find out where Miss Cotton was after we got home, and you men discovered that she wasn't in her house."

"Listen, Joan," Timothy turned to face me seriously. "I may be crazy, but I think not. I didn't ask Miss Cotton any more questions for two reasons. First, because she *might* not have been lying when she said she didn't hear or see anything before ten-thirty last night. Second, because if she *were* lying, I'd have no way of proving it. For some reason that I haven't figured out yet, Miss Emily has decided to pretend that she's on our side—and until further notice I'm going to play up to that little game. She's a smooth egg, that lady is, and the only way to break a smooth egg is to get its confidence first. Now do you see?"

"Why, Timothy—" I stared curiously, "are you saying that you're afraid of Miss Cotton?"

Timothy put his head on one side and squinted at me thoughtfully.

"Just as a matter of policy," he said, "I'm afraid of all murderers. That's one of the little trade secrets to which I attribute my very modest success. And now," he started up the path once more, "if you will follow me to the Gilbert lair, I'll try to reward your touching faith in me by showing you Lila Gilbert with her hair down—and I *don't* mean literally."

## 8

It seemed to me, when we entered the Gilbert cottage, that it was not Lila but her husband who had been caught with his hair down. Only it was actually up—ruffled and tousled in a way which altered his usual sleek appearance almost beyond recognition. Obviously Allen Gilbert was confused and dismayed by our arrival. He barely listened to Mr. Plunkett's somewhat disjointed explanation of Timothy's presence, as he stood, clasping and unclasping his thin white hands, and looking, not at us but at the closed door which led into Lila's bedroom.

"I—I'll certainly be glad to tell you anything I can," Gilbert spoke in a low, nervous tone, "but there's really nothing I can say. Mr. Fowler knows more about—about what happened last night than I do. He knows that I was searching down by the shore when the—the thing was done and ever since the discovery I've been right here in the cottage. There's absolutely nothing I can tell you that will help—"

"Just a minute, Allen," Timothy's quiet voice cut in. "We didn't come here to ask you any questions. I'd like to speak to your wife a minute." He crossed the small living-room and stood before the closed bedroom door.

"You can't do that." Instantly Allen Gilbert was at his side.

"Can't do what?" Timothy turned to regard him.

"Why, you—you can't see Lila now."

"No?" Timothy raised one eyebrow. "Why not?"

"Because," Allen Gilbert swallowed, "she's—not awake yet."

"Fine," said Timothy, and lifted his hand to knock. "This'll wake her up all right."

"I tell you," Allen protested feverishly, "you can't go in there. Lila's not well—she—" he paused a moment. "This awful business has upset her—she's not herself."

"Excellent," said Timothy, and let his hand drop sharply against the door.

For a moment there was silence. Then quite clearly I heard Lila Gilbert's voice.

"Come in," she said.

Timothy opened the door. From where I stood I could see Lila sitting up in bed, her lovely blond hair falling down over the pale blue silk jacket which covered her shoulders. If she were upset, as her husband had claimed, there was certainly nothing in her appearance to give any sign of it.

"You wanted to see me?" she asked, her words delicately clipped as always.

"I want to know," Timothy said, "why you left our cottage last night, and where you went."

Lila's shoulders were lifted in a gentle shrug.

"I left," she said, "because I wanted to, and I came straight here. Does that answer you?"

"It does not," said Timothy very clearly. "Please go on."

For a moment Lila looked as if she might be angry, but when she spoke her voice was as smooth as ever.

"If I went for a little walk," she said, "is it any business of yours?"

"It is," said Timothy. "Please go on."

"If I talked to Ruby Turner," Lila's words were as cold and pointed as an icicle, "does it mean that I killed her?"

"No," said Timothy, "if you really talked to her."

"Well—I did."

"Where?"

"On the hill path where I was walking. I often go up by the big house in the evening for the view."

"And you met Ruby coming down the hill?"

"Yes."

"You stopped to talk with her?"

"Yes."

"What about?"

"I asked her why she was there—at that hour of the night. She told me that she was after berries, that she was afraid to pick them from the good patches during the daytime because Miss Emily had forbidden it."

"You hadn't happened to meet Ruby there before, even though you frequently choose that path for an evening stroll?"

"I had not."

"What did you say to Ruby?"

"I warned her," said Lila, "to go right home."

"And what precisely were you warning her against? Did you believe that Ruby was in any particular danger?"

Again Lila's shoulders lifted in a delicate shrug.

"Possibly," she said. "For one thing, the child was trespassing against Miss Cotton's orders—and Miss Cotton is not a woman who gives orders lightly. Furthermore, there was the matter of Mrs. Benson's scare."

There was a moment's silence.

"I thought," Timothy's tone was carefully casual, "that you were inclined to doubt the cause of Mrs. Benson's fright."

Lila did not answer.

"At least," Timothy went on mildly, "you seem to have doubted the presence of danger to the point of venturing out alone. Why, in other words, should you have warned Ruby Turner against the very thing you were doing yourself?"

"I'm afraid," there was sudden sharpness in Lila's clipped words, "that I don't quite understand you."

"No?" Timothy was watching her fixedly. "Then I'll make it plain. I don't believe you, Mrs. Gilbert, when you say that you warned Ruby to go home because of the possibility of some lurking danger which had frightened Mrs. Benson earlier in the evening. Nor do I believe that you walked up the hill path at a little after midnight simply to get a view of the moon. Now will you give me a more accurate account of what you did—or shall I guess?"

There passed across Lila's face a faint shadow of emotion. Whether it was fear or anger that moved her, I could not determine, but when she spoke her voice showed not a trace of either.

"Please guess," she said. "It would be so much more interesting."

"Very well," Timothy took a long breath, "I will. I believe that you left our cottage last night because you overheard me telling Joan that I was about to search the hill path. You suspected, Mrs. Gilbert, that you would find Ruby there— and you wanted to reach her before I did, in order to issue a warning. But your warning, Mrs. Gilbert, was not concerned with the fact that Ruby was violating Miss Cotton's orders, nor with the business of Mrs. Benson's scare. You were not, I should say, anxious to warn Ruby at all—but someone who was with her. To be exact, Mrs. Gilbert, you wanted to get to your husband before I did. Am I right?"

I had a feeling, during the course of Timothy's speech, that he was taking a long shot, very much in the dark. And for a moment, watching Lila's unmoved acceptance of the amazing accusation, I feared that he had missed the mark. But I had reckoned without Allen Gilbert.

With a suddenness that made us all jump, Gilbert sprang forward and placed himself squarely between Timothy and Lila.

"For God's sake, Fowler," the words burst from his white lips, "stop it!"

"Stop what?"

"Stop making her lie for me. Can't you see," Gilbert turned toward his wife in a desperate appeal, "that you're only making things worse for me? I *told* you they'd never believe you—that they'd find out the truth somehow—" his words broke off suddenly before the look of utter scorn which crossed Lila's face.

"Very well, Allen," she sat up very straight against the pillows, "suppose you tell your story then. But if you think any fool will believe you—"

"You might," Timothy's quiet voice cut in, "give me a chance at believing him, Mrs. Gilbert. I've been known on occasions, to recognize the truth when I hear it. Now then, Gilbert. Was I right when I said you were on the hill path last night?"

"Yes."

"And you went there, as your wife guessed, to meet Ruby Turner?"

Gilbert nodded miserably. Then, as Timothy did not speak, a look of protest came over Gilbert's face.

"I don't know what you think of me," the weak chin was raised defensively, "but at least you must believe that I didn't intend to—to harm the girl in any way. Whatever you think—"

"Whatever I think," Timothy's tone was dry, "doesn't make any particular difference at this point. I'm simply interested in what actually happened last night. Where were you to meet Ruby?"

"In a little clearing just off the path, about halfway up the hill."

"And when you got there, Gilbert, what did you find?"

"I—0h God," the man drew a quivering hand across his mouth, "I saw her lying there—in the clearing.

"Was she dead?"

"I—oh, I don't know. She must have been, I suppose. But I didn't touch anything—I swear I didn't."

"I don't doubt that," Timothy nodded. "What did you do then?"

"Nothing for a minute. I just stood there, sort of dazed, looking at the kid. And then, just as I turned to go—I saw something moving on the path. A person coming toward the clearing—but I couldn't see who it was. I realized that I'd been found—with Ruby—like that, and I guess I lost my head. Anyway, I turned back and ran away from the path through the woods. I didn't stop until I got to the Benson cottage, and I waited there until the others came back from searching. It must have been about half an hour later when you came down from the hill and said you'd found Ruby. You know all the rest, Timothy. I—I would have told the truth before this," Allen Gilbert made a feeble attempt at dignity, "only Lila warned me that I'd never be believed. But I swear that now I've told you everything I know about what happened last night—"

"Except," said Timothy, "for one little thing. *Why* were you meeting Ruby Turner?"

Instantly the old, evasive look masked Gilbert's face. "Only because I wanted to—to talk to the girl," he murmured uneasily.

"Talk to her about what?"

"Something that in no way concerned what happened last night. Something that concerned only Ruby and me."

"You won't tell me what it was?"

For a moment it seemed as though Allen Gilbert was about to speak—then he glanced at Lila's set face—and held his silence. Eyes cast down once more, he shook his head.

"Very well, Allen," said Timothy slowly. "I can't force you to answer me—now." He turned toward the bed where Lila Gilbert had remained, throughout her husband's recital, still and composed as a dainty Dresden statue propped up among her pillows. "Just why," he asked, "did you consider it so important to keep your husband from telling the truth, Mrs. Gilbert?"

"Because," said Lila, "I foresaw this moment. I knew that you would doubt the truth when you heard it."

"Wasn't it perhaps," Timothy bent forward and spoke very carefully, "because *you* doubted the story yourself? Because, knowing the reason for your husband's meeting with Ruby, you feared that the girl might not have been dead when he found her?"

"*Certainly not,*" Lila's small mouth closed like a vise over the words. "I warned Allen not to tell the truth because I believed you were a fool—too much of a fool to know that Allen Gilbert is a coward—and that a coward never kills."

It was a long time before Timothy answered.

"You're wrong about me, Mrs. Gilbert," he said at last. "I'm not that much of a fool. I know that your husband is a coward—and I also know that cowards do not usually kill." He paused a moment, and then suddenly thrust out his hand. "Allow me to congratulate you," he said.

Lila laid her small hand in his, and gazed up wonderingly.

"May I ask what for?" she said.

"For your courage." Without another word, Timothy turned away from the bed and emerged into the livingroom. "Come on," he motioned to Amos Plunkett and me, "let's go."

## 9

When we reached the main path, Amos Plunkett turned to regard Timothy with a look of astonishment and somewhat bewildered admiration. "You sure move fast, Mr. Fowler." He passed a lurid bandana handkerchief across his forehead. "I don't know as I exactly see what you're drivin' at—but I'm right with ye anyways. Where do we go now? Benson's? Or that new fellow Jackson's cottage?"

Timothy shook his head. "Neither, just at the moment," he said. "I can't think of a thing to accuse those people of, and it would never do to tackle them in such a state of innocence. Besides, I'd like to mooch along on the Gilbert clue now that we've got such a pretty start. And that, I think, would best be accomplished by a chat with Ruby's mother."

The Plunkett automobile bore us over the hill with rattling efficiency, and as we emerged from the gates of Miss Cotton's property onto the main highway, Amos pointed to a smallish tumble-down frame cottage directly across the road.

"That there's the Turner place."

The car came to a jolting stop, and we got out. I hung back a bit reluctantly at first, but Timothy's hand was firm on my elbow. "Sorry," he said, "you'll have to come along, Joanie. Womanly tact and all that sort of thing."

It did take a bit of tact to maneuver an interview with Mrs. Turner. The stuffy little parlor was crowded with sympathetic and indignant neighbors who stared, half in resentment, half in awe, while Amos explained our mission. But finally we were ushered into the comparative privacy of the kitchen, and there, seated on a stiff wooden chair, we found Ruby's mother.

"It's a terrible thing that's happened," Mrs. Turner spoke dully, scarcely raising her eyes from her twisting, knotted hands. "A terrible thing. But I always knew somethin' like it was bound to happen—and my pa knew it before me. 'There's wickedness in that house over on the hill,' he used to say, 'and wickedness brings trouble on all that's near—on the good and bad alike.' Many's the time I've heard Pa say that—and many's the time I've warned Ruby to stay away from the place. But no, you couldn't tell that child anything. She'd just laugh at me and keep on goin' over with her berries and all—makin' friends with the summer folks and runnin' their errands for 'em, and it seemed like everything I'd tell her about the evil doings of old Doctor Jack and Miss Emily just made her more curious. She'd carry tales to the cottage people and listen to goodness knows what mischief they'd tell her—and now it's happened just like I always knew it would—" the heavy, toneless voice rambled on with the monotony of an often repeated story.

As soon as he could, Timothy broke in with a question, trying to bring out of Mrs. Turner's vague recital some more definite hint as to the possible cause of the tragedy. But it was uphill work. The woman's mind was so clouded with nameless fears and superstitions that it seemed quite impossible to make her focus on the fact that Ruby had been murdered by some person of flesh and blood, rather than a pervasive spirit of evil which dwelt in the old deserted house.

"This is one place, young man, where your city detectin' won't do a mite of good," Mrs. Turner eyed Timothy with dull hopelessness. "I tell ye Ruby was punished for meddlin' in things no mortal has any business meddlin' with. Things that act as sure as fate— and leave no human trace behind 'em. And now the harm's been done, you'd best not begin meddlin' yourself—for ye'll never find out what done the poor girl to death—never on this earth."

"Very well, Mrs. Turner," Timothy tried a new tack. "Suppose we go back a bit, then, to matters which we *can* learn something about. To Mr. Allen Gilbert, for instance. Had you ever heard your daughter mention him, Mrs. Turner?"

At the name, an odd gleam flashed suddenly in the woman's heavy eyes. But she looked down at her hands again when she answered. "Yes, Ruby knew him right well."

"Did she seem to like him?"

"Not lately—no. Not since that Jackson fellow's been hangin' round, talkin' to the child. He's new here this season, ye know, and he seemed to take quite a fancy to Ruby—just in a kind of friendly way. Nice enough sort of fellow he appears to be, and I let him stay around a good bit because he was always tellin' Ruby she oughtn't to be over to Miss Emily's place so much. I figured if the girl wouldn't listen to me, maybe she'd pay some attention to Mr. Jackson—so I let him talk away—but it don't seem to've done much good."

"Do you mean, Mrs. Turner, that Jackson warned your daughter particularly against Allen Gilbert?"

The woman nodded wearily. "I never rightly knew just what Mr. Jackson meant—but it seemed like he was tryin' to warn Ruby about some plan or other that Gilbert was mixed up in—and just the other day Mr. Jackson told me I'd ought to keep Ruby at home evenings. Well—I done my best about that, but it just seemed like the child was possessed of some devil's spirit, and last night, after we was all abed, she sneaked out and went over the hill again. She'd done it before—and I'd scolded her the worst I knew how, but Ruby'd just laugh at me. 'Ma,' she'd say, 'you leave me be and I'll make us all rich yet.'"

At the strange words Timothy bent sharply toward Mrs. Turner.

"What do you figure Ruby meant by that?" he asked.

"Why, I don't know as she meant anything so much," Mrs. Turner drew back a little before the intensity of Timothy's question. "Only she used to pick berries offen Miss Emily's patch, ye know, and then she'd sell 'em next day to the cottagers. I s'pose she just was jokin' about that. She had to pick the berries nights, ye see, because all the best patches are on the hill there, and Miss Emily'd never let her at 'em in the daytime. Not but what I tried to keep her from doin' it at all."

It was obvious that Mrs. Turner regarded the incident as of no possible importance, but Timothy seemed satisfied that he had made his point. Leaving the house, he led us to the car once more, and directed Amos to drive on down to the village.

"I want," said Timothy, "to have another look at Ruby—and this time, in the daylight; maybe I can learn something."

I was left to wait in the front section of the general store while Mr. Thorpe, who, besides being merchant and postmaster of Witch Harbor likewise served as undertaker, led Timothy and Amos to their gruesome errand upstairs. Standing there, idly watching the young girl who sorted the morning mail, I observed the knowing interest with which she examined each letter before pigeon-holing it—and quite suddenly I had an idea of my own. When the three men reappeared, I drew Timothy aside to whisper my suggestion, but I hesitated before the grim set of his face.

"What's the matter, Timothy? *Did* you learn something after all?"

He nodded, still looking straight ahead. "Plenty. I've seen people strangled before, but never anything like this. The kid was literally clawed to death—" he saw my face and stopped abruptly. "Sorry. But it does make a difference to know that someone hated Ruby Turner quite that much."

Glad enough to change the subject, I told Timothy about my hunch. He stared at me with raised eyebrows for a moment. "Sure," he said, "I could ask the question all right—but what would be the point?"

"I'll tell you that when you get the answer."

"Here goes then." Timothy crossed the store and faced old Mr. Thorpe. "Look," he said, "I wonder if you could tell me something very important. Do you know of anyone in Witch Harbor who sends letters to a member of Dr. Jack's family in Baltimore?"

Mr. Thorpe received the question, delivered in Timothy's best style, in an unpromising silence. He surveyed my engaging husband with a long and thoughtful stare, then turned to look me over. It was not, to be sure, the first time Mr. Thorpe had seen us—but he seemed to be giving the matter his consideration for the first time.

"So," he pronounced the verdict at last, "you folks think you're goin' to find out who killed Ruby Turner, do you?"

"We hope for something of the sort," Timothy smiled modestly.

Mr. Thorpe put on his glasses for a more thorough look.

"Well," he said, "you won't find out—I can tell you that much. And what's more, you're a couple of dern fools to try."

"No doubt," Timothy conceded politely. "But if you'll be good enough to answer that one question for me, I'd be very much obliged."

There was a further pause while Mr. Thorpe removed his glasses, polished them with exquisite care, and replaced them.

"All right," he said, "the answer is yes. There's somebody around here that writes to Mr. Russell Jack at a Baltimore address—but I can't tell you who it is because the envelopes are typed, and I ain't ever seen one of 'em mailed. Now—" he peered over the rims of his spectacles, "is that what you wanted to know?"

"That's part of it anyway," Timothy nodded cheerfully. "The other part is this: when did you first notice the letters, and about how many have there been?"

"Well now lemme see," Mr. Thorpe rubbed his chin, "I'd say the first one come along toward the end of last summer season—then there wasn't any durin' the Winter—and the end of June they commenced again. Mebbe there's been four or five altogether."

"You didn't happen to notice one today did you?"

"Nope."

"Nor yesterday?"

"Not as I recollect."

"I see." The little pucker between Timothy's brows deepened into a frown. "Well—I'm certainly much obliged, Mr. Thorpe. Now, if you'll let me use your telephone to send a message, we'll be on our way and not bother you any further."

"T'ain't no bother to me if you want to go meddlin' in trouble." Mr. Thorpe had an air of tolerant resignation. "Help yourself to the phone."

I listened curiously while Timothy negotiated a call to the nearest telegraph office and reeled off his message addressed to New York Police Headquarters:

*"Kindly wire information,"* he dictated, *"concerning present whereabouts family of late Dr. Albert Jack of Baltimore. Stop. Also dope on Anthony Jackson, lawyer, residence Newark. Stop. Thanks. Stop. Having elegant honeymoon. Stop. Joan sends love. Signed Timothy Fowler."*

## 10

The moment we were out the store, Timothy reminded me of my promise. "All right, I asked the question and you heard the answer—now tell me what your hunch was about the letters."

"Just that I happened to remember Mrs. Benson telling me that her sweet sunbeam of a husband is a director of one of the big scientific foundations. You know—research and so on."

"Well—?"

"And I wondered if he mightn't be on the trail of this great experiment of Dr. Jack's—for the foundation, of course."

"Not bad," Timothy nodded. "But where do the letters to one Russell Jack come into the picture?"

"That," I said, "is the smart part of my idea. From what we've seen and heard of Miss Cotton, I judged that Mr. Benson would hardly find her willing to cuddle up and reveal the secrets that she's been watch-dogging for so long. And so, if by any chance I'm right in assuming that he is after the stuff, I figured he must be going at it through the only other possible angle of approach. Namely: one of the surviving members of Dr. Jack's own family. Hence the hunch about Mr. Benson writing the letters."

"Don't be too sure of that," Timothy shook his head doubtfully.

"Look," I said, "I've got it all reduced. Since the letters only appear during the summer season, it must be someone in our colony who writes them—and since they began last year, it couldn't have been Tony Jackson. That leaves only the Bensons and the Gilberts to choose from—and the Gilberts have no typewriter."

"How do you know that?"

"Because Lila told me so herself. So there you are. I think that makes a pretty good case for the fact that it was Benson who wrote the letters."

"And *I* think," said Timothy, "that I married the right woman after all." Which, from him, was extravagant praise. "Just to prove my faith in you, my pet, we'll try the proposition on the old thundercloud himself when we tackle the Benson family. And that, I think, will be the next logical move in this highly illogical investigation of ours. After that—" he broke off with a sudden laugh. "After that, I think we'll have ourselves a swim and forget this damn business for a while."

We got to the swim a little after noon—but it wasn't so easy to forget the damn business. Even though we made a valiant effort to talk of other things, I knew that Timothy was still absorbed in the events of the morning. And I knew, too, that he was more disheartened than he would admit by the perplexing maze of crisscross evidence which seemed to hang like a tangled and shadowy web about the death of little Ruby Turner.

In my own mind, I went back over the two most recent interviews. The session at the Benson cottage had been a disappointing mixture of determined optimism from Mrs. Benson—and an equally determined silence on the part of her husband and son. To my regret, Timothy had not even broached the subject of the letters to Russell Jack. Afterward he had explained to me—somewhat cryptically—that he preferred to tackle the subject from the angle of Russell Jack himself. The interview with young Tony Jackson had been equally futile. He had been willing enough to talk—but he had nothing to say of the slightest value.

And what of our other suspects? Lying there on the warm sand, I checked over each one in turn—remembering always the strange words which Timothy had spoken after seeing Ruby's body. "It does change things to know that someone hated Ruby Turner that much." Allen Gilbert? I recalled his white face and trembling hands, the fearful glances he had turned toward his wife. Lila Gilbert? Impossible to imagine her fragile, poised control shattered by an emotion as violent as hatred. Miss Cotton? A woman capable, no doubt, of sweeping aside any obstacle that stood in the way of her iron will—but again, violence seemed out of keeping with her cold poise. As Timothy had observed, "If she's been up to any mischief, believe me, Miss Emily knows all the rules!" That was the trouble. Every person I thought of seemed equally impossible—and yet it *must* have been one of them.

Except, of course, for the possibility of an outsider—and I knew that Timothy strongly discounted that theory. Despite the evidence of trampled shrubbery, and general disorder outside the Benson cottage—which would account for Mrs. Benson's conviction that she heard a prowler—Timothy was steadfast in his opinion that no outsider had invaded our colony the night before. And the testimony of the villagers bore out this notion—for not one person could offer evidence that any stranger was lurking in Witch Harbor.

It was at this point in my speculations that I was startled to hear a voice behind me. I rolled over and opened my eyes to see young Jerry Benson looking down at Timothy.

"Excuse me, Mr. Fowler," the boy said, "but could I talk to you for a minute?"

Timothy raised himself on one elbow to look at Jerry.

"Sure," he said. "Sit down."

"Thanks," Jerry dropped down on the sand between us. "I—don't want to bother you," he began uncertainly, "but there's one thing I think you ought to know—and I couldn't talk very well this morning, in front of the family, you know."

Timothy nodded encouragingly.

"Go on," he said. "Tell me what's on your mind."

"Well—" Jerry took up a handful of sand and let it trickle slowly through his fingers. "I—it's about Father," he paused for a moment, as if for further encouragement, and then proceeded bravely. "I don't know whether I ought to talk about it—but Father won't tell you himself—and Mother just tries to cover everything up because she's always so scared—and they both try to keep me quiet by telling me to mind my own business. But, gee, Mr. Fowler—" the boy looked up with sudden appeal, "I think it's better to tell the truth, don't you?"

"I certainly do, son," Timothy agreed feelingly.

Jerry smiled a little uncertainly. Plainly it was a struggle for him to throw off the long habit of sulky silence and speak frankly, but he was making a valiant effort. I noticed the tenseness of his thin young body, the deadly earnestness of his face as he gathered himself for the ordeal of unburdening his conscience.

"You see," said Jerry, "it's about last night. When Father said he went out for a walk—he didn't tell you the truth."

"No?" Timothy's question was casual. I knew that he was deliberately masking his real interest, in an effort to put the lad at his ease, but he couldn't quite hide the sudden gleam of curiosity in his eyes. "What was the truth, then?"

"The truth," said Jerry solemnly, "is that Father has been going out every night at about half-past eleven or so—and I'm pretty sure it's not just for a walk."

"No?" Timothy's drawl was still carefully disinterested. "What makes you think that?"

"Because he never lets us go with him, and he gets pretty mad when Mother asks him about it. And because—" Jerry took a deep breath and hurried on, "one night about a week ago I—I followed him."

"You did?"

Jerry nodded.

"Not," he explained hastily, "because I *wanted* to—but Mother made me. She—she gets sort of nervous, you know."

"I know."

"Well—" the boy went on, "Father didn't go for a walk at all. He started down the shore path, but as soon as he was out of sight of our house he cut back, through the woods, and he went up to Miss Emily's cottage."

"He did?" Timothy sat up straight.

"Yes. He went to the back door and tried to get in—but it was locked, I guess. Anyway, he stood there for a minute, and then—" Jerry swallowed, "he opened a window and climbed through it."

Timothy's eyes narrowed sharply.

"You don't say," he murmured.

"Then," said Jerry, "I saw a light go on—it was in the kitchen—and I could see Father moving around inside. He—he *seemed* to be looking for something."

"Looking where?"

"All around," the boy made a vague gesture. "In the kitchen cupboards, and along the walls—and even in the stove. But he didn't find what he was looking for, I guess, because after a while he turned off the light, and I figured he was coming out again—so I beat it back to our house to get there ahead of him."

"Did you tell your mother what you had seen?"

"Yes."

"And what did she say?"

"Well—nothing much," the boy looked unhappy. "That is—she made a good deal of a fuss—but honestly, I don't think she knew what it was all about."

"You could hardly blame her for that," Timothy sighed. "It *was* sort of an odd performance."

"I guess it was," Jerry frowned. "Anyway, for a couple of days after that, Mother kept after Father all the time—wanting us to leave here. But he wouldn't listen. I think he sort of knew, though, that Mother had caught on, or something, because he didn't go out any more in the evenings—until last night."

"I suppose," said Timothy slowly, "that your mother stayed home from the clam-bake because she really had a headache?"

Jerry hesitated—but only for a moment.

"No," he said, "she didn't. She stayed because Father wouldn't go with us—and she didn't want to leave him here alone."

"Quite so," said Timothy, and looked at me. Then he turned to the boy again. "Jerry—what do you make out of all this?"

A troubled look came over the serious young face.

"I don't know," he said simply, "honestly, I don't. That's why I wanted to tell you about it."

"I see," Timothy nodded, watching the boy thoughtfully. "How old are you, Jerry?"

The boy's chin lifted a little defensively.

"Eighteen," he said.

"You've worried a good deal about all this business, haven't you?"

"Well—" said Jerry, "yes."

"I don't blame you," Timothy sighed again. "It's not a pretty business—and it's damned complicated. But I'm glad you told me what you did, and from now on you'd better leave the worrying to me." Timothy rose and stretched himself.

"You don't think, do you," the boy looked up anxiously, "that what I told you—about Father—had anything to do with Ruby?"

"No—oo," Timothy gave a good imitation of conviction—and I saw the strained tension of Jerry's thin shoulders relax a bit.

A few minutes later, while we climbed the shore path toward our cottage, Timothy turned to me.

"It looks, my pet, as if your hunch was right," he said.

"My hunch?"

"Don't I recall your telling me, a while back, that you suspected Benson of a commendable ambition to secure the work and data of the late Dr. Jack for this foundation of his?"

"Well—yes. But I certainly *didn't* say that I thought he'd be climbing in kitchen windows and looking inside Miss Emily's stove for the information."

Timothy opened the cottage door and looked at me with his most irritating grin.

"All right," he said amiably, "let's not argue the point—until after dark."

"What do you mean—*after dark?*"

The grin widened.

"Simply," he said, "that I intend to do a bit of stove-lid lifting myself."

## 11

Looking back on it now, I think I ought to say, in all fairness, that it was the peculiarly irritating quality of Timothy's grin and his refusal to explain the cryptic remark which went with it, that led me to walk up the hill alone. Which, in turn, led to my finding the bit of paper. And that, says Timothy, was the turning point of the case.

I cannot, however, take the slightest credit to myself for the discovery. It was simply that I was annoyed during the course of our lunch by Timothy's air of knowing—or suspecting—more than he would tell me. And when, after the meal, he retired to the bedroom and announced that he was going to sleep a while, my restlessness increased to such a point that I snatched up a pack of cigarettes and flounced out of the cottage with no particular objective beyond the slightly vindictive satisfaction of slamming the door behind me.

I just happened to pick the hill path, and it was purest chance which led me to select a certain flat rock, about half-way up toward the big house, upon which to settle myself—none too comfortably—there to meditate quietly upon my unreasonable grievances.

The piece of paper was wedged in beneath a ledge of that large rock—and again it was a mere accident that I happened to find it. For, since I was wearing rubber-soled shoes, I leaned down to scratch a match on the underside of the ledge. And there—showing quite plainly in the brief flare of the match—it lay. Still without any notion of un-earthing a vital clue, I fished out the paper. One look at the strange, neatly written words inscribed upon it, how-ever, was enough to send me plunging down the path to-ward home.

"Timothy—" I tore through the living-room and pounced upon my soundly sleeping spouse, "Timothy—look what I've got!"

He rolled over and sat up to blink at me, and at the sight of his tousled head, I inwardly repented my recent irritation.

"Hell's bells, Joanie. Whatever is eating you?"

"This. Look—" I thrust the paper at him. "I don't know what it is, but it's certainly *something*—"

Still blinking sleepily, Timothy looked. Another mo-ment and he was wide awake, sitting very straight and still while his eyes traveled rapidly over the brief page.

"Good jumping Judas, Joanie—where did you find this?"

"Up on the hill, under a rock, just off the path. Timo-thy—what *do* you think it means?"

"Hell—*I* don't know," Timothy's answer was very slow. "But look—it's a page from one of those loose-leaf note-book jiggers—"

I nodded eagerly. "And the date up there in the cor-ner—see?"

"July 19, 1934," Timothy read. "In other words," he looked up at me, "it's dated yesterday. But I'll be double damned," he frowned down again, "if I see what it's all about."

I squirmed around to look over his shoulder—and for a long minute we sat there, silent and intent, as we read over and over the words which were written in small, regular, printed script. That piece of paper is before me now, carefully preserved along with other bits of evidence which were finally woven into the solution of our riddle. As Timothy had already observed, this particular paper was a page from a loose-leaf notebook, and it had been torn away from the clamps which must have fastened it into a folder about four and a half by six inches. In the upper left-hand corner of the page was a number, neatly inscribed in black ink: 10952. In the opposite corner appeared the date: 7/19/34. And then the two baffling entries at which we stared so long and intently:

> 7 A.M.: Customary routine. Nervousness observed for past eight days noticeably abated. Appearance normal, behavior quiet. Appetite somewhat increased, probably due to recent nervous and physical activity. No sounds.
> 11 P.M.: Customary routine. Not visible. No sounds.

And that was all. Small wonder that, at the end of a long and frowning scrutiny of the words, Timothy heaved one sigh of sheer exasperation. Slowly he fished a cigarette from his pocket, lit it, and then squinted at me through a puff of smoke.

"Damned if I can make head or tail out of it," he said, "except—"

"Except what?"

"Well—of course it's an entry in some regular daily report. The date, the careful form, and the words 'customary routine' indicate that much. Also the neatness and uniformity of the printed letters show that the person is used to writing that way. But who the person could be, or what they could be reporting—or how the dickens this one page came to be torn out and left under a rock—God only knows. Anyway," he heaved himself up from the cot, "you were a smart girl to find it for me—and maybe I'll be smart enough to figure out what it means some day."

"Timothy—don't you suppose you might be able to trace it through the writing? Even though the letters are printed, someone may recognize it—"

"Amos Plunkett might," he nodded. "Or even the light-hearted Mr. Thorpe. Anyway, I'll try Amos when he comes along. He promised to bring me the answer to my wire as soon as it was phoned in—and that ought to be any time now."

As it happened, however, Amos did not put in an appearance until our supper was over and the dishes done. It was, I remember, just beginning to grow dark when I looked up from my knitting and saw the lean and lanky Plunkett figure advancing down the hill path with a weary, limping gait.

"I'm sorry to be late, Mr. Fowler," Amos flung himself into a chair and heaved a vast sigh, "but that dern car of mine's got a flat tire again. My boy's fixin' it, but he's so slow I figured I'd best walk down if you was to get your message before dark." He extracted an envelope from an inner pocket. "Here she is."

"Thanks, Amos." Timothy reached for it. "It was darn nice of you to take all that trouble."

"Oh, it wasn't no trouble. Only I never knew detectin' was so hard on the feet." Amos stretched out his sizable extremities and gazed at them ruefully. "But you know," he looked up, "mebbe it's a good thing I did walk, because comin' down the hill path there, I saw somethin' that might mean somethin'."

"And what was that?"

"Well—I don't know as it was so much, but it struck me as sort of odd at the time." Amos shifted forward in his chair, and his voice dropped confidentially. "Comin' around that turn in the path, 'bout half-way down, I caught sight of Emily Cotton. There wasn't anything out of the way about that, but she had her back turned to me and didn't hear my steps, and I hadn't watched her more'n a minute before I noticed she appeared to be lookin' fer somethin'—stoopin' down, she was, and lookin' all along under the pines and around that flat rock."

"Hold everything, Amos," Timothy paused in the middle of opening his telegram to look up with sudden interest. "Did you say the flat rock?"

Amos nodded. "It's that big one, you know, just off the path on the right-hand side—"

"Yes, I know," Timothy nodded hastily, and turned to me. "Is that the one, Joan?"

"The very one." I tried not to sound too excited.

"Go on, Amos. What else happened? Did Miss Emily appear to find what she was looking for?"

"Not as I could notice. As soon as she caught sight of me, she stopped huntin' and went along down the path—but I called right out and asked did she lose somethin'.'

"What did she say?"

"Nothin' at first," Amos chuckled with satisfaction. "But she sure was surprised. Just turned around and gave

me one of them looks of hers. Then, when I said mebbe
I could help her find it, she goes as sweet as sugar and
says, 'Oh, please don't bother, Amos—it was only a pen-
ny I dropped, and I expect it's quite out of sight in the
pine needles,'" He mimicked the honey tone to perfection.
"That's all there was to it—but I thought mebbe you'd
make somethin' out of it, Mr. Fowler."

"I think maybe I can, Amos, if you'll help me a bit."
Timothy went to fetch the precious piece of paper. "Suppose you look this over and tell me whether you recall
seeing that writing before."

It took some little time for the Plunkett spectacles to
be adjusted and the matter duly considered.

"Well now—" Amos stroked his chin in deepest per-
plexity, "it seems like I *have* seen printin' like that some-
wheres, but I don't know as I could say for sure."

"It isn't Miss Emily's writing, by any chance?"

"No—"

"Nor the writing of any person around here?"

"No 'tain't," Amos shook his head with decision. "I've
handled the mail long enough to be pretty sure of how
most of these folks write—and I ain't seen any hand like
this in years. But it seems like mebbe a long while ago—"
His shaggy brows gathered in a deep frown for a moment—
and then suddenly he remembered. "I got it, Mr. Fowler,"
Amos looked up triumphantly. "It was old Dr. Jack that
used to print his letters that way."

Timothy and I exchanged a bewildered glance.

"But Amos—it couldn't be Dr. Jack's handwriting.
Look—this paper is dated yesterday."

"I can't help that." The Plunkett conviction was not
to be shaken by a mere matter of impossibility. "I'm not
sayin' Dr. Jack did write this, mind you, but you asked

me where I'd seen letters like that before—and I'm tellin'
you."

"You certainly are." Timothy smiled a little wryly as he
took the paper from Amos' hand. He stood looking at it
for a moment, then folded the page with care and tucked it
into his pocket. "It's just possible," I heard him murmur,
"that you're not so far off after all."

We had a bit of difficulty in reading Mr. Thorpe's transcription of the telegram from New York Headquarters,
but between the three of us the message was at length deciphered.

ANSWERING YOUR QUESTIONS RE-
GARDING JACK FAMILY STOP WIDOW
OF DR ALBERT JACK DIED EARLY THIS
YEAR STOP OLDEST SON RUSSEL JACK
LIVING IN BALTIMORE EMPLOYED AS
CHEMIST HERALD MANUFACTURING
COMPANY STOP SECOND SON FREDER-
ICK JACK BELIEVED LIVING IN OREGON
SOME CONNECTION LUMBER BUSINESS
STOP NO OTHER FAMILY STOP AN-
SWERING YOUR QUESTION CONCERN-
ING ANTHONY JACKSON STOP NEWARK
REPORTS NO SUCH PERSON PRACTIC-
ING LAW THERE AT ANY TIME STOP DID
YOU KNOW SOME DAME EMILY COT-
TON MAKING INQUIRIES ABOUT YOU
STOP WHAT THE HECK ARE YOU UP TO
QUESTION MARK THE SAME TO JOAN
AND PLENTY OF IT EXCLAMATION
POINT

WALTERS

When we had finished reading it, Timothy lit a cigarette and looked at me.

"Well?" he said.

"Well—what? Are you surprised that Miss Cotton's
been on your trail?"

"Can't say that I am," Timothy shook his head. "But
the fact that Newark's rising legal light doesn't rise after
all—*that's* what I call a bit of news." As he spoke, Timothy was gathering up his coat and flash-light. Little as I
relished the idea of his prowling into the mysteries of our
neighborhood, I realized that there was no possible way of
persuading him to abandon the expedition. And so, wife-
like, I held my silence. At the door Timothy turned to
address Amos Plunkett.

"You don't mind staying here with Joan, do you? I'll
only be a few minutes—and she'd better not be alone."

Amos, who had been on the point of leaving for home
and a well-earned rest, sank back in his chair and tried to
conceal his dismay. And I, being quite as sleepy as Amos
looked, did my best to converse through stifled yawns,
after Timothy had gone.

"I reckon your husband's a right smart man," Amos
sighed presently, "but sometimes I wish I had a clearer
notion of what he's doin'."

"Sometimes I wish the very same thing," I agreed. "And
sometimes I think he wishes he had a clearer idea himself. But his cases always seem to turn out all right in the
end—" I paused on a particularly strangling yawn, and,
realizing the somewhat futile trend of our conversation,
I suggested to Amos that we might just as well make ourselves comfortable. "From past experience," I assured him,
"I know that Timothy's idea of a few minutes is likely to
include anything up to an all-night session."

With the blanket and pillow, which I provided, and numerous muttered comments, Amos draped his angular length across two chairs and prepared to wait. He could not, he declared in martyred tones, possibly get a wink of sleep on any such contraption—but before I was more than settled on my own cot in the next room, I heard a series of rhythmical and rending snores.

The next thing I knew, someone was walking on our front porch—and I opened my eyes to squint at the bed-side clock in the half-light from the living-room. It was a little after midnight.

Hunching a quilt around my shoulders, I emerged into the living-room just in time to see Amos struggling to dis-entangle himself from his blankets.

"What in thunder's goin' on out there?" He rose stiffly.

"*I* don't know, I'm sure—but I'll soon find out." I started for the door, but Amos, still trailing his blanket, stepped chivalrously between me and the possibility of lurking danger.

"Here—let me." He swung open the door and came face to face with Tony Jackson.

For a moment they stared at each other, then Mr. Plun-kett rallied—not too graciously. "Well—" he said, "what do you want?"

The young man did not answer at once. He stood in the doorway, looking (with pardonable surprise) from Mr. Plunkett in his enveloping draperies to me huddled in my quilt. He was, I observed, fully dressed himself—but in the light from our table lamp his face showed tense and a little frightened.

"I wanted," said Tony Jackson, "to see Mr. Fowler a minute."

"Then you'll have to wait, because Mr. Fowler ain't here." With great dignity, Amos Plunkett unwound his blanket and retreated to a chair.

Without another word Tony turned away, bounded down the porch steps, and started along the path at a run. Then, just as he was about to round the corner out of sight, he stopped—and I saw a flashlight turned full on his face.

"Why, hello Tony," it was Timothy's voice I heard. "I was just looking for you."

I failed to hear Tony's mumbled reply, but a moment later the two men came toward the porch. I noticed that Timothy's hand rested firmly on his companion's arm.

"As a matter of fact," Timothy went on calmly, "I went over to your cottage with the intention of routing you out and asking you to help me a bit—but luckily I find you all dressed and ready." He paused with a brief smile for me. "All right, Joanie?"

"Oh yes," I nodded hastily. "I was sound asleep when Tony's knock at the door wakened me."

"Good. Now then," Timothy addressed Tony and Amos briskly, "there's a job to be done tonight, and you two are the only ones I can trust to help me. If you're willing, and if we work fast, I think we can manage it all right. And if things work out as I believe they will—" he took a long breath—"it will mean that we can make some headway on this damned mess before daylight. Are you with me?"

The two men, Amos wide-eyed and blinking, Tony Jackson still nervously intent, watched Timothy in silence. Then Tony forced an uncertain little laugh.

"I'm afraid I don't know," he said, "what this is all about. I only came over here because I was certain I heard someone prowling around the back door of my cottage, and I thought I'd better notify you—"

"Never mind about that now," Timothy cut him short. "The important thing is that I want you to help me trap Miss Emily Cotton—"

"Hey—" for the first time Amos spoke, "what in thunder are you drivin' at now, Mr. Fowler?"

"I'll explain just as quickly as I can," Timothy clipped his words with rapid emphasis. "When I left here this evening, I went straight to Miss Emily's cottage and waited. I had a good reason to think that she'd be going out later on—and I was right. A little after eleven o'clock she left her house, and from where I was standing behind a bunch of pine trees, I saw her start up the hill path. That was the chance I'd been waiting for, and as soon as she was safely out of the way, I broke into her cottage through the kitchen window. It didn't take me long to find what I was looking for—which was this." From his coat pocket, Timothy drew a small black leather notebook, of the loose-leaf variety, and slapped it down upon the table.

"Timothy—" I sprang forward to look at it. "Is it the one the page came from?"

"It is," he nodded curtly. "Now the evidence of this notebook was all I needed to prove to me that Miss Emily was on the hill path, very close to the clearing where Ruby's body was found, at or about the time when the girl was murdered." Briefly he explained to the men about my finding the paper beneath the big rock. "There's no question," he went on, "but that the page was torn from this notebook, and that it was lost beneath the ledge of the rock. The fact that Amos saw Miss Cotton searching for something along the path at that particular place indicates that she was aware of the missing page, and of the precise spot where it had been dropped. All of which, plus the condition of other pages in the book, makes it pretty plain that some sort of a scuffle took place in the path there, on the night of the murder. To illustrate his point, Timothy flipped open the folder and showed us that several pages were rumpled and half torn from the folder—as if, indeed, the book had been involved in rough handling of some sort.

I had just time to catch a glimpse of the quickly turned pages, but a glimpse was sufficient to show several neatly written entries precisely like the one we had examined in detail earlier. Timothy was hurrying on.

"What these reports or entries are all about, I haven't the foggiest idea at the moment," he brushed aside our inevitable questions before we had a chance to voice them. "Except that they appear to be concerned with an experiment of some kind. But the really important thing right now is that this book shows definitely that Miss Cotton was somehow involved at the scene of the murder. And that, in turn, shows that she left her cottage last night and went up the hill path *for some purpose*. Whatever that purpose was, it seems damned likely that she's gone up there again tonight for the same reason, and if we can close in on her we'll stand a good chance of discovering what these mysterious errands are all about. With *that* knowledge as a lever—we may be able to get the sphinx to talk. Otherwise—" Timothy shrugged, "we'll be exactly as much in the dark tomorrow as we were today. Now—can I count on you to help?"

The two men nodded, Amos with an air of weary and puzzled duty which contrasted sharply with the alert, almost feverish intensity of Tony Jackson's signal that he was ready to assist.

Obviously, there was no time to be lost. Timothy moved about the room rapidly, fetching an extra coat for Tony, a flash-light for Amos, meanwhile outlining his scheme of action whereby the three of them, each taking a separate path, would close in on Miss Emily—wherever she might be up on the dark, mysterious hill. The men were so intent on their preparations that they did not notice my own hurried activity as I dashed into the bedroom, drew on a sweater and skirt, and bundled myself in a warm tweed coat for protection against the chill night air.

Not until they were on the point of leaving the cottage did Timothy notice me standing, flash-light in hand, close beside him.

"Where do you think you're going?" he demanded.

"With you," I said firmly. "And there's no time to argue."

## 12

I don't believe I shall ever forget the moment when we first caught sight of Miss Emily. It was as if, when Timothy parted the thick spruce boughs and we peered cautiously through, we were actually gazing upon a scene from some old legend of witchcraft. For there, in the center of the very clearing where Ruby Turner had been murdered, and oblivious of our spying eyes, Miss Cotton knelt before a strange collection of heaped-up papers and dry sticks. For all the world like one performing an ancient magic rite, Miss Emily lifted a smallish pail from the ground, and poured its contents carefully over the pile before her.

In the moment which followed, I felt, rather than saw, Timothy's quick gesture to prevent what happened next. But he was not quick enough. Before he could open his mouth to speak, before he more than raised his arm, Miss Emily had struck a match and touched off the kerosene-soaked papers.

Instantly the fire leaped up, and in the bright orange light of the roaring flames Miss Emily's grim features showed plainly. More than ever, in that moment of weird illumination, she looked like some inhuman creature. Sitting back upon her heels, the outline of her gaunt, gingham-clad shoulders showing against the bright light, she remained perfectly motionless. Save for her eyes, which seemed to glow with an almost fanatical brilliance in the reflected gleam of the fire, Miss Emily Cotton might have been a figure carved of granite.

In silent, shivery fascination I watched the curious illuminated tableau framed by the dark silhouette of the spruce branches. And then, in an instant, it was over. The quick, devouring flames died down as abruptly as they had risen, and the kneeling woman was left staring at the smoldering heap of charred ashes. The next moment Timothy had stepped into the clearing.

"Well, Miss Cotton—" his voice broke in with the harshness of reality upon the eerie silence.

Miss Cotton turned to see him standing close behind her. There was a brief pause, during which she neither spoke nor moved. Then, slowly and a little awkwardly, she rose from the ground and faced him.

"Yes, Mr. Fowler," she said. With the light of the fire gone, I could no longer see Miss Emily's face, but the quiet control of her voice indicated that whatever fear or shock she may have felt at the abrupt intrusion, was well concealed beneath an unshakable outward calm.

"I needn't tell you," Timothy's tone was as level as hers, "that your presence here, at this hour, and your action which I've just witnessed, will require an explanation."

Miss Emily's only answer was a nod.

"If, indeed," Timothy's words took on a certain sharpness, "there *is* an explanation."

But this time there was no answer at all.

"You know, of course, that I have no authority to question you, Miss Cotton, except in the presence of Amos

Plunkett. So I'll ask you to follow me to my cottage where Amos will take charge of things."

Another nod from Miss Emily was the only sign that she heard the words. Timothy waited for a moment, as if half expecting her to speak, and then, when she did not, he stepped over to the spot where, a minute before, the bright flames had leapt. Bending down, he turned his flash-light on the smoking cinders, and I saw him prod the remnants carefully with the end of a short stick. Evidently nothing—not even the tiniest scrap of the destroyed papers—remained, for after a long and intent scrutiny Timothy straightened and turned back to Miss Emily.

"Go through this way, please, and I'll follow." With his flash-light he indicated the way to the hill path.

Still silent, Miss Emily obeyed—and I, trailing along at Timothy's elbow, watched in fascination the slow progress of her gaunt figure as she led the way through the low pine brush with firm, sure steps.

As we emerged into the main path, Timothy halted for a moment, and cupping his hands, he gave a long, low whistle. A silence followed, while the sound of the whistle seemed to melt away into the brooding hush of the dark woods. Then, from further up the hill, came an answering call—almost as if it were an echo of the first sound. A pause—and then a third, fainter signal reached us from the direction of the back path where I knew that Tony Jackson had been sent to search.

"All right," Timothy nodded, "come along to the cottage."

When we had reached our place, there was a slight delay while we waited for Amos to put in his official appearance—and during the interim Timothy spoke not a word.

I was frankly curious to see how Miss Emily was taking it all—but I got little satisfaction from watching her. She simply seated herself in a straight-backed chair, and asked me, presently, for a cigarette. When I had given her one, she lighted it with fingers which were far steadier than my own. Only once did a flicker of emotion cross Miss Emily's face, and that was when she caught sight of the black leather notebook. It seemed to me, in that moment, that the odd look which flashed from Miss Emily's cool gray eyes was almost an expression of satisfaction—or even triumph of some curious sort. But that, I thought, must have been a mistaken impression, and before I had time to reflect upon it further, a loud thumping of footsteps on the porch indicated that Tony and Amos had arrived.

It must have been a strange scene that confronted the two men as they entered the cottage. There was Miss Cotton, calmly smoking her cigarette—for all the world as if she were paying a polite afternoon call, instead of sitting before a sheriff and a detective for questioning at two o'clock in the morning. Timothy stood before the fireplace, staring at the floor with an air of deep thoughtfulness. And I, not to be outdone in casual poise, had gotten out my knitting and pretended to engross myself in the business of knit four, purl two.

Amos took in the tableau with a long look, and then shook his shaggy gray head as if weary with the effort of following the night's strange events. In silence he listened while Timothy described briefly Miss Cotton's curious actions in the clearing on the hill.

"I told her," Timothy finished, "that of course you would require an explanation of such a performance—at such a time and in such a place." He paused, and fixed a meaning glance upon Amos.

"Yeah—" Amos cleared his throat with embarrassed violence. "I reckon you're right, Air. Fowler." A second clearing of the throat seemed to bring him no further ideas, and he looked appealingly back to Timothy.

But it was Miss Cotton herself who came to the sheriff's rescue.

"Don't trouble to think up a question, Amos," her tone was dry. "I came here with the intention of making a full confession."

The effect of her words was instantaneous. Amos blinked several times very rapidly and swallowed hard. Tony Jackson bent forward with a sharply audible breath, and clenched his fingers so tightly that the knuckles showed ivory white. And I dropped three stitches. Even Timothy showed signs of unmistakable interest.

Miss Emily continued quietly.

"I should, as a matter of fact, have told you frankly what I knew of last night's happenings on the hill much earlier—but there were some things to be attended to first. Those things I destroyed in the clearing a few minutes ago, Mr. Fowler, will tell you that the destruction was—complete." For just a fleeting second, Miss Emily's glance mocked Timothy's unsmiling face. Then she went on with perfect seriousness. "I have for the past several months been engaged in an experiment involving a new and powerful drug which, I believe, I am the discoverer. The nature of this drug I shall not, of course, divulge to you or to anyone else. It is my secret—and until my experiments are complete and the records turned over to the proper scientific authorities—it is my exclusive property. I will say, however, that it is a derivative of a common narcotic, and therefore I have had to employ a human subject in order to test its precise effects and possible value and importance. My discovery of the drug came about after years of research and investigation along certain lines which were begun during my years of association with Dr. Albert Jack—of whom you, Mr. Fowler, may have heard." Again the ironic glance flicked at Timothy.

"In any case," Miss Emily continued, "I can assure you that my work on this project has been thorough and exact—and that I have every reason to believe that the drug I have discovered will be of the greatest value to medicine. But before I could complete my report it became necessary, as I have said, to test the effects of this new drug upon the human system. I need hardly say that this phase of my experiment was fraught with the greatest difficulties. To locate a subject who was willing to submit to the perfectly harmless tests—and discreet enough to maintain the necessary secrecy, from this community which, as you must realize, Mr. Fowler, is not only ignorant of scientific affairs but actually hostile and suspicious toward any activity of mine—was an almost impossible task. I did, however, manage to procure a person whom I regarded as sufficiently intelligent and trustworthy—and for the past two years I have been using this person as a test subject in order to tabulate the effect of the drug in varying forms and doses. Had it not been for certain unforeseen and highly unfortunate circumstances which developed recently, the report of my discovery would now be nearly ready to submit to the scientific and medical authorities. But instead—because of these complications which rendered the experiments useless—the final section of my report now lies in a heap of unrecognizable ashes." Miss Emily pronounced the dramatic words without a shade of emphasis, but as she paused, her thin lips were twisted in a bitter smile.

"Of course," she went on, "one learns to expect these set-backs in scientific work. It is only one of the many lessons in patience that the life of research teaches. But, in this case, the disappointment is doubly discouraging, since the failure was not due to any flaw in the experiment itself, but to outside influences. It was meddling and greed which ruined my years of patient effort—meddling and greed so ruthless that they did not even stop at murder. In other words, my experiment could not be completed because my subject, Ruby Turner, is dead."

In the silence which followed the amazing words, Miss Emily turned to address me in a perfectly matter-of-fact tone, requesting another cigarette. Having obtained it, she looked at Timothy with a politely inquiring air.

"Am I making myself clear, Mr. Fowler?" she asked.

"Oh, quite."

"Who it was that murdered Ruby," Miss Cotton continued, "I cannot, unfortunately, tell you. But of the motive which prompted the deed, I am certain. This person had, by what means of spying and trickery I do not know, discovered that my experimental work was in progress, and that I had taken Ruby into my confidence to the extent which was necessary, in using her as a volunteer trial subject. The person then approached Ruby, with the intention of bribing her into turning over to them a sample of the drug which I had given her to take. This much Ruby confided in me—but, try as I would, I could not get her to tell me the name of the person. The child had, for all her garrulousness, a curious streak of stubborn loyalty—the same loyalty which, alas, had led me to select her as a helper—and I knew better than to force her confidence. I warned Ruby, of course, to steer clear of this meddler as much as possible, and meanwhile I did everything in my power to hasten the completion of the experiments, in the hope of ending the matter before any more serious attempt to steal my secret might develop. But I reckoned without sufficient knowledge of the desperate character of this intruder." Miss Emily leaned forward to flick the ashes of her cigarette into the fireplace with a careful gesture.

"Not only," she said evenly, "did this person willfully and brutally murder Ruby Turner—apparently because she would not betray my confidence and supply them with the information they wanted—but they arranged with devilish cunning to stage the murder in such a way and at such a place that suspicion for the deed would fall on me. I don't need to enlarge upon this fact to you, Mr. Fowler, for of course you *have* suspected me from the very first moment. The fact that Ruby was killed on my property, in the very place and at the very hour when I was accustomed to meeting her secretly—the fact that a page from my notebook records was deliberately placed in the path near the clearing—these facts plus the general suspicions and legends which have grown up about me among the people of Witch Harbor were, you will agree, quite sufficient to center a very dangerous circumstantial case against me. Isn't that true, Mr. Fowler?"

"Oh, quite," said Timothy again.

"Quite," Miss Emily nodded. "I had, therefore, only one course left which seemed possible to me. Under the circumstances of Ruby's death, my experiments—still incomplete—were not only impaired as scientific records, but positively dangerous to me if they were to fall into the hands of investigators who might twist their perfectly innocent contents into highly incriminating evidence. In the eyes of ignorant police and perhaps, eventually, an ignorant jury, those records would have made me a sort of modern witch—willfully experimenting with the life of a girl by administering nameless and mysterious potions. Whereas, actually the tests were quite harmless to Ruby, and were a necessary part of a work intended to be of great value to the enlightening science of medicine. I saw, therefore, that I must do two things. First, destroy all tangible records which might be used to incriminate me unjustly—and second, to tell you honestly what my part in the unfortunate affair was. Both of these things I have now done, and I trust that what information I have given will help you in discovering the identity of this unknown fiend who robbed Ruby Turner of her life—and me of my years of patient effort." As quietly as she had begun, Miss Emily stopped speaking. For a long moment she sat quite still, looking straight ahead. Then, as if recalled to the present by the stub of her cigarette which had burned, unheeded, down to her fingertips, she crushed it out carefully, and rose.

"There's one thing, Miss Cotton, I don't quite see—"

"Yes?"

"And that is—if you destroyed all records of your experiments which pertained to the test reactions of Ruby Turner, how does it happen that I discovered this particular notebook," he indicated the small black leather folder, "in your cottage, *after* you had taken all your papers out to burn them?"

"The explanation of that," Miss Emily seemed not at all perturbed, "is simple—and not very pleasant. That notebook was taken from my house last night, and was not returned until after I had left the cottage this evening. I cannot possibly say, of course, who it was that twice entered my cottage and tampered with my possessions—but it seems likely that it was the same person who was so bent upon incriminating me in the death of Ruby. However, if you have examined the contents of the notebook you must have observed that I never refer to Ruby by name, but only as X. This was a necessary precaution, since I was in the habit of carrying the book with me on certain occasions when I met Ruby—and there was always the risk that the notes might fall into the wrong hands. To further insure the secrecy of my project, I made only the briefest notes at these times—and I phrased them in such a way that they would be quite meaningless to anyone save myself. Therefore—unfortunate as it certainly is that my property should have twice been taken from my house without my consent—I can assure you, Mr. Fowler, that nothing in that notebook could be used to prove anything about me or about my work."

"I see," said Timothy, in a tone which rather belied his words. He hesitated for a moment longer—seeming to be in the grip of some puzzling uncertainty. Then, with a shrug of pure weariness, he told Miss Emily that she might go.

Everyone in the room looked relieved at the decision—Amos the most so, Miss Emily herself the least. Tony Jackson offered to see Miss Cotton to her cottage. When they had gone, and Amos had taken his limping departure, Timothy continued to stand before the fireplace—lost in thought.

"What *are* you trying to figure out, Timothy?" For all my weariness, I could not go off to bed without that question.

Still frowning, Timothy shook his head.

"Damned if I know," he said. Crossing to the table where the notebook lay, he scanned the neat pages. "Meaningless is right," he murmured presently, and closed the book with a sigh. "There's not a thing there that tells me anything more than the single page we pondered over this afternoon. Oh well—" he snapped out the light and followed me into the bedroom, "there's no use stewing any more tonight."

"*I* thought," I observed while we were undressing, "that Miss Emily's story was very convincing."

"So did I," Timothy nodded. "That's one of the things that bothers me. Maybe it's just my nasty nature—but I'm generally leery of a story that's too convincing. And there are a couple of things that I still can't figure out. One: why should those notes be written in what Amos declares is Dr. Jack's own handwriting, or a copy of it? Two: why should Miss Emily choose the hillside at midnight for a place to burn her papers when she had a perfectly good fire-place and a stove in her own cottage?"

I had, of course, no answer to suggest for either question. For a minute Timothy continued to sit on the edge of his cot, staring at my blank countenance.

"Anyway," he gave his pillow a vicious spank and settled down upon it, "thank God Miss Emily was crazy enough to choose the hillside. At least it gave us the chance to corner her."

I agreed—sleepily. And not for some time did we learn that Miss Emily's reason for choosing the hillside was not crazy—but very, very sane.

## 13

It was Mrs. Benson who gave us the second alarm. From the instant I saw her coming toward our cottage, I knew that something dreadful must have happened. For once her expression was neither cheerful nor coy, and as she hurried along the path, every line of her plump figure indicated disaster of some sort. I was, at the moment, standing by the kitchen window, engaged in measuring out our breakfast coffee—but after one glance at her set, white face, I put down the percolator and hurried out to meet her.

"What's happened, Mrs. Benson?" I took her arm as she reached the porch steps.

"Oh, Joan—" her rather pale blue eyes were wide with terror, "something *awful*—Joan, I must see Timothy right away."

I explained that Timothy had gone for an early morning dip, but would be back almost immediately. Mrs. Benson collapsed into a chair, and sat staring at me with that look of unchanging horror.

"Joan," she said excitedly, "Miss Emily Cotton is dead."

"Miss Emily—*dead?*" It was my turn to stare back—wide-eyed and incredulous. "But how—how do you know?"

"Because," Mrs. Benson's voice sank to a whisper, "I saw her."

"Where?"

"In her cottage—just now. I was passing by, and I saw that a light was burning in the kitchen. It struck me as rather strange, and I stepped up to the window and looked in. There she was—sitting in a chair in front of the kitchen table—*dead*. Oh—it was horrible, Joan—"

"But what could have killed her?"

"She was shot, I think—there was a dreadful mark on the back of her head. I—didn't go into the house or touch anything, but I could see quite plainly through the window. Joan, what *shall* we do?"

"Have you told anyone else about this?"

"Oh, no," Mrs. Benson shook her head. "I came straight here."

"Then," I said, "there's nothing to do but wait for Timothy."

For the next few minutes I forced myself to concentrate on the business of breakfast. By the time the coffee had begun to perc, I spied Timothy's tall, lean bathing-suited figure on the path, and I beckoned him to the back door. There, in a hasty whisper, I imparted the news.

For once in my life, I had the doubtful satisfaction of seeing Timothy completely surprised. When I finished speaking, he simply stared at me in blank astonishment. Then he shook back his wet hair like a shaggy and puzzled dog, and whistled a long, low whistle.

"Well, I'll be damned," he said. "I guess the old mastermind must be cracking up, Joanie. This is certainly the *last* thing I expected." A wry smile went with the words, but as he brushed past me on his way to the bedroom, I saw that the look in Timothy's eyes was anything but humorous.

As I had hoped, the hot coffee served to steady Mrs. Benson's crumbling nerves—and when Timothy appeared, after a lightning change into dry clothes, she was able to repeat her story quite coherently. Having heard it, Timothy paused only long enough to gulp a cup of coffee himself and stuff a piece of toast in his mouth before starting out to look things over. Neither Mrs. Benson nor I accepted his hurried suggestion that we had better wait where we were.

Mrs. Benson, as usual, had no thought but to return to "her boys." And I hurried resolutely in the wake of Timothy's long strides.

"If," I said grimly, "my married life is going to be composed of one murder after another—I think it's time I got used to the thing."

But I doubt if Timothy even heard my words. Having opened Miss Emily's kitchen door, he was at once completely absorbed in the details of the scene before him—too absorbed, I'm sure, even to be aware of my shrinking but determined presence on the threshold behind him. Nor was I, at the moment, aware of anything save the figure of Miss Emily Cotton—and a certain sinking feeling in the pit of my stomach.

Seated there before her bare kitchen table, her thin, strong shoulders erect against the straight wooden chair, Miss Emily's body had a strangely life-like look which made the fact of her death all the more ghastly. I was reminded that, only a few hours before, Miss Emily had sat just so on a straight chair in our living-room, recounting in precise, unhurried sentences the story of her secret experiments. And now—with her cold gray features closed in the final secret of death, there remained about her an air of forbidding dignity and poise which even the lolling, shattered head could not alter.

Timothy, less romantic and more practical than I, was obviously wasting no time in such speculations. He moved rapidly through the rooms of the small cottage, noting every detail with a sharp and practiced eye. Having finished his survey, he returned to the kitchen and considered briefly.

"Not a trace of any disturbance here," he murmured thoughtfully. "From the looks of things, I'd say the killer caught her unawares with a pot shot through the window there—" he pointed to the window, open about fourteen inches, directly behind Miss Cotton. "And there's no hope of picking up footprints outside, since Mrs. Benson tramped around enough, while viewing the remains through that same window, to obliterate any marks the murderer might have left. Which, incidentally, makes me wonder—not for the first time—whether dear Mrs. Benson is quite as simple-minded as she sometimes seems."

"You can't mean she might have blotted out those footprints on *purpose?*"

"Stranger things have happened. Anyway, I think it's fairly clear that Miss Emily wasn't killed as a result of any quarrel, or on the spur of the moment—but that the killer came here with a definite intention, carried out that intention with one carefully aimed shot, and then made off without, I'd say, even having entered the cottage."

"Don't you think it queer, Timothy, that we didn't hear the shot?"

"Speak for yourself, my pet," Timothy shook his head. "As for me, I was so darned tired by the time I got to bed, that I doubt if a volley of cannon under my pillow would have disturbed me. The only other cottage within easy earshot is Tony Jackson's—and he ought to have been as sleepy as we were. We might, however, try him out, and see whether he's smart enough to think of that excuse. In any case, he's technically the last person to have seen Miss Emily alive—so he's due for a workout."

Either Tony Jackson was asleep when we arrived, or he gave a very good imitation of it. Through the screen panel of the front door, we could see his head buried deep in a pillow of the cot. When repeated knocks failed to arouse any response, Timothy entered the cottage and walked over to the bed.

"Tony," he shook a limp shoulder, "wake up and tell me something."

With a muffled groan of sleepy protest, Tony rolled over and squinted upward.

"Have you," Timothy inquired briskly, "seen Miss Cotton this morning?"

"Huh?" Tony sat up and blinked. "Good Lord, no," he stifled a yawn that was half a grin. "What an improper suggestion." The grin didn't last long before Timothy's sober expression.

"Then tell me exactly what happened when you took her home last night—or rather, early this morning."

"Why—nothing particular. I just left her at her door, and said good-night. She went in, and I came straight on here."

"And went to bed?"

"Sure."

"And you heard nothing during the rest of the night?"

"Not a thing until you came in just now. Say—what the hell is this all about, anyway?"

Very briefly, Timothy told him—and without waiting for Tony's shocked reaction, he started to move about the room, searching the scanty contents of the shack with quick, methodical care. For a while Tony looked on in silence, then he protested mildly.

"What are you looking for?"

"Oh—" Timothy did not pause, "just wondering whether you happen to have a gun."

"Well, I haven't," Tony snapped. "And if I had, it wouldn't give you the right to come in here and search my place without a warrant."

"Quite so," Timothy agreed absently. He was standing before the open clothes-closet.

"Well then, stop it."

"But—" Timothy bent down and dragged out a pair of heavy shoes—the same shoes, I recalled, that Tony had been wearing the night before, "it doesn't take a warrant to look at a man's shoes and see that they're wet. And it doesn't take a master-mind to figure out that you've been up to something since I say you last. Because the ground was dry when you left our cottage last night, and it *did* rain sometime later on." He picked up the shoes and plunked them down by the cot. "Now then, Tony, where did you go after you left Miss Cotton? Or—*before* you left her?"

"I don't have to answer you," Tony was flushed with confused anger. "You haven't the slightest right to question me."

"True," Timothy nodded calmly. "As a lawyer, of course, you would know that," he paused for a moment, as the color in Tony's cheeks deepened visibly. "However, I *will* have the right to question you when Amos gets here—and you'll save time by answering now. Where did you go?"

"I simply went outside to look around my own place," Tony explained. "I started to go to bed as soon as I came in, but I remembered that I'd heard someone prowling about much earlier—I tried to tell you about that last night, but you wouldn't listen—and I decided I'd better take a look before turning in, to see whether the prowler had left any traces. By the time I got dressed again, and outside, it was raining. But if you think that had anything whatever to do with Miss Emily Cotton (God rest her iron-bound soul) you're quite mistaken."

"And did you," Timothy inquired with interest, "find any traces of your marauder?"

"No."

"Strange," Timothy murmured.

"What's strange about it?"

"Only that I thought you might have noticed a rather obvious trace in the form of a note that seems to have been slipped under your back door."

"*What?*" Tony turned sharply about to look at the threshold—and there, surely enough, a folded edge of white paper protruded beneath the door. Before Tony could even attempt an explanation, Timothy had retrieved the message and was examining it.

"*Black evidence no good,*" he read aloud, "*suggest wait until tomorrow night for trial as F. appears restless tonight.* Well—your marauder was brief—if not very enlightening. Also he, or she, types neatly. I suppose you haven't the vaguest idea who could have left this, have you?"

As Timothy held out the paper for Tony's inspection, I could see the two cryptic lines, carefully typed and spaced in the center of a half sheet of ordinary white paper.

"Well—?" Timothy repeated impatiently, "Are you going to tell me who left this?"

No answer from Tony, who continued to stare sullenly at the message before him.

"Are you going to tell me that Mr. Benson didn't write it?"

Still no reply.

"And are you going to deny that the words: 'F. appears restless tonight,' refer to me?"

"I'm not going to deny anything," Tony raised his eyes to look at Timothy coolly, "and I'm not going to admit anything either. And you can't prove a damn thing. You know as well as I do that this colony has gone crazy in the last couple of days—and you don't know what any of the mysterious happenings or messages mean, any more than I do. But since you've taken it upon yourself to solve the business—go to it. You've searched my place now, and you're welcome to make anything you can out of what you've found here. As for me, I'd appreciate being left to mind my own business."

"That," said Timothy, "is a privilege which will be granted to you with my compliments. It's a pity, though, that you didn't avail yourself of it a little sooner."

When we were out of sight of Tony's cottage, Timothy handed me the typewritten message.

"Why give me this?" I inquired.

"Because we're going to the Bensons'—and I want you to do a bit of special sleuthing. While I engage the assorted Benson temperaments in fascinating conversation, you, my pet, will slip quietly into Papa Benson's study and see if you can't match up this torn half of paper with its mate. Do you see?"

"I suppose so. But what do you expect to gain if I *do* manage to prove that he wrote it?"

"That," said Timothy amiably, "is by way of being a rather ticklish question—and I think I'd rather leave the answer to the inspiration, if any, of the moment. But for one thing," he added more seriously, "it will establish my long-cherished hunch that Benson and this Tony Jackson, the lawyer from Newark who is neither a lawyer nor from Newark, are in some kind of cahoots together. And if I do prove that—it'll be about the first thing that has been proved in this mess—so let's be thankful for small favors."

## 14

Fortunately for us, Jerry Benson had something on his mind—something which saved Timothy a good deal of time and questioning. We met the lad at the junction of the main path, where he had obviously been waiting for a word with Timothy.

"Mr. Fowler," Jerry began at once, "you said if I—I saw anything that bothered me I could tell you about it—"

"You certainly can, Jerry. What is it?"

"Well—" the boy glanced nervously over his shoulder toward the Benson cottage, and lowered his voice, "it's something that happened last night—and when I heard about Miss Cotton—I thought I ought to tell you. Father went out walking again in the evening—just after eleven o'clock, I think it was—and he was gone for nearly an hour. Mother was pretty worried about it—"

"How do you know that, Jerry?" Timothy interrupted. "Did your mother talk to you about it?"

"Oh, no," the boy shook his head hastily. "I was supposed to be asleep, you see. But I heard Father go out—and then I sort of got to thinking, and couldn't go to sleep. So I was still awake when he came in, and I could hear Mother arguing with him—and that's how I know she was worried, because she was kind of crying and all."

"I see."

"Mother kept saying, 'You haven't any right to go on acting this way without telling me what you're doing. Suppose something should happen—how could you ever explain your mysterious behavior?' And then Father laughed, sort of, and asked her what she expected would happen."

"Did your mother have an answer for that?"

"Well, she said, 'I don't know, but with such horrible things going on around here, and Miss Emily's so queer herself, I just know there's going to be some dreadful trouble.' Father laughed right out loud then, and he said, 'If something *does* happen, it won't be Miss Emily that it'll happen to—you can be sure we won't have any such luck as that!'"

"You're quite sure, Jerry, that your father said *'we'*?"

"Very sure," the boy nodded solemnly. "And you see, Mr. Fowler, the main reason I wanted to tell you about this, is because I'm sure it means Father didn't know anything about Miss Emily getting killed—or he never would have said what he did—would he?" Jerry's earnest young gaze searched Timothy's face appealingly.

'Well—no, I wouldn't say so," Timothy reassured him gravely. "But just while we're on the subject, did you overhear anything more last night?"

"Only that Mother asked again why we couldn't go away from here—and Father answered quite cheerfully for him. He said: 'We'll be ready to go sooner than you suppose. Inside of a week, I think, if things work out as I expect them to.' Mother seemed quite relieved then, and they didn't talk any more. But this morning she's all upset again, about Miss Emily and everything."

"Well, that's quite natural," said Timothy easily. "I guess we're all a bit on edge—but don't you worry too much about it."

"Oh, I don't," Jerry made an effort to smile. "I just wanted to tell you this so you'd know Father didn't have anything to do with—with what happened."

"Look, Jerry, do you want to help me out with a big favor?"

"Sure."

"If you could hike down to the village and tell Amos Plunkett I need him in a hurry, I certainly would appreciate it."

Jerry nodded willingly. "Shall I tell him about Miss Cotton?"

"Yes. But mind you don't tell anyone else. And be as quick as you can, will you, Jerry?"

"Sure I will, Mr. Fowler." The boy was off at once.

Timothy watched the thin young figure disappear up the path at a run, and shook his head. "Well, anyway," he sighed, "Jerry won't be around to hear me put his papa over the jumps. Poor kid," he sighed again. "Come along, Joanie, and do what I told you about the paper. If you find the other half, just give me a nod—and leave the rest to me."

I didn't, fortunately, have much difficulty in carrying out my assignment. It was simple enough to excuse myself, while Timothy stalled the Bensons with conversation, on the pretext of going to the kitchen for a glass of water. And once out of the living-room, I made for Mr. Benson's study. I sat down at his desk before the typewriter—that same typewriter which had so disturbed Lila Gilbert's communions with nature—and, feeling nervous but duty-bound, I opened the desk drawer and began to search. It

wasn't long before I saw, tucked under a neat pile of letters, a half sheet of plain white paper— and with eager
fingers I laid the torn edge against the paper Timothy had
given me. They matched—beyond a shadow of a doubt.

Back in the living-room, I gave Timothy the nod he had
been waiting for, and seated myself to wait. I was painfully aware of the atmosphere of strain within the room.
Mrs. Benson's bright glance flickered nervously from her
husband to Timothy, and back again. Even Mr. Benson,
for all his habitual stolidity, showed unmistakable signs of
uneasiness, so well had Timothy worked up the feeling of
suspense.

"Mr. Benson," Timothy walked over and stood before
him, "how long have you known Russell Jack?"

The man looked up from beneath his heavy gray
brows—a curiously penetrating glance. It was one of the
few times I had seen him look directly at anyone.

"About as long as you have, Mr. Fowler," he said.

Timothy gave himself a moment to consider that. He
took out a cigarette, lit it very deliberately—and tried
again.

"How long had you been writing to Mr. Jack before you
met him?"

"My first letter was mailed, I believe, in August of last
year."

"You sent it from Witch Harbor, I suppose?"

"Yes."

"And you have posted other letters to Mr. Jack *this*
Summer, haven't you?"

"Earlier in the season—yes."

"But none recently?" Timothy was proceeding with care.

"None, of course, since his arrival," Mr. Benson's tone
was gruffly impatient.

"Excepting the note which you left under his door last night?"

For an uncertain moment Mr. Benson's sharp glance wavered—then he apparently decided to face it out.

"That," he shrugged, "was a brief message. I'd hardly include it in answering your question about posting letters."

"I see," said Timothy—looking as if he saw a great deal, rather suddenly. The next question was more brisk. "To go back to those earlier letters, Mr. Benson, was your purpose in writing to suggest that Russell Jack should come here under the name of Tony Jackson?"

"I don't like the way you put that, Fowler," Mr. Benson's brows knotted in a bristling frown. "My proposition to Russell Jack was a perfectly reasonable one. I simply wrote to him, describing the situation here, as I had observed it, and suggested that it was high time some member of the late Dr. Jack's family stepped in and made a rightful claim upon the data and records which the doctor had left here at the time of his death. This nonsense of Miss Cotton holding on to the material until she had completed certain secret experiments struck me as utter rot. Miss Cotton was, in my opinion, dangerously close to the borderline of insanity—and to allow her to go on, year after year, as sole guardian of the life-work of a scientist as eminent and brilliant as Dr. Jack was nothing short of criminal. However loyal and helpful she may have been to the doctor during his years of work, she had no possible right to keep and conceal the records of that work after his death."

"You don't believe, then," Timothy asked slowly, "that Miss Cotton really was carrying out the work to any final conclusion?"

"Certainly *not,*" Mr. Benson's reply was a scornful snort. "That claim of hers was simply part of her determination not to reveal his material to the proper scientific authorities. I tell you, Fowler, Emily Cotton was a pathological case—she was infatuated with the idea of herself as confidante and assistant to the great scientist. And after his death, she either could not or would not give up that position of vicarious importance. The thing became a fixation with her—she insisted on keeping up all the secrecy and hocus-pocus simply because she enjoyed the role—and her absurd story about continuing the work was just another phase of this fixation. It was natural enough, I suppose, for a temperament like Miss Cotton's to take such a bent. She had, after all, lived a life of voluntary seclusion during her association with the doctor—and when that life was ended, she was left quite high and dry. Having cut herself completely off from a community like Witch Harbor, there was no chance of going back—after so many years—and becoming one of them again. Therefore, Miss Cotton had no choice but to keep up the myth of secrecy about herself—a myth which, I have no doubt, soon became a reality in her own mind. You see what I mean, Fowler?"

"Oh, quite," said Timothy.

I remembered that he had spoken those very words to Miss Cotton herself only the night before, when she had given quite a different version of this same story. How many seemingly logical interpretations, I wondered wearily, could there be of any one story? And how could one ever determine the true one?

"As I say," Mr. Benson went on, "this notion of Miss Cotton's was understandable enough, under the circumstances. But it just happened that her hallucinations

involved things which were too important to be left to her
fanatical judgment. Any work which Dr. Jack had done
was bound to be of considerable scientific value—and I,
as a member of the scientific world, felt it my duty to take
steps toward retrieving the material. And so I wrote to
Russell Jack, as I have told you, and suggested that either
he or his brother ought to do something about the situation. Since it was obviously impossible for any member
of the Jack family to come here under his true name without causing an immediate and perhaps disastrous effect
on Miss Cotton, I advised young Jack to take an assumed
name while he looked matters over."

"Just what do you mean, Mr. Benson," Timothy frowned
slightly, "when you say that the arrival of Russell Jack
might have had a disastrous effect?"

"Simply that Miss Cotton would have, I'm quite certain, gone to great lengths to increase her guard over the
records in her possession if she thought there was any danger of losing them. Just what means she would have taken,
it's quite impossible to say—but you may be sure they
would have been effective. Why, I wouldn't put it past a
woman of Miss Cotton's determination," Mr. Benson lowered his voice impressively, "to actually *destroy* those records rather than allow them out of her possession. Now
do you begin to understand, Mr. Fowler, why it was necessary for Russell Jack and me to proceed with our efforts to
obtain the material with the utmost secrecy and caution?"

"I think," said Timothy very slowly, "that I do begin to
understand." He was silent for a long moment—and I knew
that he must be remembering the scene we had witnessed
on the hillside the night before. Had Miss Emily perhaps
destroyed more than she had admitted in that weird midnight bonfire? Could it be that not only her own records,

but likewise the work of Dr. Albert Jack had been reduced, by the leaping flames, to a heap of unrecognizable ashes? I wondered whether Timothy also remembered, as I did, the tensely clenched fists of Tony Jackson—Dr. Jack's own son—when he had listened to Miss Cotton's calm account of the burning of the papers.

"I take it, Mr. Benson," said Timothy at last, "that you and Tony Jackson were planning to obtain those records by actually stealing them from Miss Cotton. Is that correct?"

"Substantially, yes," Mr. Benson shrugged. "It sounds, I admit, like an unethical method of procedure—but it was, under the circumstances, the only possible method. Legal efforts had long ago been proved futile. There was a suit, as you may remember, at the time of Dr. Jack's death, in which Miss Cotton successfully maintained her claim upon all the effects of the late doctor. And to reason with Miss Emily was even more futile. We had no choice, therefore, but to proceed by underhanded means—and I was backed, in this unconventional decision, by the full authority of the Research Foundation which, as you know, employs me."

"I wonder," said Timothy mildly, "whether the Foundation would altogether approve some of the details of this method you and Tony decided on. Whether, for instance, your fellow directors would have relished the sight of your entering Miss Cotton's house through the kitchen window for the purpose of rifling her effects—" he paused as Mrs. Benson uttered a shocked protest.

"Look here, Fowler—" an angry flush stained Richard Benson's leathery cheeks. "I've already admitted—frankly and truthfully—that I employed illegal means in this business. But it was a case where the end amply justified the means. Now that Miss Cotton is dead, and there is no further need for secrecy, I'm more than ready to come out with the whole story. I don't know who's been spying on me—and I don't give a damn—because I'm telling the whole truth. Do you understand that?"

"Oh, quite," Timothy's tone was still dangerously mild. "I was only wondering—" he hesitated briefly. "Mr. Benson, did you ever have occasion to talk to Ruby Turner about this matter?"

Richard Benson looked up with an expression of such complete astonishment that it must, I thought, be genuine.

"Why—no," he shook his head, "no—never."

"You never asked Ruby any questions, however casual, about Miss Cotton?"

"Never," said Mr. Benson firmly. "As far as I can recall, I never spoke to Ruby Turner—beyond a possible good-morning."

"That's true, Mr. Fowler," Mrs. Benson spoke with hasty assurance. "Richard always avoided the child when she came around selling berries. He said often that she was nothing but a nuisance and a chatterbox."

I reflected, with an inward smile, on the probable truth of her statement.

"Did Tony Jackson ever tell you that he had questioned Ruby?" Timothy asked.

"He mentioned once or twice having talked with the girl," Mr. Benson admitted, "but I certainly never gathered that he had questioned her in any way."

"You haven't seen Tony this morning, have you?"

"No."

"And you didn't see him any time last night?"

"No. I stopped by his cottage about eleven o'clock in the evening, but Tony wasn't there—so I left a message and came back here. I haven't seen anyone since then, except my family."

"I see," Timothy studied the tip of his cigarette thoughtfully. "Well now, about that message you left—" he came over to me. "May I have it please, Joan?"

As I took the paper from my sweater pocket, I was aware of Mrs. Benson's startled glance. Timothy unfolded the paper and frowned at it.

"Rather a cryptic message, wasn't it, Mr. Benson?"

"Not to Tony."

"And not so cryptic to me but what I can make a stab at it. *'Black evidence no good—suggest wait until tomorrow night as F. seems restless tonight.'* I'd say that meant: The evidence in the black notebook which I stole from Miss Cotton's house last night is of no use to me, so I returned it to her cottage. Fowler is prowling around tonight, and we'd better wait for a clear coast tomorrow night in order to try another search of Miss Cotton's place. Is that right, Mr. Benson?"

"Precisely right, Mr. Fowler."

"You have nothing further to add to my interpretation?"

"Nothing whatever."

"And you have nothing more to say at present?"

Mr. Benson shrugged. "I've put my cards on the table," he said, "and told you frankly as much as I know of this business. There's nothing more to say. If you want to check on the account I've given you—I'm sure Tony will bear out my story. Since Miss Cotton is dead, he has no further reason for concealing his true identity, and no doubt he'll be glad enough to tell you all he knows."

"I didn't notice any bursts of confidence from him this morning," Timothy murmured thoughtfully, "but we'll let that pass for the moment. I don't suppose," he walked slowly toward the door, "that you would care to venture an opinion on who might have killed Miss Cotton—or why?"

"Naturally not—since I have no opinion in the matter, nor any possible grounds for forming one."

"No—I thought not," Timothy sighed. At the doorway, he turned. "Just one more question, Mr. Benson."

"Yes?"

"On the various occasions when you entered the Cotton house—you counted on the fact that Miss Emily was accustomed to leave her cottage every evening at about eleven o'clock?"

"Yes."

"If you reject the idea that Miss Cotton was carrying out any phase of the work Dr. Jack had begun—just where do you figure she went on those evening trips?"

"I haven't the remotest idea," Mr. Benson shook his head blankly.

"You never followed her?"

"I never considered the matter sufficiently important to give it any particular thought—beyond the fact that her departure gave me an opportunity to search the cottage. A woman as eccentric as Miss Cotton might have had a hundred reasons for mysterious nightly outings—or she might have had no reason at all. In either case, I couldn't see that it had any bearing on what I was trying to do."

"And that," said Timothy, "would be that." He opened the door and beckoned to me.

## 15

We encountered Amos Plunkett disembarking from his car in a great state of excitement.

"Say, Mr. Fowler, is it true what the Benson kid just told me about Emily Cotton?"

"It certainly is," Timothy nodded.

"Well, say—that puts a different slant on things, don't it?"

"I suppose it does, Amos. But I can't say I'm very sure just what the slant is."

"No?" The Plunkett eyebrows indicated surprise. "Well, I'm not much of a detective, Mr. Fowler, but I'd say it looked pretty plain. If that story Miss Emily told us last night was the truth—why, it seems to me likely that she got killed by someone that was fond of Ruby Turner."

"But, Amos—" Timothy frowned, "Miss Cotton certainly didn't indicate to us that she had any hand in Ruby's death."

"Well, no. But she did say she was tryin' some dern drugs or somethin' on the poor kid. And Ruby never would have got murdered if she hadn't been mixed up with Miss Emily and her crazy doings. I say it's as plain as the nose on your face that that story of hers would make a friend of Ruby's pretty mad."

Timothy eyed the weather-beaten face thoughtfully. It was the first time Amos had displayed any signs of real enthusiasm for an idea of his own—or of anyone else's either. Now, as he stared back at Timothy, there was an unmistakable gleam of earnestness in his frosty blue eyes.

"Amos," said Timothy, "have you got any definite person in mind when you mention this friend of Ruby's?"

"Now, I wouldn't want to say for sure, Mr. Fowler—" the old man shifted uncertainly.

"If you've got a hunch, Amos, for heaven's sake spill it. I could certainly use an idea at this point."

"Well, I don't know as it's exactly a hunch, Mr. Fowler, but I was just thinking back over the people we talked to yesterday morning—and recollecting the ways they acted about Ruby's getting killed in such a terrible way. And it seemed to me, lookin' back, that the only person that was real put out about it was Mr. Gilbert."

"So—?" Timothy raised his eyebrows. "But you remember that Mrs. Gilbert's last words to us were 'My husband is a coward—and cowards don't kill.' God knows, I don't trust Lila Gilbert any further than you could throw the coast of Maine—but I do think there's really some truth in that remark of hers."

"Well, I don't know a thing about who kills and who doesn't kill," the Plunkett tone was firm, "but I do know somethin' about human nature. And if you just get him mad enough—sometimes you'd be surprised at how brave a coward can be."

Timothy received this bit of homely wisdom in silence. For a long moment he stood, gazing with narrowed eyes at the outline of the deserted house which loomed above us, high on the hill. I turned to follow his glance and wondered, for the hundredth time, what secrets had once lived behind those empty windows which now reflected the late morning sunlight with a bright, vacant glitter.

"Well anyway—" Timothy's tone was suddenly brisk. "Our first job is to look after Miss Cotton."

Amos nodded his agreement, and, as the two men started off toward Miss Emily's cottage, I turned into our own path. Walking slowly, I could still hear Timothy's voice.

"We might," he was saying, "take a squint around these woods while we're at it, and see whether there's any trace to be found of the gun that finished Miss Emily. Nobody would be foolish enough, after all, to try and hide a weapon in one of these cottages—and unless they had the sense to drop it in the ocean . . ." the rest of his words were lost in the distance, but as I climbed our porch steps I found myself remembering those muddy boots which Timothy had fished out of Tony Jackson's closet. One might, I reflected, get one's shoes muddy down by the shore—rain or no rain.

The rest of the morning passed very slowly for me. Neither reading nor knitting seemed sufficiently absorbing to distract my restless thoughts, and when at last it was time to prepare our lunch, I welcomed the task with considerably more enthusiasm than usual. The lobster stew and biscuits had been waiting for nearly an hour, however, before Timothy appeared alone.

"Where's Amos?" I inquired.

"He went home to shine his badge and slick up." Timothy drew his chair up to the table and sniffed the lunch with enthusiasm. "It seems that we're about to have visitors."

"Visitors?"

"M-h'm. Amos telephoned the Portland Police headquarters yesterday to report our local slaughter and they're sending up a detachment of distinguished bloodhounds. Due to arrive sometime this afternoon, and take charge of things, which means that A. Plunkett and T. Fowler can take the cue and bow themselves gracefully out of the picture."

"Are you sorry?"

Timothy helped himself to a generous portion of stew.

"Can't say that I am exactly," he said. "If the Portland prodigies can make any more sense out of this mess than I can—they're welcome to it. But before they get here, I am going to do one thing, just for my own satisfaction."

"And what will that be?"

"That," said Timothy, "will be to take another crack at the Gilbert household."

"Meaning that you did take the Plunkett tip seriously, after all?"

"Meaning rather," Timothy corrected me, "that it's the last chance, as I see it, to find the loose end which would unravel this tangle. Somehow, Joanie, the murder of Ruby Turner and the murder of Miss Emily are linked together—and if only I could get hold of that thread that links them, the other bits of the puzzle would begin to fall into place."

We didn't pause, when lunch was done, to clear the table. Even so, it was past three o'clock when we started for the Gilbert cottage. The sun, which had been so bright all during the forenoon, was hidden now behind a dull gray curtain of clouds, and there was an ominous stillness in the air. Through the dark trees, I glimpsed the Gilbert cottage—as gray and still as the atmosphere itself—and our approaching footsteps fell upon the soft pine needle path without disturbing the silence in which, it seemed, all sound was suspended before the threat of storm.

Not until we were half way up the porch steps did I see Lila Gilbert. She was standing just inside the screen door, watching our approach. Dressed, as always, in just the shade of pale blue silk to set off her fragile prettiness, she looked especially cool and remote—but there was, in the careful, mask-like set of her features, an impression of warning as indefinable as the heavy foreboding of the storm.

With one quick motion she opened the door, stepped outside, and faced us.

"Hello," said Timothy. His tone was casual. "Is Allen here?"

"No." Lila's small mouth shaped the word carefully and closed upon it.

"When will he be back?"

A delicate shrug of one small shoulder was the only answer.

"All right," Timothy stepped forward, "we'll wait for him."

Lila made no move to open the door.

"I'm so sorry," her tone smooth as ice, "but I was just about to take a nap."

"Well, don't let me stop you," said Timothy. He reached out for the door-knob, but Lila moved quickly to block his hand.

"Aren't you forgetting that I haven't asked you in?" she said.

"Listen, Lila Gilbert," Timothy's words held an edge as sharp as her own, "we're not playing a game. I came here to speak to Allen, and I'm going to see him."

"I tell you, he's not here."

"Then why are you afraid to let me in?"

"Afraid—" Lila's lips curled scornfully.

"And why were you waiting here—guarding the door when we came along?"

"You have no right to come here and question me like this. I won't stand for it—"

"And I won't stand for your nonsense another minute." Timothy flung open the door, but before he could enter the house, Lila made one last effort to detain him. She laid a small white hand upon his arm with a gesture of surprising strength.

"Look here, Timothy Fowler, you're meddling in something that is none of your business."

"That," said Timothy calmly, "is my chief occupation."

"Since you insist on forcing your way into my house, I will tell you that Allen is here—"

"Of course."

"And he is ill—very ill. The reason that I was guarding the door, as you so quaintly put it, is that I expect the doctor at any moment. I absolutely refuse to allow you to see my husband in his present condition."

"Just what is his present condition?"

"His illness has nothing to do with any of the recent unpleasant events, nor with anything that you could possibly wish to see him about. Allen has suffered a severe heart attack. He has had several before this, and even you must be aware that it would be dangerous to disturb him under the circumstances. At the moment he is barely conscious—and he must be kept in perfect quiet until the doctor—" At that instant Lila Gilbert stopped speaking. Her words were cut short by a sound from within the cottage—a long, low, terrifying sound. The sound of a man's voice—half a scream, half a groan of choking anguish.

Instantly Timothy sprang forward. With two long strides he crossed the living-room toward the closed bed-room door. Lila, her face frozen and white, was close behind him. And I, forgetful of the uncertainty which had kept me hovering on the steps outside, followed them across the threshold just in time to see the bedroom door flung open from within by Allen Gilbert.

One look at his disheveled, half-dressed figure, his flushed face and wildly staring eyes, was sufficient to tell me, for all my inexperience, that Allen Gilbert had suffered no heart attack. The man was in the grip of some dreadful seizure—he was mad, perhaps. But he was not ill.

For one confused moment, Allen stared blindly at Timothy's face, and then, as a dull gleam of recognition flickered in his bloodshot eyes, he sank back against the wall with a groan.

"I—I thought you were the doctor," his words came brokenly, "I—heard you talking."

"No, Allen, the doctor hasn't come yet." Lila stepped forward and took his shaking hands in her firm grip. "You must try to be quiet—"

"But you *told* me he was coming—" with desperate impatience he flung her away. "You told me that hours ago—"

"He's coming just as quickly as he can, Allen. There is nothing to do but to wait."

For once the steely edge beneath Lila's tone had no effect upon her husband. The almost hypnotic control which she had always seemed to hold over him was lost now upon his feverish mind.

"Wait—?" Allen's voice rose shrilly above her calm accents. "Don't you understand—I can't wait. It'll kill me, I tell you. You've got to do something—to help me—" He turned to Timothy once more. "You—*you* can help me. You can get Ruby. Tell Ruby to bring me something—tell her I won't let anything hurt her. Ruby will understand. She—"

"Ruby is dead, Allen," Timothy's words cut through the man's hysterical pleading. "Don't you remember?

"Yes—yes, I remember now. Ruby is dead," Allen's voice dropped to a dull whisper as he sagged back against the wall. Then, like a flash, he turned to Lila accusingly.

"You did it—" He thrust a shaking finger at her set, white face. "You killed Ruby to keep her from helping me. You won't let the doctor come here because he'll help me. *You did it—you—*"

Timothy sprang forward just in time to prevent Allen from lunging crazily at his wife. He pinned the waving arms in an iron grip, and slowly forced Allen backward into the bedroom.

"I'll handle this, Lila," Timothy flung the words over his shoulder. "I see now what the trouble is." Steadily, with easy strength, he led the man away from us. "Close the door, Joan."

Lila Gilbert had not flinched a muscle when Allen lunged toward her. Now, very slowly, she crossed the room and sat down facing me. As silent as two graven images we remained there for what seemed hours—listening—but never quite hearing the words of the strange conversation beyond the closed door. Allen's voice went on and on— now rising sharply, now sinking to an almost inaudible whisper. And occasionally I could detect the low, even murmur of a question from Timothy.

## 16

When the doctor from Pineboro finally arrived, it was Timothy who took charge of things.

"It's a drug case, doctor," he said. "An addict, apparently pretty far gone, whose supply of drugs was suddenly cut off about forty-eight hours ago. You'll know what's best to do, of course, but from what I've seen, I'd say that Mr. Gilbert ought to be taken to the hospital immediately."

The doctor followed Timothy into the bedroom. There was a short consultation beyond the closed door, and then the physician reappeared to address Lila.

"Your husband is quiet now, Mrs. Gilbert," he said. "I've given him an injection of morphine, and I agree with Mr. Fowler that he ought to be in the hospital. If you're willing, I can drive you both up to Pineboro."

Still passive, Lila signified her agreement, and set about at once preparing for the move. In the minutes that followed, watching Lila's composed, methodical actions, I was conscious for the first time of sympathy and a certain admiration for her. Only once, in that confused half hour while we assisted in preparing Allen Gilbert for his trip to the hospital, did Lila offer any remark beyond the briefest reply to some necessary question. It was when all was

in readiness, and Lila was about to take her place next to
Allen in the doctor's car, that she turned to face Timothy.

"Allen was cured of the drug habit," she said quietly,
"three years ago. But, of course, I've always been afraid of
some such recurrence as this. That is why I chose this very
remote spot for our Summers, and why I may have seemed,
at times, to be unduly watchful of my husband's behavior.
In spite of all I could do, Allen managed to obtain drugs
by having them delivered to him through Ruby Turner.
Whether the child had any notion of the dreadful thing she
was doing, I have no idea—and I suppose it really doesn't
matter now," Lila's hand passed across her eyes in a gesture of weariness. "I had begun to suspect that something
of this sort was going on, but it wasn't until after Ruby's
death that I realized how far it had gone. I don't know
what Allen may have said to you in his hysterical state, but
I swear that neither he nor I had anything to do with what
happened to Ruby. I don't seem to care very much whether
you believe that or not—but it is the truth."

A moment later we watched the departure of the automobile along the dusty road. Looking after it, Timothy
shook his head.

"No wonder the gal was a bit fishy," he murmured,
"with a problem like that on her hands."

I agreed hastily, but at the moment I had no desire to
enter a discussion concerning Lila Gilbert's probable heart
of gold. I was vastly more interested in hearing what Timothy had learned from Allen—and I said so.

"The link," Timothy answered as he followed me along
the narrow path. "You remember, I said I was after the
link?"

"Yes."

"Well—I got it."

"What is it?"

"I'm not quite sure yet *what* it is—but I know *where* it is—" Timothy paused.

When, after a moment, he did not continue, I turned. For the second time that day, I saw that Timothy was gazing intently toward the top of the hill. Without looking at me, Timothy raised his hand and pointed at the big house. Against the low-hung, darkening clouds the familiar outline was almost lost in gloom.

"The answer," he said slowly, "is there—in the house that Jack built."

"Did Allen Gilbert tell you that?"

"He did."

"But, Timothy—how could he know?"

"I'm not sure he did know," Timothy admitted. "Allen's mind was obsessed with just one thing—getting his drugs from Ruby. But in the course of obtaining the stuff, he discovered, quite by accident, the secret of Miss Emily's nightly pilgrimages."

"You mean," I suggested, "because Miss Emily was also meeting Ruby—in order to try her experiments?"

"I do not," said Timothy very firmly. "Miss Emily never met Ruby for any purpose whatever."

"But she said—"

"She said a great many things," Timothy cut me short, "and they were all intended to throw us off the real track. And I must admit," he shook his head ruefully, "the old gal succeeded pretty damn well."

"And what *was* the real track?"

"As nearly as I could gather from Allen's ramblings, it went something like this. Allen made an arrangement by which his supply of drugs was to be sent to Ruby Turner. Having been addicted before, he knew, of course, how to go about such matters—but Lila kept such a close eye on him that he couldn't receive the stuff direct. Hence the necessity of Ruby as a go-between. No doubt he paid the girl well for it (you remember Ruby's mother quoted her remark about making them all rich), and it's not surprising that the kid jumped at the chance to make easy money. All she had to do was to receive the stuff by mail and turn it over to Allen—and she probably had no idea of what she was doing beyond that simple fact. Well, having fixed up his plan, Allen had to decide on some meeting place with Ruby—and that wasn't any too easy, with Lila on the job. Apparently the only time Allen ever got away by himself was when he wandered out of an evening for a moonlight stroll—so he arranged with Ruby to meet him then. The girl, of course, used the berry-picking gag as an excuse to get away from her house—and she would bring Allen's little package along in the bottom of her berry pail.

"Allen wanted to be sure of picking a meeting place that was safely out of the way—so he settled on a certain little clearing in front of the deserted house up there. He was convinced, of course, that no one ever went near the place, and he was particularly sure that Lila would not, by any chance, follow him through the heavy underbrush that surrounded the house. Well—it seems that one night, after having several successful meetings with Ruby, Allen got to the clearing early, and while he was waiting for the girl to come along with his package, he heard some kind of noise from the house behind him—and he turned to see someone coming out of a little side door down under the porch. Before he could make a move to get away, the person came face to face with him—and Allen saw that it was—"

"Not Miss Emily?"

"Miss Emily herself," Timothy nodded. "It wasn't easy to gather a very precise account of the scene from Allen's hazy consciousness, but I think the gist of it was something like this. Both Allen and Miss Emily were pretty well worked up—since each discovered the other's secret. But Allen, being by far the more excitable, probably gave himself completely away. He was terrified, of course, for fear Miss Emily would go straight to Lila with the information—and Miss Emily was smart enough to use his fear as a bribe. The upshot of the matter was that Miss Emily promised not to give him away provided Allen swore never to tell anyone about having seen her near the house, and provided neither he nor Ruby would ever come to that place again. Allen agreed readily enough, and from that night on he always met Ruby in the berry-patch clearing half way up the hill."

"And of course," I nodded slowly, "Allen went to the clearing to meet her on that last night when he found her dead."

"Of course," Timothy agreed. "As I told you earlier, Allen was completely obsessed with his own part in this affair. The business of getting his drugs is, to an addict, the one aim and object in life. It's probable that, once certain that Miss Emily wasn't going to tell on him, Allen never gave another thought to her mysterious visits to the empty house. The only reason I got this story from him today was because, in his hysterical state of mind, he was convinced that somehow Miss Emily and Lila had plotted against him and killed Ruby in order to cut off his supply of drugs."

"And you don't believe that?" I turned to look at him curiously.

"I certainly do not."

"Well but—who *did* kill her then?"

"That," said Timothy, "is what I hope to find out—right now." He stopped short in the path. All the time we had talked, we had been slowly climbing the hill path, but so intent had I been upon Timothy's words, that I scarcely realized where we were heading. Now I saw that we were directly opposite the big house. "I'm going to have a look at that little door beneath the porch right now. You can come along, or go back to the cottage, as you like."

It didn't take me very long to decide. Another moment, and we had left the path to plunge along as best we could through the thick brush of pines and shrubs. Presently I heard a low exclamation from Timothy, who was ahead of me, and, pushing my way through a final tangle of branches, I emerged into the little clearing where he stood. There, rising before us dark and grim, were the walls of the house that Jack built.

"Timothy—" I remembered how small my own voice sounded, "Timothy, why do you suppose Dr. Jack built such a *big* house?"

There was no answer from Timothy. Slowly, with careful steps, he approached the house—moving the overgrown grass aside until he found the remnants of a neglected path. "There's just a chance of picking up a footprint along here—" he paused abruptly, and I saw him bend down. "Yes sir—a nice clear print—"

"Is it Miss Emily's do you think?" I called excitedly.

"Nope. It's a man's print—and a good big one. The ground was soft when it was made, and there hasn't been a rain in more than a week until late last night. That means, Joan, that someone was prowling around here early this morning." Timothy appeared around the corner of the long low porch which stretched across the front of the house. There was a moment's silence, and then Timothy called out from behind the porch. "Here's the door, Jean," he sounded excited. "You'd better cut straight through the brush and avoid the path."

"Look—" when I reached his side, Timothy pointed to the footprints showing plainly in the freshly dried mud before the little door. "Our prowler knew where to get in, all right—and he seems to have left the place in something of a hurry. Such a hurry, in fact, that he quite forgot to lock the door."

I looked up to see that the low door stood about an inch ajar—and as I looked, a sudden puff of breeze stirred the heavy air. On silent hinges, the door opened inward before the wind, and a faint odor of damp and musty wood came from the dim emptiness of the old house.

Timothy exhibited none of the shivery reluctance which I felt.

"Come on," he said briskly, "let's get this over with before the storm breaks." And turning, he helped me to step over the cluster of footprints and across the threshold. "Now then," he closed the door carefully behind us, "we'll see what we shall see."

Just at first, we couldn't see much of anything. But when, after a few minutes, our eyes grew accustomed to the dim light which filtered through the cobweb-veiled window panes—we looked about to find ourselves in a sort of basement storeroom. The walls and floors were unfinished, and the place was bare except for a collection of sticks and small logs, sawed to stove size, which were stacked in one corner. Timothy went over to inspect the wood more closely.

"Something tells me," he murmured, "that Miss Emily cut that fire-wood herself. Which just goes to show how important it was to keep her visits secret."

On the far side of the room a crude set of steps rose steeply, and Timothy began to climb. I followed—on tiptoe. At the top he swung open a door, and together we emerged into a large square hall.

For a long minute we stood in silence. Timothy seemed to be listening for something, and I too found myself straining to hear some half-expected sound. But except for the muffled pounding of my own heart—all was quiet in the empty house.

On either side of the hall, wide doors opened into rooms which were furnished with the barest and simplest of pine chairs and tables. Even from where I stood, I could see that those rooms had remained unused and undisturbed for a long time. The dust of neglect lay in a heavy film over all the furniture, and cobwebs fell in fluttering gray strands across the doorways.

"Well—" Timothy's voice echoed through the empty silence with a suddenness that made me jump, "it's plain enough that nothing's been going on here. Suppose we have a look upstairs." With quick steps he walked the length of the hall and started up the broad staircase.

Walking after him as lightly as I could, I was aware of the sharp creaking of the floors beneath my feet. At the top of the steps we faced three doors, all closed. Timothy hesitated briefly, and then went to open each door in turn. From the first two he turned away after a quick glance— but the third door he threw wide with an exclamation of triumph.

"Here's what we're looking for," he said.

"Timothy—" I hung back reluctantly—caught in some nameless fear of what might lay beyond, "what are we looking for?"

Before he could answer me, there came a long, low rumble of distant thunder. The old house seemed to tremble with the sound, and then, as the muttering died away, the silence hung more breathlessly than before.

"We're looking," said Timothy, "for the secret of the house that Jack built. And here it is." He stepped through the open door into the room beyond.

The room into which I walked was curiously in contrast with the other parts of the house. It too was furnished with the utmost sparseness and simplicity, and the walls and floor were barren of all decoration—but this room had obviously been in recent use. The floor was neatly swept, a large pine table in the center of the room was carefully dusted, and a bottle of ink and a row of pencils and pens gave evidence of someone lately at work. In one corner stood a large metal filing cabinet, and close beside it was a smaller table with a typewriter and a supply of fresh white paper. In the further corner I saw a Franklin stove flanked by two neat piles of firewood such as we had seen downstairs. All about the little room there was an air of orderliness and system.

"So this is where Miss Emily worked," said Timothy.

I nodded slowly. A vision, too distinct for comfort, rose before my eyes. A vision of Miss Emily's gaunt shoulders bent over that bare pine table—of her coldly intelligent eyes, her strong, gnarled fingers busy with some mysterious, methodical task in this secret workroom. Even the broom and dust-cloth, carefully placed behind the door, spoke in her silent presence with a vividness which was somehow terrifying. It seemed as if somewhere in the empty stillness of the house, Miss Emily's spirit must still be hovering close by to watch over the secret which she had so long and carefully guarded.

Timothy, as usual, wasted small time in speculation upon the metaphysical aspect of this curious retreat. With eager haste he bent to his task of examining the contents of the room. I watched him open a drawer of the filing cabinet, select a sheet of paper at random, and glance quickly down the page. I saw him frown—extract another sheet—and another. Gradually, some meaning seemed to dawn on him. His expression changed to one of wonder— of incredulous amazement. Hurriedly he opened drawer after drawer, until he reached the lowest compartment— and then, kneeling down, he searched with feverish anxiety through the close-packed records. At last he appeared to find the answer—the clue to all this painstaking record of work. From the very back of the lowest drawer, he drew out a sheaf of pages, yellowed and limp with age, and covered over with close-packed writing.

"By Jumping Judas—" Timothy cried, "this is *it!*"

"Is *what*—?" I drew closer to peer across his shoulder. In the darkening room I couldn't make out the words of the fine script—but one thing was startlingly apparent. The printed letters were identical with those we had pondered over on the pages of Miss Emily's little black notebook.

"The plan," Timothy explained excitedly, "the plan of the experiment—the key to this whole cabinet full of records. The secret of Miss Emily, and Dr. Jack—and the whole damn mystery of this place. Look here—" he flipped back to the first page of the sheaf, and pointed to the neatly printed title: *A Study of Natural Man—being an*

*outline of a projected experiment, undertaken in the year
1904 by Albert Jack, the object of which will be to discover
through observation, the mental and physical development
of a human being unaided and untrammeled by any contact
whatsoever with civilization.*

"Well—" I drew back and looked at Timothy, "it—
doesn't seem so very exciting, does it? Or so very mysterious for all the trouble they went to in keeping it secret?"

"No—?" Timothy returned my gaze with a curious
expression. "Do you realize, my girl, that all the rest of
this cabinet is filled with the records of this simple little
experiment?"

"Yes—but I still don't see—"

"And do you realize that the great Dr. Jack considered
the work so important that he gave up a brilliant career
for it?"

"Yes—"

"And that Miss Emily continued to record—and to
guard the contents of the cabinet literally with her life?"

Again I nodded—still puzzled as to the true meaning
and importance of the great secret.

Timothy paused no longer to impress his idea upon my
slow wits. He returned to the drawer and scooped out a
solid armful of the close-packed sheets. Then he rose and
faced me.

"My pet," he said, "if this stuff is what I think it is—"
he tapped the stack of papers with an impressive forefinger, "it's the most exciting, the most unbelievable—the
wisest and craziest thing that you or I will ever see." His
voice was literally vibrating with intensity.

I realized, in that moment while I stared into Timothy's
eyes across the bundle of yellowed and dusty papers, that
never before had I seen him so utterly in earnest about

anything. A sudden flash of lightning flooded the room with a brief, electric glare—and then was gone. Close on its heels came a second roll of thunder, gathering strength for a final crash which shook the house until the old boards groaned and the windows rattled in their frames. The renewed threat of storm seemed to startle Timothy out of his momentary trance.

"Come on—" he moved abruptly toward the door.

"Where to now?"

"Home—where I can get a real look at these," Timothy tucked the papers more firmly beneath his arm. "And we've got to step on it to beat the storm."

Down the stairs, through the long hall past the silent, dust-shrouded rooms, into the basement and out of the house we hurried. Once the outer door had closed behind us, I paused for one heartfelt breath of relief. Then through the thick brush, down the long hill path we ran for our cottage—and reached it just as the first heavy rain drops spattered down from the leaden sky. Inside the house, Timothy lit the table lamp, and without a word to each other we drew our chairs close, and bent to examine the precious stack of records.

The next hour passed strangely. Oblivious of the raging storm which lashed about the little cottage, we sat in silent concentration—reading, in the small circle of golden lamplight, the story set forth upon those fragile sheets of paper. The story, not only of an astounding experiment, but the story of two human beings who had sacrificed every trace of emotion, of sentiment, of civilized morality in the cause of cold science. The story of Dr. Albert Jack and Miss Emily Cotton and their child.

The whole account was set forth in the clear, lucid style of the scientific scholar—with every detail of the

plan and its actual execution precisely and fully recorded. Save for the incredible subject of the experiment, we
might have been reading the description of any learned
doctor or scientist and his study of the life cycle of some
specially conditioned guinea-pig. Never once, in all those
pages, did a single word betray a hint of the fact that Dr.
Albert Jack was writing a case history of his own son.

The exact purpose of the great experiment was given in
painstaking detail in that first sheaf of papers inscribed
in the neat, small printed letters of Dr. Jack's own writing. As a part of Timothy's records of the case, I have a
complete transcription of that introduction, but, in the
interest of space, I can set forth here only the gist of the
amazing plan. Following the inscription noted on the title
page, which has earlier been recorded, the outline of the
proposed experiment can best be indicated by a paraphrase
of Dr. Jack's own words.

"Having, in the course of twenty years' work in the
fields of medicine and psychiatry, been persistently per-
plexed and tantalized by the problem of just how much
the human creature is affected by the environment and
teachings of the civilization into which it is born, I have
decided to undertake an experiment which will furnish
a specific answer to this vexing question. Since such an
undertaking is obviously contrary to the laws and morals
of all civilized nations, and since the value of the work in
the realm of pure science could never be comprehended
by society at large, it will be necessary for me to proceed
upon the work in complete secrecy. But so deep is my conviction of the ultimate importance of the findings, that I
am resolved, in this, my forty-fifth year, to abandon all
contacts with my former life and work and to devote the

remainder of my life to the execution of this long-cherished plan.

"The precautions which I have taken to insure the necessary secrecy have been elaborate and complete. In the remote and isolated community of Witch Harbor, Maine, I have purchased a large plot of land protected on three sides by water, and on the fourth by walls which exclude all possibility of an intruder. Upon this land I have had built a house, designed especially for the purpose of my work, and it is my intention that no person shall at any time be admitted to the house save for myself and Miss Emily Cotton, my assistant.

"In the discovery of Miss Cotton, I have had the one stroke of good fortune which was essential to the success of my project. She is, perhaps, the one other person in the world beside myself who is sufficiently devoted to the cause of science and research to willingly submit her life and services to the exacting discipline which our work will require. In the event that at some future time, the world of science finds cause to be grateful for the results of our labors, I wish to make it certain that whatever small honors may be attached to my name will be equally bestowed upon the memory of Emily Cotton's devotion, loyalty and sacrifices.

"The special construction of my house, to which I have referred, has been so planned that a large portion in the center of the building will be reserved for the actual working ground of the experiment. This section, in the form of a courtyard, is completely enclosed by the inner walls of the house, but is left open to the elements from above— there being no roof over the court. The ground within the enclosure was left in its natural state—there being two good-sized trees, nearly as tall as the house, in addition to smaller shrubs of various evergreen varieties. The soil is typical of that found along the Maine seacoast—a mixture of sand and pine needles, with an abundance of rocks. In one corner of the court a large rock and several smaller ones form a natural cave measuring roughly six by four feet, and the possible uses of this shelter will, I anticipate, form a particularly interesting part of the experiment.

"It will be seen that I have provided in this enclosure, an entirely natural setting in which the subject of my experiment will eventually be exposed to the full rigors of a severe climate, save only for what protection the four surrounding inner walls of the house will provide. It will be necessary, of course, to supply food and water, but it is my intention to keep the food as primitive as is consistent with the survival and health of my subject. Detailed descriptions of the actual diet will be evolved and fully recorded in the course of working out the plan.

"For purposes of observation, I have arranged two vantage points from which my assistant and I can look into the enclosure from the house, without being ourselves visible from within the courtyard. This is achieved by means of grilled openings, screened over with branches—one placed on the second floor of the house and commanding a complete view of the enclosure, and the second so arranged that it looks directly into the sheltering cave. Alongside this second observation window, I have built a trap-door device through which food and water may be supplied to the subject without the necessity of entering the court. The greatest care will be taken in actually placing supplies in the enclosure, in order to preclude the possibility that I or my assistant will ever be seen by the subject. It is obviously essential to the success of the experiment that the subject shall never, by sight or sound, be aware of the

existence of any human being save himself. He will, therefore, develop as a creature independent of any stimuli
whatever save those which arise from his own consciousness in relation to his completely natural and primitive
environment.

"So much for the preparations and background of the
experiment. The records which follow will set forth, in
the form of daily observations, an exact description of
the growth and development of the infant which will be
placed, at the age of ten days, into this setting of natural
isolation. Henceforward he must survive entirely unaided
by human care or teaching, and the results of his behavior will constitute an actual record of the much-disputed
instincts of the human animal, the development of his
consciousness, and his reactions toward his environment.
If, as I hope, the subject—who will hereafter be referred to
as X—survives for a period of years, his life history will be
the story of natural man, recorded as fully and precisely as
my observations and knowledge allow—and for as long a
time as circumstances and my own span of life will permit."

So ended Dr. Albert Jack's outline of his great plan.
When I had finished reading it, I looked up to meet Timothy's eyes. Amazement, incredulity and horror were mingled in my mind as I stared at his sober face. For a long
minute we sat thus—looking at one another—while the
full meaning and import of Dr. Jack's plan sank in upon
us. At last I spoke.

"Timothy—is it really *true,* or are we just dreaming it?"

"It's true all right," Timothy nodded slowly. "Good
God—no wonder we thought Miss Emily was a strange
person. The real miracle is that Dr. Jack was able to find
a woman who would actually go through with a plan like

that. I thought Miss Emily was a gal of iron—but to agree
to this proposition, and then have the coldblooded nerve—
the patience—the guts to actually carry it out, year after
year—" he shook his head wonderingly.

"Oh, but Timothy—" even recalling Miss Emily's almost inhuman self-control and determination, her lack
of all normal emotion, I still found myself unbelieving,
"Timothy—they *couldn't* have gone through with it really. It's too monstrous—too awful. No two human beings
could have shut a child up in that secret courtyard prison and left it there forever. And then to peep at it, and
watch it, day after day, just to take notes on its behavior— No—I simply can't believe they would really do it—
no matter *how* valuable they thought the experiment was
going to be—"

"But, my dear girl, they did," Timothy's quiet voice cut
short my protests. "And the proof lies here, in these records—" Timothy tapped the thick stack of papers which
lay on the table between us. "Look—here's the first of
the daily entries." He held out the page, and together we
scanned the contents, written in the same neat letters. At
the top of the sheet I noted the date, June 10, 1904—and in
the opposite corner appeared the number 1. I pointed out
to Timothy that the form of the entry was identical with
those cryptic notes we had found in Miss Emily's notebook.

"Of course," he nodded. "Those notes we saw were Miss
Emily's observations, taken in code form, to be elaborat-
ed later and included as one of the pages in this record.
You remember the number on the entry you found was ten
thousand and something—and let's see—" he drew out a
pencil and figured rapidly, "Counting a daily record since
the summer of 1904—365 days to the year—that would
bring the total of days to some ten thousand."

11 a.m. The subject of my experiment, a male child aged ten days, was placed in the enclosure this morning. In order to protect the infant from the first shock of his exposure to the outdoor air, I arranged a warm bedding of straw within the shelter of the natural cave of rocks inside the courtyard.

Of necessity, the child will be given bottle feedings for the first period of the experiment, but this will be discontinued at the earliest possible time—and great care will be taken to avoid any human contact during initial period of artificial feeding.

The child X is an entirely normal infant. His weight at birth was seven pounds, eight and one-half ounces, and he appears unusually sturdy and healthy in every respect. He has an excellent physical inheritance on both the paternal and maternal sides, as will be apparent from this outline of his parentage:

(There followed here an elaborate chart of the unfortunate infant's ancestry—beginning with Miss Emily Cotton and Dr. Jack, and tracing back through several generations on both sides, with careful notes on physical and mental characteristics exhibited in the two families.)

One of the most valuable results of the experiment will be to determine, by observation, the true extent and importance of purely biological inheritance, since the usual tempering influences of environment, habit and association will be completely absent in the development of X.

2 p.m. The usual bottle feeding was administered. No particular reactions observed. X appears comfortably adapted to the new circumstances.

4 p.m. Bottle feeding. X was fretful and cried for a brief period, but quieted after feeding and slept as usual.

6 p.m. Bottle feeding.

And so it went. Page after page of the close, neat, methodical, incredible records. The fantastic record of a human life subjected to the inhuman observations of the two who watched and noted each minute detail of the infant's amazing survival and growth. Toward the end of August came one entry which I recall particularly.

It is surprising, and at the same time significant, (Dr. Jack wrote) to observe the speed and completeness with which X has adapted himself to the outdoor climate. Although fresh straw provides a warm bedding, and provisions have been made for tempering the rigors of cold weather by means of a concealed heating system, it seems unlikely at present that these precautions will be necessary for long. At an age when the civilized infant is still protected by bundling clothes from the slightest draught or exposure, X is apparently perfectly acclimated to the vagaries of the weather. Rain, fog, summer heat and the chill of the night air seem alike to agree with him. He displays not the smallest signs of distress or discomfort toward any phase of his unusual environment, and is, in fact, considerably

more contented and placid in his behavior
than any child I have had occasion to observe.

In the first weeks of November came a series of bulletins
recording the illness of X. Each symptom, each reaction,
was noted with minute care, and one could imagine the
anxiety with which the experimenters watched and feared
during the days when their subject struggled to adapt his
small organism to the increasing rigors of the winter climate. Miraculously, he did survive—and after that one
adjustment, appeared to thrive upon the strange, unnatu-
ral—or rather natural, regime.

By the second summer of his life, X was a thriving
young creature, subsisting on a diet of raw foods, and
performing feats of climbing and exploring far beyond the
strength or ingenuity of the normal child of his tender
age.

I had not read far before I observed occasional daily reports which were initialed E. C. These I judged to be written by Miss Emily, and at first the difference between her
printed writings and the doctor's was marked. But gradually, over the years, her notes became more and more like
his, until it was impossible to distinguish between the two
hand-printings. Small wonder, I thought, that Amos had
been convinced that the words in the black notebook had
been inscribed by Dr. Jack himself.

On and on, through page after page of records we read—
and, in spite of my fundamental aversion to the heartless
attitude of the two experimenters, I found myself following with fascinated interest the story of the strange development of X. The frequent notes describing the child's
vocal efforts I found particularly engrossing—while, at
the same time, I was chilled by the weird inhumanness

of his attempts to communicate with his small world by
means of speech. Being, of course, shut off from all exam-
ples of human speech, X had only the sounds of nature to
inspire him—and it was to these sounds that he responded
with an uncanny sense of mimicry. Very early X learned to
imitate the various bird calls which resounded constant-
ly in his enclosure—and these he used to express reactions of pleasure and well-being. The excited chattering
of squirrels and chipmunks, he adopted as the language of
industry and anxiety which accompanied his numerous busy
activities of exploration and play. For the comparatively
rare occasions when something distressed him, X found
expression in a curiously exact imitation of the wailing
winds which so often howled about the bleak house upon
the hill. The experimenters soon learned to recognize the
moods of this strange language, and throughout the years,
while X grew from a prattling child into a powerful man,
his sound-symbols never varied from their original mean-
ings.

Even by skimming rapidly through the copious notes,
I had hardly looked over a half of the comparatively small
portion of the records which Timothy had brought from
the filing cabinet, when a sharp knock at our door interrupted my reading. I looked up to see that the false gloom
of the storm had merged into the dusk of evening. The
torrents of rain had stopped long since, and when Timothy
opened the door, a rush of evening air filled the room with
the damp fragrance of the storm-washed pine woods.

One glance at the troubled countenance of Amos Plunkett, who stood outside, was sufficient to remind me of
the present troubles of our neighborhood—and from the
excited pitch of his normally drawling speech, I gathered
that something new and astounding had just occurred.

"Mr. Fowler," Amos began, "I think you'd better come over to Mr. Jackson's cottage right away. The police've been lookin' things over since they got here, and they've just found the gun hid down in some bushes near the shore. They're closin' in on Mr. Jackson now—but I thought I'd best get you before anything happens because—"

"Hold everything, Amos," a gesture from Timothy stemmed the tide of excited speech. "Just what gun is it they've found?"

"Why—the one that killed Miss Emily. The fellow from Portland says there ain't a bit of doubt but it's the one and—"

"What's it got to do with Tony Jackson?"

"That's what I'm tryin' to tell you. It's *his* gun—got his initials right on the side of the handle.—It's plain as a pipe-stem that Mr. Jackson killed her—but we don't know why yet—"

"I'll be right with you, Amos—" without further hesitation, Timothy snatched up his coat and started toward the door. "Your Portland prowlers may be right about Jackson—and if they are—" the screen door slammed shut, "if he really did kill Miss Emily, I can make a pretty good guess as to why." The two men clumped down the porch steps, and the rest of Timothy's words trailed back through the quiet dusk. "And I'll be damned," I heard him say, "if I could blame the kid for doing it."

## 18

Barely a full minute passed before Timothy was back again.

"What's happened?" I rose. "Didn't you go to Tony's cottage?"

"Tony's gone," Timothy flung the words over his shoulder as he crossed to the bedroom.

*"Gone?"* I stood at the threshold and echoed the word wonderingly. "Gone where?"

"Just gone. Vamoosed. Flown the coop." Timothy answered me hastily. "Must've packed his stuff and lit out while we were reading here." He hauled his suitcase from beneath the cot and bent to rummage through its contents. "The men think Tony realized they were sure to close in on him and made a quick get-away. But me—I'm not so sure. I've got a hunch that Tony wouldn't leave for good without finishing up some business on the hill. So I've persuaded a couple of the sleuths to go up there with me and have a look." He drew something from the suitcase and thrust it hastily into his pocket. But not before I had caught sight of the gleaming metal.

"Timothy—why are you taking your gun?"

"Now don't you work up a temperature, my pet," Timothy paused to bestow a pat on my shoulder as he passed

171

into the living-room, picked up his flash-light, and made for the outer door again. "There's not a thing to worry about with two doughty troopers to look after me."

"But Timothy—"

His hand on the door knob, he turned back. "Well?"

"Why *should* you go up to the house again? What do you expect to find?"

"Tony."

"Do you really think he knows about—about what happened up there?"

Timothy looked at me. "Who else," he said quietly, "do you think made those footprints around the house? And why else do you think Tony would have gone to Miss Emily's cottage window and shot her dead?"

I stood silent for a moment before the logic of the questions. "But I still don't see," I shook my head stubbornly, "why you're so sure that Tony has gone back to the house."

"I tell you," Timothy repeated, "that I don't believe Tony would leave without finishing his job."

I'm not certain how long I stood there after Timothy was gone. But presently I went in search of something to eat. It was well past our supper hour, but my usual ravenous appetite had disappeared somehow in the course of the evening's events. Halfway through a glass of milk, the resolve formed itself, suddenly and firmly, in my mind. Two minutes later, with my tweed coat belted tightly and a flash-light in my hand, I was on the path outside our cottage—headed for the house on the hill.

There was a moment when I felt my resolve weakening—the moment when I left the main path to cut through the patch of underbrush. But somehow, by keeping my torch focused on the ground straight ahead of me, and, ignoring the mysterious sounds which seemed to hover in the blackness of the pine woods, I managed to keep going—faster and faster, ducking under low branches, plunging through thick vines and brush, stumbling over rocks and roots—until at last I emerged into the clearing, close by the house.

For a minute then I stood still, smoothing down my rumpled, bramble-covered skirt, and trying to regain my breath. Straightening, I looked up at the outer wall of the house, rising black and grim above me. The windows showed dark empty squares—not a light, not a sign of life within. I listened, bending my head forward and straining for the sound of voices. There was none. Save for the murmuring noises of the woods behind me, the heavy silence of the night was unbroken. For the first time, a dreadful thought flashed through my mind. *Suppose Timothy and the men were not at the house?* Suppose they had already finished their search and gone away—or had changed their minds and not come here at all? *Suppose . . . ?*

It was only a moment before the questions wove themselves into a web of confusion and uncertainty. Out of the maze of fearful possibilities which raced through my mind, just one impulse was clear. I must get to the house and call Timothy. Gropingly I moved along the wall toward the small door we had entered earlier that day. A crisscross of shadows from the sagging boards of the old porch jumped crazily in the light of the torch that quivered in my shaking hand. Step by step I walked. And then, just as I rounded the corner of the veranda, I stumbled on something and nearly fell.

Something soft, it was. Soft, and yet strangely solid and unyielding. I think that even before I turned the flash-light down, I knew what it was that I would see. But

I could not know what horror would fill me at the sight of Tony Jackson's body—sprawled at my feet, and staring upward in the circle of bright light with the contorted grimace of death. Nor could I possibly have anticipated anything so brutally dreadful as the torn, clawed mass which was his throat. Only for a split second did I stand there—staring downward—but I remember that in that brief moment there passed through my mind a recollection of Timothy's grave face, his sober words when he had seen the body of Ruby Turner. "I've seen people strangled before—but never anything like this. The girl was literally clawed to death."

Like a great, black, icy wave, panic swept over me. With one cry of terror I turned away and plunged blindly back across the clearing and into the woods. No longer had I any thought save to escape. Escape—escape—escape. Over and over the word circled in my brain and gave me, somehow, the strength to keep moving in spite of the leaden fear which threatened to paralyze my legs. *Escape—escape.* I heard myself saying the word as I tore recklessly through the brush once more. Escape from that nameless horror which haunted the woods—which had twice reached out from the shadowy depths to deal vicious death upon its victims.

It seemed to me that I had been running for hours before I heard the sound—but actually I had only gone a few paces from the clearing. As in the grip of a dreadful nightmare, I seemed to be chained to some endless treadmill which so weighted my steps that, struggle as I would, I could make no headway. At first the sound came faintly—as if from far away toward the shore. It was the sound of wind moaning through the tall trees. Silence again, and still I plunged blindly forward. Then the sound nearer this time, and rising from a low wail into a long, high shriek, as though the wind were tearing at the treetops. I stopped. I lifted my eyes and saw the branches motionless above me, felt the still night air upon my face. *There was not a breath of wind stirring.* And then, in a final flash of paralyzing terror, I realized the meaning of that sound. It was the creature X—somehow escaped from the prison of the big house. X uttering the weird wind-cry which was his signal of distress. X *somewhere* in the darkness near me. For a frozen moment I dared not run—dared not move lest I come straight upon the creature.

Without warning, the cry sounded one last time. Shrill and piercing it came from a spot directly behind where I stood. Some instinct of self-protection told me to put out the guiding gleam of my flash-light, and I turned to strain my eyes toward the place from whence the sound had come. At first all seemed blank darkness, and then, in the depths of shadow, I saw a blacker shadow—crouching—moving toward me with silent, gliding steps. My mouth was open—I tried desperately to scream—but no sound emerged from my dry throat.

"*Timothy—Timothy—Timothy,*" cried a voice, loud and clear.

Not until I had heard the ringing cry over and over did I realize that I was listening to the sound of my own voice.

"*Timothy—Timothy—*" some power beyond my control continued to drag the words from my throat.

And still the crouching shadow moved closer and closer until it was almost upon me. Suddenly it sprang up a great towering dark form—and then—

There was a crashing of underbrush. From somewhere a light flashed full on the figure before me—and for one awful moment I glimpsed the powerful, upstretched arms, the hairy face fixed in a snarl of vicious rage. A single shot—and the great arms dropped, the head snapped backward, and with one final inhuman cry, the creature shuddered and fell.

That last wailing screech seemed to echo on and on in my ears—seemed to mingle with a roaring wave of dizziness which swept over me. And then I felt myself falling—falling into deep black silence.

The next thing I knew a dazzling light was turned blindingly on my face, and from somewhere behind the light a man's voice was speaking.

"Say—who's the snooping dame?"

And then Timothy's arm close about my shoulders, Timothy's voice, blessedly near. "It's no snooping dame—it's my wife."

The words registered upon my mind at some midway point between laughter and tears.

"You're safe, Joanie," Timothy was saying, "we're all safe. The thing is over—the creature is dead."

"But how—" I struggled to marshal my returning wit, "how did it get out of the house?"

"By a sort of tunnel over in one corner of its courtyard enclosure. Evidently X had managed to dig his way out some days ago without being discovered by Miss Emily. He probably was loose for the first time on the night Ruby was killed—"

"Oh—" I drew back, "then it was X who murdered her?"

Timothy nodded slowly. "And it was X that Mrs. Benson heard prowling around her cottage earlier that evening. He must have wandered back up the hill and happened to find Ruby where she was waiting to meet Allen Gilbert. We'll never know exactly what took place there—but I'm pretty well convinced that Miss Emily came along the path in time to see that X was out. There must have been some kind of a scuffle—you remember Miss Emily's note-book got mussed up, and a page torn out. Anyway, she managed to get away without being hurt by the creature. Whether she made any effort to get him back to the house—or whether he went of his own accord—God only knows."

"Then you think Miss Emily really knew all along that X killed Ruby?"

"I've no doubt but what she did," again Timothy nodded. "And that was why she made such elaborate efforts to throw us off the track. Whether Miss Emily suspected that Tony was really Dr. Jack's son, and that he was here to claim his father's records and papers—I'm not certain. But, at any rate, the old gal was sure that we were on the trail of Ruby's murderer—and so she staged that whole bonfire scene on the hill just for our benefit—and, of course, the story about the secret dope and her experiments on Ruby was a pure fake. She was willing to do anything to keep us from focusing our suspicions on the big house—"

"But Timothy—" indignation gave me the strength to sit up straighter, "she *couldn't* have been willing to let that awful creature go on roaming around?"

"Oh no. She did her best to prevent any further trouble of that sort. After X was back in his enclosure, Miss Emily evidently discovered the tunnel through which he had escaped, and she put up a pretty good barricade of heavy wood, nailed across the opening. That's probably what she was doing after Ruby was killed. You remember she wasn't in her cottage as late as two o'clock that night. She undoubtedly thought the barrier would be strong enough to keep X where he belonged—and no doubt it would have been if only she hadn't been killed herself sometime last night."

"What's that got to do with it?" I frowned.

"Simply that X got hungry," said Timothy calmly. "He depended on Miss Emily for food, you see, and when she didn't come last night, nor today, the creature got terribly hungry. So hungry that he managed to break through the barricade. When we got up to the house tonight we found the inner courtyard, just as Dr. Jack described it in his records. But the place was empty, and over in one corner we saw the tunnel down under the foundations of the house—and at the end of it was the remnant of Miss Emily's wooden barrier. When we saw that—we knew what had happened to poor Tony. You see, Joan, Tony was evidently the only one of us who doubted the story that Miss Emily told last night the fake story about the drugs and so on. And after he had taken Miss Emily home, he must have come up to the big house and discovered what her secret really was. Either Miss Emily came up herself, and Tony followed her—or else he had a hunch to investigate the place for himself. At any rate, he did go there—which accounts for his muddy boots, and the footprints we found near the door. And he must have discovered the secret of X."

"Do you suppose, Timothy, that Tony actually *saw* X last night?"

"Maybe," Timothy shrugged, "and maybe not. He might have simply looked through those records that we found. But anyway, he learned enough to make him certain of one thing. He was going to kill Miss Emily. You can't really blame the poor kid. It must have been a terrible shock to him to discover the thing his father had done. And, naturally enough, he took out his shock in blaming Miss Emily. Among other things, you remember, her association with Dr. Jack had damn well wrecked the lives of Tony and his mother and brother. So, as I figure it out, he went straight to Miss Emily's cottage and shot her—without further ceremony. Then, having done that, he waited for his chance today to come back to the big house and finish off the creature X. If he had succeeded in that—the whole wretched business would have been ended. But, unfortunately, he didn't succeed. By the time Tony reached the house, X had escaped again, and the poor kid never even got as far as the door. We found him there, Joan, when we came up—and he was—" Timothy hesitated in the effort to break the news gently.

"I—I know about Tony," I said. "I saw him too."

"Poor Joanie," Timothy's arm tightened around my shoulder. "It must have been awful for you."

"I was trying to follow you," I went on. "It was terribly silly of me, I realize now—but anyway I got as far as the house—and then, when I saw Tony, and there was no sign of you in the house, I got panicky and tried to run away. I let out sort of a yell—and I suppose it was that sound that made the creature follow me. The next thing I knew, I saw him coming toward me through the darkness—and somehow I managed to call you—"

"You managed to call me, all right," Timothy agreed heartily. "I'll bet they heard that yell of yours clear up in Pineboro. We were scouting the woods over on the other side of the house when we heard you—and believe me, I set a new world's record for speed getting around here. You were a damn silly little goose to get yourself in such a mess—but you certainly gave us a clue to find X. And we did find him, and you're safe now—and everything turned out all right after all. And now—" Timothy got up and swung me lightly off the ground.

"Now what?" I murmured against his tweed-coated chest. "Do I get a scolding?"

Timothy motioned to one of the detectives to guide the way with a flash-light, and we started off through the brush. "You do not," he answered me firmly, "get a scolding—yet. First, you get carried all the way home—and then you get a mighty swig of rye—and then you get some sleep. By the time you wake up, I'll have the scolding all worked out."

He carried out the plan exactly as he had outlined it. When I had imbibed the mighty swig of rye, I suddenly remembered that we had had no supper.

"I really ought to fix you men something to eat," I murmured through a comfortably warm haze.

For an answer, Timothy put a quilt over me and turned out the light.

"Sure," he said, "you can fix us some supper when you wake up. We'll just be ready for it when you've had a nap."

When I opened my eyes, the room was flooded with brilliant sunlight, and Timothy was standing over me with a cup in his hand.

"Timothy—" I sat bolt upright, "what about supper?"

"Breakfast, you mean," Timothy grinned, "and here it is." He thrust the cup of steaming coffee into my hand. "Now drink it like a good girl, and then put your hat on—because we're going places."

"Going *where?*" I stared about the room and discovered our bags, neatly packed and lined up ready to be closed.

"To a place called Sunset Bay, about fifty miles from here," Timothy answered calmly. "The Portland men told me about it, and they're going to drop us off on their way back home. They've sworn up and down that it's a quiet place, full of old maids and retired ministers and that the only exciting event of the day is sunset. No mysteries, no

murders, no witches, no house that Jack built. So I think
it's just the place for us."

"But Timothy—"

"Drink your coffee," my husband commanded, "and
don't argue. So far this trip of ours has been ten per cent
honeymoon and ninety per cent bloodshed and sudden
death. But from now on, it's going to be one hundred per
cent honeymoon."

And, I may add, it was.

# MURDER IN AMBER

(1937, *periodical serial*; 1938, *novel*)

This Book is for
Dr. A. A. M.
In Gratitude for His Friendly Interest
And a Very Good Idea

## 1

# A RED SILK ROSE

On a Saturday afternoon in mid-July, I stepped over the threshold from the elegant lounge of the *S.S. Orion* onto the promenade deck. Looking down the long row of chairs, it was easy to find my place by the fact that my husband's long legs protruded a good six inches further than those of anyone else, and I made my way down the deck reflecting thankfully that, with his usual foresight, Timothy had chosen the side which was shaded from the glaring afternoon sun. Three weeks of stifling heat in Shanghai had made me wonder whether I was ever going to be really cool again. Not even the sight of the Pacific, stretching out calm and deeply blue, nor the sound of frosty spray which fell away from the *Orion's* bow, could lift the feeling of sweltering oppression that had hung like thick, damp mist over the crowded confusion of the strange city.

I settled myself in the chair beside Timothy and tried to take a breath of sea air deep enough to drive out the lingering memory of varied and pungent harbor aromas which still hovered in our stateroom below.

Timothy looked up from his book. "Hello. All through unpacking as soon as this?"

I shook my head. "I gave up when the stateroom got to the boiling point. The stewardess tells me it will be a charming bower of refreshing breezes by dinner time—owing to prevailing winds in Latitude XYZ or something like that. Anyway, I'm *not* going down there again until some of the local color atmosphere of dear old China evaporates—not if I have to stay right here all night." I fetched up my knitting bag and opened it.

Timothy leaned forward with a great show of interest. "That's something new, isn't it?" He inspected the beginnings of a white bouclé sweater with a professional air. Ever since, as a child, he was taught to knit two rows on some unfortunate soldier's muffler, Timothy has considered himself a *connoisseur* of knitting.

"Very nice," he nodded approvingly.

"I'm glad you like it. There's one good thing about it, anyway—the pattern is so complicated I have to keep my eyes glued on the needles and mutter to myself all the time I'm knitting. So I won't always be disturbing you with my bright remarks while you're trying to concentrate on unraveling the clues in some detective story. Which one are you reading now?" I peeked across Timothy's shoulder as he opened his book. "Oh. Agatha Christie again. Well, then I expect it doesn't matter whether I interrupt or not—you never *can* guess the answer to her stories."

"Never," Timothy shook his head cheerfully. "I may be good enough for the Homicide Squad back on a simple island like Manhattan, but Agatha can still twist me around her finger any time she wants to."

"You're not queer enough, very likely," I said. "If you could just have handle-bar moustachios like Hercule Poirot, or walk in your sleep, or grow orchids, it might help you. Although I can just imagine the Commissioner's face if you asked him up for steak and mushrooms some night and he found out you grew orchids."

Timothy laughed, but the next moment he looked gloomy. As gloomy, that is, as Timothy can ever manage to look. "As a matter of fact," he said, "I've been trying not to think too much about the Commissioner's face. Especially when I have to tell him what a fine wild-goose chase this trip to China turned out to be. The department will be out one round-trip fare, and nobody knows any more about that little dope-ring than they did before—least of all me."

"I wouldn't worry too much." I stopped counting stitches long enough to look up comfortingly. "It isn't your fault you didn't find what you were looking for. After all, everybody knows China is a big country."

Timothy gave me a sideways glance, just to make sure I didn't really mean to be nasty.

"And, anyway," I went on, "the trip isn't over yet. You may still distinguish yourself and bring glory to the Force on the way home."

"How, for instance?"

"Well, you might save fifteen or twenty orphans and row them back to Shanghai with your bare hands, in case we have a shipwreck. Or you might discover a sea-monster, or maybe there's a celebrated criminal amongst our fellow-passengers."

Timothy made a sound a little like a snort. "If there is," he said, "he—or she—is definitely not one of our merry band at the doctor's table. The collection I met at lunch is far too old to be considered in the criminal class. Criminals are getting so standardized these days. Result of mass-production, I daresay." He sighed.

"I've been meaning to ask you whether I missed much by not going down to lunch," I said.

Timothy shook his head. "You can see for yourself at dinner, if the dining-room cools off enough to be bearable. The doctor himself isn't so bad, except that he has one of those intense, two-watt brains that glows white hot over some trifle and blinds him to everything else that's going on."

"How reassuring," I observed. "In case we should get sick."

"Very. And there's an old sawbones of a missionary, mouth dragged down, soul dragged up—both equally painful—and his miserable looking wife. Shaw, the name is. Three lone men: a Nicholas Brande, the type who seems to think you ought to have heard of him and quibbles with the steward about wine; an elderly and vague soul named Samuel Norman; and a young Tod Hutten, who appears to be a student in the Yale graduate school and a rather classic example of a pain in the neck . . ."

"Odd combination."

"Not as rare as you might think. That finishes off the bachelor males. Our only unattached lady is Mrs. Gideon Hertz of Paterson, New Jersey, who looks exactly she sounds, bless her heart. She runs to bosom, conversation and common sense—and she's a nice lady. That's all, except for a dashing young couple named Covell, who came in late with a distinct glaze of Martini in the eye and annoyed the steward by asking for a plate of scraps to take to their dog."

"Well, *they* sound nice, anyway."

Timothy nodded. "But the others, as you must have gathered from my deft portrait sketches, are not what you'd call an inspiring group. Which means, my pet, that you're likely to be thrown rather exclusively on my society for the voyage."

"And what could be nicer—my dear Inspector?"

"Excuse *me*—" a woman's voice at my elbow made me turn just in time to see a large lady settle herself in the deck chair next to mine, "but aren't you Mrs. Fowler? We met your good husband at lunch and we did hope your not being in the dining-room didn't mean you were sick or anything."

"Oh, no. Only the heat, and the—the rather complicated atmosphere of the harbor—"

"I know just exactly what you mean," she nodded emphatically. "Mr. Hertz is the same way. Sensitive. He says foreign travel is just one long smell to him. But with me, it's just the other way. I love anything strange, even a smell. . . ."

We were off—and within ten minutes I had an adequate understanding of the precise points wherein the attitude of Mrs. Gideon Hertz toward travel differed from that of her husband. It hadn't taken Timothy's murmured introduction to tell me who my new acquaintance was. One look at her friendly blue eyes, the firm but generous set of her mouth and chin, and the extreme amplitude of her figure had recalled his description: "She runs to bosom, conversation and common sense." And at the end of an hour I was pretty well versed in the affairs of Mrs. Hertz, the little Hertzes, and the more intimate details of Mr. Hertz's character, convictions, and mental attributes.

I thought I knew all there was to know about the Hertzes when, in the comparative coolness of early evening, we descended to our stateroom to dress for dinner, but just as I settled the folds of my thinnest chiffon dress and shouted some remark at Timothy, lost in the depths of the shower, there was a light tap at the stateroom door, and I turned to see the beaming countenance of Mrs. Hertz peeking at me.

"Are you dressed? Oh, and *how* sweet and cool you look, Mrs. Fowler, in that yellow chiffon. Just like lemon ice. I *do* feel hot in black, but Mr. Hertz always thinks it's more dignified." A layer of light pink powder did not quite conceal the glowing warmth of Mrs. Hertz's face and neck. "Now I *don't* want to disturb you—but there are just two things—First, should I wear this *here*—or *here?*" Like a prestidigitator, she produced a tremendous red silk rose from somewhere, and holding it first at her waist, where it seemed lost beneath bosom, and then on her shoulder, where it seemed lost above bosom, she waited for my verdict.

When I had, somewhat tentatively, suggested the shoulder, Mrs. Hertz clamped the flower into place with a competent jab of a pin, and proceeded to her second question. It concerned a note, written in a spidery and not too steady handwriting on ship's stationery.

"What," Mrs. Hertz demanded, "do you think I ought to do about this? I found it under my door when I came down to dress."

I scanned the courteously worded invitation, signed by Samuel Norman, asking Mrs. Hertz to join him in the lounge for a cocktail before diner. Recalling Timothy's description of Mr. Norman as a vague and elderly soul, and being more than confident of Mrs. Hertz's ability to deal discreetly with a chance gentleman acquaintance, I would have advised her to accept, were it not for a rather peculiar postscript at the bottom of the page. In letters which were noticeably unsteady, a single sentence was scrawled downward across the lower corner.

*"In reference to the matter we discussed this afternoon,"* it said, *"I have something of importance to say to you."*

The final word trailed off the edge of the paper, almost as though the writer had been unable to finish—and yet the note was neatly folded and the envelope carefully sealed and addressed.

"Doesn't that strike you as kind of—well, queer?" Mrs. Hertz eyed me anxiously. "Particularly as I don't remember having said anything very special to Mr. Norman, though we did talk for a few minutes this afternoon. As I recall, he did most of the talking."

This last statement I had reason to doubt, but I handed back the note after only a moment's hesitation. "Well, I'd certainly go and see what it's all about, anyway. It could hardly do any harm—and if this Mr. Norman seems a nice old gentleman . . ."

"Oh, *very* nice," Mrs. Hertz nodded quickly, "and do you know, I think he's kind of lonesome. It struck me that he wasn't so awfully well, either—or else he was worried about something . . ."

"I think you certainly ought to go and cheer him up, then," I said decisively. "He sounds as if he needed it."

"I suppose you could look at it that way—but I'm sure I don't know what Mr. Hertz would think—" Mrs. Hertz glanced at the note in her hand, hesitated one last minute, and then spoke with firmness. "There's no use beating about the bush—I'm too curious a woman not to go and find out what under the shining sun Mr. Norman can possibly have to tell me 'of importance.' So thanks for giving me the advice I wanted to hear." She tucked the folded paper into the frontal expanse of her black lace dress. "And if I only have *one* cocktail," Mrs. Hertz added earnestly, "I don't believe Mr. Hertz could possibly object, do you?"

## 2
# A MESSAGE FOR THE DOCTOR

When Timothy and I reached our places in the dining room, only the missionary and his wife and Dr. Sloane were at the table. My impression of the Reverend Asa Shaw was immediate—and complicated. The man looked so terribly worn out and threadbare and sincere that you couldn't help feeling sorry for him—yet one glance at the lines of care and weariness in his wife's face, at the pathetic effort of her made-over taffeta dress, at her red, work-roughened hands which she tried so hard to keep out of sight beneath the table, all made me instinctively resent the gleam of fanatic righteousness in the Reverend Shaw's eyes. Nor did his conversation, consisting mostly of telling us things we already knew about China, do much to improve my opinion of him.

Dr. Sinclair Sloane seemed, on the whole, rather more attractive than Timothy's description would have led me to expect. Aside from a tendency to eat too fast and twitch at his small, black mustache, I saw no indications of the "intense two-watt brain," and I observed that he was careful to give at least momentary attention to Mrs. Shaw each time she ventured a timid remark or smile. Which more than could be said for young Tod Hutten when he arrived from a rather evident session at the bar. He proceeded, in the course of two minutes, to contradict flatly one statement of Mrs. Shaw's, and to dismiss her second effort with such obvious disregard that she lapsed into an unhappy silence.

Meanwhile Hutten held forth with great authoritativeness on a bit of ship's gossip he had just gleaned in the smoking-room.

"It seems," he said, "that J. T. Ezry—*the* Ezry—is aboard the *Orion,* traveling incognito, and taking a consignment of absolutely priceless Oriental antiques home for his collection. The Captain is busy denying the story right and left, but one of the stewards saw some letters and baggage. marked with Ezry's name, and it's a pretty good bet that the old gent really is aboard—particularly since he's been in China for the past few months on the trail of some special manuscripts and pottery businesses that have been dug up lately."

Since, despite our interest, we all must have seemed a trifle vague as to the precise identity and position of *the* J. T. Ezry, Tod Hutten obliged us with an account of his tremendous importance as an art connoisseur and collector, his fabulous wealth, and—a fact which appeared to give Tod the greatest satisfaction—Ezry's reputation for somewhat bizarre peccadilloes. Warming to his subject, Tod was in the midst of a detailed and unfortunate anecdote involving the learned and cultured Mr. Ezry and a certain nurse in a New Haven hospital, when the arrival of a handsome and breezy young couple interrupted him. Introduced to me as Mr. and Mrs. Covell, the new arrivals—very bright of eye and glib of tongue—launched into their version of the Ezry rumor. While their remarks were by no means lacking in spirit, I was relieved to note that

they lacked the extreme explicitness of Tod's story which
had brought spots of color to Mrs. Shaw's sallow cheeks,
and made her reverend husband look as if, for all his obvious Protestantism, he were mentally crossing himself with
every breath.

"The absolutely *marvelous* part of the rumor," Mrs.
Covell was saying, "the absolutely priceless thing *is*—
that while everybody's perfectly sure that Ezry really is
on board—no one has the dimmest notion what he looks
like. He's such an old bear about being photographed, you
know, that it seems he can go practically anywhere and not
be recognized. The result is that every time an unidentified
male over twenty-five walks up to the bar, conversation
absolutely *withers,* on the assumption that the stranger
may be old J. T. Ezry himself. *I* really think the Captain
owes it to his passengers to let us in on the secret, don't
you, Dr. Sloane?" Mrs. Covell leaned across the table.

"For Pete's sake, Sally," Ned Covell squelched his wife
good-naturedly, "you don't expect the doctor to answer a
question like that, do you?"

"Well—maybe not here, in front of everybody," Sally
Covell was undismayed, "but later—maybe—"

"As a matter of fact," Dr. Sloane cleared his throat,
fidgeted with his napkin, and then coughed slightly, "I
don't know anything at all about it, Mrs. Covell, but very
likely there's no foundation at all for the rumor. Gossip
starts very easily on shipboard, as you doubtless know, and
I've found it better to—ah—ignore any such stories . . ."

"Of course, you have, Doctor," Sally Covell agreed.
warmly, "and you're perfectly right, too. But at the same
time—" her smile dimpled again, "you wouldn't want to
keep us gossipers from our fun, would you? Now *I* have a
theory about this business. Ned says I'm crazy, but I *know*

which one Ezry is, and furthermore—" she lowered her voice and bent forward with such an air of confidence that even the Reverend Shaw leaned closer to listen, "furthermore—*he sits at this table.*"

"Oh, dear," Mrs. Shaw drew back in fluttering alarm.

"Not *really?*" Tod Hutten played up to the drama of the moment.

"Absolutely," Sally nodded solemnly. "And the reason I know is because he—"

"Shut up, my sweet, shut *up,*" Ned Covell hissed the words with a warning nudge in his wife's ribs. I looked up to follow his glance and saw that a tall, distinguished looking man was approaching our table.

Sally, likewise sighting the newcomer, had just time to murmur "Speak of the devil—" below her breath, and change the subject before the handsome, gray-haired stranger drew out a chair next to Timothy, nodded to Dr. Sloane, and seated himself. He glanced once in the direction of Sally, who had plunged into a rather pointless story about her dog, named Haile Selassie. He lifted one eyebrow very slightly, bowed to me when Dr. Sloane introduced him as Mr. Nicholas Brande, and then turned his attention to the menu. A question of the wine list, evidently taken up from where it had left off at lunch, occupied Mr. Brande and the steward in a lengthy and technical discussion.

Under cover of Sally's anecdote about the charms of Haile Selassie, I bent toward Timothy. "What *do* you suppose has become of Mrs. Hertz and her date?" I demanded.

Timothy shrugged. "Either she's so far forgotten herself and Mr. Hertz as to have two cocktails, or else Mr. Norman, dazzled by the glory of that red silk rose, is pouring out his life story on her motherly chest. But either way, they're taking a devilishly long time about it."

Neither of Timothy's suggestions turned out to be correct. Just as we were finishing our cheese and crackers, Mrs. Hertz came to the table alone.

Catching my questioning look a moment later, Mrs. Hertz flushed a little. "Really," she murmured, "I can't imagine what could have happened to Mr. Norman, but it *was* embarrassing for me, waiting in the—" she glanced toward Mrs. Shaw and lowered her voice confidentially, "bar." She turned to the head of the table. "Dr. Sloane, you haven't by any chance seen Mr. Norman, have you?"

"Norman?" the Doctor seemed to recall his thoughts from some distance. "Why, no."

"Well, I just wondered—he had an appointment with me and when he didn't come *I* thought possibly he might be ill. He doesn't *look* like a well man to me."

"I can't say that I'd noticed anything wrong about his appearance, Mrs. Hertz." Dr. Sloane twitched at his mustache. "As a matter of fact I had quite a talk with him this afternoon and he didn't mention being ill in any way."

"I shouldn't call that much of a test," said Mrs. Hertz—rather tartly, I thought. "But he's likely to miss his dinner if he doesn't come in soon—and, personally, *I* think he's a sick man."

"I agree with Mrs. Hertz," quite unexpectedly Mrs. Shaw spoke up—and then instantly subsided before a look from her husband. "I—only mean I saw him this afternoon," she murmured, "and he didn't seem just quite as—as well as he might."

"Don't you think, Mr. Fowler," Mrs. Hertz appealed to Timothy, "that perhaps someone ought to go to Mr.

Norman's cabin—just to see? After all, you know, he *might* be in need of a doctor."

"You're quite right, Mrs. Hertz, he might," The gravity of Timothy's answer made me turn to see whether he were in earnest. Apparently he was.

"Then would you do it, Mr. Fowler?" Mrs. Hertz pursued the question anxiously. "Go and see about Mr. Norman, I mean."

"Well, really—" Timothy hesitated.

"Don't you bother, Mr. Fowler," the Reverend Shaw pushed back his chair. "We've finished our meal, and I'll be very pleased to look in on Mr. Norman and see if by chance there is any service I can do him." He made it sound as though he were accepting an impressive challenge in the line of Christian duty. "Come, Pearl." He rose.

"Do you know, Shaw, I shouldn't if I were you." It was Nicholas Brande who spoke, very quietly. Everyone turned to look at him.

"What do you mean, I shouldn't?"

Mr. Brande passed his long, elegantly-groomed fingers back over his close-cropped gray hair, and shrugged slightly. "Oh—nothing very definite. But it strikes me we're making rather a fuss over the simple fact that a man has exercised his simple privilege of not coming into this crowded, overheated dining-room and sitting with ten strangers while a not particularly good dinner is not very efficiently served to him. In all probability Mr. Norman has dined on deck, or in his cabin—and if he should be in need of what you call 'service,' Mr. Shaw, I think it quite likely that he understands the meaning of a small, printed card which says 'ring for steward.' That's quite all I meant." Without any particular emphasis, Mr. Brande concluded his speech and bent his attention to the portion of fish which had just been placed before him.

Mrs. Shaw, who had half-risen to follow her husband, sank back in the chair and fingered a small string of pink coral beads at her throat while her gaze wavered uncertainly between Mr. Brande's bent head and the expression of angry embarrassment on the Reverend Shaw's face.

"Well—I'm sure I wouldn't want to intrude," said Shaw stiffly.

There was no reply from Mr. Brande, who continued to regard the filet of sole on his plate without noticeable approval.

Dr. Sloane looked up, rather as though he would like to say something which would smooth over the awkward moment. But apparently nothing occurred to him, and he remained silent.

"Are you ready, Pearl?" the Reverend Shaw turned toward his wife again, and this time she rose quickly and followed her husband as he turned away from the table.

I looked after the two of them, he with his gaunt, drooping shoulders beneath the rusty black coat, and she in her bunchy blue taffeta, as they walked self-consciously through the dining-room.

It must have been about ten minutes later when a steward came hurrying toward our table and bent down to murmur something in Dr. Sloane's ear. Despite the fact that I was only two places away from the Doctor—and frankly curious—I failed to hear a word of the steward's message, but I did observe the startled expression with which the news was received. Twice the Doctor nodded quickly, and then, as the steward departed, he rose, and without looking directly at anyone, made a sort of explanation.

"If you will excuse me," Dr. Sloane said, "I—ah—must—" He coughed slightly, gave one last twitch to his napkin, and put it down. "That is—if you will excuse me, please." He turned abruptly and was gone, leaving me, at least, still intensely curious.

If the others were as preoccupied as I in wondering about the mysterious message they gave no sign of it—and the conversation presently resolved itself into a sort of competition in monologues between Mrs. Hertz and Tod Hutten. Mrs. Hertz, slightly in the lead by virtue of superior enthusiasm and sheer bulk, had just launched into an account of her first grandchild, the arrival of whom had provided the motive for her visit to her married daughter in Peiping, when the steward who had come to fetch Dr. Sloane appeared once more. But this time it was Mrs. Hertz whom he sought, and the message he delivered was plainly audible to all of us at the table.

"Pardon, Madam, but the Captain would like a word with you. In his quarters on the boat deck, please."

Mrs. Hertz, caught squarely in the middle of a sentence about the uncanny fact that her grandson, at the age of six weeks, had exhibited an antipathy for cats which was plainly inherited from Mr. Hertz, paused at the steward's words, closed her mouth, and stared up at him with wide eyes.

"The *Captain*—wants to speak to *me?*"

"Yes, madam. At once, if you please."

"But I—my dinner," Mrs. Hertz looked at the generous helping of steak on the plate before her. "I was just in the midst of it."

"And the Captain asked me, Madam, to deliver this to you," the steward produced a square white envelope.

"This—for *me?*" Mrs. Hertz made a fluttering gesture and pressed one hand dramatically against her black lace bosom.

"The Captain said, Madam, that he thought you would understand."

Slowly, wonderingly, Mrs. Hertz turned the envelope, and then, as she caught sight of the address, I saw the quick change which came over her face.

"Yes," she said, "I think I do understand." Without pausing to open the note, Mrs. Hertz pushed back her chair and struggled a little to rise. "Please tell the Captain I'll be there right away."

As the steward turned away, Mrs. Hertz murmured some excuse to the table at large, and then for just a moment—she caught my eye. I was puzzled at first by the expression of anxiety, almost of fear, which seemed to hover over her normally cheerful and sensible countenance. But in the second when she turned away, I caught sight of the address on the envelope in her hand—and I thought then that I understood her anxiety. For the thin, spidery handwriting was plainly identical with that upon the note she had showed me earlier that evening—the note from Mr. Samuel Norman.

# 3
## A NOTE AND A PACKAGE

Sally Covell put down her knife and fork and stared after the retreating form of Mrs. Hertz. "Well—will somebody please tell me," she demanded, "what this is all about?" She looked at those of us who were still left at the table, but no one seemed inclined to answer.

Tod Hutten was occupied with a cigarette, and Mr. Brande was trying to convey something to the steward about the difference between bernaise and hollandaise sauce. Timothy seemed absorbed in the business of folding his napkin. Ned Covell, apparently, was oblivious of the question.

When none of us showed any signs of rallying, Sally fixed her bright gaze on Timothy. "Mr. Fowler, why don't *you* have something to say about all this hocus-pocus? You're a detective, aren't you?"

"Of sorts," Timothy admitted. "But that doesn't, fortunately, make me a mind reader. And besides, I can't see that anything particularly detectable has happened—" he paused.

Mr. Nicholas Brande did not look at Timothy. But I noticed that for the first time since he reached the table, he seemed momentarily distracted from the subject of food.

Very casually, but quite deliberately, he drew a handkerchief of sheer white linen from his coat pocket, touched
it lightly to his lips, to the palm of each hand. Then, still
without looking up, he replaced the handkerchief with
care and went on buttering a bit of roll.

Tod Hutten, on the other hand, registered frank interest when Timothy's occupation was mentioned. "So—" he
blew out a match, "you're a detective, are you, Mr. Fowler?
That interests me, because it happens I've done some work
in criminal psychology."

"Have you?" said Timothy.

"Quite a bit, as a matter of fact. Some rather surprising
things came out in a series of laboratory experiments we
tried at New Haven last winter—"

"How *fascinating,* Mr. Hutten," Sally Covell fixed
him with a look of passionate attention. "With apes and
things?"

"Get on with your dinner, my girl," Ned soothed his
wife good-humoredly, "and never mind the bright remarks.
Here—if you're through with those we can take them to
Haile Selassie." Without waiting for her permission, he
fished two half-eaten chops from her plate and added them
to a growing collection of scraps at his own place.

Mr. Brande, catching sight of the action, frowned
slightly. "Isn't it customary," he inquired, "for the dogs to
be fed by a steward or something?"

"Oh, yes," Sally and Ned nodded in cheerful unison,
"but, you see, they give them regular dog food and Haile
hates it. He only likes what we like. Besides, this is his
sixth trip across and we feel sort of a conscience about
taking him so often—he doesn't have a very good time, so
we try to make it up to him in every way we can."

Tod Hutten cleared his throat and went on as though nothing had interrupted him. "The experiments were mostly concerned, Mr. Fowler, with the use of drugs that lowered the threshold of normal inhibitions—on the theory, of course, that criminal impulses are frequently present in non-criminal types—and that the only difference between the person who actually commits the crime and the one who only thinks of it lies in the potency of his inhibitory reflexes. The same relationship holds good for confession of crimes also."

"Very novel idea, I'm sure," said Timothy. "We must have a talk about it sometime, although I'm afraid I won't have much to contribute. It's always been my impression that the psychology of criminals was surprisingly like the psychology of everyone else—but no doubt that's due to the fact that I have to work with laws instead of laboratories, and little helps like drugs are pretty much ruled out." He put down his napkin, looked at me, and we rose to go. "See you later."

Tod Hutten crushed out his cigarette, popped a last bit of cheese and cracker into his mouth, and pushed back his chair to follow us. "I'll come along now, if you like," he said. "That's rather a good point you made about the difference between the law and the lab. . . ."

I caught a fleeting glimpse of the look on Timothy's face, and then, as my eye met Sally Covell's, we both laughed.

"Why don't you come along with us, Mrs. Fowler?" Sally suggested, "while we feed Haile Selassie—and then we might do the movie and leave the great criminal brains to bulge in peace."

I was on the point of agreeing with pleasure, when I saw Ned Covell frown and shake his head. "Aren't you forgetting, Sal, that we promised the plushy couple from Des Moines a rubber of bridge?" His tone was as light and casual as before, but it brought a curious change in his wife's expression. For the first time the gay sparkle in her eyes faded, and she glanced down quickly.

"Yes, of course, I—did forget," she murmured almost inaudibly. But the next moment she was all vivaciousness again as she scooped up the collection of scraps from Ned's plate and, quite without self-consciousness, carried the heaping bowl aloft between the tables of diners who turned to observe her curiously. "At least we've got time to feed Haile Selassie," Sally said to me over her shoulder, "and you really must come down and meet him. He's an enchanting pooch, and I can tell to look at you that you're the doggy type."

But Haile Selassie was doomed to wait for his supper that evening. For we were met in the outer lounge by Mrs. Shaw, with a message which drove all other thoughts from our minds for the next few minutes.

Very warm and red of face, Mrs. Shaw bore down upon us. "Oh, Mrs. Fowler, excuse me, but I have a message for you. Will you go to the Captain's quarters right away, please."

"I—to the Captain's quarters?" Very much in the manner of Mrs. Hertz, I pressed a fluttering hand against my bosom. "What for, for heaven's sake?" More than anything else I was struck by the sudden importance of Mrs. Shaw's manner. Her blue taffeta dress fairly rustled with assurance and general efficiency as she addressed me.

"I don't know exactly what's wanted, Mrs. Fowler," she said, "but it's quite urgent. Mrs. Hertz is with the Captain now—and I've no doubt it's something about poor Mr. Norman—"

"*Poor* Mr. Norman? What's the matter with him?"

"Oh—why hadn't you heard?" Mrs. Shaw was all concern. "I hope, my dear, the news won't shock you—but you
may just as well be told straight out. Poor Mr. Norman
passed away this evening."

I did not wish at the moment, and do not wish now, to
be thought heartless, but I was certainly able to hear without undue shock that an elderly man whom I had never
seen had died. But Mrs. Shaw was intent on making the
most of it.

"Of course," she went on solemnly, "it was a terrible
blow to Mrs. Hertz—and I expect that's why she asked the
Captain to send for you—"

"What did Mrs. Hertz have to do with it?" I failed to
see why she should be concerned in the unfortunate man's
fate any more than I.

"Why—I don't know, *exactly,*" Mrs. Shaw seemed a little
hurt by my tendency to question everything she said. "But
the Captain sent for her almost immediately after Mr. Shaw
notified him that poor Mr. Norman had passed on—and
Mrs. Hertz has been in the Captain's quarters ever since."

I looked over Mrs. Shaw's shoulder at Timothy and Tod
Hutten. Tod was obviously bored and restive, as he fiddled
with his cigarette lighter and shifted from one foot to the
other—but it didn't take my wifely eye to see that Timothy was distinctly interested in our little scene. Hoping to
please him, I played up like a true detective's wife with a
question.

"Was it Mr. Shaw," I inquired, "who discovered that
Mr. Norman had died?"

"Yes, it was," Mrs. Shaw answered me with a sort of sad
triumph in her voice. "In spite of the—well, the rather
hasty remarks Mr. Brande made, my husband still felt that

it was his duty to inquire for Mr. Norman—and when he got there he found the poor old gentleman dead. And now wasn't it a fortunate thing that Mr. Shaw *did* go—otherwise there's no knowing how long the poor soul might have lain there before anyone found him. Oh, dear, it does seem such a sad thing to pass away alone like that—" She broke of suddenly and her pale blue eyes filled with tears.

"What did Mr. Norman die of?" Sally Covell inquired. Her tone was polite enough, but coming after Mrs. Shaw's remarks, the question sounded strangely abrupt.

"Well, I wouldn't want to say for *sure.*" Mrs. Shaw removed her *pince-nez* and polished the lenses vigorously. "But I *think* I overheard Dr. Sloane say something about an accident. Of course, Mr. Shaw sent for the doctor the moment he found out what had happened to poor Mr. Norman, and the two of them were in Mr. Norman's cabin, you see, when— Oh, dear—" She stopped suddenly, "There's Mr. Shaw looking for me now. I shouldn't have stayed here talking when there's so much to be attended to, and Asa is depending on me to help him." Having reminded me once more that I was expected immediately in the Captain's quarters, and replaced her *pince-nez,* Mrs. Shaw hurried away—fairly exuding officious energy from the folds of her rusty blue taffeta.

I looked toward the doorway where the Reverend Shaw awaited her, and observed that his habitual expression of one who has just swallowed a beneficial but extremely unpleasant medicine was more pronounced than ever. Watching the two of them go off together, Timothy shook his head wonderingly.

"It certainly takes a death," he said, "to bring out the best in the Shaw family. And now, my girl," he took my arm, "to the Captain with you."

"But Timothy, you really needn't—"

"Oh, yes, I need," he guided me firmly toward the stairway. "You don't think I'm going to miss out on this, do you?" he demanded when we were out of earshot of the Covell's and Tod Hutten. "*I* want to know what's going on, what with Comrade Norman dropping by the wayside and leaving notes for Mrs. Hertz. Besides—it gives me a swell excuse to escape the toils of the boy criminologist."

Captain Cobb was standing, feet braced apart, fingertips in his blue coat pockets, in the center of his small office when we entered. A rather short man, very square of chin and shoulder, very shaggy of brow and blue of eye, I thought he looked precisely like one's traditional notion of a sea captain. It occurred to me furthermore, that he thought so, too.

Nodding in the direction of Mrs. Hertz, Captain Cobb explained very briefly about Mr. Norman's sudden death, and added that the reason for Mrs. Hertz being involved in the matter concerned a legacy which the old gentleman had left her.

"Rather unusual, of course," the Captain said, "to make a bequest of that sort to a comparative stranger. But then—ah—Norman seemed an odd chap, if I may say so without offense. At any rate, I'm afraid it's upset Mrs. Hertz—ah—most unfortunate occurrence all round. I thought perhaps you people would be good enough to stay with her awhile."

"Why, of course—" I went directly to the large chair where Mrs. Hertz, looking as nearly crushed as her bulk would allow, sat quietly. In one hand she held a sheet of crumpled note-paper and an oblong white box, and with the other she dabbed a handkerchief against her eyes from time to time. I patted her shoulder and murmured something which I hoped would sound comforting.

Mrs. Hertz looked up at me gratefully. "It was nice of you to come," she said. "I don't want to be foolish about this, but the shock of the poor man dying—and then to find that he'd left me a note and *this*"—she held out the box—"it just all seems so terribly queer, you know . . ." Her voice trailed off in a long sigh, and she dabbed at her eyes again.

Looking down at the package in her hand, I felt an almost overwhelming curiosity. "What—?" I began, but Mrs. Hertz was proceeding with the explanation in her own way.

"It all happened so very strangely," she said. "You see, we were talking this afternoon, Mr. Norman and I. He seemed such a nice man and somehow we got onto the subject of jewelry. I suppose I shouldn't have said it, but somehow it just slipped out about how, all my life, I've wanted to have a really beautiful amber necklace. I've hardly ever mentioned it to anyone—not even to Mr. Hertz—because I never dreamed I could possibly afford to own one half so lovely as I wanted, but Mr. Norman was so sympathetic about it, and he seemed to know so much about all kinds of jewelry, that the first thing I knew I was telling him exactly how I imagined the necklace would look, and I even admitted that I'd looked at amber while I was in China—hoping I'd find a bargain in one of those dirty little shops." Mrs. Hertz paused to look up at me in genuine distress. "I don't need to tell you that I *never* for one *moment* meant to hint for anything when I talked like that to a strange man . . ."

"Of course you didn't," I could barely restrain a smile at the thought of Mrs. Hertz in the role of gold-digger: "What you said was the most natural thing in the world."

"Well—you're very kind to look, at it that way," she sniffed a little, "but I'm afraid Mr. Hertz would say. if was just a plain case of my talking too much again. Anyway—*I* never gave the conversation a second thought, and when I got Mr. Norman's note saying he had something of importance to say to me, I didn't even remember what we had talked about. Then—at the dinner table—the steward brought me that second note, and I still couldn't understand what it meant at all. It wasn't until Captain Cobb told me that poor Mr. Norman was dead—and that they had found *this* in his room, along with the note—" Again she indicated the oblong package in her hand. "Then I realized that Mr. Norman had meant to—to give me—" Mrs. Hertz's voice faltered and broke. She thrust the crumpled sheet of notepaper toward me. "Here—you read what he says—"

I smoothed the page. The old man's handwriting was so delicately traced that I could scarcely make out the words.

"Dear Mrs. Hertz,
This package is for you, with sincere good wishes. I am sure you will understand.
　　Faithfully yours,

　　　　　　　　　Samuel Norman."

In silence I handed the brief message to Timothy, and watched his expression.

"So—" he glanced up, "it looks as though the old chap had a notion he might die, doesn't it?"

At his words, I felt Mrs. Hertz's substantial shoulder heave convulsively beneath my hand. But the Captain frowned, and cleared his throat briskly.

"I'm afraid I can't see how you make that out, Mr. Fowler," he said. "I think you go too far in assuming that Mr. Norman was in any way forecasting his own death."

"Perhaps you're right at that, Captain," Timothy agreed mildly. "It's rather a habit of mine—reading between the lines, so to speak. Better, no doubt to put the thing down to coincidence."

"M'mm—yes," the Captain's face cleared. "Well, coincidence you know, plays strange tricks on us all sometimes. But I take it that you agree with me," he went on more briskly, "that Mrs. Hertz should quite properly accept the gift, despite the unfortunate and—ah—rather unusual circumstances under which it comes to her?"

"Oh—absolutely," I spoke up with great conviction, but, to my surprise, Timothy remained silent.

"And you, Mr. Fowler?" the Captain asked.

"I'd say yes," Timothy answered slowly, "if—" he hesitated, "if Mrs. Hertz really wants to own the gift—whatever it is."

"Oh—I do, Mr. Fowler," Mrs. Hertz raised her eyed and regarded him through a blur of tears. "Even though it all happened so strangely—and I do feel so sorry for poor Mr. Norman—and although I don't know how I can ever explain it to Mr. Hertz—" she paused and gulped. "Even so, I want the necklace more than I've ever wanted anything in my whole life. It's so lovely—it's like—" she groped helplessly for a word and then, failing to find it, she opened the oblong box in her hand and slowly, almost reverently, she lifted out an amber necklace.

I can remember to this moment the thrill I felt as I watched that long, shimmering strand uncoil. I had certainly not been prepared for anything half so gorgeous. The amber beads were square-cut instead of rounded in the usual way, and the effect was like a rope of sparkling, honey-colored sunlight strung on the long, gold cord.

"A most unusual necklace, don't you think?" Captain Cobb's voice cut through the silence. "I may say I know a bit about amber—I've picked up a few pieces myself, as a matter of fact, traveling here and there—but, by Jove, I don't think I ever saw any better than that. I said so to Dr. Sloane right off, when I found the package there in Mr. Norman's room—"

"Oh—?" Timothy sounded surprised. "So it was you who discovered the beads?"

"Well—quite naturally, Mr. Fowler," the Captain looked up sharply. "The package and this—ah, note, addressed to Mrs. Hertz, were lying on the desk in Norman's cabin."

"Doesn't it strike you as a trifle odd," said Timothy, "that Mr. Norman should have left a written note with the package? After all, he had an engagement to meet Mrs. Hertz for cocktails—why shouldn't he have given her the necklace in person?"

The Captain beetled his eyebrows. "Well, there's no accounting for the sudden notions a chap like Norman might take. He'd crossed with me several times before, as a matter of fact, and I'd always set him down as an odd sort of fish. Nothing wrong, you know—only a bit queer in his ways."

There was a moment's silence, then Timothy spoke carefully. "I was just wondering," he said, "whether in this case Mr. Norman might have had his mind changed for him. I mean, for instance, that some unforeseen circumstance might have prevented his meeting Mrs. Hertz as he planned."

"What circumstance did you have in mind, Mr. Fowler?"

"Death," said Timothy.

"Oh, I say—come now, Mr. Fowler—" the Captain's beetling frown deepened as he looked quickly at Mrs. Hertz and me, "isn't that a bit strong? I mean—to put it that way—"

"Well, of course," said Timothy. "I don't quite know how to put it—really—since I haven't happened to hear what killed Mr. Norman, nor when he died."

"Heart," said Captain Cobb, and tapped his chest significantly. "He's been ailing quite some time, I believe. I remember speaking to him this afternoon shortly after we sailed, and he told me then that his heart had been troubling him lately. I didn't gather from what he said that there was anything acute—but then, with the heart, we never know. Evidently the attack came on suddenly—at least I knew nothing of it until a steward came to me just as I left the dining room and said I was wanted at once in Norman's cabin. Bit of a nasty shock, it was, getting there and finding the poor old chap gone—" The Captain shrugged his broad-set shoulders and gazed out through the window at the distant horizon of deep blue sky and water. "But then—" he sighed, "we all go sometime—and that's the best way, I should think. Heart just stops, I'm told—and it's all over in a second. No fuss—"

"Oh, quite," said Timothy. His drawl was a shade more pronounced than usual. "*If* that was the way it happened. I thought I heard Mrs. Shaw say something about an accident, though—" he hesitated as the Captain shifted his glance quickly from the horizon to Timothy's face.

"Shaw? Oh, yes, the missionary woman. Excitable sort of creature she seemed. I don't quite know what she meant by *accident,* unless—"

"She was there," Timothy went on calmly, "when Dr. Sloane was first called to look at Norman. It was Mr. Shaw who sent for the Doctor, you know."

"Oh, yes. Yes, I recall now," the Captain's face cleared. "No doubt what Mrs. Shaw heard was a remark Doctor Sloane made concerning the possibility that Norman may have struck his head against something as he fell. Very sudden, those heart things, you know—and it seemed as if the poor old chap had bumped against the corner of the desk as he collapsed. Not a very pretty subject—" Captain Cobb glanced apologetically at me. "That's likely what the Shaw woman overheard—and twisted it around to make some story of an accident. You never know what a woman is going to make of what she hears, if you'll allow me to say so, Mrs. Fowler." This time he gave me a slight smile. "Ah, well, that explains your point, I believe, Mr. Fowler."

"Yes—very nicely, thank you, Captain. All except the matter of *when* Mr. Norman probably died."

"As to that, I'm afraid I can't say," the Captain shook his head. "Personally, I can't see that it makes very much difference—but in any case, Dr. Sloane would have a fairly accurate notion, I presume. These things are all figured by science nowadays—"

"Yes," said Timothy. "Yes, I believe they are. Well—" He rose from the edge of the desk where he had been sitting, "If that's all you wanted of us, Captain—"

Mrs. Hertz looked up suddenly. She had been staring at her necklace, apparently as oblivious to the conversation of the two men as if she had been hypnotized by the glittering strand of amber. She raised her eyes and looked directly at Timothy.

"Do you see, Mr. Fowler," she asked, "why I want to keep the necklace?"

Timothy walked over to her chair and nodded slowly.

"Yes," he said, "I think I do see."

## 4
## MONDAY NIGHT AT MIDNIGHT

Sunday morning we rose late, and came out on deck just as the sound of a rather wheezy hymn indicated that divine services had gotten underway in the main lounge.

Mrs. Hertz was already in her chair, and Sally Covell stood in front of her, with a black cocker spaniel on the leash.

"Well, he was a good doggie, yes he was. He was a *nice* Haile Selassie." Mrs. Hertz puffed a bit with the effort of leaning forward in her deck chair as she stroked the spaniel's silky ears.

Sally beamed with approval while Timothy and I came up to admire her little dog. He was, quite as Sally had said, an enchanting pooch—and our enthusiasm was perfectly sincere, a fact which Haile Selassie obviously sensed. Wriggling all over with almost unbearable delight, he turned his soft brown eyes on first one and then another of us, and waved a front paw ardently in the direction of Mrs. Hertz's caressing hand.

The next moment Sally was jerking back the leash in sudden alarm. "Haile—*careful*—" She managed to drag him away just in time—for the eager black paw had caught on the long string of amber beads which swung forward

217

from the bosom of Mrs. Hertz, and in another second the beads would have scattered far and wide on the smooth deck floor.

"Just for *that,* sir," Sally addressed her pet severely, "you'll have no more attention and compliments today. Come along—we'll finish our mile." With a wave for us, she was off down the deck, a slim figure in her little girl's frock of white linen with a high round collar, and bright green belt matching Haile's leash. The spaniel bounded amiably along beside her.

When they were out of sight, I glanced at Mrs. Hertz and saw her hand still closely clasped about her precious necklace. "Maybe," she caught my eye, "I oughtn't to wear my beads just for every day like this when there's the danger of—of some accident." The words were vague enough, but I gathered somehow that Mrs. Hertz was thinking of some danger other than a spaniel's paw. "But, oh, dear—" she went on, "I just can't bear *not* to wear them—and after all, lovely as the beads are, amber can't be so *terribly* valuable, can it? I mean, not as if they were real pearls or something—" Her voice trailed off questioningly.

I looked at Timothy, and he looked at the open book on his lap. Mrs. Hertz frowned a little anxiously. *"Do* you think I'm foolish, Mr. Fowler?" she inquired.

For another moment Timothy's glance remained fixed on his detective story, then he said slowly: "I really wouldn't know, Mrs. Hertz. Only Mr. Norman seemed to think quite a lot of the necklace. I mean, he made quite a point of giving it away, don't you think?"

"Well, but after all, Mr. Fowler, don't you think Mr. Norman was just a little bit—well, queer? Not that I'd breathe one word against a man who did such a wonderful thing for me—but everybody that I've told the story to thinks it *was* odd of him to give me the necklace that way."

Timothy raised one eyebrow slightly. "Have you told that story to very many people, Mrs. Hertz?"

"Oh, I *know* I shouldn't even have mentioned it, Mr. Fowler." Mrs. Hertz's amiable face was instantly flushed with distress. "Mr. Hertz would look at me just the way you're doing, if he were here. But I only actually told Sally Covell and that nice young Mr. Hutten. There couldn't be any harm in telling Sally, of course, and Mr. Hutten didn't seem to be especially interested, so I expect he just forgot about it as soon as I'd finished, don't you think so?"

Timothy took his time about answering, and just as he opened his mouth to speak, he looked up to see one of the deck stewards coming toward his chair.

"A message from the Captain, Mr. Fowler. He'd like to speak with you as soon as you can come up to his office."

Timothy nodded to the steward and turned to grin at me. "Well, that puts me in the social swim, anyway." He rose and stretched himself. "I began to feel that I was the only passenger on board that the Captain *hadn't* sent for. Lord knows what's on his mind this morning, but at least I'll lay a bet that nobody's left *me* an amber necklace. So long, pet," he bent down to chuck me under the chin in a way which he knows I dislike, "I'll be back to tell you all about what's on the great Sea Rover's mind."

I reflected, when he had gone, that Timothy had certainly wasted no time in answering the Captain's summons. I picked up the detective story he had left, but I had scarcely reached the gory and unexpected corpse at the end of chapter three when I caught sight of Timothy coming down the deck as fast as his long legs would bring him.

"Hi, Joanie," he stopped in front of my chair, "how's for a turn around the deck before lunch?" He sounded excited, and as I murmured some excuse to Mrs. Hertz, and tried to avoid her frankly curious look, he took my arm and swung me off down the deck at a great pace.

"For heaven's sake, Timothy, what is this all about? Have you discovered a fire or something?"

"Better than that! What do you think the Seafarer wanted to see me about? Well, of course you wouldn't know, but he wanted to break right down and tell me all about this J. T. Ezry business. Who the old gentleman is, and why he's traveling incognito and so on. It seems that the responsibility of being the only one in on the secret has been weighing on our Captain's brain—and I think only a relatively small weight would be required to bring it to earth—*so* he decided to confide in me—"

"Why on earth did he pick you?"

Timothy glanced down sideways at me. "It would be more tactful," he said, "if you would try to remember my profession."

"Yes, darling, I *know* you're a very fine detective, but why would that make the Captain tell you about his big-shot passenger?"

"Because, darling," Timothy's tone was very sweet indeed, "it just happens that our big-shot passenger is dead."

*"Dead?* But I thought that snooty Mr. Brande at our table was really Ezry—"

"Which, my pet, was precisely what Mr. Brande hoped you would think. Actually—it appears that old Norman was our man."

"You mean Norman was J. T. Ezry?"

"I do."

"Well, I still don't see why the Captain should tell you about it. After all, if he's dead, he's dead."

Timothy gave me another slanting look.

"Are you by any chance the gal who remarked yesterday that I might yet distinguish myself by doing a bit of brilliant detective work on this trip?"

"Timothy—what do you mean by all this?"

"I mean," said my husband seriously, "that we've got a case on our hands—and a good one, too. A corpse, and plenty of suspects, and counting in the amber necklace, we've even got beautiful joo-ells."

"Even ignoring the last of your speech," I said, "you're still not making sense. Mr. Norman is a corpse, all right, but there isn't any mystery about a man dying of heart failure. And there aren't any suspects, because he wasn't murdered."

"Oh, yes he was," said Timothy very firmly.

I stopped and stared. "Did the Captain tell you *that?*" I demanded.

"Certainly not. I told the Captain. As a matter of fact, he already suspected it, deep down in his subtle mind. That's why he sent for me, but of course he hadn't a notion of how the dirty deed was done or who did it."

"Don't tell me you answered those questions, too?"

"Oh, no," Timothy shook his head cheerfully. "I only know two things so far. One is—we've got to keep our eyes open, you and I. And the other is—that those amber beads may be worth more than you think. Old J. T. Ezry wouldn't have made such a fuss over any ordinary necklace, and I think Mrs. Hertz ought to be warned about that before she tells the entire passenger list the story of her legacy."

I agreed to that readily enough, but first I pressed Timothy for more details. "If you're so sure Norman was murdered, how was it done?"

"Hit on the head," said Timothy. "You may remember all that dainty hedging the Captain gave us last night to the effect that Norman must have tapped his head on the edge of the desk as he went down with the heart attack."

"Oh, yes—and what about that heart attack?"

"Nothing about it. For all I know, Norman may have had heart trouble—but he didn't die of it any more than I did. He died when someone plunked him on the head with something good and heavy. But who did it, or with what, or when—I don't know yet."

We walked in silence for a few moments.

"Timothy, if what you've said is true, then Dr. Sloane must have known it last night. I mean—he couldn't make a mistake like that."

"He knew, all right," Timothy's tone was grim, "and he told the Captain, too—but the Captain couldn't see things that way."

"You don't mean the Captain would *dare* try to hush up a murder? And especially of anyone as important as this—"

"He dared *try*—" Timothy nodded, "but he had a sudden change of heart when he heard there was a cop on board."

"Oh."

We rounded the corner of the deck. "Here's where we break the news to Mrs. Hertz," said Timothy. "Oh, hell," he stopped as he saw that her chair was empty. "She's probably gone down to lunch—and ten to one it'll be too late to do any warning by the time we get there."

Timothy was right. When we reached the doctor's table Sally Covell was regaling the entire group with the story, plus various flourishes of her own, of the late Mr. Norman's amazing bequest to Mrs. Hertz.

"And *I* shouldn't be surprised," Sally finished, "if it all had something to do with that Ezry person being on board. He collects jewels, you know, and why should he keep himself such a secret unless he's planning something about—well, something." She finished vaguely and stared hard at Mr. Brande, who was regarding a rather flat omelet on his plate with a detached sort of air.

Dr. Sloane tried, as usual, to turn the conversation into a less precarious vein, and I, remembering Timothy's instruction about keeping my eyes open, looked around the table for signs. There weren't any that I could see. Mrs. Shaw was the only person who was not giving strict attention to her lunch, and she seemed entirely lost in fascinated wonder as she gazed at the beautiful amber beads draped proudly across the front of Mrs. Hertz. The pale blue eyes of the missionary's wife were wide with a look of wistful admiration, and I wondered whether she had even heard Sally's words. As for the Reverend Shaw, Tod Hutten and Ned Covell, they looked, respectively, as pious, bored and cheerful as usual.

After lunch Timothy and I agreed that there was no use warning Mrs. Hertz, now that the story was out.

"After all," Timothy said, "no one but us knows that Mr. Norman was Ezry, and I doubt if the Captain lets that fact out. He seemed very much inclined, in spite of his suspicions, to Let Matters Rest, unless something further should happen. And maybe nothing more will happen. Maybe."

Until a little after midnight on the following night, which was Monday, nothing more did happen. In spite of our resolute policy of keeping our eyes open in the meanwhile, Timothy and I had found nothing more suspicious to observe than Dr. Sloane's rather futile efforts at a flirtation with Sally Covell, who was attempting, in her turn, to make an impression on Mr. Brande. Ned Covell was likewise aware of this double play, and commented on it while I was dancing with him.

"Trust Sally," Ned said good-naturedly, "to pick the toughest proposition on the ship and try to make a dent in him." He looked across the lantern-lit after-deck where we were dancing, at the couple standing by the rail. Nicholas Brande, more elegant than ever in a white dinner jacket, was watching the churning wake that lay in a phosphorescent path against the blackness of sea and sky. Sally, close beside him, leaned back with her elbows on the rail and did her best. A warm night breeze blew the soft, dark curls away from her upturned face, and outlined her figure beneath the white crepe evening gown. Ned, obviously appreciative of her points, shook his head slowly. "At that, I shouldn't be surprised if she managed it," he said, "until she tackles him for a job for me. That'll be curtains—as usual."

There was a bitterness in his tone which made me glance up curiously.

"You see," Ned explained, "Sally has a theory that Brande is really this Ezry person, and she also has a theory that every rich man she meets has been scouring the earth for a nice, useless person like me to fill a long-felt vacancy in his business. Somehow it never seems to work—and Sally never seems to learn." He broke off with a short laugh as the music stopped, and the next moment he changed the subject abruptly. "What do you say we tackle the missionaries for a dance? They look a bit forlorn, you know, in spite of their faith."

Fortunately Timothy appeared at my elbow just then, which spared me the possibility of having to dance with the Reverend Shaw, but a few minutes later Ned waltzed past us with Mrs. Shaw. Under his expert guidance she quite forgot her embarrassment and really danced. Her cheeks were flushed with unaccustomed pleasure, and when her eye-glasses steamed up, she took them off and looked almost pretty.

"All the same," said Timothy, when our dance was ended, "it's still too warm for all this exertion. A highball, my pet, and then to bed we go."

Tod Hutten was at the bar when we got there, and with him, to my considerable surprise, was Mrs. Hertz. To my further astonishment, I realized that Tod was listening, with apparent patience, to an account of the wedding of Mrs. Hertz's daughter, for which occasion she was explaining, Mr. Hertz had given her the handsome beige lace dress she wore. And as she talked, Tod Hutten sipped his drink and watched the glittering amber beads as they rose and fell with each energetic breath Mrs. Hertz drew.

In spite of an enthusiastic signal from Mrs. Hertz to join them, Timothy steered me to a table as far as possible from Tod's range of vision—and when we left to go below at a little after eleven o'clock, Mrs. Hertz was still talking, and her escort was still watching.

In our cabin, Timothy retired to the upper berth with his detective story, which he vowed he must finish before he could possibly hope to shut an eye, but I dropped off to sleep almost immediately, and awoke only with the greatest difficulty to the sound of insistent knocking at our stateroom door. I opened my eyes to see Timothy's lengthy frame clambering down from the upper berth, and I could hear him muttering something to himself. I glanced at the clock and saw that it was only ten minutes past twelve. The next moment Timothy had opened the door and Mrs. Hertz, clad in a kimono of the largest and most striking flowered pattern I had ever seen, was leaning against a corner of the dresser and breathing heavily.

"Why—" I sat up in bed, "for heaven's sake, what's happened?"

"Oh, my dear—" Mrs. Hertz clutched the kimono about her dramatically, "my dear—I'm almost *scared* to *death!* Someone—" she paused to gasp for breath, "someone broke into my cabin to *steal* my necklace. I—"

"Good Lord," Timothy broke in, "as soon as this! Tell me—did they *get* the beads?"

Mrs. Hertz shook her head, and Timothy looked relieved. "That's something, anyway. Now—what did happen?"

"Oh, it was too dreadful—" Mrs. Hertz sank down upon the foot of my bed. "I had just gotten to bed, and I must have gone to sleep right away. It usually takes me quite a while, but I'd had a little drink with that nice Mr. Hutten—he *said* I wouldn't feel it, but I *did*—and I expect that's what made me drop off so quickly. Anyway, I'd *barely* closed my eyes when I woke again, and I *realized,* that way you do, that *someone* was in the cabin. I just lay still for a moment and waited. Of course, the first thing I thought of was the necklace—but I didn't think anyone would ever guess where I had it hidden, so—"

"Where did you have it, Mrs. Hertz?"

She leaned toward Timothy and lowered her voice. "Under my pillow. And the strange thing is, Mr. Fowler, that they seemed to know where the necklace was. At least— while I was lying there, frightened out of my wits and not making a *sound,* I could absolutely *feel* this person coming nearer and nearer to my berth—and then the pillow sort of moved under my head, and I realized suddenly that a hand was reaching for my necklace. Well—I *couldn't* keep quiet then, so I let out a scream—rather loud I'm afraid, and at the same time I reached out and *grabbed* the hand."

"You *did?*" I leaned forward eagerly.

"Yes—but all I touched was a coat sleeve, and then the arm was snatched away and the next thing I knew the person had gotten out of my stateroom and banged the door shut behind him. By the time I got up to look, the corridor was empty—and after a moment I decided to come and ask you people what you thought I ought to do. You know—whether I ought to report it to the Captain or something—" Mrs. Hertz looked at Timothy.

"I do not," said Timothy firmly, "think you should. Not now, anyway."

"Well—" Mrs. Hertz seemed relieved. "I'm awfully glad you feel that way. I *do* hate to make a fuss. But, do you know—" she rose and went slowly toward the door. "I can't quite forget feeling that hand moving under my pillow."

"Suppose," said Timothy, and did not look at me, "you stay here for the rest of the night, Mrs. Hertz, and let me go to your cabin. That hand might come back, you know, and I'd rather like a chance at grabbing it myself. By the way, did it seem to be a lady or a gentleman hand?"

"I really couldn't tell, except that the arm felt quite solid—strong, you know—and there was something on the coat sleeve that felt like—" Mrs. Hertz hesitated a moment, "I hate to say this when I'm not *sure,* Mr. Fowler, but I could have sworn there was gold braid trimming on that sleeve. Like the ship's officers wear, you know."

"Yes," said Timothy slowly, "I know."

"That's why I sort of didn't want to report it to the Captain."

"Yes," said Timothy, "I can understand that, too. Well—" he belted his dressing gown and opened the state-room door, "sleep soundly, you two, and maybe I'll have some news by morning. Oh—" he turned back, "by the by, where are the beads now, Mrs. Hertz?"

"Right here," she answered promptly, and fetched up the long strand from the front of the flowered kimono.

"Good," Timothy nodded. "You keep them there." He answered my look with a bright smile. "You don't mind, do you, Joanie?" he asked—and shut the door before I could reply.

## 5
## A BANDAGE WITH ARNICA

As a matter of fact, I didn't mind particularly. I couldn't blame Mrs. Hertz for not wanting to go back to her cabin alone, and she was plainly very grateful for Timothy's offer to change places with her. Also I was more than a little curious to know what, if anything, Timothy would encounter during the remainder of the night. Which, I reflected, only went to show what a good detective's wife I was becoming.

Since it was obviously impossible for Mrs. Hertz to negotiate an upper berth, I climbed topside and left her to take, with many protestations, my bed. For a few minutes after we were settled there was no sound in the darkness except for the heavy throb of the ship's motors and a sound of creaking metal beams as we rose and fell in the slight swell of the sea. Then, from beneath me, I heard a plaintive sigh.

"You know," said Mrs. Hertz, and her voice sounded almost forlorn, "I think this is all kind of a judgment on me."

"Nonsense." I leaned over the edge of the berth. "In the first place, nothing really has happened, and in the second place, what on earth would it be a judgment for?"

"Well, Mr. Hertz would say it was for talking too much—and he'd probably work in something about that drink I let Mr. Hutten give me. But *I* think it's a punishment for my selfishness. You see, I wasn't going to tell anyone this, but I do think you'll understand—something happened this afternoon and I've felt perfectly miserable ever since. It was just after lunch today while you and Timothy were playing shuffleboard. I was sitting in my deck chair and all of a sudden the Reverend Shaw came and took your place beside me. He seemed terribly embarrassed—as if he were trying to work up his courage to say something, you know. Of course I hadn't the vaguest notion what was on his mind—but the poor man looked so miserable that I tried to help him along by talking. And then—right in the middle of something I was saying, he blurted out the fact that he wanted to buy my necklace for his wife."

"*What?*" in the darkness I opened my eyes wide with astonishment. "But I shouldn't imagine he could possibly afford it—both the Shaws look as poor as church-mice."

"That," said Mrs. Hertz, "was the worst part of all. He told me his wife had never had any jewelry, and that she'd always wanted it—so he'd been saving up some money with the intention of buying her a really nice present when they got back to the States. Well, it seems he'd been saving for more than a year, and he has twenty-five dollars—"

"Oh, surely he couldn't offer you so little!"

"He could—and did," Mrs. Hertz assured me solemnly.

"And what's more, he did it in such a sort of—well, *humble* way, that I almost felt as though I should say yes. I don't say I exactly *like* Mr. Shaw—and I can just imagine what Mr. Hertz would think of him—he feels so strongly on the question of missionaries—but honestly, Joan, there

was something about the way Mr. Shaw looked. . . . That
dreadful black suit he wears, you know . . ."

"I know," I said. I sympathized with Mrs. Hertz's distress when I pictured the scene. Mr. Shaw, with his gaunt
face and ill-fitting clothes, sitting awkwardly on the edge
of a chair and offering his only twenty-five dollars to buy
a gift for his wife . . .

"Still," I said, "you just *had* to refuse an offer like that."

"Oh, I did," Mrs. Hertz sighed, "and he took it with the
most awful meekness. It made me feel worse than ever—
and then when I saw Mrs. Shaw at dinner tonight in that
same bunchy blue taffeta—I'll bet it's her only evening
dress—and saw the way she looked at my beads, I can tell
you I just felt like an everlasting worm. So you see, Joan,
that's what I meant when I said it seemed almost like a
judgment on me when the necklace was nearly stolen."

Even while I tried to reassure Mrs. Hertz, another possible explanation of the attempted theft flitted through my
mind. I dismissed it as probably too fantastic, but resolved
to ask Timothy's opinion the first thing next morning.

It was, however, well on toward noon on Tuesday before I said anything at all to Timothy, and by that time all
theories about Mr. Shaw and the amber beads had tempo-
rarily fled from my mind.

Mrs. Hertz first suggested that we ought, perhaps, to
go to her cabin and see what was delaying Timothy—for
we had slept late ourselves, and at nearly ten o'clock, there
was still no sign of him. It was a nasty morning, I remember, with a warmish rain that dotted the gray sea with a
speckle of heavy drops. The swell had increased during the
night, and we had run into a choppy sea that sent us side-
slipping with each pitch of the vessel. As we approached
Mrs. Hertz's stateroom, I saw that the door was unlatched

and flapping slightly on its hinges with every motion of the ship.

Even before I pushed open the door I had a horrid premonition that something had happened—and it was with a feeling of positive relief that I caught sight of Timothy, stretched out on the lower bunk, with one hand dangling limply over the edge. For, although it was obvious that something certainly had happened, it was equally obvious that Timothy was alive. Alive—but sleeping so heavily that at first I thought he must somehow have been drugged. Then I stepped closer and saw the bump on his head. A nasty bruise it was, about as big as a walnut, just above one eye.

Mrs. Hertz, close behind me, took one look at Timothy over my shoulder. She made no comment, but went at once to get a towel and soak it with ice water from the thermos pitcher.

"Here," she handed the towel to me, "hold this on his forehead while I go for the doctor. And don't worry—Mr. Hertz fell down our cellar steps once and got a bump much worse than that and he was as good as new inside of two hours." At the doorway she paused a moment and looked doubtfully down at the flowered kimono. "Oh, well," she drew it closer about her, "in an emergency I don't suppose it matters."

Timothy stirred a little when I put the icy compress against his head, but he didn't open his eyes or answer when I spoke. In the few minutes that passed before Mrs. Hertz returned with Dr. Sloane, I had time to look about the cabin for signs of disturbance. But there was nothing out of order—except for a small bundle of letters which apparently had been taken from an open drawer of the desk and strewn over the top. I left Timothy long enough to go over and glance at them, and saw that the letters were purely personal correspondence. The warning sound of footsteps in the corridor gave me just time enough to get back to my place beside Timothy.

Dr. Sloane took a quick look at the patient.

"Nothing to worry about," he said, "nothing at all. Just a bump—possibly a slight concussion, but no harm done."

His manner, as he rummaged in his medicine case and produced a bottle of brownish lotion, was extremely brisk and efficient. Just a little too brisk, I thought. I was perfectly certain that the dressing he used was nothing more than ordinary arnica, but he applied it with all the professional ceremony and concentration of a major operation— and I had the feeling that Dr. Sloane was deliberately using this routine to cover some underlying nervousness.

Not until he had taken Timothy's pulse, peered into his eyes, and done everything but examine his teeth, did Dr. Sloane ask the one obvious question. "How did it happen?"

I looked at Mrs. Hertz, uncertain of how much she had already told the doctor, and how much she wanted me to tell, but I got no answering glance from her. She was, at the moment, standing by the desk and carefully collecting her scattered letters. Mrs. Hertz being the neatest and most methodical of persons, I could not believe that she had left her correspondence strewn about, therefore it must have been the mysterious intruder who had rifled the desk drawer. And yet there was Mrs. Hertz, replacing the letters without a word of comment, and closing the drawer as quickly and inconspicuously as possible. For a moment I sat there, open-mouthed, wondering—and then I realized that the doctor was still awaiting my reply.

"Oh—" I recalled myself, "I don't know yet how it happened, Dr. Sloane. You see, my husband changed places with Mrs. Hertz because she had been frightened, and when we came in this morning—he was just like this."

It was certainly the sketchiest of explanations, but the doctor did not seem disposed to follow it up. "H'mm yes, I see—" he twiddled his small, black mustache and frowned for a moment. "Well, in any case, I should say a day in the hospital was the best thing for your husband, Mrs. Fowler. Even though it's nothing serious, absolute rest is very important for the next few hours, and we should want to—ah, be on the safe side. You don't object, do you?"

"Certainly not." I tried a question of my own. "What would you say Timothy was hit with, Dr. Sloane?"

"Well, now, that's quite impossible for me to say." He busied himself repacking his medicine kit. "It may very well be that Mr. Fowler knocked his head against something in the dark—there was quite a choppy sea last night." The doctor rose and straightened his coat. "You see, Mrs. Fowler, your husband is very tall."

Being already well aware of this fact, I made no reply.

"And he might easily have struck against the edge of the upper berth here," Dr. Sloane tapped the metal bar. When I still failed to answer, he coughed slightly and turned away. "Excuse me just a moment, I'll ask the steward to assist me with Mr. Fowler."

The two men practically carried Timothy down the short passageway to the ship's hospital quarters, while Mrs. Hertz and I followed anxiously along. Not until the moment when Dr. Sloane lowered his patient's head onto the pillow, did Timothy show any signs of returning consciousness. The bandage compress had slipped down across his eyes, but I saw Timothy put out his hand and touch the doctor's arm. As his fingers found the gold braid insignia on the uniform coat sleeve, Timothy smiled. "Hello," he said, "is that you, Doctor?"

I happened to be looking at Mrs. Hertz at that instant, and I saw her glance quickly at Dr. Sloane.

"You're quite all right, you know, Mr. Fowler," the doctor pushed the bandage away from Timothy's eyes. "Your wife is here."

Timothy turned his head and looked up at me. "Sure, I'm all right," he said, "except for a little pat on the head." He raised his hand, felt the lump gingerly, and made a face.

"Timothy, who hit you?"

He made a wry face. "You ask me that before you ask how I feel?" he said. "Who's the detective in this family, anyway? *I* don't know who hit me."

"Of course he doesn't," said Mrs. Hertz suddenly. "It's as dark as a blind man's pocket in that cabin when the lights are out. I—" She glanced at the doctor and a nurse who had come up to the bed, and stopped abruptly. "There, Joan," she turned to me, "he's come around just as I told you he would, hasn't he? This is exactly like Mr. Hertz was that time he fell. Perfectly all right inside of a couple of hours—"

"But he needs rest," Dr. Sloane repeated firmly. He looked at Timothy. "I should strongly advise you to stay here, Mr. Fowler, for at least the remainder of the day. After that—we'll see . . ." He laid a finger on Timothy's pulse and pursed his lips thoughtfully. "We'll see . . ."

Timothy looked up at him in silence. Knowing my husband, and seeing that he looked quite thoroughly recovered, I expected him to decline further care very emphatically indeed. Instead, to my vast surprise, he laid his head back against the pillow and closed his eyes with a weary sigh.

"I think you're quite right, Doctor," said Timothy in
the meekest tone I had ever heard from him

And I had a fleeting impression that Dr. Sloane was as
surprised as I.

I had scarcely finished a belated breakfast and gone up
on deck before I was approached by passengers who had
heard of Timothy's mishap and wished to convey solicitous
remarks to me, accompanied by questions which veiled,
in varying degrees of subtlety, the underlying motive of
curiosity. Apparently Mrs. Hertz and the doctor had given
conflicting versions of the affair, for everyone seemed to
have heard a different story—but they were agreed in feeling that something dire, if rather vague, lay behind it all.
By dinner time that evening, our table was a hot-bed of
gossip and theory, tempered somewhat by my presence and
Dr. Sloane's usual efforts at changing the subject.

After I left the dining room, I stopped in to see Timothy and tried to entertain him with some of the rumors I
had heard—particularly one to the effect that he had been
mortally wounded—but he was not amused. Instead he
frowned at the tip of his cigarette, then he sat up in the
hospital bed and thumped his pillows.

"Joan," he said, "this is a bad business." It is only in
his completely serious moments that he calls me Joan.
"We knew, of course, that something was up—and I had a
hunch that if I stuck around the hospital I might get a line
on what it was all about. That's why I stayed here today."

"I thought as much."

"Well—my hunch was partly right anyway. I haven't
made any discoveries that are actually world-shaking, but
I did manage to woo Miss Thompson, the nurse, into a
confidential mood."

"Oh—? And what did she have to tell?"

"Nothing very exciting, so don't get your hopes up," Timothy smiled. "The main thing is that she got a good look at Norman the other night—and what's more important, she was in on a little argument between Dr. Sloane and the Captain about how they were going to make out the death certificate. It seems the Captain got all upset at the idea that there'd been foul play—and he gave the Doctor some pretty definite hints on the desirability of hushing the story up. After a few remarks, Sloane seemed willing to fall in with the Captain's plan—in fact, Miss Thompson felt that he was just a shade too willing to be quite convincing. She, fortunately, has a conscience—and she's been pretty much bothered ever since by the idea of diagnosing a cracked skull as heart disease. This is Thompson's first trip with the *Orion,* and just between us, I don't think she likes the doctor's little ways any better than we do."

"Timothy," I said, "do you think Dr. Sloane—"

"I don't think the doctor killed Norman, if that's what you're going to ask. For one thing, it doesn't look like that sort of a job. Doctors have such perfectly swell opportunities for murder, if they're inclined that way, that they seldom resort to anything as crude as a wallop on the head."

"Yes, but mightn't he have chosen that method just as a blind?"

"He *might,*" said Timothy, "but I don't think he did. It's my notion that Dr. Sloane isn't any too bright—which may account for the way he acts. If, for instance, he knows—or suspects—just enough to worry him, it would explain his you-chase-me manner."

"He'd do better," I observed, "to come out with it-—if he does know anything."

"Not necessarily," Timothy shook his head. "There's such a thing, you know, as getting involved in a matter that turns out to be more serious than it seemed. I've seen smarter men than Dr. Sloane get themselves in a position where explanations were damned awkward—and in his case there's one thing to remember: Norman had traveled on this boat several times before. See?"

"I'm beginning to."

"Now, listen, Joan. I feel swell, but I'm going to stay right here for the night—"

"But why?"

"Simply because I have a notion that things will progress better with me out of the way. Get Mrs. Hertz to sleep in our cabin again, and leave her stateroom vacant. You know my pet theory of giving these playful murderers plenty of space to play in. Unless I miss my guess, our friend will be up to his pranks again tonight. After two unsuccessful attempts, he'll probably figure that the third time never fails."

"Are you going to have Mrs. Hertz's cabin watched then?"

"I am not. In the first place, I have no authority to have anything watched, and in the second place, I mean to give our villain a real chance. If he got the idea he were being spied on, he might get too careful—and not leave any convenient little traces for us to pick up in the morning."

"Has it occurred to you, Timothy, that the person who was in Mrs. Hertz's stateroom last night might *not* be after the necklace?"

"It has," said Timothy. "Frequently."

I told him about the incident of the letters which had been scattered about on the desk. "What do you suppose that could mean?"

"God knows," he said cheerfully. "At any rate, it makes the outlook for tonight's hunting even better. Meanwhile, will you do one bit of snooping for me?"

"Of course." Helping Timothy with two previous cases had quite dulled my sensibilities about prying into things that were none of my business.

"I want you," he said, "to get me a sample of the hand writing of each of our pals at the doctor's table. You can manage quite easily by asking each of them to sign your passenger list. Souvenir of the trip, you know—"

"I know, all right." I had visions of myself requesting an autograph from Nicholas Brande. "They'll think I'm the original hick from Four Corners—but I suppose I must sacrifice my vanity to the cause of your art. You might tell me, though, what the point is?"

"Very simple, my pet. You remember asking me about the impulsive person who socked me in the eye last night? Not being as quick on the uptake as Mrs. Hertz, I didn't manage to contact any gold braid on the coat sleeve. But you may also remember telling me about finding the stuff in Mrs. Hertz's desk upset. Well—I have a theory that our prowler was interested in the desk because he, or she, was anxious to have a look at those notes from the late Mr. Norman. But who it was that wanted the notes, or *why*, I won't know until you bring me those samples of writing. And probably," he added cheerfully, "I won't know even then."

## 6

## TUESDAY NIGHT AT MIDNIGHT

When I had found my passenger list and dutifully made
the rounds, requesting signatures, I took the list back to
the hospital and made my brief report.

"All right-handed," I said, "and apparently of sound
mind."

Timothy glanced at the names. "How did the elegant
Brande react? And Tod Hutten?"

"Raised eyebrows department. As for Ned Covell—he
looked as if he would never feel quite the same toward me
again. But they all signed, as you see."

"M'mm," Timothy was still studying the list. "Damned
characteristic autographs, too. Hutten's writing is small
and neat, quite befitting the gentleman scholar; Sally Covell makes big, round letters like a school-girl; and our
Reverend Shaw's name looks as cramped and angular as
his face. Pearl S. Shaw is colorless Spencerian, of course;
and Dr. Sloane writes in a nervous rush." He paused and
smiled as his eye lit on *Luella Hoskinson Hertz*, inscribed
in a flowing, energetic script. "Ned Covell is neither here
nor there," Timothy went on, "which is to be expected,
but Nicholas Brande—now there's a curious thing—" He
paused again.

"What's curious about it?" I leaned over his shoulder and inspected the small, unpretentious letters: *N. C. Brande.*

"Well, for a person as studied as Brande, it just looks kind of homespun, that's all. And it's certainly not the signature of a person who writes his name very frequently or impressively. Signing fifty thousand dollar checks, for instance."

I was amazed at the seriousness with which he was taking all this.

"Great heavens, Timothy, you're not going to start telling fortunes by handwriting, are you?"

"No, I'd rather begin with crystal-gazing. All the same," he folded the list and tucked it into his pajama pocket, "I'm going to hang on to this. It was an interesting experiment, even if it didn't work."

It wasn't until I was almost ready for bed that night that I suddenly remembered an incident which had occurred in the afternoon, while Sally Covell and I were watching deck games. Ned had just been beaten at the golf-driving machine when Sally said: "Poor Neddy, he usually wins the ship's tournament on that thing, but there weren't any left-handed clubs around today." When I remarked that I hadn't noticed Ned being left-handed, Sally Went on to explain. "He's really ambidextrous—or amphibious—or whatever you call it. I mean, he can use either hand to write with—only the two handwritings look entirely different. But for anything that calls for *strength*—he always takes his left hand."

I had paid scant attention to the remark at the time, but now, recalling it in the light of what Timothy had told me, I wondered whether it might mean something important after all. With one stocking half off, I sat transfixed in thought until Mrs. Hertz, already settled in the lower berth for the night, noticed my preoccupation.

"What in the wide world is the matter with you, Joan?" she demanded. "You look as if you were hearing voices, or seeing a ghost."

"I just remembered something." I started to pull my stocking on again. "Something I forgot to tell Timothy."

"Oh, is that all?" Mrs. Hertz sank back against the pillow. "Well—" she yawned, "you can tell him first thing in the morning."

But I had no intention of waiting till morning. I had already slipped on a yellow negligee.

"I shan't be but a minute," I said to Mrs. Hertz. "I'll just go down and speak to Timothy now."

"But, child—" she raised her head to protest, "you can't do that. It's already past midnight."

Nevertheless, I went directly down the corridor to the hospital quarters. Fortunately, Timothy was still awake and reading, and he received my information with gratifying interest.

But it wasn't until I was on the way back to my room that I made my really important discovery. Halfway between the door of the hospital and our cabin I passed Mrs. Hertz's stateroom, which was supposedly empty for the night, and just as I came opposite that door, I heard a small, clicking sound.

For some reason, the sound stirred something familiar in my memory—I wondered why, for a moment. Then I realized that it was precisely the same sound I had heard that morning when we found Timothy in Mrs. Hertz's room. I looked—and sure enough, the door of her room was unlatched and swinging slightly to and fro, just as it had been in the morning.

In that second while I watched, the door swung inward with the motion of the ship, and I saw that the room within was dark.

I hesitated. Perhaps the door had simply blown open in the wind . . . perhaps . . .

And then, from the darkness beyond the door there came another sound—a sound which left me standing there in the deserted passageway, hugging the satin negligee closer about me, and shivering in a sudden grip of icy fear.

I listened—and it came again. A long, slow, agonized moan. Silence for a moment—then the sound once more, fainter this time, and ending in a long-drawn, gasping breath.

My instant thought was that Mrs. Hertz must have returned to her room for some reason, and encountered the mysterious prowler. I stepped forward, and with a hand that felt like a lump of ice, I pushed open the door. To this day I can close my eyes and feel again the creeping horror that I felt at that moment—the horror that I might step inside and stumble over the body of Mrs. Hertz. But somehow I forced myself to go on, groping through the dark until my fingers touched the light switch—and the next moment I was staring down at the floor with a curious mixture of amazement, terror and relief. For there was a body lying prostrate before me—but it was not the body of Mrs. Hertz.

Sprawled face upward across the small space between the bed and desk lay the Reverend Asa Shaw. His long arms were flung out, the bony wrists protruding from his coat sleeves, and his face showed ghastly pale and still in the brilliant overhead light.

I stood quite still, frozen in a sort of fascination by the dreadful sight, until the ship gave a sudden lurch which jarred the limp figure on the floor—and from the half-open mouth came another groan, still fainter this time, and painful to hear.

It was then that I realized that something must be done—and done quickly. Obviously the Reverend Shaw was not dead, yet there was a look about his face that warned even my inexperienced eye that I must hurry if anyone else were to see Asa Shaw alive. I turned toward the door.

It seemed a million miles that I walked—swiftly, like one in a dream, yet getting nowhere. Along the corridors, up the steps to B Deck, through deserted passageways until at last I came to Dr. Sloane's quarters. For all the confused thoughts that raced through my mind, I never once paused to think of what I should say to the doctor. And when, after a long wait, he answered my knock, I found myself groping helplessly for words.

"Dr. Sloane—quick—you must help Mr. Shaw. . . . He—he's ill—"

"Ill?" The doctor's face registered sleepy surprise. "What's the matter with him?"

"I—I don't know," I shook my head. "Only you must hurry. He—I'm afraid he's going to die or something . . ."

Dr. Sloane blinked at me. "But how does it happen that you—?"

"Never mind that," again I shook my head. "Just hurry —please. He's in Mrs. Hertz's stateroom, down on C Deck."

"Mrs. Hertz?" Dr. Sloane ran his hand through his tousled dark hair. "But I thought you said it was Shaw who was ill—"

Somehow I managed to persuade him that this was not the time for explanations, and at last he disappeared to fetch his emergency kit.

While I, stood waiting, my glance strayed nervously about the doctor's small room, and I saw that his bed, on the far side against the wall, was neatly made up. In the excitement of the moment, the significance of this observation did not dawn on me. It wasn't, in fact, until we were halfway back to Mrs. Hertz's stateroom that I suddenly realized the discrepancy between the doctor's disheveled and drowsy appearance, and the obviously unslept-in bed. But there was no time to reflect on the matter just then.

For in the next half hour I had all I could do to follow the doctor's orders. The Reverend Shaw lay just as I had first seen him, except that he no longer made any sound, and his face looked even whiter than before. Dr. Sloane knelt beside him and gave one quick look, then he spoke to me over his shoulder.

"Get down to the hospital," he said. "Ask for Miss Thompson, the nurse. Tell her to come here at once. I'd go myself, but I don't dare leave him for a moment. If anything's going to help him, it'll have to be quick." As he spoke, the doctor was preparing a hypodermic with deft speed.

At least, I thought, as I went down the short corridor to the hospital, Dr. Sloane was functioning this time far more efficiently and with less fuss than when I had called him for Timothy that morning.

Miss Thompson responded immediately, and I had only a moment, while she slipped on her dressing gown, to get to Timothy with the news. He took one look at my face and sat up in bed.

"Well—who's been knocked in the head this time?" he asked.

"It's the Reverend Shaw, Timothy. I don't know what's the matter with him, but it's pretty bad. I'm afraid he's going to die—at least Dr. Sloane seems to think so."

"Sloane?" Timothy sat up straighter, "is he alone with Shaw now?"

"Only for a minute. He sent me down to call Miss Thompson, but—" I stopped short as Timothy threw back the covers and hopped out of bed to fetch his dressing gown from the wardrobe. "Do you think you ought to get up, Timothy?"

"Hell, *I'm* all right, except for a patch over one eye. If you think I'm going to lie there while things like this are happening, you're wrong. There's a limit to my policy of letting nature take its course, you know—and if something serious has happened to Shaw, that's more than I bargained for."

"But don't you think you ought to ask Miss Thompson?"

"Unless I'm crazier than I think," Timothy started for the door, "Thompson will be glad enough to have another witness handy."

As a matter of fact, neither the doctor nor Miss Thompson appeared to take any notice of Timothy when we reached Mrs. Hertz's cabin. The two of them were bending over their patient, and Dr. Sloane barely glanced around as we came in. His first notice of my presence was another abrupt order a minute or two later.

"Mrs. Fowler, will you take a message to the Captain, please?" the doctor said. "Have him come down here as quickly as he can."

I looked at Timothy. He nodded.

"By all means," he murmured.

Once out in the corridor again, I wondered just how I should send a message at this hour. The purser's office was long since closed, and I scarcely thought a steward should be trusted with such serious news. There seemed to be nothing for it but to fetch Captain Cobb myself—so I started for his quarters on the boat deck.

There was no question about rousing the Captain from a sound sleep. He answered my knock immediately, and when he opened his door I saw that Nicholas Brande was seated in an easy chair near the big desk in the Captain's office. Despite the fact that it was now past one o'clock, the two men had evidently been engrossed in conversation, for Mr. Brande was sipping a highball in a leisurely manner, and the Captain was smoking his pipe. He received my message and my somewhat unconventional appearance with entire presence of mind and, after a word of explanation to Mr. Brande, he followed me down to C Deck, at once.

I was relieved to see that Mr. Shaw had been lifted onto the bed when we got back. Dr. Sloane was still close beside him, and Miss Thompson, her face set and expressionless, stood by. Timothy, I observed, was perched on the edge of the wash-basin in a far corner of the small cabin, smoking a cigarette and looking quite detached. Dr. Sloane straightened up when the Captain entered and addressed him gravely.

"Mr. Shaw is dead, sir."

The Captain frowned, glanced at Timothy, cleared his throat and said nothing.

There was a pause. Everyone waited for Dr. Sloane to go on, but for some reason he seemed reluctant to speak.

"Well—" the Captain's voice rapped out sharply, "this is—ah, unfortunate. Most unfortunate, indeed. It appears to have been quite sudden, and under—ah—" he glanced about the room, "rather peculiar circumstances. This is not Mr. Shaw's own cabin, is it?"

"No, sir, the room is occupied by Mrs. Hertz."

"M'mm," the Captain raised his eyebrows. "And the—ah—presence of Mr. and Mrs. Fowler?"

I started to explain my presence, since it seemed extremely unlikely that the doctor would do it for me, but an abrupt gesture from Captain Cobb cut me short.

"Never mind that now," he said. "The—ah, the main thing is to get at the facts." He turned back to Dr. Sloane. "What was the cause of death?"

Dr. Sloane pressed his hands tightly together and looked down at them. "I—it was an acute heart attack, sir."

I looked quickly at Timothy, and for an awful moment I was afraid he was going to laugh. But the Captain failed to see any humor in the situation. He flushed angrily.

"Look here, Sloane—are you quite serious?"

"Quite, sir," the doctor lifted his chin slightly. "When I was brought here by Mrs. Fowler, I found Mr. Shaw very ill indeed. I tried an injection of stimulant, of course, but—" he spread his hands, "it was already too late. I can assure you that every symptom indicates an acute coronary thrombosis—but if you care to consult another medical opinion, I'm quite willing—"

Captain Cobb made a sound of impatience. "You know damn well that's impossible," he said shortly. "But, see here, this thing is getting a bit thick, you know. First one death under—ah, questionable circumstances, and now—" he swung around suddenly and faced Timothy.

"What's your opinion of this, Fowler?"

If Timothy was startled by the sudden question, he gave no sign of it. His answer was prompt. "I should call it a second death under questionable circumstances, Captain," he said quietly.

"Just what do you mean by that, Fowler?"

"I imagine," said Timothy, "that Dr. Sloane can tell you what I mean."

I was practically certain that Timothy was taking a shot in the dark—and it was a good shot. The doctor looked startled for a moment, then he nodded.

"I—as a matter of fact, I was going to say the same thing myself, Captain." Dr. Sloane pushed back his hair with a gesture of weariness and his glance rested on Timothy's cigarette. "Do you mind, Fowler?" he put out his hand. "I haven't any with me."

Timothy fished a package of Chesterfields from his dressing gown pocket.

The doctor's hand was perfectly steady as he struck a match. "Bad luck we've had this trip, sir—bad luck, and something else, I'm afraid—"

"What are you driving at, Sloane?" Captain Cobb frowned. "You said a moment ago that Shaw died of perfectly natural causes—"

"I said every symptom pointed to a heart attack, sir, but the circumstances are puzzling, to say the least. When you consider the death of Mr. Norman Saturday evening, and Mr. Fowler's accident this morning—"

"Yes—quite," the Captain's frown deepened as he turned toward Timothy again. "I understand you, ah—had a bump. I hope you're quite fit now?"

"It was nothing, really," Timothy touched the patch above his eye. "I often get bumped—one way and another. I'm afraid I'm rather clumsy by nature."

There was a short silence. Everyone looked at Captain Cobb, obviously expecting him to take the lead.

"Well—" the Captain cleared his throat. "I expect the first thing is to find out as nearly as we can just what happened here tonight."

It didn't take long to piece together the little we knew. But why the Reverend Shaw should have visited Mrs. Hertz's cabin, and what sudden attack he had suffered there, remained as much a mystery as ever. When everything we knew had been said, the Captain turned to Timothy once more.

"Mr. Fowler," he said, "a few minutes ago you suggested that the circumstances of Mr. Shaw's death might be questionable. Does that mean that you disagree with Dr. Sloane's diagnosis of heart attack?"

Timothy looked surprised. "Certainly not, Captain," he shook his head. "I wouldn't presume for a moment to have an opinion on that point—far less dispute a doctor's diagnosis."

"M'mm, yes. Yes, of course," the Captain nodded impatiently. "But have you, quite apart from medical knowledge, any reason to believe, or suspect, that Shaw's death might have been caused by some—ah, by something else?"

Timothy looked thoughtfully at the tip of his cigarette.

"If there were any other cause," he said at last, "I'm quite certain that Dr. Sloane would know of it." He paused and then added: "It would be interesting, I should think, to ask Mrs. Shaw how long her husband had been suffering from heart trouble. Unless, of course, Mr. Shaw had happened to mention his complaint to Dr. Sloane?"

"Shaw never said two words to me," said the doctor, "aside from casual conversation at our table. And I should strongly advise against questioning Mrs. Shaw in any way, for the present. This thing is bound to be a bad enough shock for her as it is."

"Yes, yes—quite so, no doubt," the Captain said. "But before I notify Mrs. Shaw—are you quite certain you have no further—ah, theories as to what might have occurred here, Mr. Fowler?"

We all looked at Timothy, and Timothy still looked at
his cigarette. "Nothing very definite, I'm afraid," he said
slowly. "There's always the matter of the amber necklace,
of course—"

"The necklace—yes," Captain Cobb looked distinctly
relieved. "Quite. I was just on the point of mentioning
that myself. You think perhaps Shaw came here with some
idea of—ah, stealing the necklace?"

"Possibly," Timothy nodded without enthusiasm. "But
I scarcely think that would account for his dying here."

"Nevertheless," the Captain was not to be diverted, "I
think Mrs. Hertz should be consulted. At least she can tell
us whether the beads are missing and—" he turned to me.
"You say she's sleeping in your stateroom, Mrs. Fowler?
Would you be good enough to ask her to come in here?"

I hesitated briefly, glancing toward the still figure on
the bed, and in that moment I noticed, for the first time,
something which dangled from a corner of the dead man's
coat pocket. Something which caught the bright overhead
light and sparkled like spilled honey.

"Look—" I pointed. "What's that in his pocket? Isn't
it—?"

Dr. Sloane stepped forward quickly and bent down. The
next moment he faced us wonderingly. "By George—" he
said, "here's the evidence against poor old Shaw." And in
his hand he held the long strand of gleaming amber beads.

"For heaven's *sake,* what are you all doing in my stateroom?"

We turned at the sound of the new voice, and there was
Mrs. Hertz in the doorway—flowered kimono and all—her
curl-papers bristling angrily about her face as she surveyed
the curious scene.

"Oh, excuse me, Captain," Mrs. Hertz tempered her voice slightly, "I didn't see you at first. I got worried about Joan when she didn't come back, and I thought I'd better see what had happened to her—" She stopped as her glance fell upon the figure on the bed. "Whatever is the matter with Mr. Shaw?"

"Mr. Shaw is dead," said Captain Cobb with the bluntness of a sea-faring man.

"Oh—" Mrs. Hertz's eyes widened in an expression of genuine distress. "Oh, the poor man."

"He died," the Captain went on relentlessly, "in your cabin here, while he was in the very act of stealing your necklace."

"Oh, no," Mrs. Hertz shook her head. "No, you must be mistaken."

"I'm sorry, Mrs. Hertz, but the evidence is unmistakable. Dr. Sloane found your necklace in Mr. Shaw's pocket just a moment before you got here. There's not the slightest doubt—"

"*No,*" said Mrs. Hertz even more firmly. "The whole thing is some dreadful mistake. He *couldn't* have stolen the beads—they weren't mine any more—don't you see?" Her voice rose excitedly.

"Hold everything, Mrs. Hertz," Timothy stepped forward and put a soothing hand on her shoulder. "Take it calmly, and tell us what you mean."

"I mean—" she, steadied herself with a long breath, "I mean Mr. Shaw couldn't have come here to steal the necklace because it was already *his.*"

"My God," said Timothy, "you don't mean he'd taken it earlier?"

"No. Oh, no. I—I *gave* it to him."

"You *what?*"

"I gave it to him tonight, after dinner—for his wife."
Mrs. Hertz took one look at the circle of astonished faces
and collapsed wearily on the nearest chair. "Oh, *don't,* ask
me to explain any more—Joan will tell why I just *had* to
give it to him."

## 7

## AN IVORY KNIFE

"Mr. Fowler," said the Captain, "I need your help. Quite frankly, I'm more than a little confused by these unfortunate events."

"Quite frankly, Captain," said Timothy, "I'm damned confused myself."

The Captain permitted himself a small, grim smile. The two men were in conference in the Captain's study on Wednesday morning—the morning following Mr. Shaw's death. I was permitted, at Timothy's suggestion, to sit in a corner and listen.

"Nevertheless, Mr. Fowler," Captain Cobb answered him seriously, "you're better fitted to handle—ah, confusing situations, than I am. Murder, theft, and so on—rather out of my line, you know."

"They're not exactly my favorite pastimes," Timothy murmured. "But I'll take a hand if you say so—making no promises, of course."

"Good," the Captain nodded in an executive way. "Now then—to begin. The first step, I presume, is to—ah, check the alibis. Is that correct, Mr. Fowler?"

"I see you read detective stories, too, Captain. Yes, that's quite correct—in theory. Unfortunately, people in real life so seldom have alibis. When I strike a really good one, I'm usually suspicious of it. However, I've already done a bit of checking concerning the whereabouts of our friends on the afternoon of Mr. Norman's death. That was Saturday, you remember, the day we sailed, and I thought it was best to look around a bit before everyone got the idea they were being checked on. So I found out what I could—"

"Indeed?"

"Unofficially, of course," Timothy smiled rather apologetically. "It wasn't exactly my business—but then, I'm used to not minding my business."

"H'mm," said the Captain, "I see. And just what did you manage to find out, Mr. Fowler?"

"Nothing very definite, I'm afraid, except that any one of our group *might* have been in Norman's stateroom between four and six o'clock that afternoon. You see, I learned from Nurse Thompson that Mr. Norman had probably been dead about four hours when his body was discovered by the Reverend Shaw—"

Captain Cobb cleared his throat. "I should have thought Dr. Sloane would be better qualified to give an opinion on that point," he said.

"Oh, yes—he certainly would," Timothy nodded. "But for some reason, the Doctor seemed a bit reluctant to discuss the matter. It appears that he'd had some sort of order not to give out any information concerning Norman's death—"

"I see," said the Captain a trifle hastily. "Yes—quite. Well, to get on—"

"To get on," Timothy proceeded amiably, "I think it reasonably safe to take Miss Thompson's word for it. She seems a very intelligent woman, as well as conscientious.

So—if we grant that Norman was killed somewhere between four and six on Saturday afternoon—"

"Just a moment, Mr. Fowler—there's one point there you might have overlooked. I seem to recall that Mrs. Hertz mentioned having a note from Mr. Norman during the late afternoon—around six o'clock, I believe she said. It was an invitation to have cocktails, or some such thing. Now wouldn't that argue that Norman was alive and quite well at that time?"

"It would argue it, yes," Timothy nodded. "But it wouldn't prove the point, Captain. Thus far, at least, we have no way of being certain that Mr. Norman either wrote or dispatched that note to Mrs. Hertz himself."

"Oh, come now, Mr. Fowler," the Captain frowned. "Isn't it going a bit too far to suppose that someone would deliberately concoct a thing like that?"

Timothy shrugged. "When a person goes as far as murder, Captain, he seldom hesitates to go a little further. And it *might* have been rather convenient for someone to make it appear that Norman was, as you said a moment ago, alive and well at six o'clock Saturday evening. However, to get back to the matter of the alibis. It appears that Mrs. Hertz went directly to her room after her conversation with Mr. Norman in which they discussed the topic of amber necklaces. She was alone there, resting— you may remember it was rather uncomfortably warm on Saturday—until about five o'clock, when she came up on deck and got into a conversation with my wife. That leaves Mrs. Hertz alone and unaccounted for, except by her own statement, between four and five—"

"Oh, Timothy—" in spite of myself, I put in an objection, "you surely can't be suspicious of Mrs. Hertz!"

The Captain turned to frown at me. "In a case of this sort," he said officially, "we are none of us above suspicion. None of us. You agree with me, Mr. Fowler?"

"Oh, absolutely," said Timothy mildly. "I have the highest opinion of Mrs. Hertz—but, after all, she's about the only one who has any motive that I can see for being glad Norman was called to his Maker. She got an amber necklace out of it, anyway. To get on, Dr. Sloane tells me he was in his room during the entire afternoon Saturday. He, unfortunately, was also alone the greater part of the time—"

"In the case of Dr. Sloane," said the Captain, "I can give you my personal assurance that his actions are entirely above questioning—"

"A mere matter of form," Timothy murmured, "in a case where none of us is above suspicion. As for Mr. and Mrs. Covell, it appears that they were playing bridge with a couple from Des Moines. The game broke up shortly before half-past five, however."

"That leaves them unaccounted for between five-thirty and six, then?" the Captain looked hopeful.

"Not quite," said Timothy. "I had a word with Mrs. Des Moines this morning, and it seems that when the Covells left the smoking room, Mrs. Covell remarked to her husband that they mustn't forget to go down below and give Haile Selassie a pan of warm milk—"

"I *beg* your pardon?"

"Haile Selassie is their dog," Timothy explained. "A cocker spaniel."

The Captain's brow cleared, but only partially. "Rather an odd time to be feeding a dog, I should say. Doesn't it strike you as a somewhat—ah, implausible alibi, Mr. Fowler?"

"Oh, decidedly implausible," Timothy agreed. "But, as I told you, Captain, it's the plausible alibis that I find harder to believe. Anyone could invent a more likely story than giving a dog a pan of milk. To proceed—Mr. Tod Hutten was a bit under the weather that afternoon. Apparently they failed to teach him at Yale that brandy does *not* mix well with hot weather and a touch of seasickness. Result: he took to his bed with Mothersills a little after four o'clock. His steward looked in just before going off duty for his supper, and found the shades drawn and Hutten evidently asleep. That was about quarter past six. As for Mr. Nicholas Brande—"

"There's no question about Mr. Brande," said Captain Cobb firmly. "I happen to recall that on Saturday Brande spent the late afternoon with me, here in my office. He's traveled on the *Orion* before, you know, and we're rather well acquainted. Most interesting sort of chap, Brande is. He's done an amazing amount of traveling."

"I don't doubt it," said Timothy, just a trifle drily. "But you may also recall, Captain, that you went up to the bridge between five and five-thirty and that Brande was alone here while you were gone?"

Captain Cobb looked distinctly surprised. "Why, yes, I—" he coughed, "I did go up for inspection, Mr. Fowler. But it was a matter of fifteen, possibly twenty minutes— and I found Mr. Brande here when I returned. It's scarcely possible that in that short time—"

"It doesn't take so very long," said Timothy mildly, "to go down three flights of stairs and crack a man over the head, Captain. However, I'm only mentioning the possibilities. That accounts for all of our group except Joan and myself—"

"And me," said the Captain. "You're not forgetting me, I trust."

"Far from it," said Timothy politely. "And Mrs. Shaw. I expect you know more about Mrs. Shaw than I do, Captain, since you went to break the news to her as soon as we left Mrs. Hertz's room last night."

"Well, I hardly think it's necessary to consider Mrs. Shaw in this matter. After all, the man's own wife—"

"From the little I saw of the Reverend Shaw," said Timothy, "I'd say his own wife was very much to be considered in the matter of his sudden death. By the way, how did she take the news?"

"Terribly cut up, poor woman," the Captain shook his head. "It was a nasty business, having to tell her. Of course, she hadn't the slightest warning that her husband was likely to drop dead like that. So suddenly, I mean—"

"She didn't mention whether Mr. Shaw suffered from any sort of heart trouble, then?"

"N-no—" The Captain ran one finger around the inside of his collar. "Quite the reverse, as a matter of fact. She said more than once that her husband's health had always been—ah, extraordinarily good."

A curious expression came over Timothy's face as he stared over the Captain's shoulder at a marine map which hung on the far wall. He looked half as if he had expected the news he had just received, and half as though he were somehow disappointed by it. But he said nothing, and presently the Captain went on.

"As for the notion that there might have been any—ah, any sort of foul play in the matter of Shaw's death, Mrs. Shaw took exception—I may say, rather violent exception—to any such suggestion on my part. She said that it was absolutely inconceivable that anyone could possibly want to bring any harm to such a good man as her husband."

"Quite so," Timothy sighed. "And had she any idea for what high-minded purpose Mr. Shaw might have been visiting Mrs. Hertz's cabin in the middle of the night last night?"

"None whatever," the Captain answered seriously. "Except that Mrs. Shaw did suggest the possibility that her husband might have been led there through some hoax. By a person who wished to—ah, discredit Mr. Shaw's character, or something of the sort."

"Of course," Timothy cleared his throat. "I don't suppose, Captain, that you happened to touch upon the subject of the amber beads in your conversation with Mrs. Shaw?"

"I did," said Captain Cobb promptly. "Matter of fact, I purposely brought the matter up—in an indirect way—just to see how the land lay, so to speak."

"That was very clever of you, Captain," said Timothy admiringly. "And how *did* the land lay?"

"Beg pardon? Oh, yes—well, there was a curious thing, Mr. Fowler. Do you know, the woman knew nothing at all about the matter of the necklace—and yet you remember Mrs. Hertz said quite distinctly that she gave the beads to Shaw as a gift for his wife."

"M'mm, quite distinctly—yes," Timothy narrowed his eyes thoughtfully. "I wonder—" he paused for a moment, and then said briskly: "Well, Captain, there's as much of the picture as we've seen so far. Not a pretty picture—and damned complicated. But I'll do what I can to help, if you want me to."

"I'd be much obliged, Mr. Fowler. You may consider that I have, ah—delegated my authority to you in the investigation of this matter."

"It sounds good, anyway," Timothy smiled as he pushed back his chair. "I can't say that I'm sure yet just what I'll do with the authority, but perhaps a bit of searching will show me where to begin."

"Searching?" The Captain registered instant alarm. "You mean deliberately going through people's—ah, possessions?"

"In a nice way, yes."

"Well, now—I can't say that I exactly favor that sort of thing," Captain Cobb shook his head. "Is it strictly necessary, Mr. Fowler?"

"No—but it's often quite useful. You needn't worry, though—I'm the soul of discretion in matters of this sort. It's part of the technique they teach us on the New York Force. Being little gentlemen and all that sort of thing, you know."

The Captain looked a trifle baffled, but on the whole, relieved. "M'mm—well, I'd appreciate it if you'd go easy with anything like that. I never like to antagonize a passenger if I can help it. Very easily offended—passengers—not very reasonable in a case of this kind. However—" he rose, "I leave it to you, Mr. Fowler. Absolutely to your discretion," he struck one of his Captain-in-command-of-a-sinking-vessel poses, feet braced, arms folded, chin set and eyes narrowed. "Call on me when I can help, of course."

"Of course," Timothy rose also, and I noticed how tall he looked next to Captain Cobb's stalwart figure—he even stooped slightly, lest the top of his dark head should touch the beams of the low, curving ceiling. "Oh, by the way, Captain. I was noticing your paper knife there. Odd design, isn't it?"

"Paper knife? Oh, yes, that." The Captain took it up and handed it to Timothy.

The knife was about twelve inches long, slightly curved, and very heavy. It had apparently been carved from a single tusk, the blunt end forming the handle, and the tapering point being sharpened into a slender ivory blade. When Timothy had finished examining it, I took the paper-knife in my hand, and I was astonished by the weight of the solid ivory handle. It must have been a good three or four pounds. I gave it back to Timothy, and he turned it over and traced the deep, intricately carved design with one finger while the Captain talked.

"You know," Captain Cobb was saying, "it's a curious thing, your mentioning that knife—because it just happens that it was Mr. Brande who gave it to me. He dropped in here for a night-cap with me last night—Mrs. Fowler may recall seeing him here when she came up to give me the doctor's message about poor old Shaw. Anyway, in the course of conversation we touched on the subject of ivory, and I mentioned the fact that I'd always been fond of the stuff. Brande said he'd fetch up this piece to show me—and then he quite insisted that I keep it. Said he'd picked up no end of such things in his travels. Decent of him, wasn't it?"

"M'mm, I should say it was," Timothy raised his eyebrows. "It looks to me as though all you have to do on this boat, is admire something—and it's yours. Mrs. Hertz gets amber—you get ivory. I think I'll just sigh for a diamond or two and see what happens." While he talked, Timothy weighed the knife in the palm of his hand and turned it thoughtfully. Without looking up, or altering the tone of his voice in the slightest degree, he said: "By the by, Captain, did the handle of this thing have blood on it when Mr. Brande gave it to you?"

The effect of the question on Captain Cobb was distressing to observe. It took a moment for the point to

register—but when it did, his ruddy face went so red that
I feared for him.

"I—what's that you say, Fowler? You can't be in earnest!"

"Oh, but I am," said Timothy, still mildly. "Look here,"
he held out the knife "Two small spots on the carving of
the handle, do you see? I can't swear they're bloodstains,
of course, but I think it's worthwhile letting Dr. Sloane
have a look."

The Captain bent to examine the spots, then he raised
his eyes and stared at Timothy. "And if they are bloodstains—what then?"

"Then," said Timothy, "it will be interesting."

"You mean you think Brande murdered Mr. Norman
with the handle of that knife?"

"Not necessarily—"

"But, damn it, man—what else can it mean?"

"Various things." Timothy refused to respond to the
Captain's explosive tone. "For instance, it might mean
that Brande wanted it to appear that you had a hand in
Mr. Norman's undoing."

"See here, Fowler, this is no matter for joking," the
Captain's face darkened angrily.

"Or," Timothy proceeded, "it might indicate that someone else would like things to look bad for Brande. Either
way, it's worth considering—if you don't mind lending me
the knife for a while?"

"I—oh, certainly not. Certainly not," the Captain's
effort at assurance sounded a trifle hollow. "Best to have
it cleared up, by all means."

At the doorway Timothy looked back.

"It may not mean a thing, you know," he said.

But the Captain, drumming his fingertips on the desk and staring straight ahead of him, made no reply. He seemed lost in unaccustomed thought.

I could scarcely wait until we were outside to pounce on Timothy.

"*Do* let me see." I took the knife from Timothy's hand and peered at the two brown spots—disappointingly small. "What do you really think it means, Timothy?"

"If they're bloodstains," Timothy shrugged, "it's probably a plant, and not a very smart one. Still—it gave the old Rover a pretty jolt, didn't it?"

"Practically a stroke. But even a plant means something—I've heard you say so yourself."

"Sure, when you can figure out—" Timothy paused as we rounded a corner of the deck and caught sight of Tod Hutten leaning on the rail and gazing morosely out to sea. "Now, there's the very man who may be able to help us." To my surprise, Timothy abandoned his usual policy of avoiding Tod and made straight for him. "How are you this morning, Hutten?" he inquired genially.

Tod turned a face which was anything but genial toward us and nodded faintly.

"As a matter of fact," Timothy breezed on, "I was just hoping I'd run into you. You've heard what happened to Shaw, of course?"

Tad nodded again, but with no trace of enthusiasm. "God, yes," he said wearily. "The whole boat's buzzing with it."

"Any theories?" Timothy asked.

"Any what?"

"Theories. I thought you told me you were interested in criminal psychology."

"Only when there's been a crime," said Tod. "I'd call the person who helped that missionary on his way to the Happy Hunting Ground a benefactor rather than a criminal."

"A natural point of view, perhaps—but hardly professional."

"I leave the professional side to you," said Tod, rather aptly, I thought.

But Timothy was undaunted. "You hadn't by chance observed anyone who seemed particularly to dislike Mr. Shaw?"

"I really hadn't given the matter any thought," Tod's indifference was tinged with impatience, "except to suppose that everyone probably disliked him heartily. He struck me as a peculiarly repulsive specimen."

"Indeed?" said Timothy on a rising note. He let a short silence fall. "Well, see you later, Hutten. Let me know if you have any more thoughts."

Down in our stateroom, I slipped off my woolly sweater and skirt, and put on a sleeveless pink cotton dress. The sun had suddenly came out, and the air was bright and warm. Through the porthole I could see the stretch of sea, as calm and clear as a huge, dark blue mirror.

"It's really far too nice a day to think of murders," I sat down before the dressing table to fix my hair, "but since I've brought up the subject, would you mind telling me what was the idea of that asinine conversation with Tod Hutten. Or *was* there an idea?"

"There was," said Timothy, "but I think it rather laid an egg. Still—I gathered that the Hutten didn't care much for poor old Shaw."

"You must be psychic, Inspector."

"Never you mind, my girl. I'll startle you one of these days with a real idea." He leaned over my shoulder and peered into the mirror. "Do you think I'd better shave again? This damn sea air has a strengthening effect on whiskers."

"Oh, no—leave the beard. It'll help to awe your suspects." When Timothy made no reply I glanced in the mirror and saw him standing, still rubbing his chin thoughtfully and staring straight ahead. "Seriously, Timothy, what are you going to do next?"

"Eat lunch," said Timothy.

## 8
# A GENTLEMAN'S BELONGINGS

"Do you know, Joan," said Mrs. Hertz, "it sometimes seems to me that I'm just fated to do the wrong thing. I suppose Mr. Hertz would say I'm blaming fate for my own foolishness—but honestly, no matter how hard I try, everything I do seems to turn out a dreadful blunder."

"You might try doing nothing at all," I suggested.

"Oh, I *have* tried that often," Mrs. Hertz sighed, "but it doesn't help enough to be worth the effort. I feel as if this whole awful business were somehow my fault—but I don't think even Mr. Hertz could have foreseen such trouble from my making one little remark to Mr. Norman about liking amber necklaces."

We were stretched out in our deck chairs after lunch. The sun was just warm enough to be comfortable, and the monotonous throb of the ship's engine reduced me to a stage of drowsiness quite beyond the reach of Mrs. Hertz's troubles. Even the fact that Timothy was at that very moment conferring with Dr. Sloane about the matter of the ivory paper knife left me entirely unmoved. "Don't worry about it, anyway." I lay back and closed my eyes. "Nobody could possibly blame you for anything that happened."

"I can't help but blame myself, Joan," Mrs. Hertz's energetic anxiety was in nowise soothed. "This morning when I saw that poor Mrs. Shaw—honestly, I couldn't have felt more guilty if I'd actually murdered her husband with my own hands. Of course, in a way," Mrs. Hertz lowered her voice, "I should think she might almost be relieved— but I really shouldn't say that. I suppose, when you come right down to it, a husband is a husband—and perhaps Mr. Shaw had more good qualities than it seemed. Anyway, Mrs. Shaw is taking it terribly hard. When I went in to see her this morning, she was just sitting there on the edge of the berth—in that awful stuffy little cabin down on D Deck—just sitting there, not crying or anything, but staring at her hands and twisting her handkerchief. All the time I was there, she never looked up, Joan. Even when I handed her the necklace, she just reached out and took it as though she were in a kind of a daze—"

My eyes flew open, and I sat up straight. "Mrs. Hertz— you didn't give your necklace away *again?*"

"Why, yes—" She seemed startled by my sudden exclamation. "I intended her to have it in the first place, you know. And it really was the least I could do. Besides—you don't suppose I'd want to keep the necklace after—after the awful thing that happened last night?"

"I shouldn't suppose Mrs. Shaw would want to keep it either—for the same reason."

"Well, I don't know," Mrs. Hertz's tone was troubled. "I was just trying to do the right thing, Joan. And, anyway, she *did* take it."

"Then no doubt you were right," I sighed, and took up my knitting.

I was quite lost in the intricacies of *k one, p two,* yarn over, *k two together,* when Timothy's voice made me look up suddenly.

"Well, Madame La Farge, or whoever it was that knitted while Rome burned, are you weaving the story of our great marine disaster in an undecipherable but imperishable tapestry?" He plumped himself down in his deck chair beside me and looked quite pleased with his speech.

"I judge from your spirited manner, Inspector, that you have just unearthed a clue of vital importance."

"Not vital, perhaps, but interesting—ah, me, yes, damned interesting. For one thing, the dark-eyed Sloane has decided, for reasons best known to himself, to be just a pal."

"Probably thought he'd be safer on your side."

"I hope he's right," Timothy sighed. "Anyway, he says the spots on the knife handle are bloodstains, all right—and what's more, he told me he'd seen the knife before. Not, as you might suppose, in the possession of Mr. Brande—but in the Shaws' cabin."

"*Where?*"

"That's what he said," Timothy nodded solemnly. "It seems Mrs. Shaw sent for the doctor shortly after we sailed, and asked him to prescribe for a headache, or something—and there, plain as the nose on your face, was the ivory paper knife lying on top of a steamer trunk in her cabin."

"Well—" I was a little disappointed, "I've no doubt there is a point, but I'm afraid I don't quite see it—"

"Neither do I," Timothy admitted cheerfully. "But I hadn't come to the really interesting part yet. Which is that Mrs. Shaw herself just finished telling me that Dr. Sloane had never, to her knowledge, been inside her cabin."

"Oh—" I took a moment to think this over. "Well, that means someone's lying, doesn't it?"

"Brilliant, my dear."

"But which one—and *why?*"

"That," said Timothy, "is what *I'd* like to know." He leaned back in the deck chair and stretched his long arms over his head. "And the way to find out, as I see it, is by a bit of that discreet searching I mentioned to the Captain—but I think the dinner hour is the logical hour for that. So how's it for a game of ping-pong to kill the rest of the afternoon?"

"Swell." I put down my knitting.

"By the way," said Timothy, "where's Mrs. Hertz?"

"She went into the writing room about half an hour ago. Probably pouring out her soul in a letter to Mr. Hertz."

"Not likely, since she'll get to Paterson, New Jersey, sooner than the letter would. However—I'd like a word with her."

The broad back of Mrs. Hertz was turned toward us as we entered the writing room. She looked up suddenly when Timothy approached, and placed her hand across the page of her letter.

"Oh, it's you," she said. "You startled me for a moment." But she did not move her hand.

"I was wondering," said Timothy, "whether you'd let me take another look at those two notes you got from Mr. Norman. The one asking you to meet him for cocktails, and the second one about leaving you the necklace?"

"I'm sorry, Mr. Fowler, but I haven't got them," Mrs. Hertz answered evenly. But from where I stood, I could see the deep blush that stained her plump neck. "I—I destroyed them."

"Did you now?" Timothy said mildly.

Still flushed of face, Mrs. Hertz looked him straight in the eye. "I hadn't any idea, naturally, that the notes would be wanted for anything."

"Of course not," said Timothy. "Well—it really doesn't matter much."

But when we were outside he looked annoyed. "Damn," said Timothy, "there goes the Hertz hatching a little mystery of her own."

"Why did you want those notes from Mr. Norman?"

"I didn't particularly."

As we reached the ping-pong table, Timothy selected a racquet and handed it to me.

"Then why ask Mrs. Hertz for them?"

"Simply because I'm still remembering what you told me about the stuff in her desk being pawed over—and I thought I'd better see whether the Hertz had a guilty conscience in the matter."

"Well?"

"Well—" Timothy balanced the ball on his racquet thoughtfully, "she didn't flush purple for nothing."

"But, Timothy, what motive could Mrs. Hertz possibly have?"

"Don't talk to me about motives at this point, my chick," he cut me short. "So far as I can see, nobody on this boat has a motive for anything. Get over in your court and let's begin the grueling contest."

At the end of four games Timothy was leading three to one and quite inflated with victory when Sally Covell appeared in the doorway and waved at us.

"Hello, you two," she said. "May I cut in on your game?"

"By all means take over the champion," I handed her my racquet, "and see if you can reduce his self-esteem a bit." I sat down to watch.

"My, but this air smells good." Sally threw back her head and sniffed the fresh salt breeze appreciatively. "I've been lost in the darkest corner of the smoking room for the past hour—listening to a travelogue by Mr. Brande.

But, you know, he's really quite interesting when he thaws out a bit. He's certainly traveled a lot."

"So I understand," said Timothy. "He didn't by any chance offer to give you a piece of rare old ivory from his collection, did he?"

"No. Why?" Sally looked puzzled.

"Only that he seems rather inclined that way."

"Well, as a matter of fact," Sally served a ball, "Mr. Brande *is* frightfully generous. When I happened to mention that Ned has been sort of—of drifting between jobs, he took the greatest interest and asked me all about him. It seems that Mr. Brande has business interests all over the world, and do you know, he says he *thinks* he may be able to place Ned in one of his branch offices. Isn't that *marvelous?*"

"I should say it was." Timothy held up his racquet and studied it carefully. "Just what line of business is Brande in?"

"Oh—shipping and things." Sally made a vague gesture. "Some sort of importing, you know—or exporting. I never can remember which is which. Anyway, he's talking it over with Ned now."

"Ned must be pleased with you for getting him the chance," I said.

Sally frowned a little. "It's hard to tell sometimes whether Ned's pleased or not," she said slowly. "But anyway, I'm sure it'll be all right when he's talked to Mr. Brande."

Later, when we had gone down to dress for dinner, I asked Timothy what he thought of Ned's possible new job.

"It's difficult to say." Timothy bent close to the mirror and struggled with his tie. "I don't know whether anything good will come of Sally's valiant efforts or not. After all, there are worse ways of making a living than playing bridge with couples from Des Moines."

"Oh, Timothy, you don't think the Covells are what-do-you-call-'ems, do you?"

"Sharpers? Why, yes, of course." He turned to glance at me. "What else did you think they were?"

"Well, I *had* wondered about it, but I don't know, I like them so much that I sort of hated to think—"

"Good heavens, don't take it so seriously," Timothy smiled at my troubled expression. "The fact that they make a living off of other people's bad bridge doesn't make them crooks, you know. They may play a perfectly honest game."

"Just the same," I said, "it's hardly a profession to be proud of. And obviously Sally hates it. Look at the way she's worked on Mr. Brande to wangle a chance for Ned."

"True, my pet, quite true," said Timothy soothingly. "All I said in the first place was that our gal Sal may find she's jumped neatly out of the frying pan and so forth. Ask me again after our evening round of snoops and maybe I can tell you more—if you're still interested." He gave his tie a final jerk and picked up his coat. "And here goes for the searching party."

I was concentrating on a matter of lipstick. "Happy hunting," I murmured between dabs.

"What do you mean, happy hunting? You're coming along, my pet."

"Oh, no, I'm not." I clamped the top of the lipstick firmly. "I'm only a detective-in-law, you know."

"Come along," said Timothy, "and don't argue. This job needs a woman's intuition and all that sort of thing. Besides, if we get caught prowling I can always explain that you walk in your sleep."

I gave in, as usual, and after a final glance in the mirror, turned to follow obediently. "Where first, oh, Master Mind?"

"We'll try the Hertz diggings—just to get our hand in. The dinner gong rang ten minutes ago, so she's sure to have gone down. And I'd still like to know what's become of those letters from Norman."

"But Mrs. Hertz said she'd destroyed them."

"And I happen to doubt that," said Timothy gently.

We reached the stateroom door, and, after a glance up and down the empty corridor, Timothy opened the door and we stepped quickly inside. "In fact," he made for the desk at once, "I doubt it like hell. Either the notes were taken—and for some reason Mrs. Hertz won't admit it— or else she's hidden them for some other reason. But you ought to realize that she's the type that practically never destroys a letter. I'll bet she's got bales of old correspondence in her attic in Paterson, New Jersey—and no arguments from Mr. Hertz would persuade her to part with a single picture postcard. Look here, for instance—" Timothy drew a fat bundle of letters from the desk drawer. "This package is labeled 'Steamer Letters received when sailing for China.' And here's another: 'Letters received when leaving China.' You see my point, I trust?"

"Yes, but that still doesn't prove—"

"Will you kindly look at this," Timothy held up a large scrap-book, inscribed in gilt letters: "My Trip." It was crammed and bulging with every conceivable sort of memento to illustrate the closely-written pages. Menus, pressed flowers, ticket stubs and photographs had all been carefully pasted in.

"Now unless I'm a pretty lousy detective, those notes ought to be in here somewhere—" Timothy flipped through the pages hastily and then looked up in sudden triumph. "What did I tell you," he exclaimed, and showed me a page from which two entries had been torn away, leaving only the dabs of pasted paper. At the bottom of the page Mrs. Hertz had written: "Letters from Mr. Samuel Norman, explaining his strange gift." And the date.

"Just as I thought," Timothy shut the book and returned all the contents of the desk neatly. "Mrs. Hertz was basely deceiving me. She would no more have destroyed those notes than she'd have torn up her passport. But someone—for some reason—wanted them. Which remains just one more little problem for us to solve." He straightened up and glanced about the orderly room. Every trace of last night's disturbance had been carefully cleared away. "Nothing else here," he said. "Shall we proceed?"

"Where now?"

"Everything considered, I'd say Brande's room. We've only time for one more, and still get to dinner in time not to look suspiciously late, and I'd rather like a peek at the shipping tycoon's quarters."

"I suppose Mr. Brande has one of the elegant suites up on A Deck?" I paused as we reached the staircase.

"Wrong again, my chick." Timothy led the way down the steps. "Nobody in a suite would spend half as much time and energy being a gentleman as Brande does. Actually, he has the very cheapest cabin on the boat, forward on E Deck; and his elegant manner, well, the theory is called over-compensation. Tod Hutten will explain it to you, if you ask him."

"Thanks," I said, "but I've had some of the advantages, too."

There was no need to be careful about being seen as we approached Mr. Brande's stateroom. The short corridor was quite deserted, and after a moment's pause, Timothy tried the door. It was locked.

"So now what do you do?" I inquired. "Break it in?"

Timothy took a bunch of keys from his pocket and glanced at me reproachfully over his shoulder. "Give me credit for *some* foresight," he said. "I borrowed these from the Captain."

The door opened and we stepped quickly into the smallest and stuffiest cabin I had ever seen. There was barely room for the two of us to stand between the narrow bunk and the wall, and I stared with amazement at the curious display of Mr. Brande's possessions. Across one end of the room was a makeshift clothesline on which hung a pair of socks, several handkerchiefs, and a suit of underwear. An improvised ironing board and a small electric iron were carefully stowed in a corner, and beside them a neat shoe-shining kit and a mending basket. On a peg hung a single dark blue suit, perfectly pressed. It was, I recalled now, the only one I had seen Brande wear, aside from his dinner jacket.

"Behold," said Timothy, "the makings of a gentleman. Or how to be your own valet in six easy lessons." He picked up a small book from the foot of the bed, glanced at the title, and then held it toward me with a grin. It was called *The Epicure's Guide to Wining and Dining*. "If we look far enough," Timothy said, "we'll probably find a copy of Emily Post. I'll bet he even presses his pants under the mattress." He lifted a corner of the bedding, and there, sure enough, were the white flannels which Mr. Brande had worn at lunch. They were smoothed out carefully between two towels.

"But Timothy," I shook my head in utter amazement, "what *is* the idea? Why would anyone go to such trouble to put up a bluff of looking rich?"

"That," said Timothy, "is one of the mysteries of mankind which will probably never be solved." He dropped the mattress and bent down to pull an ancient leather suitcase, plastered with foreign labels, from beneath the bunk. He opened it and began, with expert care, to search the meager contents. A few pairs of neatly rolled socks, some shirts and pajamas, and miscellaneous toilet articles were laid aside one by one. There remained only a battered writing case in the bottom of the bag.

"Our last hope," Timothy murmured, as he unfastened the clasp and spread it open. Nothing, at first glance, could have looked less hopeful. A small supply of plain white writing paper, a fountain pen, a few stamps and a blotter—and nothing else. No letters, diaries, memorandums, or scribblings. Not even an address book. "Damn," said Timothy.

"You might try the blotter in the mirror," I suggested.

"An old trick, my girl, but any port in a storm," Timothy got up and went over to the small mirror on the wall. Out of the welter of crisscross lines on the blotter, only two words emerged in the reflection which appeared to have any particular meaning. One was the word "stateroom." The second was the name "Ezry."

And neither of them was written in the small, undistinguished script with which Nicholas Brande had autographed my passenger list the night before.

## 9
### THE KORAN

We weren't, after all, the last ones to reach the dinner table. Our not very fruitful search had taken barely a quarter of an hour, and when we got to the dining salon, the Covells had not yet appeared. Mrs. Shaw's place was likewise empty, but I scarcely expected that she would be coming to dinner—even though her husband's chair had been taken away, and the space tactfully filled in by moving the other places on that side of the table.

As we sat down, it appeared that Tod Hutten had been holding forth with some long and complicated anecdote, and he paused only long enough to nod a greeting to us. While he wound on with the details of his story, I had a chance to observe his three listeners. Dr. Sloane, at the head of the table, was rather less nervous than usual, and he welcomed Timothy with very much of a we-in-the-know smile. Mrs. Hertz, making her way daintily but efficiently through a large portion of steak, seemed preoccupied with some placid reflection of her own. If, as I now believed, she *had* deliberately lied to Timothy about the notes from M. Norman, there was certainly not the slightest indication of a guilty conscience in her calm and far-off gaze.

I sighed, realizing the duplicity of even the best of human natures, and turned my attention with new interest upon the immaculate elegance of Nicholas Brande. The perfection of his dinner clothes, the glistening white shirt front with discreet gold studs—even the corner of the fine linen handkerchief which peeped from his pocket, took on a new significance as I remembered the clothes-line and the electric iron. Over the rim of his wine glass, Mr. Brande was watching Tod attentively, without, I felt morally certain, hearing one word of the story.

"And then there was a chap in one of Tinker's classes at Yale—" Tod was well launched on the second chapter of his narrative when Mrs. Hertz emerged suddenly from her reverie.

"Yale?" she said. "Oh, that's right, Mr. Hutten, you did tell me you went to Yale, didn't you? How wonderful for you. I've always thought I'd love to go there—if I were a young man, I mean. They have such wonderful cheers at their football games. Not that I've ever seen a game—Mr. Hertz doesn't care much for football. He prefers wrestling," she stifled a sigh. "But then, I can listen on the radio. And one year I went with a group of ladies from our club to hear William Lyon Phelps lecture in Trenton. Oh, he was marvelous. Did you manage to get into any of his classes, Mr. Hutton? I should think it would be an education just to listen . . ." Mrs. Hertz paused abruptly, and an expression of concern came over her face. "Why—whatever is the matter, Mr. Hutton?" she asked sympathetically. "Did you get one of those bad olives? We really ought to speak to the waiter . . ." She turned to look for the steward, but the next moment her complaint was lost in sudden surprise as she caught sight of Mrs. Shaw coming slowly toward our table through the crowded room.

One by one the rest of us followed Mrs. Hertz's gaze, and one by one we were caught in a silence which held us in an almost tangible grip. It was not so much the surprise of having Mrs. Shaw join our group, after the tragic events of the night before—it wasn't even the fact that she wore the amber beads. It was a sense of the subtle change which had come over the woman herself.

Slowly, deliberately, and with perfect poise, Mrs. Shaw advanced to the table, nodded an unsmiling greeting at each of us, and took her place. Gone were the fluttering, inadequate gestures we remembered; gone was the air of downcast apology with which she had faced the world so long. And in their place was a new assurance that gave to her plain, mouse-like features an almost impressive calm, and lent dignity even to the rusty blue taffeta dress.

The rest of us, still locked in awkward silence, made a feeble pretense of returning our attention to the matter of dinner—but from the corner of my eye I saw the involuntary gesture with which Mrs. Hertz lifted her hand to the front of her black lace dress, now bare of adornment, while she stared with wistful eyes at the beautiful amber beads that hung about Mrs. Shaw's thin neck.

It was Mrs. Shaw herself who came to the rescue by uttering some trivial remark about the weather in her flat, toneless voice. Timothy managed some sort of a reply, and we others chimed in as best we could. But despite our efforts, the conversation limped painfully until the arrival of Sally and Ned, full of their usual high spirits, returned us all to something like normal.

I, for one, drew a breath of relief when the dinner was over and we rose to go. Mrs. Hertz took my arm as we left the room, and whispered that she had something important to say to me. Once outside, she drew me aside and began abruptly:

"Joan, I haven't drawn an easy breath since I talked to your husband this afternoon."

I registered what I hoped was a blank expression.

"I don't quite know how to say it, Joan," she hurried on, "but he asked me a question, and I—well, I lied to him. It was about those two notes from Mr. Norman. He asked to see them—and before I realized it—I'd gone and said something that wasn't true. You see, I *didn't* have the notes any longer, but I'd promised someone not to tell where they were, so I just said the first thing that popped into my head, and told your husband that I'd torn them up. I could see that he believed me, Joan, and afterwards I got to thinking that telling a lie was just as bad as breaking a promise—maybe worse."

"Timothy would bless you for that sentiment," I said sincerely.

"Well—" said Mrs. Hertz, "I want him to know the truth. But I'd rather have you tell him. I'd sort of hate to admit to his face, you know, that I'd deceived him."

"I don't think Timothy would really mind very much," I suppressed a smile. "He's quite used to being deceived. But what *did* happen to the notes? Were they stolen from you?"

"Mercy, no," Mrs. Hertz looked startled. "Whatever gave you that idea, Joan?"

"Oh, nothing," I said hastily. "Nothing at all."

"Well, the fact is," Mrs. Hertz glanced about and lowered her voice, "that I lent them to someone. I suppose I probably shouldn't have—but he said it would help clear up the mystery, and he seemed so in earnest—"

"*Who* seemed in earnest?"

Mrs. Hertz hesitated for a second. "Mr. Hutten. There now—I've broken my promise, but you know the truth."

"For heaven's sake, why did Tod Hutten want the notes?" I stared in astonishment.

"Why, he has some kind of a theory, Joan, about—well, about everything that's happened. And he told me that if he just had those letters to work with, he thought he could clear everything up. It seems that he's a sort of detective himself. Not a professional, you know, but he's studied a lot about criminals and so on. He told me—"

"Wait a minute, Mrs. Hertz. When did all this happen?"

"Night before last, in the bar. You remember you saw us together there? I guess Mr. Hutten was just being nice to me because he wanted something from me—but still, he's such an agreeable young man. And clever, too, Joan."

"So I'm beginning to think," I murmured. "But go on."

"Well, Mr. Hutten said that he believed those notes from Mr. Norman were forgeries, and that he could prove it if he had a chance to study the writing. So after awhile I went down to my stateroom and got them—and then I promised Mr. Hutten I wouldn't tell anyone a word about it. You see," Mrs. Hertz bent forward earnestly, "he explained to me that if anyone found out that he was working on this theory, it might be dangerous for him. So will you ask your husband not to say anything about it, Joan?"

"You needn't worry," I assured her. "Timothy practically never tells anyone anything."

"Well, that's a relief," Mrs. Hertz drew a long breath. "Because I'd really feel perfectly awful, you know, if anything were to happen to that nice Mr. Hutten when he's only trying to help."

"Wasn't it fortunate," I observed, "that you happened to have kept the letters." I couldn't resist it.

"Yes; well, it was just the purest chance, you know. I'd slipped them in my desk and forgotten all about them."

I could scarcely wait to take this latest news to Timothy, but as I rose to leave, Mrs. Hertz delayed me.

"By the way, Joan, I meant to tell you that I'm moving my things to another stateroom tonight. The Captain sent a message that I probably wouldn't want to go back to my cabin after what happened there last night, and he offered to put me up on B Deck. Wasn't it thoughtful of him?"

"Very."

"So I'm doubling up with Mrs. Shaw and—"

"Oh—did the Captain suggest that, too?"

"No. But, of course, the poor woman couldn't stay on in her cabin alone, under the circumstances, and so I suggested that she move into the large one with me. She seemed very grateful, and the purser said it would be all right. In a way, she's not exactly the kind of a traveling companion I'd select—but I suppose I shouldn't say that. As Mr. Hertz says, we're none of us perfect." Mrs. Hertz sighed as she heaved herself up from the big armchair. "Well—I must go see to my packing."

I found Timothy stretched out in his deck chair, reading by the last rays of fading daylight.

"Hello," he looked up. "Why the self-important face?"

I told my story as quickly as I could. Timothy listened to the part about Tod Hutten without making any comment, but when I came to the fact that Mrs. Hertz and Mrs. Shaw had signed up as roommates, he stopped fiddling with the pages of his book and sat up straight.

"Hell's bells," he said, "did you say Mrs. Shaw was moving her stuff this evening?"

I nodded.

"Where do you think she is right now?" he demanded.

"Who? Mrs. Shaw? I haven't the faintest idea. Why?"

"I'll tell you why, my girl," Timothy laid aside his book and got up. "I want you to find her, wherever she is, and keep her busy for the next fifteen minutes or so—while I go down and take a look at the Shaws' room."

"But, Timothy—" I spread my hands helplessly. "I scarcely know the woman. How in the world am I going to keep her busy?"

"Talk to her," said Timothy. "Ask her questions. Get her to quote the Bible to you. Tell her you've got a rich old uncle who's about to die and wants to leave his money to some worthy missionary project. Ask her what she thinks of the morals of Chinese women. I don't care *how* you do it—but *do* it. It's damned important to me to get a look at old man Shaw's haunt before she packs up all his stuff to move upstairs." While he talked, Timothy led me toward the entrance to the main lounge, pausing only long enough to make certain that Mrs. Shaw was not there.

At the doorway of the ship's library, Timothy stopped to look in, drew back quickly and nodded at me. "There she is," he said, "and mind you keep her there until I get back. I'll be as quick as I can—so do your stuff." With a vigorous thump between my shoulder-blades, which I judged was intended as a pat of encouragement, Timothy turned and departed.

Propelled thus suddenly into the library, I found myself face to face with Mrs. Shaw. She had just replaced a book on the shelf and turned toward the door as if to leave, when she caught sight of me and looked a little startled by what must have been an altogether odd expression on my face.

"Oh—it's you, Mrs. Fowler. I was just returning a book to the library," she spoke in her flat, colorless voice.

"Yes," I said, a trifle irrelevantly. And then, as it became apparent that Mrs. Shaw was waiting for me to get out of the doorway so she could leave, I clutched desperately at the only idea I could summon. "Are you very fond of books, Mrs. Shaw?" I made the tone brightly conversational.

Mrs. Shaw's look of surprise deepened, but she answered me civilly enough. "Well, no, I don't suppose you'd call me much of a reader. I don't get the time mostly, with all I've got to do. Sometimes the folks used to send me magazines from home, though, and I read some of the stories. There was one that came out in a serial last winter that was real interesting. It was all about a young girl who was a private secretary and she was engaged to marry her millionaire employer and then he ran off with another woman. I think it was by Kathleen Norris. Anyway, my sister forgot to send me the last part, so I never did know how it turned out. Maybe you read it, Mrs. Fowler?"

"No—I'm afraid I didn't happen to."

"Well, I guess I'll have to wait and ask my sister about the end of it. I was kind of curious because the heroine was such a sweet girl." Mrs. Shaw paused a moment, and took another step toward the door. "I suppose I'd better be going. I've got some things to do downstairs."

"I was hoping maybe you'd help me find something to read." I didn't budge from the doorway. "What about the book you just returned? Was that good?"

"Oh, that wasn't my book. Mr. Shaw took it out." There was only the faintest trace of a sigh in Mrs. Shaw's flat voice as she spoke her husband's name. "I don't think you'd enjoy it very much, Mrs. Fowler. It was all about some ancient religions. Heathen, you know. Mr. Shaw was a great hand to read deep books like that," again the threatened sigh beneath her words. "But I don't imagine you're so much interested in religion, are you?" She sounded almost wistful.

I took a deep breath and plunged in.

"Well, as it happens, Mrs. Shaw—I am. I—I made quite a study of ancient religions when I was in college. Especially the Koran." In my agitation, the Koran was the only item of religious literature I could bring to mind. "I'd like ever so much to look at that book you mentioned, if you wouldn't mind finding it again."

"Why, no, of course I wouldn't mind," said Mrs. Shaw mildly. She went over to the shelf and extracted a heavy blue volume on primitive cults and customs. "Here it is."

"Ah, yes." I thumbed through the solid and uninspiring pages. "It looks fascinating, doesn't it? I remember reading about this man's work," I pointed to, the author's name. "As a matter of fact, Mrs. Shaw, I was going to ask you to tell me some of your experiences sometime. You must have seen a great many—ah, temples and things like that."

"Well, yes, I did travel around quite a lot with Mr. Shaw. There were some heathen monasteries we visited where I guess I was the only white woman who had ever been inside. Mr. Shaw was very highly thought of by the natives and—" Mrs. Shaw was off. She talked on without pausing, and I made bright and interested sounds—not hearing a word of her long and rambling discourse.

I was positively startled when, after what seemed a passage of several hours, I looked up to see Timothy in the doorway.

"Oh, *there* you are, Joan," said my husband brightly. "I've been looking all over the ship for you—but I should have known I'd find you here." He turned to Mrs. Shaw. "My wife's a great little reader," he said, and patted my shoulder with fond pride.

I could have murdered him where he stood.

"I wonder if you'd be interested in seeing my photographs, Mrs. Fowler?" Mrs. Shaw was not to be diverted from her subject. "I've got some very pretty ones of those monasteries I was telling you about—"

"Joan would just love to see them tomorrow, Mrs. Shaw," said Timothy. "But come, my dear," he took me firmly by the arm, "they're waiting downstairs for us—and we really mustn't keep them any longer. Good night, Mrs. Shaw—"

We escaped together.

"Who's waiting for us downstairs?" I demanded, the moment we were out of the room.

"Two Planters' Punches," said Timothy, "in the bar."

# 10

## SALLY WALKS PAST ME

Timothy sat at a table in the bar and looked long and appreciatively into the depths of his glass. "You certainly had Mrs. Shaw rattling when I got back," he said. "What was the magic trick?"

"Very simple, really—it's all done with mirrors, you know." I stirred my drink. "We started with a little number that the late Reverend had been reading. *Primitive Cults, Their Cause and Cure*—or some such thing—and I told Mrs. Shaw my specialty was ancient religion. She started on heathen temples, and from there on it was a non-stop flight. You needn't have hurried back—she'd have gone on indefinitely."

"So I gathered. By the by, don't you think widowhood has improved the little woman remarkably?"

"She's changed all right," I agreed, "but I'm not altogether certain it's for the better. There's something—I don't know—I'd almost say something frightening about that sudden poise she's developed. I think I liked her better in the timid mouse stage. Or at least, I trusted her more. But do tell me how your searching party came out. Was it worth all the trouble?"

Timothy sipped his punch slowly. "Everything considered, I'd say yes. For the most part, of course, the Shaws' belongings are quite typical—and therefore meaningless. But a couple of things turned up that *might* prove something—" he paused.

"Prove what?"

"I don't quite know yet," he answered thoughtfully. "But look, Joan, you remember Dr. Sloane told me about seeing the ivory paper knife in Shaw's cabin?"

"Yes."

"Well, God knows I'm no judge of rare old ivories, but at least I'm sure that knife is no mere trinket. Doesn't it strike you as a bit odd that a missionary so poor that he could only save twenty-five dollars in a whole year should have a valuable thing like that lying around?"

"It might have been given to him," I suggested, "by a grateful potentate or something like that. My impression of the Orient is that they fling around priceless bits of jade and ivory quite carelessly."

"Sounds a bit like the movies to me," said Timothy doubtfully. "And I can't imagine why any potentate should be grateful to the Reverend Shaw. But there's more to the story, anyway. Tucked away among some of Shaw's papers labeled sermon notes, I found communications from no less than three banks—one in San Francisco, one in Seattle, and one in Honolulu. All the letters were addressed to Shaw, and all referred to recent deposits he had made. Now does that fit into the picture of the poor and struggling man of God?"

"No, it certainly doesn't."

"Furthermore," Timothy continued earnestly, "I found two copies of the *Wall Street Journal* in his suitcase, underneath a stack of much mended and patched underwear.

And finally there was one of those jolly little notes from the Bureau of Internal Revenue, asking, Oh, so discreetly, why they had not heard from the Reverend Asa Shaw concerning his income for the years 1930 to 1935? Now—is that evidence, my girl, or is it evidence? And, if it is, what do you make of it?"

"Good Lord, Timothy," I put down my glass and surveyed him solemnly, "don't tell me we've got another case of mistaken financial standing on our hands! Less than two hours ago you proved your theory that Mr. Brande is a whole lot poorer than he looks and acts—and now you've decided that the Shaws, for all their church mouse appearance, are actually in the money. It just doesn't make sense, you know."

"I know," Timothy agreed wearily, "it sounds crazy as hell. But I'm just telling you what I found."

"I can vaguely understand," I went on, "a person putting up a bluff to seem richer than he is—but I *can't* see why anyone in his right mind would deliberately pretend to be poor, and carry it to the point of being actually threadbare and traveling in miserably, stuffy quarters—"

"Still," Timothy interrupted, "it happens every day. You know the stories that are always coming out in the newspapers—tattered old lady in Bronx dies of starvation, leaving fifty thousand dollars hidden in broken milk bottle. It's a common enough occurrence, but whether the people who do it are in their right minds or not—that's another question."

"It's almost," I said, "as though Brande and Shaw ought to have exchanged places."

Timothy looked at me sharply for a moment, then he laughed. "Come, come, my chick, what would that make of Mrs. Shaw?" He finished the last of his drink and pushed back his chair. "I know this much, anyway. I'm going to find Brande and see what sort of a story he can produce to account for his having the ivory knife. Want to come along?"

"No, thanks. I'm going down to the stateroom to powder my nose. I'll see you later on the afterdeck if you care to dance."

Timothy waved his hand and departed.

Downstairs I attended to the business of powder and lipstick, took a light velvet jacket from the wardrobe, and started through the corridor toward the elevator. Halfway along, I was suddenly aware of a muffled sound from behind one of the closed doors. I paused a moment, listened more closely, and realized that it was the sound of someone weeping. The long, choking sobs mingled curiously with the faint echo of dance music from upstairs. Just as I was about to go on, I glanced up at the number on the door—C17. That, I remembered, was the number of the Covells' stateroom. Good heavens, what could have happened to Sally Covell to make her cry like that? On a quick impulse, I stepped up to the door, and my hand was literally raised to knock when a footstep in the corridor behind made me glance around.

The next moment I was staring in open-mouthed astonishment at Sally herself as she came swiftly toward me.

"Why—Sally," with my hand still uplifted, I drew back from the door, "I—I thought you were—" but the sentence was never finished. For without a word or a glance for me, Sally swept past and into her stateroom. The door clicked sharply behind her, there was a low murmured voice from within, and the sobbing died away in a last, long-drawn breath.

I was left standing, still rooted in surprise, with only the distant sound of music to break the silence of the

empty corridor. Slowly I turned and made my way toward
the elevator.

When I came out onto the afterdeck, Timothy had not
yet arrived. I wandered about for a few minutes, looking
for someone I knew. The dancers looked carefree enough
in the soft light of the colored lanterns strung overhead,
and it was difficult to reconcile the gay, summer night's
scene with the reality of mystery and death which had followed our ship. I made my way toward the stern rail where
the blare of the band was dissipated somewhat in the dark
stillness of the night, and looked down at the swishing
black water.

"Hello," said a voice. "Not contemplating illness, I trust?"

I turned to see Tod Hutten.

"If I stay and talk to you," he said, "will you please not
expect me to ask you to dance? I don't dance."

"Oh, that's all right. I'm used to dancing with Timothy,
and he doesn't dance either. But I'm quite willing to stand
here and moon, if you like."

"It's nice, isn't it? Cigarette?" Tod was considerably
more genial than I remembered seeing him before. He
struck a match and smiled at me in the brief flare of light.
"Do tell me," he said, "how's the investigation of our great
murder mystery coming on? Is your Timothy making much
headway?"

"Tolerable, thank you. And how about you?"

"How about my what?"

"Headway. How's your little private investigation coming?"

"Oh," Tad looked surprised, but not in the least dis-
concerted. "Well, quite frankly, I'm not doing so well. You
see, I started on the wrong assumption."

"And what was the assumption—if you wouldn't mind
telling a girl?"

"Not in the least," said Tod easily. "I simply had a quaint notion that when Mrs. Hertz promised not to tell a thing, she would keep her word. But I see," he held his cigarette over the rail and kicked the ash very delicately. "I see I was mistaken."

I was thankful that it was too dark for Tod to see me blush. He would have assumed, and rightly, that his random shot had scored.

"I wouldn't let one little mistake bother me, if I were you," I said. "The business of detecting is mostly trial and error—you'll learn that when you're more experienced."

"Thanks so much for the advice," Tod sounded amused. Then, as he saw Timothy coming toward us, "I expect it would be discreet of me to withdraw," he said. "No doubt, you two want to discuss all the latest clues." He flipped his cigarette over the rail and sauntered away.

"Hello. What's all the huff about?" Timothy looked after Tod's retreating figure.

"Nothing much. Only your little helpmeet tried to ask questions and got snubbed for his pains." I told him what Tod had said.

"And what did you do then?" Timothy grinned.

"Oh, I handled the situation with great finesse, never fear. But seriously, Timothy, what do you think Tod's up to? I mean his getting those letters from Mrs. Hertz, and handing her such a line about proving that they were forged?"

"Seriously, my chick, I do not know. He may really have an idea about the notes, or he may have wanted to get hold of them for some other reason—or he may be just playing horse. It's hard to tell just at this stage."

"But what do you intend to do about it?" I persisted.

"Do? Well, after all, what can I do? If Tod has an idea, it's probably wrong—so there's no use bothering him about it. If he has a motive for taking the letters, he certainly wouldn't be fool enough to tell me—so why ask? And if it's horseplay—well, I've always been in favor of letting horses have their fun. Meanwhile, would you care to dance?"

"All of which is very glib, Inspector—but I'd say it simply means you haven't the vaguest notion what Tod is trying to do. Yes, I'd care to dance." I tossed away my cigarette, and led the way back to the lantern-lit deck.

For a few minutes we danced in silence, then I looked up at Timothy. "And what luck did you have with the Brande?" I inquired.

"About what you'd expect," Timothy shrugged. "The moment I brought up the subject of the ivory knife, he was full of information. Volunteered the fact that he'd gotten the knife from Shaw—said he'd admired it casually, and Shaw jumped at the chance and offered to sell it. According to Brande, he bought it more to help out the poor missionary than because he really wanted the thing, then, when Captain Cobb took a fancy to it, Brande was glad enough to pass the trinket on. He told me the whole story with many shrugs and lifted eyebrows—you know, one man of the world to another stuff."

"And when you came to the part about the bloodstains?"

"Then," said Timothy, "he took the line of amused concern. Said it made the thing look deuced awkward for him, but really, upon his word, he hadn't the faintest idea how the spots got onto the knife. I said I hadn't either—and that was that."

I looked up again as Timothy finished speaking. "What did you think of the story?" I asked.

"Briefly, I thought it was as fishy as a shore dinner."

"And yet, you let Brande get away with it?"

"What else could I do?" Timothy sighed. "After all, *I* don't know how he happened to get the blasted knife away from Shaw, or why he gave it to the Captain—or who planted the bloodstains." He was silent for a moment. "By the by, this isn't a waltz they're playing, is it?"

"Now that you mention it," I said gently, "it is."

Timothy shifted his step obligingly.

Presently I recalled the incident that had occurred outside the Covells' stateroom, and when I had finished telling Timothy about it, he heaved another long sigh.

"Odd," he said. "In fact, damned odd. This is practically the worst mess *I* ever stepped into. I wish now I'd told the Captain I was a barber, or a writer of greeting-card verses—or anything except a detective. God knows what Ned was howling about, but—"

"Oh—" I glanced up in surprise, "do you really think it *was* Ned?"

"Why else," Timothy countered logically, "would Sally have acted as she did?"

"Well, I don't know—but Ned hardly seems the type."

"My dear girl, people seldom seem the type. At any rate, the Covells appear to have recovered their spirits—for the moment at least."

I turned to follow Timothy's look, and there, surely enough, were Sally and Ned, as gay and carefree as any couple on the floor. They danced beautifully together, both tall and graceful, and Sally's full white skirt billowed out as they dipped and turned. A moment later they passed close by us, and Sally smiled and waved cheerfully as she caught my eye. Perhaps it was a trick of the dim lantern light, but it seemed to me that Ned's handsome face looked unusually pale even as he echoed Sally's gay greeting. And I noticed that they left the floor before the dance was finished.

Timothy and I stayed on a while longer. Just as we were leaving to go below, a steward tapped Timothy's arm.

"Beg pardon, sir, but the Captain would like to have your report for the day, if it's convenient, before he retires."

"My report for the day," Timothy murmured, as he watched the steward's retreating figure, "is a large and well-rounded cipher. Still—" he stifled a yawn, "I suppose it would sound more impressive if I delivered it in person. So trot along to bed, my chick, while I break it to the Skipper that he's picked a lousy detective to solve his little mystery for him."

# 11
## THE GIDEON BIBLE

I awoke next morning with a sense of some great commotion and opened my eyes to see Timothy, clad in striped shorts, struggling to do his setting-up exercises in the distinctly confined space between my bed and the dressing table.

"Well," I sat up and watched his long arms thrashing the air, "if it isn't Lionel Strongfort himself!"

Timothy made a face at me between bends, but a moment later he abandoned his efforts with a sigh. "No use," he said. "Every time I lean down I crack my head against something. I guess I'll just have to let nature have its way with the old waistline for the rest of the trip."

"You can always stand in front of the port-hole and breathe deeply a hundred times," I suggested helpfully, "remembering, of course, to expand the chest, draw in the abdomen and relax the arms. But first tell me the news of your pow-wow with the Captain last night. You took so long about it that I abandoned my lonely vigil and went to sleep."

"I took ten minutes and six turns around the deck, to be exact," said Timothy, "and the news is this." He took a key from the dresser and dangled it before my nose.

"Not the key to the old strongbox, Inspector, where-in you expect to discover the missing papers which will Explain All?"

"Better than that, my pet," said Timothy calmly. He sat down to pull on his socks. "It happens to be the key to the late J. T. Ezry, alias Norman's, stateroom, and if we don't find something worth looking at *there*, I'm a Dutch baboon."

"Inconceivable, Inspector," I murmured politely.

"I had a hell of a time wangling the key from the Cap-tain," Timothy went on, "but I finally convinced him that I wasn't going to steal the old man's art treasures."

"Pooh," I said, "I'll bet he didn't even have any with him. Just because Mr. Norman was supposed to be J. T. Ezry, everybody acts as though he had the Mona Lisa rolled up in a pair of socks. *I* think he was just an eccentric old man who traveled incognito because he liked to make him-self feel important."

"That," said Timothy, "is a theory you can prove for yourself very shortly. So hurry up and get dressed, and we'll have a look at his quarters right after breakfast."

Mrs. Shaw was the only one left at the table when we reached the dining room, and she greeted me with an ex-pectant smile.

"I was just wondering, Mrs. Fowler, if you'd be inter-ested in looking at those photographs I was telling you about last night. I've got them all out, and it wouldn't be a bit of trouble—"

Before I could answer, Timothy spoke for me.

"That certainly is nice of you, Mrs. Shaw. It'll mean a lot to Joan—in her studies you know. But she's promised to help me for a while after breakfast, with some—" he coughed slightly, "some research work. So if about eleven o'clock would suit you—?"

"Oh, yes, that would be just fine," Mrs. Shaw looked pleased. "I think it's very interesting to find a young girl like Mrs. Fowler studying such a serious subject. Sometimes I wonder whether young people nowadays have any serious side at all, it's so discouraging trying to work with them. I just wish she could have talked with Mr. Shaw about her work—he could have told her so much about the Oriental religions."

Timothy made a noncommittal sound.

"Well—he's gone now, poor soul." Mrs. Shaw drew a long sigh and touched her handkerchief to her eye in appropriate widow fashion. It struck me, however, as a slightly perfunctory gesture.

"I suppose," said Timothy, "that your husband and Mr. Brande must have had some interesting talks. I understand Brande is quite a student himself, as well as a traveler." His tone was just a shade too casual to convince me, but Mrs. Shaw accepted it without suspicion.

"Well, no," she said. "I don't believe my husband got to know Mr. Brande at all. I don't think he seems very friendly, do you? Mr. Brande, I mean."

"Scarcely effusive, no," Timothy admitted.

"It seems kind of too bad, in a way." Mrs. Shaw put aside her napkin. "I think meeting different people is one of the most interesting things about traveling, don't you? Mr. Shaw always felt that way, too. He used to say he didn't care a bit whether a person agreed with him or not, just so they had something to say. But then, I suppose everybody isn't as broadminded as he was."

"No," said Timothy, "I suppose not."

Mrs. Shaw rose. "I'll be expecting you about eleven o'clock, then," she said to me.

When she had gone, I looked at Timothy.

"Well, I'm sorry," he said, "but what else could I do? It's your own fault for telling her you collect idols—or whatever it was. And besides, I think it's a swell idea for you to get chummy with Mrs. Shaw. Look at the way she's blossoming out with conversation now that old sourpuss isn't at her elbow every minute. She probably hasn't dared express an opinion on anything more important than the weather for the past twenty years! Cuddle up to a person who's been that thoroughly squelched—and she's practically certain to spill something."

"If," I observed, "she has anything to spill."

Timothy drank the last of his orange juice and put down the glass with a thud. "I wouldn't worry about that, sister," he said, "if I were you."

When we unlocked the door of the late Mr. Norman's stateroom (a comparatively modest cabin on B Deck) I stepped inside and looked about me with a distinct feeling of disappointment. I don't quite know what I expected, but there was nothing about the room or its contents to suggest the slightest interest. The scattered and somewhat untidy possessions which were strewn about the room might have belonged to any ordinary traveler. Two leather suitcases, of moderately good quality, but unmarked, were standing open on the floor. One of them was empty, and the other partly unpacked. The wardrobe door stood half ajar, revealing a row of undistinguishable dark suits, a grey topcoat, and a rack of somber ties. The usual collection of masculine toilet articles were lined up on the dresser top, and the desk was bare, save for inkwell and pen, a few sheets of the ship's writing paper and an overturned tumbler from which some water appeared to have spilled. On the rumpled surface of the single bed lay a dark blue sack suit and a discarded shirt, and on the floor close by stood a pair of high laced black shoes with socks stuffed in them. Surely, I reflected, a most unpromising array.

Timothy, however, seemed to share none of my disappointment. He walked slowly around the small room, pausing to look at each object, but touching nothing.

"Swell," he said at length. "Perfectly swell."

"What's so swell about it, if I may ask?"

He turned to look at me reproachfully. "My dear girl, the man who had this room was murdered."

"I'm aware of that."

"And nobody's touched a thing! Thanks to the Captain's quite remarkable foresight, the place was locked up and left precisely as the late Norman himself left it—and take it from me, that's a rare advantage in the business of solving puzzles. In a long career of crime I've come across darn few murdered people who left as clear a record of the last hour of their lives as this"—his sweeping gesture indicated the entire contents of the room.

"I suppose you mean fingerprints?" I suggested doubtfully.

"Good Lord, no," Timothy shook his head with impatience. "You sound like the people in that detective story I'm reading. I mean the evidence of what old Norman was actually *doing* in the last few minutes before he died. I mean *this,* for instance." He pointed to the bed and the mussed clothes which lay on it.

I shifted from one foot to the other, and tried, without success, to observe intelligently. "It simply looks to me,"

I said, "as though the poor man had changed his clothes for dinner."

"Precisely," said Timothy with enthusiasm. "And does that suggest to you that Mr. Norman was *not* expecting to keep his cocktail date with Mrs. Hertz?"

"N-no—unless he were taken sick or something. After he'd dressed for dinner, I mean."

"And in that case, do you think he'd sit down and write a note to Mrs. Hertz, presenting her with the necklace?"

"All right," I said, "you win. So what does that prove—except that poor old Norman was pretty eccentric, which, if I may say so, we knew anyway."

"It proves," said Timothy, "that Tod Hutten may be smarter than I think."

"Meaning?"

"Meaning that whether he knows it or not, Tod's theory about those notes from Norman is probably right."

"You think they were forged?"

"I'm beginning to," Timothy nodded soberly. "Now then, let's go at this thing systematically." He planted himself in the center of the room. "Norman was here in his cabin say an hour or more before time to change for dinner Saturday evening. He lay down on the bed to rest for a while—that's evident from the rumpled spread and the dent in the pillow. Sometime or other, the idea occurred to him of asking Mrs. Hertz for a cocktail—you remember they'd been talking earlier in the afternoon. Very well—he gets up, starts to dress for dinner, and somewhere during the process, he sits down at the desk and writes a perfectly conventional invitation to Mrs. Hertz. *But*—before he gets around to dispatching the note, or even sealing it—he's interrupted by someone at the door. Whoever it is must either be well known to Norman, or else have some convincing excuse for barging in—for there are not signs of a struggle anywhere in the room—"

"Except for that upset glass," I pointed to the water tumbler on the desk and the blistered spot on the blotter where the water had spilled.

"I'm coming to that," said Timothy. "Now—Norman chats with his visitor, and the visitor watches for his chance—or her chance. The chance comes when Norman stands here in front of the desk, and picks up a glass of water. While he's drinking, the visitor gets set—and cracks the old man's skill with a blow from behind. Norman goes down—probably without a sound—and drops the half-empty tumbler on the desk as he falls—"

"Hold everything, Inspector. You're letting your imagination run away with you there. How can you possibly prove—?"

"Never mind the proof," Timothy waved aside my objection impatiently. "I'm only supposing—and the point I'm trying to make is simply this: When Norman was killed, that invitation to Mrs. Hertz was still lying on the desk here—*and it was not Norman, but someone else who added the P.S.*—"

I was amazed at the conviction of his tone. "But Timothy—how can you be so sure?"

"Because," said Timothy, "it was a perfectly ordinary note except for that last sentence tacked on the bottom: 'I have something important to tell you concerning our conversation of this afternoon.'"

"Yes, but who, besides Mrs. Hertz and Norman, would have known about the conversation?"

"Who indeed?" said Timothy. "If I could answer that question, my girl, I could answer a lot of other questions, too. Just the same, I'll bet you anything you care to name that P.S. and the whole of the second note about the amber necklace were *not* written by Norman."

"The handwriting was the same—you saw it yourself."

"That's where Tod Hutten's theory of forgery comes in. And it wouldn't take much of a forger to copy the old man's shaky writing—particularly when he had the chance to sit right down here at the desk and use the same paper, the same pen and the same ink. I haven't had much experience with that sort of thing—but I'll bet I could make a fairly convincing job of it myself."

"Let me get this straight," I said slowly. "You think someone sat down here, *after* Mr. Norman was killed, and calmly put a postscript on one letter, and invented another one—and then went out and left the poor man lying here dead?"

"That's what I think," Timothy nodded.

I stared in silence for a moment. "Good Lord, Timothy—it's not possible. It's *too* cold-blooded, and besides, it's utterly fantastic."

"It's never been my experience," Timothy answered me seriously, "that murderers are particularly warm-blooded. As for the fantastic part—well, I'll admit it seems so. But don't forget, we don't know any of the reasons behind this thing. If only we knew, there's probably a perfectly rational explanation—or, at least, rational as murders go. Someone, for some reason, wanted Norman dead—and someone, perhaps the same one, wanted Mrs. Hertz to have that necklace. And there you are." He spread his hands. "Now for a bit of that proof you've been longing for." Timothy crossed the room and surveyed the contents of the wardrobe. "*If*, indeed, there's any proof to be found."

During the next few minutes, Timothy went over the remainder of the late Mr. Norman's possessions with rapid efficiency. Not until he reached the very bottom of the last suitcase did he find anything worth commenting on, then he laughed, and held up a square, black book for me to see.

"A Bible," he said, "and a well-worn one at that." He turned through the limp pages, and over his shoulder I could see that numerous passages had been checked and underscored. At the title page he paused and pointed to the familiar inscription, stamped in red letters: 'Property of the Gideon Society of America.' "So that's where he got it," Timothy grinned up at me. "Just the same, it's an odd sort of thing for old J. T. Ezry to be carrying around with him."

"Maybe he was studying up on how to get to heaven," I suggested. "You know, the rich man through the camel's eye, or whatever it is."

Timothy turned the pages again and selected one of the underscored passages at random:

> *"It was planted in a good soil by great waters, that it might bring forth branches, and that it might bear fruit, that it might be a goodly vine."*

He read the verse aloud, and then closed the book. "Not much information there on how to get to heaven," he said, "for a rich man or a poor one either. Well, I guess that finishes the job here—" Timothy replaced the suitcase in the closet and straightened up with a sigh.

"There was nothing very exciting to see, after all," I observed.

"Nope—" Timothy dusted his hands thoughtfully. "Only—you know it's a curious thing that there's not a single mark of identification in this whole room. Not an initial, nor a letter, nor a baggage label to be seen—"

"That's not so curious when you remember that the man was traveling incognito."

"All the same," said Timothy, "that doesn't mean you can travel without a passport." He was silent for a moment, then he glanced at his wrist-watch. "Five minutes of eleven—you've just got time to keep your date with Mrs. Shaw and her picture postcards."

I sighed.

"Meet me for sherry before lunch," Timothy opened the door for me, "and tell me all about it. And *don't* forget what I told you about being just girls together with Mrs. Shaw."

## 12
## A BOX OF CANDY

I found Mrs. Shaw all ready and waiting for me in the large stateroom which she now shared with Mrs. Hertz. The Captain, I reflected, had certainly done right by his two lone women passengers—for the room was decidedly the handsomest I had yet seen on the ship. The mahogany beds, jade green brocade hangings, and upholstered furniture were far grander than anything in the simple cabin I had just left, despite the late Mr. Ezry's reputed millions.

Mrs. Shaw, not in the least awed by her new surroundings, welcomed me with considerable graciousness.

"I've just put everything on the bed here so we can have plenty of space," she indicated the collection of photographs spread out upon the counterpane. "Now then, if you'll just take this chair, Mrs. Fowler, and make yourself comfortable, we'll begin at the beginning. . . ."

My heart sank at the prospect, but, remembering my duty to Timothy and the Cause, I set my face in an appreciative smile and resigned myself.

"How I do wish Mr. Shaw could have explained some of these temple interiors to you." Mrs. Shaw uttered the customary sigh, and then proceeded at once and briskly. "But I'll try to remember everything just as he used to tell it. Now here's a group we took on our first trip into the mountains of the northern interior . . ."

We were off. For the next hour I listened to a jumble of province names, monasteries, missions, ruins and ancient cults—and gazed upon at least a hundred views of the Buddha's *embonpoint,* while making what I hoped were appropriate murmurs of interest. I stole a look at my wristwatch and saw that it was already past noon. There were plenty of photographs still to be seen, and I had certainly not yet succeeded in hearing anything from Mrs. Shaw which shed the slightest light on the life or death of her departed spouse. I was reflecting on this and planning a somewhat bitter speech to Timothy on the subject of my duties as his assistant, when a stray word in Mrs. Shaw's speech caught my attention. The word was *paper-knife.*

I focused for the first time on the photograph I held in my hand, and realized that I had been gazing unseeingly at a picture of Mr. Shaw. He was posed beside an ancient and wizened Chinese magi, who was grinning toothlessly and rather foolishly for the benefit of the camera. And Mrs. Shaw was explaining to me that this photograph had been taken on the occasion of their first visit to the palatial home of the Chinese gentleman, who, despite his toothlessness, she assured me was one of the wealthiest merchants and collectors of art in his province.

"No one but Mr. Shaw," she said, "would ever have dreamed of trying to convert such an important person—but Mr. Shaw just kept going back, again and again, and finally he succeeded. And when the old man was baptized, he gave Mr. Shaw the most beautiful carved ivory knife just as a token of his gratitude." She smiled proudly, with just the proper touch of sadness. "Everyone thought it was a great achievement for Mr. Shaw—and for the mission,

of course, to have made such a prominent convert." She
started to pass on to another photograph.

"I wonder if I could see the knife, Mrs. Shaw? Carved
ivory has always been rather a hobby of mine—" I paused,
wondering guiltily whether she would begin to suspect
that these hobbies of mine came on only at the most op-
portune moments—but it was evident that something else
was troubling her.

Mrs. Shaw hesitated briefly, and then looked straight at
me. "I would gladly, Mrs. Fowler," she said, "but—I may
as well tell you—the ivory knife has disappeared in the
strangest way. I hate to say it, but I'm perfectly certain it
was stolen."

"Stolen?"

Mrs. Shaw nodded solemnly. "It happened the very first
evening after we sailed—Saturday, that was."

"You're quite certain?" I asked.

"Oh, absolutely. I know that the knife was in our stateroom, because I unpacked it myself that afternoon, and I
left it on top of Mr. Shaw's steamer trunk."

"And when did you first miss it?"

"About nine o'clock that evening," the reply was prompt.
"I'd gone down to our room early—I had a little headache,
and I was sort of upset—all that terrible business about poor
Mr. Norman, you know, and Mr. Shaw thought I ought to
get right to bed. Well, I was all undressed and ready to turn
out the light when I just happened—I declare, I don't know
what made me think of it—but I looked over at the trunk
and saw that the knife wasn't there. Of course, I thought
it must have slipped down behind—but I looked and it
wasn't there, either. Then I hunted high and low—and the
knife just wasn't to be found. If I hadn't been all ready for
bed I'd have gone straight to find Mr. Shaw and tell him

that very minute—for I knew how upset he'd be. But as it was, I thought best to wait till he came down."

"Well," I said as she stopped speaking, "did you?"

Mrs. Shaw nodded. "I told him the very first thing next morning, and asked him what he thought we'd better do. Of course, I never like to say a thing's been stolen unless I'm absolutely sure, but in this case I just *knew*—"

"What did Mr. Shaw say about it?"

"Well, he felt the same way I did—but he thought the best thing would be to say nothing. 'just let it rest a few days, Pearl,' he said, 'and I have kind of a feeling the knife may turn up.' But it hasn't yet—" she sighed.

"You don't suppose Mr. Shaw might have loaned it to someone?" I suggested. "Or even given it away?"

"Mercy, no," Mrs. Shaw looked startled, almost shocked by such an idea. "Why, Mr. Shaw wouldn't have parted with that ivory knife for anything in this world. I guess you don't understand how much it meant to him."

"Well, I only thought—" I let the sentence trail off lamely.

"Yesterday I decided I'd best speak to the Captain about it when I had the chance, and so last night—just after our conversation in the library—I told him."

"What did he say?" I tried not to sound too eager.

"Well—nothing much," Mrs. Shaw frowned. "He said he was sorry, of course, and he told me not to worry, he'd try to locate the knife for me. And in the meantime, he said, it would be best to say nothing about it. But I'm sure he wouldn't mind my telling you."

"Oh, no, I'm sure he wouldn't."

There was a silence, then Mrs. Shaw sighed and seemed about to turn back to the photographs when I made a sudden decision.

"Mrs. Shaw," I said, "have you any idea why your husband was in Mrs. Hertz's cabin the night he—he died?"

She blinked a little at the directness of my question, but her pale blue eyes met mine squarely, and when she answered, her voice was steady.

"I think," said Mrs. Shaw, "that he went to—take these—" her hand clasped the long amber necklace which hung round her neck.

"Oh, but Mrs. Shaw—surely you know that's impossible. Mrs. Hertz said she had *given* your husband the necklace—"

"Yes, I know Mrs. Hertz *said* that, but—" she stopped short, and a dull flush crept over her sallow cheeks.

"You don't believe her?"

"No." She was silent for a moment, then she looked up again and said simply, "Mrs. Hertz is a good woman. I believe she was only trying to spare me when she said that. Maybe you think it's awful of me to say such a thing— when my husband is dead. I don't know why I'm telling you, only you seem so honest, and—well, I thought maybe you'd understand—" She broke off with a sigh. "But I guess only a person who's been poor themselves can know what it's like to scrape along years and years and years and never have anything you want—*never*—" Her voice rose sharply, almost fiercely. It was the first time I had seen Mrs. Shaw really emotional about anything. The next minute the spark had died out of her eyes, and her voice went flat again. "Well, sometimes a person will do something he shouldn't—even a good person. I guess we can't any of us stand but just so much."

"No, I suppose not—" I shifted a little uncomfortably.

"If you don't mind, I guess I'd rather not talk about it, any more." Mrs. Shaw took off her glasses and passed her hand wearily across her eyes. "It kind of upsets me."

"Naturally," I nodded sympathetically. "Still—you do want to know what happened. If your husband died in some mysterious—I mean, if there was something peculiar about his death—"

Mrs. Shaw looked straight at me. "There wasn't anything peculiar about it," she said.

"Well, no—of course not peculiar. But I only meant if there were some reason to suspect that he was—that his death wasn't entirely natural—" I was floundering miserably, but I got no assistance from Mrs. Shaw. She continued to regard me with no expression whatsoever. "Well, anyway—" I finished half-heartedly, "I should think you'd want to be perfectly sure."

Mrs. Shaw replaced her glasses. "Yes," she said, rather absently, "yes, of course." But there was not an ounce of conviction in her tone. The next moment she stood up, murmured something about lunch time, and glanced around the room in a vague sort of way. Suddenly her eye heightened as she caught sight of a candy box on the table next to Mrs. Hertz's bed.

"Oh, now do try one of these, won't you, Mrs. Fowler?" She held out the large box containing an assortment of rather stale-looking chocolates mixed in with a great many fancy paper wrappers. "I'm sure Mrs. Hertz won't mind—she told me I was to help her eat as many as I could. I think she's dieting, sort of."

"Thanks, I don't believe I will before lunch." I eyed the candy without enthusiasm.

"Well, if you don't mind, I guess I'll have just one. Now, let's see, where are those caramels I like so well?" Mrs. Shaw rustled the empty wrappers and peered into the box with more animation than I had ever seen her display.

Having located the desired caramel and popped it into
her mouth, Mrs. Shaw smiled at me a little apologetically. "I'm afraid I just have a regular old-fashioned sweet
tooth," she said thickly. "And then, it's been so long since
I've had any real good American candy. Mr. Shaw's sister
used to send us some now and then, but she stopped after
Mr. Shaw went on a diet."

"Surely he wasn't reducing, was he?" I recalled his
gaunt, lean frame.

"Oh, no," Mrs. Shaw shook her head. "It was some
kind of trouble he had—stomach trouble, I think—and
the doctor wouldn't let him eat any kind of sweets, not
even sugar. It was kind of hard for me, you know, having
to cook with that saccharine stuff. Oh—must you go?" As
I rose, Mrs. Shaw followed me to the door, candy box still
in hand. "Well, you must come back some other time, and
we'll go over the rest of the pictures. There are some real
interesting ones you haven't seen yet."

A minute later I was in the corridor outside, and as Mrs.
Shaw's door clicked shut I had a feeling, vague and not
particularly pleasant, of having been dismissed—promptly
and rather cleverly.

Down in the bar I found Timothy waiting with a glass
of sherry for me.

"Hurry up and start," he said. "I'm two up on you already. And between ladylike sips, tell me what you got out
of the Shaw."

"Well, if you still think the little lady is just waiting
for a friendly ear to spill her life story into, you're wrong,"
I said with decision. "You told me to cuddle up to her, and
I did."

"But she didn't?"

"Right the second time, Inspector. She told me just exactly as much as she wanted to—and no more. And before you could say Benito Mussolini, I was alone in the hall with my thoughts. However, I did learn one thing by professing a lifelong interest in old ivory."

"I wonder," said Timothy, "that God doesn't strike you dead for the lies you tell. But go on."

I retailed the story of the ivory knife, and wound up with Mrs. Shaw's theory of why her husband had gone to Mrs. Hertz's cabin that night. "Do you suppose she's right about that, by any chance?"

"No," said Timothy promptly. "But the more important question is whether she really *thinks* she's right. Personally, I don't believe she'd accuse her late husband of trying to steal a necklace unless—" he paused, "well, unless she knew, or at least suspected, that he was actually prowling around for some worse reason. But what that reason could possibly be—" he frowned and shook his head. "Ah, well, if we knew that, we'd know everything. And we don't. Not by a hell of a lot, we don't."

"Right again, Inspector. And if you think that you or anyone else is going to find out anything further from Mrs. Shaw, you'll discover that she's neatly changed the subject and is telling you all about the late Reverend's diet—and the next thing you know, you'll be out in the hall."

Timothy smiled. "Don't tell me old sawbones was actually on a diet?" he said.

"That's what I said, too. But Mrs. Shaw explained that he had a delicate stomach or something, and couldn't eat sweets. She's making up for lost time now, though. You should have seen her go for a chocolate caramel—" I stopped suddenly and stared at the expression on Timothy's face. "What on earth—" I began.

"Jumping Judas—I believe that's *it!*" He brought his fist down on the table with a whack that made the empty glasses jump.

"Timothy—what *are* you talking about? You look as though you'd seen a ghost or something."

"Who knows, my girl—maybe I have." Timothy pushed back his chair. "You run along to lunch, will you, and order something for me—"

"But where are you going?"

"I've got to look at something down in the hold. It won't take very long—but if I see what I *think* I'll see—" he broke off with a short laugh. "Well, we'll be having a chat with Dr. Sloane this afternoon."

I opened my mouth to ask another question, but Timothy patted my shoulder before I could speak. "Sorry," he said, "but it would take too long to tell you what I have on my mind right now. And besides, you'd be far too excited to eat any lunch—much less join in the gay and witty table talk. So trot along like a good girl, and I'll see you, in a few minutes." With a final pat, he was gone, leaving me to finish a last sip of cherry and make my way to the dining room alone.

## 13

# A PRETTY PLANT

As a matter of fact, table talk had never been more difficult for me than at luncheon that day. The others seemed
calm enough, but I had begun to feel as if the web of
mystery and death which hung over our oddly assorted
group at the doctor's table were an almost tangible thing.
Looking about at the circle of faces, listening to the commonplace conversation, I realized how closely we were all
caught up in the tangle of clues and counter-clues—yet
each of us separated from the rest by his own secret undercurrent of thought. Dr. Sloane, with his thin face and
restless dark eyes; the Covells with their bright, incessant
patter of jokes; Nicholas Brande, with his pose of studied
aloofness; Tod Hutten, with his interminable anecdotes;
Mrs. Shaw, with her newfound assurance resting oddly
on the long habit of diffidence and self-effacement—even
Mrs. Hertz's genial and natural manner. What suspicions,
what knowledge, what guilt or innocence lay behind these
now familiar masks?

I longed to tell Timothy how I felt about it all. And
then, when he arrived, it occurred to me suddenly that
Timothy's own candid expression, his amiable contribu-
tions to the talk, were likewise masks to hide the watch-
fulness of his casual glance, the eternal questioning of

his mind. I shook myself mentally with the reflection that Timothy would undoubtedly dismiss this entire train of thought as piffle. And doubtless he would be quite right.

After lunch, true to his prophecy, Timothy asked Dr. Sloane if we might have a word alone with him. The doctor agreed readily enough, and, at his suggestion, we went to his quarters.

I rather imagine Dr. Sloane thought he and Timothy were going to have a friendly little pow-wow—one honest man to another. But Timothy lost no time in coming to the point. The doctor had just asked us to be seated and was offering cigarettes when Timothy asked the first question.

"Dr. Sloane," he said, "why didn't you tell me that you had been giving Shaw hypodermic injections of insulin?"

At that particular moment, the doctor was holding a pack of Chesterfields toward me. His expression did not change by so much as a flicker, but when I shook my head, he continued to stand—the cigarettes in his outstretched hand. I shook my head again, and still he did not move.

"No, thank you," I said clearly, "I don't care for a cigarette just now."

There was a moment's pause after my words, then Dr. Sloane dropped his arm and turned slowly to face Timothy. "What was that you asked me, Mr. Fowler?"

Timothy repeated the question. His tone was mild, but very distinct.

"Oh," the doctor drew out a cigarette, tapped it on the pack, and frowned thoughtfully at it. "Why, I didn't tell you because I really couldn't see that it had any bearing on—" he hesitated slightly, "on anything that happened afterward."

"No?" Timothy's eyebrows rose. "Very well, let's put it this way. A few minutes after Mr. Shaw had died, you told

Captain Cobb that a heart attack had been the cause of
death—"

"We've been all over that before, Fowler," the doctor
cut in curtly. "My diagnosis remains the same today as it
did that night. Mr. Shaw had every symptom of coronary
thrombosis . . ."

"I'm quite aware of that," Timothy's voice was level.
"My point is a simple fact which you doubtless know.
Death caused by an overdose of insulin is frequently, and
with good cause, diagnosed as heart disease. The symp-
toms are identical, even to the professional eye, and even
an autopsy will often leave a margin of doubt."

While Timothy was speaking, I watched the effect of
his words. The doctor's face darkened and one corner of
his thin, set lips twitched visibly. But when he spoke, his
voice was controlled and quiet.

"Good God, Mr. Fowler, if you're trying to say you
think I killed Shaw with an overdose of insulin—why don't
you say it?"

"Oh, but I'm not saying that, doctor. You go too fast.
I was only going to ask whether you suspected that too
much insulin was the cause of Shaw's death?"

"Well, I—I hardly know how to answer that," Dr.
Sloane seemed both disarmed and confused by Timothy's
explanation. "It's a possibility, of course, but on the other
hand, there's considerable room for doubt. As you say
yourself, an exact diagnosis is virtually impossible in such
a case and—"

He stopped speaking as Timothy rose, walked over to
where he stood, and faced the doctor squarely.

"Stop stalling," said Timothy. It was a tone he rarely
used, and when he did, the effect was generally prompt.
"Now then—you as good as knew that it was insulin that

killed Shaw, but you didn't say so because it was you yourself who had given him the injection—and you were afraid
you might be blamed for his death. Isn't that it?"

"Look here, Fowler, I don't have to explain—" Dr.
Sloane began indignantly, and then, quite unexpectedly,
he walked over to a chair and sat down. "Yes," he said,
"that's it exactly."

"Good," Timothy helped himself to a cigarette and
drew up a chair facing the doctor. "Now we're getting
somewhere." He paused for a light, and took a deep breath
of smoke. "I can't say that I blame you for trying that
dodge, Dr. Sloane. It was a nasty mess—still is, for that
matter. But now that we understand each other, we may
be able to straighten it out. Now first—about the dose of
insulin. I suppose it was Shaw's own prescription that you
gave him?"

Dr. Sloane nodded. He seemed, now that the original
admission was made, to be almost eager to get the whole
story out.

"Mr. Shaw came here to my room shortly after we
sailed from Shanghai last Saturday," the doctor said. "He
brought his own hypodermic syringe with him, and a box
of ampoules, and explained that he required a daily injection. He asked me whether I'd give him the shots during
the voyage. Of course, most diabetic patients would rather
give their own injections—less bother, and all that. But
Shaw said he'd only begun the treatments lately, and was
still a bit squeamish about it. I agreed to give him the
shots, naturally, and I also agreed to keep his equipment
for him. He made rather a point of that . . ."

"Did he, now?" Timothy bent forward quickly. "And
for what reason, would you think, doctor?"

Dr. Sloane shrugged. "I really couldn't say. He made some sort of excuse, I believe, about not liking to have the stuff about in his room. Sensitive about needing treatments, or some such thing. To tell you the truth, Fowler, I didn't pay much attention at the time. I just thought Shaw was an odd kind of chap, and let it go at that."

"Not so odd but what he tried to save his skin," Timothy murmured. "But go on. You agreed to keep the stuff for him—and then what?"

"I took the needle and the box of ampoules and put them in my desk drawer here."

There was a moment's silence, then Timothy said, very quietly: "Oh."

"Later that afternoon," Dr. Sloane went on, "I think it must have been around five-thirty—a steward brought me a message that Shaw would like to have his treatment. So I took the things and went down to his cabin—but when I got there, Shaw wasn't in the room."

"Was Mrs. Shaw there?"

"No. I went in and waited a bit, and after a minute or so, Shaw came in and asked if we could come back up to my place for the injection."

"What was his excuse that time?" Timothy inquired.

Dr. Sloane smiled a little. "Well, it seemed that Mrs. Shaw didn't know about the treatments—and her husband didn't want to worry her."

"So—" said Timothy, "that was why you thought you could get away with the heart attack story, was it, doctor? You figured that if Shaw's own wife didn't know about the insulin injections, it was damned unlikely that anyone else on board would be in on the secret."

Dr. Sloane cleared his throat, but he made no reply.

"As a matter of fact," Timothy went on, "you almost did get away with it, except—" he paused.

"Except for what?"

"Well, it's a long story—but if Joan hadn't gone to look at some photographs, and if she hadn't asked Mrs. Shaw something that Mrs. Shaw didn't want to answer, and if Mrs. Shaw hadn't changed the subject by remarking on the fact that Mr. Shaw wasn't allowed to eat candy—if all those things hadn't happened, I wouldn't have gone down to the hold just before lunch and bribed a porter to let me have another look at the late Mr. Shaw, and I wouldn't have seen the hypodermic spots on his arm. And, for all I know, your theory of the heart attack would have stuck for good. But that's pretty much beside the point now. To get back to your story, you brought Shaw back up here and gave him an injection. Right?"

The doctor nodded. "We talked a minute or two about the weather, I think, and that was all."

"I see," said Timothy. "I suppose it was while you were in Shaw's room that you saw the ivory paper knife?"

Dr. Sloane looked down quickly. "Well—yes, as a matter of fact, it was. When I mentioned that to you yesterday, I think I said something about having gone there to see Mrs. Shaw, but—" he hesitated.

"But, as it happened, you weren't telling the truth," said Timothy easily.

"Sunday afternoon," the Doctor went on a trifle hurriedly, "Shaw came up here again, and I gave another injection. Precisely the same routine. And again on Monday and Tuesday—same needle, same ampoules—" he stopped.

"But on Tuesday," said Timothy quietly, "there was a different reaction."

Dr. Sloane did not answer at once. He stared down at his hands, then suddenly, almost angrily, he raised his eyes and looked straight at Timothy. "I tell you, it's crazy," he blurted out, "it doesn't make sense! Those injections were identical, and yet the first three were regular treatments, and the fourth—" again he stopped.

"After the fourth," said Timothy, "Shaw died from an overdose of insulin."

Dr. Sloane nodded. A moment later he ground out his cigarette and jumped up from his chair. "Do you see—?" He walked the length of the room and swung around to face Timothy, "Do you see now why I—I rather lost my head the night Shaw died?" When Timothy made no reply, the doctor turned away sharply and flung himself down in the chair again. "It's crazy, I tell you, Fowler. That a diabetic should be fatally poisoned by a prescribed dose of insulin—a dose that had been given again and again with normal results. . . . And yet," he spread his hands helplessly, "there's no other answer . . ."

Timothy eyed him soberly for a long moment. "There's just one other answer," he said at last. "Perhaps you've thought of it, too . . . ?"

Dr. Sloane placed the tip of one forefinger very carefully against the tip of his thumb. "Quite frankly, I don't see what you're driving at, Fowler."

"No? Well, I'll explain. You put a box of say, half a dozen ampoules of insulin in your desk drawer here. Each ampoule contained the exact dose of insulin prescribed for the treatment of Mr. Shaw's condition. But suppose some-one entered your room, removed one of the ampoules from that box, and substituted another one—looking precise-ly the same, but containing enough insulin to kill Shaw within a few hours after injection. Now—you go on giving the treatments, selecting the ampoules at random. *Sooner or later, you're bound to strike the one with the fatal dose.* By George—" Timothy broke off suddenly, "that's damned neat, isn't it?"

The doctor took out his handkerchief and drew it across his forehead with a hand that was not quite steady. "I—I'm afraid I can't quite share your impersonal enthusiasm, Mr. Fowler," he said stiffly. "I expect you realize that if this—this quite fantastic suspicion is correct, it places me in a most awkward position. In plain words, it means that I—" his voice faltered.

"That you killed Shaw," Timothy finished it quietly. "Yes, of course I realize that, doctor. But the actual murderer was the one who switched the doses of insulin—whoever that person may have been." He eyed the doctor's face thoughtfully for a moment. "And that person must have known that Shaw was taking insulin, that he had asked you to give him the injections, and that you had placed the box of ampoules in the drawer of your desk here."

Once more Dr. Sloane passed the handkerchief across his brow, and he made an obvious effort to steady his voice. "There's—something else, Fowler, that I expect you ought to know," he hesitated. "Sometime Monday afternoon, the coat of my dress uniform was taken from the closet there—"

"You— Good Lord, you don't say—" Timothy started forward.

I supposed he was remembering, as I was, what Mrs. Hertz had said: *The coat sleeve with gold braid on it.*

"And it was returned to the closet," said the doctor, "on Tuesday morning, while I was down in Mrs. Hertz's room, looking after you."

Timothy got up and crossed the room in three long steps, then he plunged his hands in his pockets and stared at Dr. Sloane. "It's amazing," he said slowly. "It's—almost too good to be true."

"I assure you," said Dr. Sloane levelly, "that it is true. Every word of it." Then, as Timothy continued to stare, his control snapped suddenly. "My God—" he burst out, "do you wonder I didn't tell you all this sooner? Don't you think I know how the thing looks? I've been framed, Fowler, and damned cleverly. You've got a perfect case against me—and I haven't a single scrap of proof to show that the whole thing was planted. My only witness is dead—" He laughed bitterly, but the next moment he turned away, and his voice dropped into weariness. "Oh, Lord—what's the use of talking? Of course you don't believe me—and why should you?"

Timothy took rather a long time with his answer. "It's a pretty plant, I'll grant you that," he said mildly. "But it just happens that I've seen some pretty plants before, in my day—and sometimes they bear surprising fruits. Sometimes."

## 14

# A BRIGHT RED LEASH

After we left the doctor's room, we went straight down the corridor and stepped out on a section of the deck, which, save for a couple of dear old ladies engrossed in needlepoint embroidery, was deserted. Timothy walked over to the rail and took a deep breath of the fresh afternoon breeze.

"Well—there's this much about it," he looked down at the water. "The doctor's story is either all right or all wrong. And if it's all wrong, he's a better liar than I think he is."

"Even the part about the switched doses of insulin and the stolen coat?" I inquired.

"Especially those parts," Timothy nodded. "I know it sounds like a dime novel—but I tell you, I don't think Sloane would be very good at inventing dime novels."

"Someone else may have invented it for him."

"M'mm—maybe," Timothy sounded doubtful. He turned around and leaned back with his elbows on the rail. "But I'm not making any guesses anyway until after I've tackled my next prospect—"

"Who's the lucky winner this time?"

Timothy looked sidewise at me. "You won't like it," he said.

I waited.

"There are a couple of questions I'd like to ask Ned Covell," Timothy said.

When I still made no reply, he glanced at me curiously. "What's the matter," he asked, "aren't you going to defend your pet?"

"Certainly not. If you want deliberately to pick on Ned Covell—it's no affair of mine."

"Suppose I were to tell you that I'm not, as you so flatteringly put it, deliberately picking on Ned—that I've got good grounds for asking him some questions?"

"What grounds, for instance?"

"For instance, that Ned Covell went to Mr. Norman's cabin about five-thirty last Saturday afternoon—and that half an hour later a steward saw him put a note under Mrs. Hertz's door—a note that was supposed to be from Samuel Norman—"

"Oh—*no,* Timothy! No—it couldn't be—I simply don't believe it!"

"I knew you'd sputter," said Timothy calmly, "but there you are—it's true all right. I got it straight from the steward."

"I don't care what anybody told you," I said firmly. "Ned Covell never sat down in the room with a dead man and forged two letters. I may not be a detective, but I know that much. And besides—how can you be so sure that Ned was ever in Mr. Norman's room?"

"Well—how else would he have gotten that letter?"

"Lots of other ways."

Timothy gave me another side glance. "Name two, for instance."

"Naturally, I can't think of any, off-hand like that. But there *could* be dozens of explanations—and I'll bet anything there's some good reason why Ned had the letter— if he really did—"

"My dear girl," said Timothy, "I don't doubt that in the least. But, as you may or may not recall, this argument was precipitated by my simple statement that I was going to ask Ned Covell a few questions. And if he has any explanations to make—he'll probably make them. And then he'll be happier, and I'll be happier, and you'll be happier. So what's wrong with that plan?"

"Very well," I said, still huffily, "if you want to ask Ned a lot of silly questions—go ahead. But don't expect me to be a party to it. I refuse to sit by like a ventriloquist's dummy and listen to you put the poor lad through a grilling like the one you just gave the doctor."

"Wait till you're invited, my pet. As a matter of fact, all I want you to do is to keep Sally's mind off her troubles while I chat with Ned."

"I won't do that, either," I said promptly.

"Very well, then," Timothy offered me his arm with an amiable smile, "suppose we go sit in our deck chairs a while. I trust that's not asking you to violate any of your high-minded principles?"

"Timothy—what are you up to?"

"Nothing, upon my word. Only—if we play mountain, there's just a chance that Mohammed may come along. Of course, with your knowledge of Oriental religions, I needn't explain the reference."

We hadn't been in our chairs for more than a quarter of an hour before I looked up from my knitting and saw Sally Covell coming along the deck with Haile Selassie on the leash. As she came nearer, she waved at me and I waved back. Timothy, deep in his book, paid no attention. Sally walked past us, Haile Selassie trotting along at her side, and then, having got about half way down the deck, she stopped. For a moment I saw her stand quite still, as though making up her mind to something before she turned and marched resolutely back toward us.

"Can I sit here a minute?" she asked, indicating Mrs. Hertz's vacant chair.

"Of course," Timothy glanced up for the first time at the sound of her voice, and rose hastily.

"Thank you." Sally perched herself on the edge of the chair and looked around as if to make certain that no one was within earshot. In her bright yellow sweater and skirt, she looked as much as ever like a pretty little girl, but her solemn face did not brighten as she watched Timothy stoop down to pet Haile Selassie. The little spaniel greeted him like an old friend, and when Timothy snapped his fingers, Haile climbed onto his lap and settled himself with a sigh of contentment.

Sally shook back her dark curls and regarded us with round eyes. "I wanted to talk to you," she said, "about something. Something serious."

"Would you rather see Timothy alone?" I started to get up, but Sally shook her head vigorously.

"No, you stay, Joan. It's about—" she stopped and looked down at the bright red leash in her hand, twisting and untwisting it around one finger. "About Ned," she said.

We waited in silence, and then, all of a sudden, Sally burst out with it.

"Ned's in trouble—awful trouble. It's not his fault—I absolutely *know* that—but he won't tell you himself, because he says no one would be a big enough fool to take his word for anything, and he hasn't any proof for what he says."

Sally hurried on. "I hate to bother you, and Ned would absolutely *kill* me if he found out I'd told you, but I just *know* that if Ned goes on hiding everything this way, that someone will find out something and then it'll look as if he—" she hesitated, "as if he'd done something that he really hasn't."

"You're certainly not bothering us, Sally," said Timothy, "and we'll do anything we can to help you—and Ned. But could you be just a little more specific about what the trouble is?"

"Yes, of course," Sally nodded earnestly. "You see, I didn't know anything at all about it until last night about ten o'clock. I don't think Ned would have told me even then, only that I happened to come down to the stateroom and found him there—maybe you remember when it was, Joan, you were standing just outside our door?"

I nodded.

"Well—when I went in, I found Ned sitting on the edge of the bed, and he was terribly upset. He was almost—well, sort of *crying*. I've absolutely *never* seen Ned like that before, and I just *made* him tell me what was the matter. At first he wouldn't, but finally he told me the trouble was about Mr. Brande—"

"You mean something about the job he promised Ned?"

"Well—yes. You see, I don't exactly understand what happened, but I guess there was something wrong about that job and—and Ned blames me for getting him into it." Sally bit her lip.

"That's certainly very unfair of Ned," I said indignantly. "After all, you were only trying to help, and Ned has no right to say that you're to blame for anything."

"Oh—he doesn't *say* I'm to blame," Sally shook her head quickly, "but I can tell he *thinks* so, just the same. And that's not the worst of it, anyway. The worst part is—" she raised her eyes to look at Timothy, and took a deep breath, "is that Ned knows I told you about it."

"You mean about the job?" Timothy sounded surprised. "What difference does that make?"

"I don't *know*—" Sally's voice rose in a wail, "that's what Ned simply *wouldn't* explain to me. All he said was that now he was in a frightful mess, and that you'd be sure to blame him for something he hadn't done—and that it was all because I'd told you that Mr. Brande said he might give him a job."

Timothy looked at her for a moment, then he shook his head slowly. "It doesn't make much sense to me, Sally," he said, "unless there's more to the story than you've told me."

"All Ned would say," Sally repeated, "was that Mr. Brande had just used him—and now he'd be blamed for everything. Ned, I mean."

Timothy shook his head again. "It still doesn't make sense," he said. "Everybody seems to be worried about who'll be blamed—but blamed for *what?*"

Sally looked down at the leash in her hand. "I—I don't know," her voice was almost a whisper, "but I thought perhaps you'd know what he meant. And if—" she swallowed, "if Mr. Brande tries to tell you anything about Ned, you mustn't believe him, Timothy, because it isn't true—honestly, it isn't. Why, Ned wouldn't hurt a fly—you *know* he wouldn't—"

For a fleeting second I saw a curious change come over Timothy's face, but when Sally raised her eyes to his, he smiled reassuringly.

"What I do know," he said, "is that you're worrying a lot over very little—probably nothing at all. If I were you, I'd forget the whole thing and have a game of shuffle-board."

"Oh—" Sally's face lighted up hopefully, "then Mr. Brande *hasn't* told you anything?"

"Far from it," Timothy laughed shortly. "And unless I miss my guess, he never will."

"Well—I *do* feel better, then," Sally rummaged in her sweater pocket and pulled out a handkerchief. "Only—" she dabbed at her eyes, "I did think I ought to explain to you that it was all my fault, about Mr. Brande, I mean. Oh, dear," she sighed, "and I thought everything was going to be so lovely. I thought Mr. Brande must be terribly rich—he talks so much, you know—"

"Yes, I know."

"And all that about his big shipping interests," Sally blinked indignantly. "Why, he was just stringing me."

"So it would seem," Timothy sighed. The next moment he rose, deposited Haile Selassie carefully on the deck floor, and looked down at Sally.

"Are you—?" the girl met his sober glance anxiously. "What are you going to do, Timothy?"

"I just remembered I had a date with the Captain," Timothy's tone was brisk. "See you both at dinner—" he turned away with a wave of his hand. "And don't forget you two are going to play shuffle-board."

But after he was gone neither of us said anything about the game. Sally looked after his retreating figure with an expression of childish anxiety.

"Timothy seemed kind of funny about it, didn't he, Joan? I mean, not very cheerful."

I had to admit that Timothy's manner had not been altogether reassuring. "But then," I said, "you never can tell about Timothy. He may have been thinking of something else entirely."

Sally nodded. "Well—" she rose and smoothed her yellow skirt, "it's after four-thirty. I guess I'd better take Haile Selassie down and give him his dinner."

At the mention of dinner the spaniel cocked his ears with interest, and a moment later he was bounding off down the deck, straining at his bright red leash as Sally walked slowly beside him.

Left alone, I tried Timothy's book—but even the most feverish activities of Scotland Yard seemed tame beside the puzzles of our own mystery, and each time someone approached my chair I looked up with the expectation of seeing Timothy. But he did not come, and at six o'clock I went down to dress for dinner alone. At seven I was dressed and ready, and still no Timothy. Resigned to wait, I took up my knitting and sat down on the bed, but I had scarcely finished one row when there was a sharp knock at the door. Before I could speak, the door flew open and Sally Covell faced me with an expression of tragic excitement. She was still dressed in the yellow sweater and skirt, and her dark curls were all awry. For a moment she stood, leaning back against the closed door, breathing rapidly.

I scrambled up off the bed. "Why, Sally—what—?"

She caught her breath and blurted it out. "Joan—Timothy's arrested Ned."

"Oh, no, Sally. He—he couldn't. Timothy has no authority—"

"He had the Captain do it," she said. "They've got Ned up there this minute—in the Captain's office. I saw him, just now, but they wouldn't let me talk to him—and they won't tell me anything—"

"Who's *they?*"

"Timothy and the Captain and Dr. Sloane. They're asking Ned a lot of questions and—"

"Dr. Sloane?" I asked in astonishment. "What's he doing there?"

"Oh, I don't *know,*" Sally's voice rose to a wail. "But he's there—I saw him. Joan—" she came over and put her hand on my arm, "you've got to stop them. Ned's not guilty—he doesn't know anything about what happened to Mr. Norman. I swear he doesn't."

"Well, when they find that out, they'll let him go. You mustn't get so excited, Sally."

"But, Joan, you don't *understand,*" the girl tightened her grip desperately. "You don't *know* Ned. If they keep accusing him of things, he's liable to admit something that isn't true. He's so terribly cynical and sort of bitter about everything that he never expects anyone to believe him anymore. Honestly, Joan—you've just got to make Timothy stop."

Still I hesitated. "I don't see how I can very well interfere—"

"But you can, Joan. You can tell Timothy what I've just told you—that he mustn't believe what Ned tells him. Oh, don't you see, Joan, I've got to do *something* to help Ned because this is all my fault. If I hadn't gone and told Timothy everything, he'd never have thought of suspecting Ned—" Sally stopped short and stared at me for a moment. There must have been something in my expression that gave her warning, for presently she spoke again, and her voice was curiously flat. "He *didn't* have any other reason for suspecting Ned—did he, Joan?"

With Sally's dark eyes, pleading and fearful, fastened on my face, I didn't dare answer her directly. "Look," I said, "I can't promise anything, but I'll go up to the Captain's quarters and see if I can speak to Timothy—"

"Oh, thank you a *million* times, Joan," a smile of relief broke over the girl's anxious face. "Come on, we'll have to hurry—"

"But," I added firmly, "I think I'd better go alone. I'll be more apt to get in, and besides, you'll have to hurry and dress or you'll miss dinner."

"Oh, Joan," she shook her head reproachfully, "I *couldn't* go in the dining room, feeling the way I do. I couldn't choke down a single mouthful."

I took her by the arm and marched her out into the corridor. "You're going to put on your prettiest dress, Sally, and go to dinner just as usual. If anyone asks about Ned, say he's been detained by—by a bridge game." As we came to the door of her cabin I gave her arm a final pat. "Now go on, and remember—if Ned's innocent, then everything will be all right."

"But if—" Sally's eyes widened fearfully.

"The more mouthfuls you choke down," I turned hastily toward the elevator, "the better it will be for both of you."

When I reached the door of the Captain's office, I paused and listened to the low murmur of voices from within. Only the memory of Sally's pleading eyes gave me the courage to lift my hand and knock. There was a wait, the voices inside stopped, and then Timothy opened the door.

"What do you want, Joan?" His face was very serious.

"I—I've just been with Sally and—" I paused, glancing over his shoulder at the Captain's stocky figure. Beside him, smoking a cigarette, and looking very calm and collected, stood Dr. Sloane. And over behind the desk, I saw Ned Covell. He was just sitting there, staring straight ahead.

"Timothy, I—may I speak to you alone, for just a minute?" I asked.

Timothy frowned, but he closed the door behind him. "Good Lord, Joan, what's this all about?"

"I'm sorry, Timothy, but Sally absolutely made me come. She told me that you'd arrested Ned."

"I did nothing of the sort, of course," said Timothy briskly. "The Captain has the only authority—"

"But you had the Captain do it," I cut in quickly. "Didn't you?"

"Well—?" Timothy's shrug was impatient.

"Oh, Timothy—*why* did you? You surely didn't believe that silly business about Ned being to blame for something? Why don't you have Mr. Brande arrested, if you Want to pick on somebody? You *know* he's up to something—lying to Sally about his business—"

"Listen, Joan," Timothy eyed me sternly. "I know Sally put you up to this—it's not like you to butt in of your own accord. I know you're sorry for Sally, and so am I—but I knew what I was doing when I had Ned arrested. Now will you please take my word for it, and leave me alone until I can explain everything to you?"

He started to turn away, but I tried once more.

"I know I'm talking out of turn, Timothy, but Sally told me one thing you ought to remember. She said if you kept on accusing Ned, he might admit something that wasn't true. He just isn't the kind of person who can stand being browbeaten and questioned—"

"You're damn right he isn't," Timothy laughed shortly. "I'm afraid even Sally underestimates Ned's powers of resistance. He hadn't been up here more than five minutes before he melted like an ice cream cone on a summer's day."

"Timothy—" I drew back, "you don't mean—"

"I mean," he said quietly, "that Ned Covell has admitted everything."

## 15
## THE SUBJECT OF INCENSE

It took me a minute to realize the meaning of what Timothy had said. Then, before I could speak, he patted my hand briefly, and turned to the door again.

"Sorry," he said, "but you asked for it. Not a hint—to anyone. And now will you run along like a good girl and have some dinner?"

I nodded, still speechless, and then I remembered. "Oh, but what about Sally? How can I face her, Timothy? What can I possibly say?"

"You'll have to figure that one out yourself, my girl." Timothy's tone was kind, but firm. "I'll be down just as soon as I can get away." The next moment the door clicked shut and he was gone.

I stood quite still, staring at the blank panel before me. The low voices had started again inside the room. Then I turned and walked slowly along the passageway, down the stairs, across the lounge, and toward the dining room. But I didn't venture in until I'd stopped at the bar for an old-fashioned.

Mrs. Hertz, Mrs. Shaw, Tod Hutten and Mr. Brande were at the table. And Sally Covell. As I approached, Sally had just seated herself next to Tod, and she was in the

middle of a laughing remark when she looked up and saw
me. For a fleeting second she stopped speaking, and the
bright smile seemed frozen on her lips as her eyes questioned mine. On the strength of the old-fashioned, I managed a reassuring nod, but I turned away hastily from the
look of relief that lighted Sally's face. She had dressed,
quite as I had told her to, in her prettiest frock—a soft,
corn-colored chiffon which swirled away from her shoulders in flowing pleats—and her dark curls were brushed
back, smooth and gleaming, from her forehead.

Rather desperately, I plunged into conversation with
Nicholas Brande, at my side. The first topic which came
to my mind was, for some obscure reason, incense; and I
heard myself asking whether he had brought any with him
from the Orient. Mr. Brande looked distinctly startled
by my abrupt question—and small wonder. He stopped a
forkful of smoked salmon halfway to his mouth, lowered
it to his plate again, and turned to survey me with lifted
eyebrows. He replied civilly that, no, he had not brought
any incense, and added the information that the best incense was not to be purchased in China, anyway, but from
a certain importing house in San Francisco. With that, he
returned his attention to the smoked salmon, and it appeared that my effort at conversation had come to an end.

But Mrs. Shaw leaned forward from her place beyond
Mr. Brande. "What did you want to know about incense
for, Mrs. Fowler?" she asked in her flat, matter-of-fact
voice.

To my dismay, I found that everyone at the table was
looking at me, waiting for my answer. I offered the only
explanation which I could summon at the moment, and
said that I had just recalled that I hadn't bought any in
China, although I had intended to. I could only hope

that this would end the subject—but not so. It was one of
those trivial topics upon which, for some curious reason,
everyone fastens with passionate intensity. The next thing
I knew, the attention of the entire table was concentrated
on the dilemma of my not having purchased any incense.

Tod Hutten was the first one to offer a practical suggestion. "Why don't you send for some when you get home?
You remember the name of that big store in Shanghai—"

"Better than that," Mrs. Hertz interrupted eagerly, "I
can ask my daughter to buy some and send it to you, Joan.
She'll be sure to get the very best—she's really marvelous
about dealing with those native merchants and not getting
cheated. She's always been clever that way, she gets it from
Mr. Hertz. You just give me your address when you think
of it, Joan, and Dorothy will be only too glad to send the
incense right to you . . ."

Before I could answer, Mrs. Shaw broke in again. "No,"
she said with decision. "I don't think that's a very practical idea, Mrs. Hertz. I'm sure Mrs. Fowler appreciates it,
but it's very foolish to try sending packages from China
with the mails so uncertain and all. Why, I couldn't begin
to tell you all the things I know for a fact were lost that
were sent to Mr. Shaw and myself. No, the best thing,
Mrs. Fowler, is for you to let me give you some of the
incense I've got right with me."

"Oh, really," I murmured, "I couldn't think of—"

"You'd be doing me a favor to take it," Mrs. Shaw insisted. "I've got I don't know how many packages in my
trunk that Mr. Shaw was bringing to friends at home. He
was always a great hand to bring home souvenirs like that.
Last time we crossed, I remember it was perfume he decided on. Honestly, we must've had dozens of little bottles.
But, my goodness, I wouldn't know what to do with all

those packages of incense, and you might just as well have some of it, seeing that you're so fond of the stuff. There's not a bit of use my taking it home. The folks in my church would think it was wicked. So you just let me give you a couple of packages. If you'll stop by our room after dinner—"

"Take my advice, Mrs. Fowler," Mr. Brande was drawn into the general concern, "and don't touch any of this Chinese stuff. Not meaning to slight your—ah, late husband's judgment, Mrs. Shaw, but the native product is distinctly inferior. If you care about getting the real thing, Mrs. Fowler, you go straight to that importer in San Francisco. I'll be glad to give you my personal card of introduction, if you like."

"You're all so very kind," I said, "but really, it doesn't matter particularly. I only happened to think of incense, I don't quite know why—" I paused, not wishing to seem too ungrateful for all their offers, and before I could think of any way to lead the conversation away from the whole cursed subject, I heard a step behind me and turned to see that Timothy had arrived.

"Well—" He sat down beside me and unfolded his napkin. "Am I too late for the regular dinner, and if so, will some of you be good enough to collect me a plate of scraps?" His voice was rather overly cheerful, but his eyes looked distrait and a little weary, and I observed that he had not stopped to change for dinner. He smiled as he saw the plate of dinner which Sally had, as usual, garnered for Haile Selassie. "I see the pooch got ahead of me in the scraps racket," Timothy bent over the menu which the steward reluctantly produced, and it seemed to me that he was pretty pointedly avoiding Sally Covell's fixed glance.

But Sally was not to be put off. She leaned across the table. "Timothy—you didn't happen to see Ned, did you?"

Timothy frowned at his menu. "Nope."

"I was just wondering," Sally said, "how long that game is going to last. If he doesn't come down soon, he'll miss his dinner."

"Perhaps he's having something to eat upstairs," Timothy suggested.

"But after all," she said, "a game can't go on forever, can it, Timothy?"

"That depends on who's winning."

"I'm afraid," Sally sighed, "that Ned's not awfully good at games. You don't suppose he's being cheated, do you Timothy?"

Timothy put down the menu and looked steadily into the girl's eager eyes. "I wouldn't know, Sally," he said, and turned to give his order to the steward.

After the others had left the table, I waited for Timothy to finish eating. When we were alone, I turned to him at once.

"For heaven's sake, Timothy, what's the idea of keeping up all this hocus-pocus? Ned mysteriously shut up in the Captain's office—and poor Sally on pins and needles—"

Timothy laid down his knife and fork and faced me seriously. "Listen," he said, "I think it's very sweet and quite touching of you to stand up for Ned and Sally so loyally. But it's getting just the least little bit monotonous. Now I'll tell you, as graphically as I can, what this is all about. I'm sorry I can't accompany the speech with colored slides, but if you listen attentively, I think you'll catch the drift. Point one is that Ned Covell does know something about the hanky-panky that's been going on around this ship.

Point two is that he doesn't want me to know what he knows. So—in order not to tell me the truth, he makes up a fake confession to the whole business, murder and all, and tells a story so obviously full of holes that he knows damn well that no one but the Captain could possibly believe it. Now—if I admit to Ned and the doughty skipper that the confession is a dud, there's nothing to do but let little Neddy go free. Which would please you, no doubt, but would scarcely be serving the gods of justice as is my bounden duty. Therefore, I take the only alternative which my dim wits allow me, and keep Ned shut up on the ground that I have accepted his story. That makes the Captain happy as a lark to think we've caught our criminal so promptly, and it gives me a chance to look around and try to make a better guess next time. Meanwhile, our Ned will have the sweet bliss of solitude and reflection, and he *may* come to the conclusion that honesty pays, after all. If he *does* come clean with whatever his part in the doings really was, so much the better for us all. And if he doesn't—then no harm has been done, apart from a bit of ladylike nail-biting on the part of Sally and yourself. Now, have I made myself clear?"

"Crystal clear, Inspector."

"And do you, by any chance, approve of the idea?"

I sighed. "I think it sounds a little cock-eyed, but I've learned from past experience that when you seem to be wandering in your mind, you sometimes turn out later to be right."

"Well," Timothy smiled, "I shouldn't call that exactly base flattery, my pet, but I *am* grateful." He buttered a piece of roll and gazed at it reflectively. "As a matter of fact," he said suddenly, "it all comes down to just three questions."

"What comes down?"

"The whole business. If we just knew those three answers, we'd know everything. One: who knew that Shaw was taking insulin injections?"

"I can answer that one," I said. "Dr. Sloane knew."

"Two: who knew that Shaw had that ivory paperknife?"

"I can answer that one, too. Dr. Sloane did. He said so himself."

"Three: what, if anything, has the damned amber necklace got to do with it?"

"That one stumps me," I admitted. "But I don't exactly see where Ned Covell fits in on any of the questions."

"He fits in all right," Timothy put down his napkin and stood up, "and I *think* I see where. But I'd rather not commit myself until I'm sure I'm right—except to say that I'm pretty darn sure Ned tried to do one thing, and suddenly discovered he'd bitten off more than he could chew. There's quite a gap between a little larceny—and murder."

We left the deserted dining room and went toward the lounge. In the doorway, Timothy paused to light a cigarette for me and one for himself.

"Larceny's stealing, isn't it?" I asked.

"In a nice way, yes."

"Then you mean Ned was trying to steal the necklace?"

"Well, unless he was planning to steal Mrs. Hertz's virtue, I can't think why else he was in her stateroom Monday night."

"I don't believe he *was* there," I said flatly.

"All right then, suppose we ask Sally. She's over there watching a bridge game right now."

"Oh, Timothy, you can't—" I put out my hand to stop him, but it was too late. He had caught Sally's eye and signaled her to come over. In horrified silence I watched while Sally, looking the very picture of unsuspecting inno-cence, approached us with a smile.

"Hello," she said. "Were you waving at me, Timothy?"

I would have plunged into the breach with some neu-tral topic if I could have managed it quickly enough, but Timothy gave me no chance.

"I wanted to ask you something, Sally," he said. "Was Ned particularly interested in the string of amber beads that Mrs. Hertz had?"

I needed only one look at Sally's stricken face to know that Timothy had hit something near the truth. She glanced from Timothy to me and back again with piti-ful confusion. She opened her mouth to speak and closed it again without having uttered a sound. Then she took another breath and tried once more.

"Did he—" she began, "did Ned—"

Timothy took pity on her. "Ned wouldn't tell me him-self," he said, "but I think you realize that it would be a whole lot healthier for him to admit he was after the neck-lace than to stick to the story he did tell me."

"What did Ned say, Timothy?"

Timothy told her. Sally's face went very white, but she lifted her chin bravely. "That's not true, Timothy," she said evenly. "Ned never killed anyone. He didn't even mean to hurt anyone when he—" She stopped short and bit her lip.

"When he went to Mr. Norman's room?" Timothy prompted her gently.

Sally nodded. "But you can't do anything to him," she hurried on, "because he didn't even see the beads. And he's never done anything like that before. He'd never have done this only we needed money so terribly. You see, Ned didn't tell me how poor we really were, and I'd been spending a lot of money for clothes and things. I'd *never* have done it if I'd known Ned couldn't pay for them. I wish now I'd never even *seen* these horrible old dresses," she held up a fold of her lovely yellow frock and flung it aside bitterly. "Just because Ned had plenty of money when we were married, and I liked to buy pretty things, he thought that was all I cared about. Why—I'd take all the clothes in the world and throw them over that rail into the sea before I'd hurt Ned, but he didn't tell me how things were until—too late—" Her voice broke, and she covered her face with her hands.

"Steady, Sally," Timothy patted her shoulder soothingly. The scene was getting a bit too strong for a public lounge, and he signaled to me to take her other arm. Together we guided Sally out into the corridor and up the stairs to our stateroom. When we were safely inside and the door closed, the girl sank down on the edge of the bed and stared at Timothy with dull eyes.

"You see," she said slowly, "it's really all my fault that Ned ever had this trouble. But I didn't know about it— not until last night when I found Ned so upset. And the reason that business about Mr. Brande frightened him so awfully was because Ned *was* mixed up somehow with the necklace. He told me last night that the reason we'd taken this trip to the Orient was because we were so dreadfully in debt at home that he had to get out of the country. He managed to borrow just enough money for our round-trip fares. He said he was sure something would break for him while we were traveling, and sure enough, he said he'd struck what he thought was a great opportunity."

"What was the great opportunity, Sally?"

"I—I don't know," she shook her head. "That was the one thing Ned wouldn't tell me. I thought at first he meant something about gambling. We have picked up quite a bit

here and there playing bridge, just because we've always
happened to play a fairly good game. I thought we only
played in fun until Ned told me that money was what we'd
been living on. But this big scheme didn't have anything
to do with gambling, Ned said. And that was all he'd tell
me."

Timothy bent down until he was looking straight into
Sally's eyes. "You're quite certain," he said, "that's all Ned
told you?"

Sally stared straight back for a moment. Then she
frowned a little and shook her head. "Only," she said, "just
one other thing. I didn't understand what it meant, and
maybe it doesn't mean anything. But just when Ned was
feeling the worst last night, and I was getting him a drink,
he was sitting on the bed and sort of—well, talking to
himself. And all of a sudden I heard him say, 'My God—if
only I'd never laid eyes on that damn psalm-singing Shaw.'
That was all he said, Timothy, and I still don't know what
he meant by it."

"Did you ask him?"

"Oh—yes."

"And what did he say?"

Sally closed her eyes wearily. "He told me he'd never
said any such thing. But he *did*, Timothy. I *heard* him."

# 16

## A PACKAGE OF INCENSE

It took Timothy more than an hour to get the story from
Ned himself. When he came back from the Captain's room,
I was waiting in the stateroom alone. Sally had gone off,
rather forlornly, some time before, to wash her face and
powder her nose. "So that Ned won't know I've been snif-
fling when he sees me," she had said.

Timothy stretched himself out on the bed.

"Well," I went over and sat down beside him, "did you
get your story?"

Timothy nodded. "It was a cinch," he said, "the minute I told Ned that Sally had spilled the beans, he came
out with the whole works, and something else besides. In
fact," he wadded up a pillow and leaned back against it,
"I know practically everything now except who killed old
Norman and who killed Shaw, and why. Which is what I
started to find out in the first place."

"Never mind," I said, "you're making progress anyway."

"Rapidly," Timothy said, "in every direction but the
right one. What Ned explained was the tie-up between
himself and the amber necklace. Damned interesting
story, but it doesn't seem to include any plans for murder.
It seems that while Ned was in Shanghai, still hoping for

that lucky break which was going to keep the wolf away from Sally's door, he went to a bar one afternoon and fell into conversation with a parson, of all people. And the parson was—"

"Not Mr. Shaw—"

"None other," Timothy nodded gravely. "After they exchanged remarks about the weather, and Shaw had explained his presence in such a sink of iniquity by saying that he was the barkeep's spiritual adviser, they progressed to more serious matters, and the parson got chummy and told Ned an amazing story. I gathered that Ned had had a few more drinks than were strictly necessary, and the chances are that he'd let slip the fact that he was getting pretty desperate about locating the lucky break that was going to save his precarious financial life. Probably Ned gave the very distinct impression of a man who would do damn near anything to make some money and make it quick.

"Anyway, whatever the provocation, Shaw decided to let Ned in on the big secret, and offered to pay him handsomely for doing a bit of business for him. The point of the proposition, which Shaw finally got to, after a couple more drinks for Ned and a slug of ginger-ale for himself, was simply the fact that he, Shaw, in addition to being a bringer of light, was a U. S. Government agent—and had been for some years. At this juncture, Shaw flashed a badge at Ned and took out a handful of impressive-looking credentials to prove his point. Ned, poor lad, was all too ready to believe each and every word. Shaw's particular province, he said, was catching up on smugglers, and as a missionary he had excellent opportunities for picking up tips, et cetera, while mingling with the lower classes in bars, opium dens and other haunts of vice.

"Now, Shaw said, he was at this very moment on the point of making the biggest catch of his career. He had been summoned on this very day to this very saloon, by the barkeep who was one of his henchmen, posted to listen for suspicious bits of conversation among his customers. The barkeep had told Shaw that he'd overheard two men talking about a certain piece of jewelry which they were planning to take into the United States without letting the customs in on the secret. The item in question was an amber necklace, and it was to be carried by a man who would sail from Shanghai on the *S.S. Orion,* under the name of Samuel Norman. That was the tip, and Shaw was all set for the catch—but for one serious fly in the ointment.

"At this point he hitched his chair closer to Ned and lowered his voice. 'The one thing I need,' he said, 'is a man to carry out the job for me. A man I can trust—who will be ready to sail on the *Orion* in three days.' Shaw went on to explain that the chap who usually did this sort of a job for him had been taken to the hospital with acute appendicitis, and operated on the night before. So that, said Shaw, left him high and dry with a hot tip and no one to carry it out for him."

"Why didn't he go to the American Consul and get someone?" I demanded.

"An excellent question," Timothy nodded. "And Ned, be it said to his credit, asked the very same thing. But Shaw was ready with an answer. He said that he'd already been, and the Consul couldn't possibly send anyone on such short notice. Then, said Ned, why didn't Shaw go himself? To which Shaw replied that was exactly what he intended to do—*but* he must absolutely have someone with him, someone who was in his confidence, otherwise he couldn't hope to pull off such a big, and also such a tricky job."

"Excuse me," I interrupted once more. "No doubt I'm ignorant, but just *why* should an amber necklace be worth all this trouble? As Mrs. Hertz said herself, the night she got the beads, amber *can't* be so terribly valuable."

"Ned thought of that, too," said Timothy, "and again Shaw was ready for him. He explained that this was a very special amber necklace, a collector's item, in fact, and was worth a hell of a lot of money. As you may or may not be aware, the customs business is conducted on commission basis. In other words, the bright person who tattles on a smuggler gets a fat percentage cut from the fine that's slapped on the smuggler. And the fine sometimes goes as high as twice the value of the article in question. Hence Shaw was dealing in pretty high stakes, and he only had to mention the probable size of the commission to dazzle our Ned.

"The long and short of it was that Ned agreed to go in on the proposition, and Shaw laid down a nice little hundred dollar bill to clinch the bargain. That gave Ned enough to settle his hotel bill, and he took passage at once for himself and Sally on the *Orion*. He was to meet Shaw the next day to settle the details of the plan, and that was that."

Timothy paused to reach across me for a pack of Chesterfields, then he fumbled in his pockets for a match, gave the pillow beneath his head a violent plumping, and settled down to continue the story.

"The plans, at the time Ned and Shaw boarded ship, came briefly to this: They were not, of course, to give the slightest indication of knowing each other at any time during the voyage. Their first object was to spot the man traveling as Norman, which they did. The second point was to maneuver an acquaintance, preferably by being placed at the same table in the dining room. The third, and most important thing was to make absolutely certain that Norman had the necklace with him. More than that, it was necessary that the beads should actually be *seen* in the old gentleman's possession. That took a bit of strategy —but Shaw planned it carefully—"

"Wait a minute," I said. "I don't get this business about the necessity of seeing the necklace. After all, if Mr. Shaw was so sure that Norman had the beads with him, what difference did it make whether they were seen or not?"

"Because, my pet," said Timothy, "Shaw had carefully impressed Ned with the fact that he must witness the beads *in the possession of Norman* in order to claim his reward at the customs."

"I still don't get it," I protested again. "If Norman had the necklace with him at the time he smuggled it in, should think that would prove his possession of it beyond any doubt."

"And so it would," Timothy nodded. *"But*—the point was that Norman had no intention of taking the beads into the country himself. And Shaw was smart enough to foresee that dodge." He paused a moment for the meaning to sink in upon me.

"Did Mr. Norman have an accomplice, then?"

"Right the first time."

I thought for a minute. "Someone on this boat?"

"Correct."

"But, Timothy—*who?*"

He gave me an odd look. "I'll give you three guesses and a hint," he said. "Who's the person who radiates so much honest conversation and good will that not even a customs inspector could possibly suspect her of evil intentions?"

"*Her* intentions?" I echoed in amazement. And then: "Oh, Timothy—you don't mean—you *can't* mean—?"

"But I do," said Timothy calmly. "The accomplice of Mr. Norman's selection was none other than Mrs. Gideon Hertz of Paterson, New Jersey."

I stared in astonishment.

"And your open mouth, my dear," Timothy went on, "just goes to show what an excellent picker Mr. Norman was. No one, as your expression so plainly indicates, would ever suspect Mrs. Hertz of being a smuggler—nor would they have any reason to suppose she would even own any jewels of particular value."

"I simply can't believe," I shook my head, "that Mrs. Hertz would enter into any such scheme."

"Well, to put you out of suspense," said Timothy, "I don't believe she did enter into it knowingly. Old Norman was too clever to try anything like that. What he intended was that Mrs. Hertz should bring the necklace through the customs as her own possession. You see how simple it really is. During the course of the voyage he forms a friendship with a lady of no particular means, and with an obviously and impressively honest front—profound apologies for the pun—and he makes her a present of the necklace. She takes it through the customs, probably declaring it at a nominal value, and lo—the dirty deed is accomplished, and the necklace is safely into the United States."

"Yes, but what good does that do Mr. Norman? I mean, if the beads belong to Mrs. Hertz?"

"Quite simple, my pet. Norman lets a few weeks pass, during which Mrs. Hertz has the pleasure of owning and showing off her trophy, and then he sends an agent to the Hertz dwelling in Paterson, New Jersey. The agent, ostensibly acting for some firm of jewelers, offers Mrs. Hertz a tidy sum, spot cash, to purchase the necklace. He then returns the beads to Mr. Norman, who adds them to the rest of his priceless collection—and there you are."

"Well—but suppose Mrs. Hertz refused to sell the necklace?"

Timothy lifted his eyebrows. "If Mrs. Hertz were actually so benighted as to refuse, say, a thousand dollars in cash in these dark dog days, do you think for one moment that *Mr.* Gideon Hertz would permit such folly?"

"I suppose not," I admitted. "But look—suppose Mrs. Hertz didn't have the necklace when the agent came? Suppose she'd lost it, or sold it to someone else—or even given it away, as she actually did?"

"Presumably," said Timothy, "Mr. Norman was willing to run that risk. He was a gambler by nature—that much is evident from this whole crazy plan of his. Crazy—but clever. He liked to run risks, you see, he liked to plot and plan and be complicated—"

"Wait a minute," I broke in suddenly. "You've forgotten to mention whether, in the light of all these new revelations, you still think that Norman *was* J. T. Ezry."

"I'm just as sure as I ever was," Timothy nodded.

"Well, then, for heaven's sake, what was the point of such an absurdly complicated scheme to avoid paying duty on the necklace? Even if the duty was plenty high, it would have been only pin money to Mr. Ezry—that is, if the stories about his fabulous wealth are even a quarter true."

"I guess they're true enough," Timothy said, "but that doesn't make it impossible that the old man would go to a hell of a lot of trouble to avoid paying duty on his imported knicknacks. Strange as it may seem, rich men are not always noted for their patriotism, nor for their devotion to the laws of the land. As a matter of fact, some of the cleverest and most persistent smugglers have been, and still are, people so rich that the customs duties would never have been missed from their personal checking accounts. I remember seeing a certain plump gentleman down at the docks in New York one icy cold day, arguing for fully three-quarters of an hour with a customs inspector over the value of a tortoise shell cigarette case which the inspector said must have cost at least two hundred and fifty dollars. The man had declared it at six shillings, and he was sticking to his story if the North River froze over—and it damn near did. Afterward the inspector told me the man was wearing cufflinks made of four pigeon blood rubies that were worth about fifty thousand apiece, and that he could have bought and sold the whole French Line, if he'd felt like it. But my whole point is this. The fact that Norman was J. T. Ezry, and therefore lousy with money, does not, *in itself,* prove that he wouldn't go all around Robin Hood's barn *and* garage to keep from paying the duty he owed."

"All right," I murmured when Timothy stopped for breath. "I'm convinced."

"Now then—to get back to Ned's story. The plan that Shaw evolved for getting Ned into Mr. Norman's room was, briefly, this: Ned was to go to the old gentleman's cabin at five-thirty on the first afternoon after we sailed, and ask Mr. Norman's opinion of a certain article which he, Ned, had ostensibly bought during his stay in Shanghai. And the souvenir in question was to be none other than a carved ivory paper knife, loaned to Ned by Mr. Shaw, for the occasion. The knife was unusual—and probably fairly valuable—so it was pretty certain to interest anyone with a collector's turn of mind. Then—while Ned

and Mr. Norman were discussing the knife Shaw promised
to send a steward to the door with a message saying that
the radio operator had an urgent wireless phone call for
Mr. Norman. And while the old gentleman went up to
take the call—Ned would have a chance to look around his
room and spot the necklace. And that would be that.

"Well, at a few minutes before five-thirty, Ned, true to
his word, left his bridge game, collected the paper knife
from Shaw, and went to Norman's room, with the knife
safely in hand. But things didn't work out as he had expected—quite. The first thing that happened was that Mr.
Norman failed to answer his knock. And the second thing
was that Ned found the door unlatched and slightly open.
After a few moments' wait, Ned decided to have a look for
the necklace, anyway. So he pushed in the door, and the
next thing he knew, Ned found himself inside Norman's
room—and Norman lying stretched out on the floor, dead
as a doornail."

"Good Lord, Timothy—" I leaned forward in astonishment. "Is this really true?"

"And just to complete the picture," Timothy went on,
"there was the fact that Norman had died from a crack on
the head—and Ned was standing beside him, holding an
ivory knife with a handle heavy enough to have done the
job—*and on that handle a couple of bloodstains.*"

"What *did* Ned do?"

"Well—" Timothy shrugged, "he just stood there a
minute, taking in the situation—and then he did the only
thing he could do under the circumstances. He turned
around and got out of the room just as fast as he could.
But bad luck was still with him. Just as he opened the door
into the hall, he came face to face with Nicholas Brande."

*"Mr. Brande?"*

Timothy nodded. "And it didn't take Brande more than one look at Ned's face to see that something pretty bad had happened. Ned thought fast, and realized that now he was framed for fair. It was only a matter of time before Mr. Norman's death would be discovered—and here was a witness who could testify that he saw Ned Covell leaving the dead man's room—with a face as white as a sheet—and carrying a heavy-handled ivory knife in his hand." Timothy took a long breath. "And so—again Ned did the only thing he could do. He took the long chance and told Brande what he'd just seen inside Norman's room. Fortunately for Ned, Mr. Brande didn't seem to require many explanations. Quite the opposite, in fact. Before Ned knew what was happening, Brande had the situation in hand. He took the knife from Ned, told him to wait upstairs in the bar, and without further ado, disappeared into Norman's room and shut the door."

"And then what did Ned do?"

"Went to the bar, just as he'd been told. After a couple of drinks his hand stopped shaking and he began to feel a little bit better. He didn't know, of course, what Brande was going to do—but, Ned supposed that he would take the proper steps—notify the Captain and the doctor of what had happened to Norman, and so on. Well—" Timothy smiled slightly, "that's where Ned was wrong. Whet Brande appeared, after about fifteen minutes, he had just two things to say to Ned. The first was that Ned was not, under any circumstances, to let anyone know either of them had been to Norman's room—and the second was that Ned must deliver a certain note to the door of Mrs. Gideon Hertz's stateroom at once. The sealed note which Brande handed over was, apparently, the well-known invitation asking Mrs. Hertz to have cocktails with a dead man. Ned tried to argue a bit at first. Said he didn't think they were exactly proceeding along cricket lines—but, as you may imagine, it didn't take long for Brande to talk him out of that idea."

"I certainly can imagine it," I nodded feelingly.

"Brande simply said," Timothy went on, "that if Ned did as he was told—and said nothing—that everything would be all right. But otherwise, he wouldn't answer for the consequences. And so—Neddy did as he was told. He put the note under Mrs. Hertz's door, and said nothing to anyone—and for a few days, everything *was* all right."

"And then—?"

"And then, Tuesday night, at about midnight, as you may recall, the Reverend Shaw was found dead in Mrs. Hertz's cabin."

"I recall it, all right. But what did that have to do with Ned?"

"Just this," said Timothy. "On that same Tuesday evening, Brande had come to Ned with a proposition. He said he understood from Sally that Ned wouldn't be averse to turning a few honest pennies—and it just happened that he had a job open in his importing business for a man who could do what he was told. That part was all right—but when Brande went on to say that the particular bit of importing he was interested in at the moment concerned an amber necklace—our Ned began to smell a large and rather alarming plant. So, before hearing the rest of the proposition, he said no thank you very much. But that, strangely enough, did *not* end the matter. Very delicately, but firmly, Mr. Brande pointed out that he knew certain things about Ned's whereabouts on the afternoon of Norman's death which would not be altogether healthy for

Ned—and he went on to say that he *would* greatly appreciate Ned's help in the matter at hand."

"Tut, Timothy—that was plain blackmail—"

"Quite so, my girl," Timothy nodded. "But just being able to call it blackmail didn't help Ned a great deal at the moment. He had a choice between two things—and neither of them was a bit pretty—so he chose to take Brande up on the job. And then he got his orders. It seemed that Brande was very keen on the necklace Mrs. Hertz had inherited—"

"Good Heavens—don't tell me Mr. Brande was after it, too!"

"Well—not in so many words," Timothy said. "He told Ned that he was simply interested in the thing from an impersonal point of view. Said he was rather a fancier of jewels and so on, and that he had a notion the beads were more valuable than you might suppose. As a matter of fact, Brande said he wanted to make Mrs. Hertz an offer to buy the necklace, but *not* until he'd had a chance to look at it first—and that was where he needed Ned's help. All Ned had to do was to keep a look-out that night while Brande got the beads from Mrs. Hertz's room and gave them the once-over—and in the end Ned agreed to do it. But the more Ned thought over his position, the less he liked it. Here he was, supposedly helping the Reverend Shaw as a Government agent, and at the same time agreeing to help Brande in what looked like a fairly shady bit of business. The upshot of Ned's reflection was that it would be healthier to stick on the side of the law. So later that evening, Ned took his chance and tipped off Shaw to the fact that Brande would be in Mrs. Hertz's room at a few minutes before midnight—just to have a look at the necklace. That was all Shaw needed. He told Ned to go to bed and forget

the whole business—and that he'd handle everything himself. Well—you know, and I know, what happened next.
Ned went to bed all right, but when he woke up the next
morning he found out that Shaw was dead. And *then* Ned
thought he saw things clearly at last. Brande had been up to
dirty work in Mrs. Hertz's room, and when Shaw popped in
on him, Brande had killed him. And that left Ned in the
prettiest spot he'd been in yet. His ally, Shaw, was dead—
and *the man that Ned had double-crossed had turned out to
be not a probable thief and a blackmailer, but a murderer—*"

"But Timothy—how *could* Mr. Brande have murdered
Shaw? If it was insulin poisoning that killed him, and the
doctor gave the injection—"

Timothy sighed. "That, my dear, is precisely the point
I'm trying to put across. Of course Brande didn't murder
the Reverend Shaw that night in Mrs. Hertz's room. If
only he *had,* things might be a hell of a lot simpler for
me. I'm only telling you what Ned *thought* had happened.
Actually, I don't know any more about who fixed that insulin dose than I did Tuesday night. But Ned was scared
damned near out of his wits. He didn't know just what
to expect from Brande—but he waited, and waited—and
nothing happened at all. Then Sally, bless her heart, decided to interfere with her idea of getting Ned a job with
Brande—and before Ned could think of any way to stop
her, short of telling her the whole truth—she came out
with the fact that she'd told me that Ned was going to tie
up with Brande and that I thought it was a swell idea. Ned
knew that I was some sort of a cop— and that was when
Ned hit the ceiling—and he didn't come down again until
about an hour ago when he finished telling me the whole
story. He'd have saved himself and me a lot of trouble
if he'd only taken me to his bosom earlier—but he was

absolutely certain that Brande would somehow hang every-thing on him and he had some crazy notion that I wouldn't believe him. As a matter of fact—" Timothy paused.

"You *do* believe it?"

"Somehow or other," said Timothy slowly, "I do. It's a fantastic yarn, God knows, and I still don't know what it's all about—but you know my weakness for believing the impossible. Anyway, I'm letting Ned's story stand until I find a better one."

"I take it then, that you let him go with your blessing?"

Timothy got up off the bed and stretched his arms. "Something like that," he said, "only I don't remember any blessing. And now don't sit there with that idiotic expression on your face. I let Ned go for two reasons. One, because on shipboard he can't go far. Two, because I'm probably a damned fool. But your being soft on the lad had nothing whatever to do with it."

"Of course not," I murmured politely. "It's doubtless the effect of the sea air, or your long years of grinding service in the cause of justice that are responsible for this amazing crack-up. Whatever the cause, I think it was very sweet of you."

Timothy made a face at me over his shoulder. "So now what do we do with what's left of the evening?" he in-quired. "Go up and dance awhile? Or settle down to a nice quiet game of cat's cradle?"

"Personally, I'm a bit sleepy." I strangled a yawn.

"Me, too, come to think of it," Timothy stretched again. "I've got to go upstairs and send a radio message, and after that—"

"What radio message do you have to send?" I paused in the act of taking off my jacket.

"Oh—nothing much. Only I thought maybe the United States Government might be interested in learning of the death of their faithful servant, the Reverend Asa Shaw."

"Well—" I unfastened my earrings and swallowed another yawn, "don't forget to hurry back. We ought to think up our costumes for the party Saturday night."

"What party?" Timothy turned back from the door.

"I forgot to tell you, Mrs. Hertz came in while you were with Ned and brought me the news. She was in quite a dither about it, and wanted to know whether I thought she should go as Portia or the Goddess of Liberty. I didn't exactly like to encourage either. It seems the Captain told her he was especially anxious to have the party a big success—so that everyone would sort of forget the more unfortunate occurrences of the voyage."

"I can understand that all right," said Timothy dryly. "I suppose you promised her we'd both go?"

"Well, I didn't quite promise, but she's very anxious for you to go as Mahatma Gandhi. She offered to make your costume out of two Turkish towels."

"I should have thought one was enough."

"Oh, and she brought me this, too." I went over to the dresser. "A package of incense from Mrs. Shaw." I held up the box, and Timothy glanced at it.

"What do you want incense for?" he demanded.

"Well, I don't really—but the subject came up somehow at dinner, and Mrs. Shaw offered to give me a package." I looked at the box in my hand and sniffed the pungent, spicy smell. "As a matter of fact, I hate the stuff."

"Chuck it out of the porthole then," Timothy suggested. "It'll give some unsuspecting fish a fine case of indigestion." Then, just as I was about to obey, he stopped me.

"Wait a minute—why not give it to the stewardess? I'll bet she likes to take home souvenirs to the kiddies."

"All right," I said. I turned back from the porthole, laid the box of incense in the top of my suitcase.

The next moment I yawned once more—and this time I made no effort to stifle it.

# 17
## A DRESDEN SHEPHERDESS

The greater part of the next two days, Friday and Saturday, were given over to preparations for the party. It developed that the Captain had decided to combine the traditional ship's concert with the masque ball, so the occasion was to be definitely gala.

I don't think any of our group at the doctor's table felt particularly gala, except for Mrs. Hertz. But she threw herself into the thing with such spirit that by lunch time Saturday, we were all discussing the matter of costumes with surprising intensity. Mrs. Hertz herself had suddenly switched her plan of disguise, owing to the fact that she had been induced to sing a solo as a part of the entertainment. After a good deal of agitation, she decided on a Dresden Shepherdess as an appropriate costume for her Performance—and with that decision out of the way, she could give her attention to the rest of us. The high point of her inspiration was reached when she told Mr. Brande he really ought to appear as Dr. Dafoe with the quintuplets in tow—a suggestion which he quite unexpectedly accepted.

During the afternoon, while the costumes were actually being evolved, there was a great deal of going about to each other's staterooms, in order to lend advice, assistance, and various items of apparel. I spent most of the time up on B Deck with Mrs. Shaw and Mrs. Hertz. For one thing, their stateroom was the only one large enough to serve as a fitting room, and for another, Mrs. Hertz's ideas of a Dresden Shepherdess were so elaborate that it required the ingenuity of Mrs. Shaw and myself, and our full time, working at top speed, to carry out her plans.

I think it must have been about four o'clock when Mr. Brande surprised us by coming to the door and asking to speak with me. Only a minute before, Sally and Ned—in the most excellent of spirits since Ned's release the night before—had dashed in to return three palm leaf fans to Mrs. Shaw, and ask for one of Mrs. Hertz's dresses instead. It seemed that they had changed their plans, and instead of going as a pair of tropical Sally Rands, with palm leaf fans, they planned to impersonate Siamese Twins—both of them to be enveloped in one of Mrs. Hertz's ample skirts. After they had gone, Mrs. Shaw and I resumed the business of cutting and pinning a pink satin slip to form the foundation of the shepherdess dress, but we had scarcely knelt down to adjust the hem when there came a second tap at the door.

"Oh, *dear.*" Mrs. Hertz reached for her flowered kimono and wrapped it modestly about her. "What can those children want now?"

"Come in," Mrs. Shaw spoke through a mouthful of pins, and the next moment she very nearly swallowed them as the door swung open and revealed Mr. Brande, composed and elegant as always, on the threshold.

"Well— I—" Mrs. Hertz gathered her kimono more closely around her, and reached up to pat her hair into place. "This is a surprise, Mr. Brande. I do hope you'll

excuse us— I'm afraid we weren't quite expecting a caller—" She laughed a little nervously, while Mrs. Shaw
scrambled to her feet and managed to transfer the pins
safely from her mouth to the tomato pincushion.

Mr. Brande bowed ever so slightly, and smiled. "It's I
who should be excused," he raised a deprecating hand, "for
intruding this way. But I was told that I might find Mrs.
Fowler here—" He paused and looked at me.

"Well—yes," said Mrs. Hertz rather unnecessarily,
"she's right here. Won't you come in, Mr. Brande, and—
and sit down?"

"Thank you, no," he shook his head gently. "But if I
might have just a few moments of Mrs. Fowler's time?"

"Of course." I handed scissors and tape measure to Mrs.
Shaw, and rose. "I'll be back shortly, Mrs. Hertz, and we
can finish your costume in no time."

As I went toward the door, Mr. Brande explained with a
slight laugh. "A little costume trouble, you know. I'm not
quite so adept with needle and thread as I might be, but I'm
sure Mrs. Fowler can help me out of the difficulty in a trice."

There was a moment's silence, then Mrs. Shaw spoke
just as the door closed. "Well, yes," she said flatly, "I'm
sure she can help you, Mr. Brande."

Out in the hall, Mr. Brande turned to me. "You won't
mind if we go to your stateroom instead of mine?" he
asked. "I think we're a bit nearer."

"Right down these steps and around the corner," I nodded. "The first door to your left." I could well imagine
why Mr. Brande preferred not having me see his quarters.

Once inside the cabin, Mr. Brande made a rather feeble
pretense at consulting me about the matter of his costume.
And then, quite suddenly, he faced me and came to the
point.

"Mrs. Fowler," he said, "no doubt you think this is strange of me—but I had to see you alone—right away." There was an odd note of urgency in his usually suave tone. "It's—ah, just a bit difficult to explain—" Mr. Brande brushed one slim hand back over his clipped gray hair, "but the point is, Mrs. Fowler, quite frankly, I'm alarmed."

"Well—I'm sorry," I murmured. It was all I could think of at the moment.

"You see, it all came about quite suddenly—when I went to the doctor's cabin a few minutes ago to borrow one of his surgical gowns for a costume. You may recall that Mrs. Hertz asked me to appear as Dr. Dafoe tonight? I consented, although it was quite absurd of me," he laughed apologetically. "But no matter about that. What alarmed me was something that Dr. Sloane said. While he was getting the surgeon's gown, I happened to notice an ivory knife lying on his desk. I—I wondered how it came to be in the doctor's room—and I made some comment about it, quite casually, I assure you. To my amazement, Dr. Sloane turned on me with the most ridiculous accusation. He said—I hope you'll excuse my quoting his words, Mrs. Fowler—he said: 'You've got a hell of a nerve pretending you've never seen that knife before, Brande. You know damn well that Mr. Norman was killed with the handle of it, and that you tried to get rid of the thing by pawning it off on the Captain.' I did my best to explain to the doctor that I hadn't the vaguest idea what he was talking about— but he quite refused to listen. He simply said: 'I'm warning you, Brande, for your own good, that Inspector Fowler knows exactly what you did—and if you know what's good for you, you'll make your explanations to him and not waste breath on me.' And with that he handed me the gown, and literally shut the door in my face. Of course, I came straight to you, Mrs. Fowler. I hope you'll excuse my troubling you—but after all, such a serious charge—" He paused to draw the linen handkerchief from his pocket and pass it delicately across his brow.

"I'm afraid I don't quite see why you should come to me, Mr. Brande," I said, "if it's my husband you want to talk to."

"No—that's just it, Mrs. Fowler," he shook his head. "I—please forgive me—but I *don't* want to talk with your husband. It's rather difficult for me to say this, but the fact is that your husband might not understand my predicament. I've no doubt he's a very clever detective, but sometimes detectives take a most unfortunate attitude toward innocent persons. Or at least," he added hastily, "I've always heard that they do. Particularly in America."

"You're quite mistaken about that, Mr. Brande," I said firmly. "Timothy is entirely reasonable, and if you tell him your story frankly, I'm sure you won't have the slightest difficulty."

"All the same," Mr. Brande insisted, "I do wish you'd do me a good turn and explain to him for me that I had absolutely no knowledge of this dreadful business. I expect it's very foolish of me, but the very thought of being interviewed by the police quite paralyzes me."

"I think you're being a little over-sensitive, Mr. Brande. If you care to have my advice, I assure you that the only thing for you to do is to go straight to Timothy with the whole story. I really haven't the least authority in this matter, you know—and if I did tell Timothy what you've told me—he'd want to talk to you anyway." I made my tone as final as I could, but it took more than finality to discourage Nicholas Brande.

"I do indeed appreciate your advice, Mrs. Fowler. But I wonder—I'm not altogether certain you realize the seriousness of my position. You see, this whole incident goes back to the evening Mr. Norman was—eh—" he coughed delicately, "met with his unfortunate accident. On that evening, when I happened to go to my room shortly after dinner, I discovered a most extraordinary thing. Lying on my bed was this same carved ivory knife. I hadn't the remotest idea how it came to be there, so I rang for the steward and asked if he could explain the matter. He couldn't—and I was left thoroughly puzzled. I wasn't in the least alarmed, however, until I examined the knife more closely, and discovered that on the handle there were—"

"Several small bloodstains," I said.

"Why—yes," Mr. Brande looked startled. "At least, I supposed they were bloodstains, although I assure you I have no experience in such matters. But how did you know?"

"Timothy found the knife in the Captain's room, and the Captain explained that you had given it to him."

"Eh—yes. Yes, quite," said Mr. Brande. A very faint color stained his usually pale face. It was as near, I imagine, as the suave Nicholas Brande ever came to blushing.

"And you told Timothy later," I went on, "that you had bought the knife from Mr. Shaw because he told you he needed money."

"Yes," said Mr. Brande. "Yes, I did. And that is precisely what I wanted to explain to you. I felt that you would perhaps understand how, in a moment of confusion and alarm, one might say something that is not strictly the truth. And I ventured to hope that you might help me out of this extremely awkward predicament by explaining the matter to your excellent husband."

"I understand perfectly, Mr. Brande," I said, "and so will my excellent husband, without any explanations from me. But what I don't quite see, is how you knew that the ivory knife had actually belonged to Mr. Shaw, if, as you say, it simply appeared in your room?"

"Ah, yes," he said quickly. "I was just coming to that. It happened, you see, that Mrs. Shaw chose to confide in me about the disappearance of the knife from her husband's room. From her description, I recognized it at once—and so, when your husband questioned me, I—I'm afraid I rather lost my head. It was foolish of me to lie, but I'm so very unaccustomed to this sort of thing—and frankly, I was alarmed. Now that I see clearly what the whole thing means, I am exceedingly anxious to have your husband understand my foolhardy action."

"Oh," I said, "you *do* see clearly what it all means?"

"I'm very much afraid I do," he answered seriously. "It means simply that someone—for some unfathomable reason—is trying to implicate me in the—eh, most unfortunate series of events which have taken place during this voyage. After all—the knife being placed in my room, you see . . ."

"Yes, I see, Mr. Brande, and my advice is still the same. Go straight to Timothy and tell him the whole story." I went to the door and opened it, and turned to look directly into the man's troubled eyes. "It's your one chance, Mr. Brande," I said. "And now, if you will excuse me, I expect Mrs. Hertz is waiting for me."

For a moment Nicholas Brande said nothing. He took the fine linen handkerchief which he still held, folded it neatly, and tucked it into the breast pocket of his dark blue coat. Then he patted the handkerchief lightly, and faced me with something like his usual composure.

"Thank you so much for your patience, Mrs. Fowler, and for your excellent advice. Believe me, I shall act upon it—at once." He bowed, very slightly, from the waist, and walked quickly from the room.

For a moment after he was gone, I stood with my hand on the door-knob, looking down the empty corridor. Then I closed the door behind me, and went slowly toward the steps and up to Mrs. Hertz's cabin.

It took the rest of the afternoon, with Mrs. Shaw and me working for dear life, to complete the transformation of Mrs. Hertz into a Dresden Shepherdess—but when it was done, and we sat back on our heels to survey the results, we felt that we had indeed accomplished something. Over a simple and form-fitting pink satin slip we had built an elaborate over-skirt, with two cretonne laundry bags (stuffed with newspapers) as panniers. Around Mrs. Hertz's neck and over her bosom, we had draped a lace fissue, and her head was resplendent in a gloriously intricate white wig, made of cotton-batting and adorned with a blue satin bow and jeweled comb. Two canes, joined together and wrapped in gilt paper, formed her shepherd's crook—and the final touch, added by Sally Covell, was Haile Selassie, loaned for the occasion, and upholstered with white cotton to impersonate a lamb.

Mrs. Hertz gazed at her reflection in the mirror with radiant satisfaction. "But I just can't help wishing," she sighed, "that Mr. Hertz could see me—even though he'd probably say I looked like a darned fool. Well—I can't tell you how much I appreciate all your help—" She turned to pat my shoulder. "And now, what about your costume, child?"

"Mine's simple enough," I said. "I'm going as Aimée Semple McPherson, and all I need are a few sheets and safety pins. Oh—and a Bible. I almost forgot that."

"Oh, dear," said Mrs. Hertz. "I expect it's quite awful of me—but I *haven't* got a Bible with me. But maybe—" She turned questioningly in the direction of Mrs. Shaw.

"Why, certainly," Mrs. Shaw said at once. "I've got Mr. Shaw's Bible right here—and there isn't any reason in the world why Mrs. Fowler shouldn't borrow it."

I felt a trifle hesitant about accepting, but Mrs. Shaw quite pressed the matter.

"Of course you must take it," she handed over the rather ponderous volume. "It's a good, big one, and everyone will be sure to see it. I'm sure Mr. Shaw would have been only too glad to have you carry it—he was always such an admirer of Mrs. McPherson, you know."

"Well—if you're quite certain you don't mind, Mrs. Shaw—I'll be very careful of it."

I had barely time to get back to my room and adjust the draperies of my costume before the first gong sounded for dinner. Timothy was even later than I, but it was a simple matter for him to slip off his clothes and don the bath-towels which transformed him into a large, but convincingly thin edition of Gandhi. I was bending down to fasten his most vital bath-towel, when I thought to inquire, through a mouthful of safety-pins, whether Mr. Brande had sought him out for the interview I had advised.

"Yup," said Timothy, and screwed himself around to look over his shoulder at me. "By the way, my lass, what is it that you're supposed to represent tonight? Those sheets sort of suggest something out of Poe—but I don't exactly see the point of the volume of Holy Writ."

"Aimée Semple McPherson," I said. "I thought she'd make a good partner for you."

"I get it," Timothy nodded. "One good faith healer deserves another."

"But what I wanted to ask, before you changed the subject so adroitly, was what you thought of Mr. Brande's revelation?"

"I thought his latest story of how he came to get the ivory trinket was even fishier than the first version."

"That's what I thought, too—but what on earth do you suppose made him switch stories at this point?"

"Oh, I don't know—" Timothy's tone was vague. "Lots of things might have made him change his mind. Now, look, if you'll help me black out all my front teeth but one, I'll be all set."

And that was as much as I was to learn of what Timothy thought about Nicholas Brande. Just as we were taking a final look at ourselves in the mirror, however, Timothy volunteered another remark.

"I forgot to tell you," he said, "that I got a wireless this afternoon."

"Who from?"

"My darling pals at New York Headquarters. It was an answer to that information I wirelessed them last night about the late and Reverend Asa Shaw."

"Well—?" I bent closer to the mirror to arrange the folds of my draped gospel gown.

"Well, it turns out that there's no record of any government agent in China or any other place by the name of Shaw."

"Oh—" I swung around to face Timothy, "then—does that mean that Ned—"

"It means that Ned was a sucker," said Timothy shortly. "And it also means that we'll be late for dinner if we don't hurry up. The last gong rang ages ago."

Dinner, with everyone in costume except Mrs. Shaw, was more of a success than I had expected. Sally and Ned

Covell, strapped together as the Siamese Twins inside of Mrs. Hertz's skirt, provided a good deal of amusement by their struggles to eat while sitting back to back on one chair, while Mr. Brande, in surgeon's gown, had to lift his gauze mask for each mouthful of food. Dr. Sloane, with golden curls and a black velvet jacket, made an excellent Lord Fauntleroy, and Tod Hutten, in a slinky black satin gown borrowed from Sally and a blonde wig made of straw, was entirely devastating as Greta Garbo. But it was Mrs. Hertz who quite carried off the honors in her Dresden Shepherdess costume—and later, when we had adjourned to the ballroom for the grand march, Mrs. Shaw and I were rewarded for our afternoon's work when the Shepherdess, leading Haile Selassie as a noticeably reluctant lamb, marched up to claim first prize for her costume.

Just before the concert program began, Mrs. Shaw slipped away from her place next to me. She whispered, a trifle regretfully, that she scarcely felt right about staying for the party—and not even the prospect of hearing Mrs. Hertz sing could induce her to change her mind. But the rest of our group applauded and cheered loyally when the Dresden Shepherdess, quite flushed with triumph, rendered *At Dawning* in a deep contralto voice embellished with a tasteful tremolo. It was a flawless performance save only for the persistent efforts of Haile Selassie to squirm out of the Shepherdess' grip and rush back to Sally and Ned in the front row.

The high spot of the concert was the big love scene from *Grand Hotel* played by Tod Hutten in the role of Garbo, and Timothy, still wearing his Gandhi towels, as the most ardent of Barrymores. They were called back for bow after bow by the quite hysterical audience, and the applause continued even after Timothy had returned to his place beside me.

It was during the intermission, which followed an appeal by Captain Cobb on behalf of the Disabled Seamen's Fund, that Timothy's eye happened to light on the large Bible in my lap. He reached over to take it, and examined the worn, dark binding curiously.

"Where on earth did you dig up this relic?" he inquired.

I explained that it had been loaned to me out of deference to the late Mr. Shaw's admiration for Aimée Semple McPherson.

Timothy opened the volume and began to turn idly through the pages, pausing here and there to read a penciled notation in the margin. I had become quite engrossed in the gossipy conversation of two women sitting behind me, when a sudden exclamation from Timothy made me turn toward him. He was frowning over a page of Scripture, and the next moment he dug me violently in the ribs and pointed to an underscored passage.

"Look—" he said, "did you ever see that before?"

For a moment I stared blankly at the verse:

> *"It was planted in a good soil by great waters, that it might bring forth branches, and that it might bear fruit, that it might be a goodly vine."*

And then suddenly something clicked in my mind.

"That Gideon Bible—" I whispered excitedly, "the one we saw in Mr. Norman's room—the very same verse was underlined."

Timothy nodded quickly. From somewhere in the back of the Bible he lifted out a slip of notations, Chapter and Verse. The list was headed "Sermon notes, July 14."

I pointed to the date. "That's only three days before we sailed from Shanghai, Timothy."

He nodded again. "Wait a minute now—we'll see—" He read the first notation: "*Ezekiel* 8:2—now just a second—" he thumbed the flimsy india paper pages with clumsy haste, "Where the hell is *Ezekiel* . . . Oh, here—" He found Chapter 8, second verse, and together we scanned the words:

*"Then I beheld, and, lo, a likeness as the appearance of fire: from the appearance of his loins even downward, fire; and from his loins even upward, as the appearance of brightness, as the color of amber."*

*"Good jumping Judas*—" Timothy exclaimed under his breath, "that's *it!*" He slapped the book shut and got up. "Look, Joan," he said, "you wait here. I've got to go see—" he stopped short and never finished the sentence—for at that very instant there was a sudden commotion at the back of the ballroom, and a woman's scream, long-drawn and piercing, cut like a knife through the hum of laughter and talk.

There was an instant of frozen silence, and we turned to see a stewardess standing in the open door. Her voice rose again and echoed through the room.

*"Help*—someone—quickly," the words rang out desperately, "there's a woman out here—trying to jump overboard. I can't stop her—someone—"

For one moment more everyone seemed paralyzed—then there was a sudden rush for the doors. But Timothy was the quickest of all. With a single motion he had thrust the Bible into my hands and bounded out into the aisle and half-way across the floor. Gathering up my sheeted draperies, and clutching the Bible tightly, I followed him as quickly as I could. When at last I had pushed my way through, the milling crowd and reached the open deck, I saw with a sharp breath of relief that Timothy had been in time.

It was a curious tableau there in the warm, still darkness of the night. After the brightly-lighted ballroom, I could scarcely make out what was happening at first. Only two figures, both in white, were visible near the stern railing of the deck, outlined against the dim background of black water and a starless sky, as they struggled silently.

All around me everyone was talking at once, excitedly and incoherently. Now and then a woman would scream. Questions, asked of no one and answered by no one, sounded on every side. And then, quite suddenly, I was free of the crowd and running down the deck to Timothy's side.

When I got there, he had the woman in a firm grasp—her elbows pinned behind her back, and one long arm around her waist. But even so she struggled toward the rail—twisting and turning her slight body beneath the long, white coat she wore. For a moment I could not see who it was. Then, with one desperate lurch, she threw back her head—and I saw the white face of Mrs. Shaw, her eyes gleaming wildly in the darkness. One last time she lunged with failing strength toward the rail—and the next moment, without uttering a sound, she fell back limply in Timothy's arms and lay still.

For a few minutes everything was hectic. People crowded around, and the babble of questions rose again. Someone cried out close behind me, "My God—she's dead."

Then Timothy's voice answering quietly, "No—she's not dead—only fainted. Stand back, please."

From somewhere the little stewardess who had given the warning appeared, and standing close to Timothy, she gasped out the explanation.

"I saw her here by the railing—throwing something into the water. I came up, and when she saw me she screamed at me to stay away. Then she started to climb up on the rail—I tried to stop her, but she was too strong for me— she fought like—like a tiger. Then I ran for help—"

"It's all right," again Timothy's voice came quietly. "I got her just as she slipped over the side of the railing. Everything's all right now, she's quite safe—" He swung the light body up in his arms and turned away from the rail. "I'll take her down to the hospital at once. Will some-one please ask Dr. Sloane to follow me?"

There was a moment's hush as the crowd fell back to make room for him to pass. In the moonlight they looked strangely grotesque in their motley costumes, and every eye was fastened on the limp burden in Timothy's arms as he stepped quickly past them and disappeared through a lighted doorway into the ship.

# 18
# A PASSPORT

Mrs. Shaw lay on a narrow hospital bed, her body slight and motionless beneath the counterpane. The room was very quiet as we stood waiting, Dr. Sloane and Nurse Thompson on one side of the bed, Timothy and I on the other. All of us were watching Mrs. Shaw's face, so white and still against the pillow. The only sound was the distant throbbing of the ship's engine, and an occasional rustle of Miss Thompson's starched uniform as, from time to time, she bent over the patient with a bottle of ammonia spirits.

The minutes passed slowly, and still there was no sign of returning life. I saw Dr. Sloane frown slightly as he lifted Mrs. Shaw's limp wrist between his fingers, then he nodded to Miss Thompson, and again she leaned forward. The pungent fumes of ammonia drifted upward from the uncorked bottle. There was another minute of waiting— and then, ever so faintly, came a sigh that fluttered through the patient's half-open lips. Her eyelids quivered, and she turned her head on the pillow as though to avoid the light from the shaded bedside lamp. Miss Thompson moved the bottle gently.

"Look," said Timothy quietly, "hadn't you better take off the wig, doctor? If Mrs. Shaw wakes up and sees you . . ."

Dr. Sloane nodded unsmilingly. Without moving his eyes from the patient's face, he reached up and slipped off the blonde curls.

As though roused by the sound of Timothy's voice, Mrs. Shaw opened her eyes and looked straight into the face of Dr. Sloane. Her lips moved a little, but there was no sound—then she sighed once more. Miss Thompson murmured something to the doctor.

"Oh—" Mrs. Shaw breathed the word gently. She sounded weary and surprised. "Then I didn't—?" She left the question unfinished as Dr. Sloane spoke quickly.

"You're quite all right, Mrs. Shaw. It was just a matter of nerves—very natural, under the circumstances—"

"No," said Mrs. Shaw with surprising conviction, "no—it wasn't nerves." She shook her head, and then, as if exhausted by the effort, her eyes closed again. "They're gone," she said distinctly, "every one of them. Gone."

Above her head Timothy's glance met the doctor's, then Timothy bent down and spoke close to Mrs. Shaw's ear.

"What's gone?" his voice was urgent. "What do you mean, Mrs. Shaw?"

She stared at him quietly for a minute, then her glance shifted to me, and she frowned suddenly. "No," she said, "you've got some of them, Mrs. Fowler. You must get rid of them—right away—if they find out about them, you'll be arrested. I know—he told me so. Go get them and throw them away—in the ocean—like I did. Then they can't ever be found—but hurry—" Her voice grew stronger with anxiety, and she struggled to raise her head.

"No—no, you mustn't worry now, Mrs. Shaw," I reached out to ease her back against the pillow. "Everything will be all right—" But she only gripped my arm with icy hands, and went on more urgently than before.

"You don't understand—you think I'm just dreaming. But I'm *not*—you're in danger, I tell you. You've *got* to throw them away before they find out—"

"Throw what away, Mrs. Shaw?" Again Timothy's voice.

"The package I sent you," Mrs. Shaw answered him, but her pleading glance still rested on my face. "The—the incense. You remember?"

"Yes, of course I remember. But why—?"

Mrs. Shaw drew a deep breath. Her tongue flicked against her dry lips. "Because it's not really incense—I know now. He told me why my husband carried those packages—so carefully. Inside those tablets—the ones on the bottom row—there are diamonds and pearls and everything hidden. He told me Asa hid them because they were stolen—and now that Asa is dead—*he* tried to take them. But I was too quick—I took every one and I threw them in the ocean where they'll *never* be found. Never. And no one can ever know," her voice rose in triumph, and then died away. "I would have gone, too," she said quietly, "only—"

Dr. Sloane leaned forward. "Mr. Fowler saved your life," he said.

For a moment Mrs. Shaw stared upward into Timothy's face. "I don't think I thank you very much," she said dully, "right now. Later—perhaps—" Her voice trailed away again.

"Never mind that," Timothy shook his head impatiently. "It was a stewardess who did the trick, anyway. But this man who told you about the jewels—who was he?"

Mrs. Shaw made an effort to rouse herself once more, but she seemed scarcely able to focus her mind on the question. "The man?" she murmured weakly. "Those things he said—about my husband—they're not true. Asa *couldn't*—I know—" her eyes were open again, pleading. "You mustn't believe those things—my husband was such a good man—"

"Yes, yes, I'm sure he was," said Timothy hastily, "but *who was the man?*"

Mrs. Shaw's lips moved, and Timothy bent close to catch the words—but no sound came. "Look here," he spoke quickly to the doctor, "isn't there some stimulant you can give her—just for a few moments?"

Dr. Sloane hesitated, catching his lip between his teeth. "I'd rather not disturb her, if you can wait—the shock's been pretty severe for her already—"

Timothy gave him one look, then he turned to Nurse Thompson. "Here," he put out his hand, "give me that bottle." Before she could protest, he had the ammonia spirits uncorked. As Mrs. Shaw breathed the sharp fumes, her eyelids fluttered—did not quite open—

There was a sudden sound at the door. A quick exclamation. We turned to see Mrs. Hertz, one hand pressed dramatically against her heart.

"Oh—" her voice breathed excitement and relief, "*Oh*— I'm *so* glad I've found you—Timothy, you must come a once—" she paused to gulp for breath. Her bosom heaved beneath the lace fissue, and the elegant shepherdess' wig had tumbled rakishly over one eye. She pushed it back with a trembling hand. "There's someone in my room, Timothy—locked in. I went to the door just now, and I couldn't open it—but I could hear someone inside, moving around. When he heard me rattle the knob he called out, 'Let me out of here, for God's sake.' I—I don't know how he ever came to be there, Timothy, but I—"

"Whose voice was it, Mrs. Hertz?" As he spoke, Timothy picked up a bathrobe someone had left on a chair, and slipped it on over his scanty costume.

"Well, I—" Mrs. Hertz paused uncertainly. "I couldn't be certain, Timothy—but it *sounded* like Mr. Brande. But whatever he could be doing locked up in my room—

"Good," Timothy nodded without surprise. "That saves me a lot of time. Now if you'll let me take your key, Mrs. Hertz, I'll see to your visitor." He moved toward the door, but paused as Mrs. Shaw spoke suddenly.

"It's—the man—" The words came faintly from her white lips. "I locked him in—careful—" Her voice faded and Mrs. Shaw lay still once more.

"All right," Timothy opened the door and spoke to me over his shoulder. "You, Joan, go get that package of incense and bring it straight to me—in Mrs. Hertz's room. And be quick about it. The rest of you stay here—" He took the key from the quivering hand of Mrs. Hertz, hitched the bathrobe closer about him, and was gone.

What with fumbling around in the suitcases, and the general suspense and excitement, it took me awhile to locate the package of incense. But when I had it safely in hand, and got up to B Deck, I saw that Timothy was just approaching the door of Mrs. Hertz's room. At Timothy's side was Captain Cobb, quite red of face and hurrying along as fast as his dignity would allow in an effort to keep up with Timothy's long strides.

I judged from the Captain's baffled expression that he had no very clear idea of why he had been summoned on this sudden errand, but Timothy wasted no time in explanations. He unlocked the door, and after one quick glance into the stateroom, he stood back and motioned for the Captain to enter.

"All right," said Timothy, "there's your man, Captain."

I stepped into the room behind the two men and closed the door, and I had just time to glance at Mr. Brande, seated on the edge of Mrs. Shaw's bed, before a sharp exclamation from Captain Cobb made me turn toward him.

"I—why, good Lord—it's Mr. Brande," the Captain sounded both astonished and angry.

"You're darned right, it's Mr. Brande," said Timothy with a touch of grimness.

"But, look here, Fowler—I thought you said we'd find the man here who tried to steal the necklace—"

"So I did," said Timothy, still grimly.

The Captain's flush of anger deepened. "But, my God, man—that's impossible. Why—you don't know what you're talking about!" He drew himself up and took a somewhat calmer tone. "Am I to understand, Mr. Fowler, that you brought me here because for some insane reason you locked up Mr. Brande in this room?" Before Timothy had a chance to answer, the Captain turned to Mr. Brande and addressed him anxiously, almost pleadingly. "I can only offer you the most sincere apology, Mr. Brande. Whatever has happened has been, I assure you, a mistake on the part of Inspector Fowler. A most *unfortunate* mistake—"

"If there's been a mistake, Captain," Timothy's voice cut in coolly, "it wasn't mine, but Mrs. Shaw's. It was Mrs. Shaw who locked Mr. Brande in here—for the very good reason that he was attempting to steal some property belonging to her. An amber necklace, to be exact. And, in addition to that, Mr. Brande made certain statements concerning the late Mr. Shaw which I would like very much to have more fully explained. I suggest you use your authority, Captain, to ask Mr. Brande to make those explanations . . ."

"*Mr. Fowler—*" The Captain's deep voice was a bellow of rage, "I shall use my authority to order you to be quiet! You must realize that what you are saying is utterly preposterous as well as insulting. Mr. Brande is—"

"Never mind that, Captain." It was Brande himself who spoke for the first time, and we all turned to look at him.

Still seated on the bed, Mr. Brande had neither moved nor glanced up since we entered. He simply sat there,

hunched over and staring disconsolately at his hands which
lay folded in his lap. He seemed, somehow, a strangely
different Nicholas Brande. Gone was the poise, the assurance, the air of studied elegance. This was just an elderly
and rather tired-looking man.

We waited for Mr. Brande to go on speaking, but he said
nothing. After a moment, the Captain cleared his throat.

"I—ah, am not at liberty to reveal Mr. Brande's identity to you, Mr. Fowler," said the Captain stiffly, "but I
must ask you to accept my assurance that any accusation
you make against him is completely false—and I suggest
that you apologize to Mr. Brande and end this—this mis-
understanding at once."

Timothy made no move to follow the Captain's advice.
Instead, he crossed to the desk chair and sat down.

"No apologies are necessary, Captain." Again Nicholas
Brande spoke without looking up, and his voice sounded
curiously hopeless. "What Inspector Fowler thinks is quite
natural under the circumstances."

"You're damned right it's natural," said Timothy firmly.
"And what Mr. Brande's name may or may not be doesn't
alter those circumstances in the slightest. His name can be
Herbert Hoover, for all I care—but this is far too serious
a matter to stand on ceremony—"

"*Fowler*—" Once more the Captain's face darkened dangerously, "Kindly remember that I am in charge here, and
that I have ordered you to stop this. You can't possibly
know what you are saying—but I am forced to tell you
that you are being a fool—and a very meddlesome fool—"
He stopped short as Nicholas Brande looked up suddenly.

There was a moment of silence, then Mr. Brande rose
from the bed and walked over to where Timothy sat. From
his pocket he drew out a passport and handed it over.

"Ezry is the name," said Nicholas Brande distinctly. "J. T. Ezry." And without another word, he went back to the bed and sat down again.

I looked at Timothy, and for once in his life, I saw him completely and entirely astonished. He stared at the passport in his hand, then at Brande, then at the Captain's expression of righteous triumph, then back at the passport in his hand.

"Well, I'll be damned," said Timothy. His voice was scarcely more than a whisper.

Captain Cobb cleared his throat. "Now perhaps you see, Mr. Fowler, why this ridiculous performance can go no further. With your permission, Mr. Ezry, I think we can close the incident and say no more about it . . ."

"Not quite yet, I'm afraid, Captain," said Mr. Ezry quietly. "I've told Inspector Fowler this much—I think he's entitled to the rest of the story. He might be interested in knowing, for instance, that I *did* come to this room tonight after the amber necklace. It wasn't my intention to steal it, however, but only to examine it. And Mr. Fowler might also like to know that the necklace was originally mine; that I bought it from a street peddler in Shanghai a few days before we sailed; that I paid exactly two dollars and twenty cents for it; and that it was I, and not the late Mr. Norman, who gave the necklace to Mrs. Hertz. Does that clear things up a bit for you, Mr. Fowler?"

Timothy swallowed. "A bit—yes," he nodded slowly. "But there are still some things I'm afraid I don't see—"

"There are some things I don't see, either, Mr. Fowler," said Ezry. "I did my best to find out about them—but it seems that I'm not particularly good at that sort of thing. I made one attempt last Tuesday night in Mrs. Hertz's stateroom, but Mr. Shaw got there ahead of me. Tonight I made another attempt here—and this time Mrs. Shaw was too quick for me. If you want to have a try at it, Inspector, you'll have to get the necklace from Mrs. Shaw—"

"Sorry," said Timothy, "but I'm afraid that's impossible. Even if she wanted to, Mrs. Shaw couldn't show me the necklace now."

Mr. Ezry looked up sharply. "What do you mean, Fowler?"

"I mean," said Timothy, "that Mrs. Shaw threw that necklace into the ocean—along with all the other evidence you discovered against her late husband." Then, as Ezry dropped his head on his hands with a gesture of utter weariness, Timothy turned to me. "Let's have that incense, Joan." He took the box from my hand, opened it and lifted out the top layer of small brown pellets. From the second layer he took several tablets, placed them on the desk, and crumbled them with the point of a pencil. A moment later he held up some small, dust-coated stones, and rubbed them clean against his bathrobe. In the lamp light I could see the sparkle of green.

"Emeralds," said Timothy. "Is that what you found in the other boxes of incense, Mr. Ezry?"

"Yes." Mr. Ezry did not raise his head from his hands, but Captain Cobb started forward with interest and took one of the dusty green stones from Timothy.

"Emeralds—*by Jove!* Does that mean that old Shaw was actually a smuggler, Mr. Fowler?" His recent animosity toward Timothy appeared to be quite forgotten.

"A smuggler," said Timothy, "and likewise a thief. Am I right, Mr. Ezry?"

"Oh—what does it matter?" Mr. Ezry's answer was a long-drawn sigh. "The necklace is gone—and Shaw is dead. What's the use of prying into questions that can never be answered?"

"Because," said Timothy quietly, "I think those questions can be answered. You know some things, and I know some things, and Mrs. Shaw knows some things—and if we put the three together—"

"But I tell you the necklace is *gone*—" Mr. Ezry shook his head stubbornly, "so what can it matter now whether we know things or not?"

"It still matters," said Timothy, "who killed Shaw, and who killed Mr. Norman—not to you, perhaps, but to the law. And it will be a whole lot simpler for the law, and for you, if we settle the thing now." He paused a moment, and still Mr. Ezry showed no signs of reacting. Then he shifted his tone. "Just for instance, Mr. Ezry, it might interest you to know *why* that amber necklace was worth so much trouble—"

Mr. Ezry glanced sharply at Timothy, then he turned away with a shrug of impatience. "Rubbish," he said. "What could you possibly know about that?"

"Well, for one thing," Timothy was undaunted. "I know that the beads weren't real amber. With your knowledge of jewels, of course, you realized that—"

Mr. Ezry looked up again, and this time he did not turn away. "Why—yes," he said slowly, "I was aware of that. But how did you—?"

"I'll tell you exactly how I know it, Mr. Ezry," Timothy hitched his chair closer, "if you'll tell me all you know. Is it a deal?"

"Yes—yes, of course," Mr. Ezry brushed aside the question hastily. "But, look here, Fowler—if the stuff wasn't real amber, then *what could have been so valuable about it?*"

Timothy did not answer the question. Instead, he turned to me. "Joan, where's that Bible you were carrying tonight?"

"Down in our room," I said. "Do you want me to get it?"

Timothy nodded. "And while you're down there, you might stop in the hospital and ask Nurse Thompson how soon we can have a talk with Mrs. Shaw?"

When I came back with the Bible, I handed it to Timothy. He drew out the slip of paper labelled "Sermon notes, July 14," and laid it on the desk.

"There," said Timothy, "is the answer to your question about the amber necklace, Mr. Ezry."

Mr. Ezry rose and came over to the desk. He stood between Captain Cobb and me, and for a minute the three of us stared at the list of chapter and verse notations in puzzled silence.

"Exodus 28:18
Exodus 40:34
Genesis 4:8
Ezekiel 8:2
Ezekiel 17:8
Genesis 4:8
Zechariah 3:2
Psalms 90:4
Matthew 11:12
Acts 26:3
Job 17:11"

"Well—" the Captain was the first to speak, "this is all very fine, Mr. Fowler, but what difference can it possibly make to us what texts the late Mr. Shaw chose to preach on?"

"Because," said Timothy, "the late Mr. Shaw chose his texts to far more purpose than most missionaries. You may notice, Captain, a list of numbers here at the bottom of the page—" he pointed to a row of numerals, and again we all bent to examine the slip.

"13, 4, 4, 37, 3, 4, 26, 19, 9, 11, 4"

"I still don't see it, Fowler," the Captain drew back again and shook his head. "Looks like a lot of aimless scribbling to me—"

"Hold on a minute, Captain," Mr. Ezry spoke suddenly. "Look here, there are eleven of those numbers—and eleven of the references in the list above. Isn't it possible that they tally in some sort of a—ah—a code system?"

"Right you are, Mr. Ezry," said Timothy. "The numbers tell you which word in the verse is important—and just to save you the trouble of looking up the message for yourselves—here it is, already worked out." From the pocket of his bathrobe, Timothy drew a small memorandum. "There's the message, Mr. Ezry—I figured it out down in the hospital while we were waiting for Mrs. Shaw to wake up. Reading down the list of references, the words are these: *Diamonds covered with amber planted with brand watch until customs passed.* I assumed, of course, that 'brand' refers to your incognito of Brande, Mr. Ezry. If I'm right, then the message would read: *Diamonds planted with Brande. Watch until customs passed.* That means that Mr. Shaw's accomplice was sending him a message indicating a plan for getting the diamond necklace transported to America, and taken safely through the customs—after which—"

"*Diamond necklace*—" Mr. Ezry seized upon the words.

"Good God, Fowler, is it possible that the thing I bought for two dollars and twenty cents could have been—"

"Could have been, and *was*," Timothy cut him short. "In other words, Mr. Ezry, you were being used as a dupe by a pair of clever smugglers—damned clever, in fact. Their little plan was as slick a one as I've seen in a long while—but, like many another slick plan, it was spoiled by a disagreement between the planners. If Mr. Norman hadn't tried to double-cross Shaw—"

"Wait a minute," the Captain frowned. "What's Norman got to do with this thing?"

"Oh—" Timothy waved his hand casually. "I forgot to mention that Norman was the accomplice—the partner who sent this message to Shaw." He tapped the memorandum in his hand.

"How can you be certain of that?" The Captain's frown deepened. "Norman is dead, and Shaw—"

"Is dead," Timothy finished it calmly. "That's the very point I'm trying to make in my roundabout way. Don't take my word for it, though," he rose and faced the two men. "The person who can really tell us what's what, is Mrs. Shaw—and according to Joan, she's wide-awake now, and ready to talk. So I suggest, Captain, that we go down to the Hospital and hear what she has to say. After that, I can add my piece, and Mr. Ezry can add his piece—and with a little imagination to fill in the chinks, we'll have the whole story, and you, Captain Cobb, will have your mystery solved."

## 19
## FOUR AT A DESK

In spite of Timothy's optimism, it was getting on toward midnight that night before we had the various bits of the puzzle fitted together into something like a coherent pattern. First there was Mrs. Shaw to deal with—and it took all of Timothy's persuasive charms to worm out of her the amazing truth about the late Reverend Asa Shaw—missionary, thief, smuggler, and penitent. Then there were Mr. Ezry's actions to be explained, and Timothy's knowledge to be added to that. At last it was done, and we sat back, in the Captain's office—Timothy, Mr. Ezry, the Captain and I—and realized with weary relief that our story was complete.

It was a story that began more than twenty years ago, with a chance meeting between a young missionary named Asa Shaw and a certain Mr. Samuel Norman. It was in a restaurant in Shanghai that they met, quite casually, and fell into conversation. At that time Shaw had been in China for only a little more than a year—but in that short time he had already learned the bitterness of poverty and hardship. Worse than that, he had seen the heartbreaking futility of one small mission—struggling like a single flickering match-flame to light the dark strongholds of ignorance and custom. The young Shaw had flung his arrogant and spirited head against the immovable wall of indifference built by centuries of a civilization which had learned the wisdom of inertia and the hopelessness of hope—and the young Shaw had lost. He had seen his future stretch out before him, an endless battle to hold back the ocean of doubt with the sheer will of faith—and he had seen his faith swallowed up and lost in that dark ocean. He was ready to turn back, disillusioned forever, when he met Samuel Norman, in a small café in Shanghai.

Norman, not quite so young, was also new at his career; but he was not in the least discouraged. He was engaged in building up an elaborate and highly successful business which was built on the simple principle that all sorts of valuables, usually stolen goods, can be picked up for very little in the Orient—provided one knows the native merchants and traders—and smuggled into more (or less) civilized countries to be retailed at a handsome profit. All that stood between Norman and the complete success of his plan, was the necessity of acquiring a partner who would handle the native contacts angle, and at the same time serve as an impressive and apparently innocent front. For this dual purpose no one could have been more ideally suited than the Reverend Asa Shaw at that particular moment. Discouraged, disillusioned, desperate—but still retaining his title of Reverend and the rights, privileges and aura of unworldliness generally pertaining thereto—Shaw was indeed the perfect prospect for Samuel Norman.

The partnership was formed, apparently, on that very day and it endured for twenty years. Having agreed to act as scout, agent, buyer, and general undercover man in the business, the Reverend Shaw returned to his remote and crumbling little mission with such renewed courage

and zest that his wife thought a miracle indeed had been
wrought. An important part of the plan, of course, was to
have Shaw continue with his missionary work, both as a
shield of ultra-respectability, and as a means of contact-
ing those obscure sources of jewels, tapestries and other
valuables which are to be found among the truly provin-
cial Chinese merchants. Since Shaw's mission happened to
be in the northwest interior section of China, there was
a small but constant traffic in stolen or confiscated Russian jewelry which trickled across the border into China
and provided occasional high spots among the more ordinary run of unset gems and precious metals. At one time,
it seemed, a considerable portion of the Imperial Crown
jewels—melted up, reset, and otherwise disguised—were
acquired by Shaw after infinite haggling with a Chinese
war-lord merchant, duly passed on to Norman, and smuggled by him into France, where they were sold for a quite
fabulous sum to a certain prominent American family win-
tering on the Riviera.

(At this point in the story, I remembered the photograph Mrs. Shaw had showed me of her husband and the
ancient Chinese merchant—and I recalled what she had
told me about their many visits to the old man's stronghold until at last the Reverend Shaw had succeeded in
"converting" his prospect.)

And so, for years, the business partnership had pros-
pered. With an irony which Mr. Ezry seemed to find characteristic of life, it appeared that once Shaw had forsaken
the pure cause of good, his missionary work bloomed and
developed until his parish became famous for the number
and enthusiasm of its converts. Throughout the years, the
Reverend Shaw was able, somehow, to carry on his amazing dual career—and to do it so cleverly that even his own

wife remained ignorant of the true and considerable extent
of her husband's worldly estate. It had galled Shaw, apparently, to have to keep up the pretense of poverty in the
midst of riches—to see his wife scrimping along on missionary pay while his accounts in foreign banks fattened
and grew on the proceeds of his "exporting" business. But
he comforted himself by looking forward to the time when
he could retire from the mission work, and, having managed some story of a mythical inheritance to appease Mrs.
Shaw, establish himself in some byway of the world and
finish his life in a manner befitting his accumulated fortune. And meanwhile he knew that if he were to die before
that time, his wife would be left provided for by unexpected but abundant wealth.

Now, after more than twenty years of profitable partnership, Shaw and Norman had hit upon their greatest
piece of good fortune. But it was an enterprise so daring—so important—that the greatest care was necessary in
the actual details of its working. Some three weeks before
the sailing of the *Orion,* the partners had met in Shanghai to lay their plans. The object of the conference was a
certain necklace, strung of flawless and perfectly matched
diamonds, which Shaw had obtained through his longtime friend, the war-lord merchant. Pressed on the one
hand by the dangers of bandit tribes, and on the other by
the increasing vigilance of Chinese government officials,
the old merchant had been forced to abandon his mountain stronghold, and dispose of his accumulated treasures
as best he could. And to the lot of the Reverend Shaw
had fallen, among other lesser items, the superb diamond
necklace. With his experience in such matters, Shaw had
only to look at the necklace to realize its almost staggering
value. But with his sudden stroke of good fortune came

the necessity of some scheme, more cunning than he and Norman had ever evolved before, by which so spectacularly valuable a piece could be brought safely across the ocean and into the United States.

Together Norman and Shaw had planned and plotted until at last they hit upon a method by which they believed the thing could be accomplished. It was a scheme at once so simple and so bold that they were agreed to risk everything upon its success. And if it were to succeed, it would mean a profit greater than the whole accumulation of twenty years' work. The plan was to have someone else take the necklace to America for them. *Someone who had no possible knowledge of its value*—and who, if discovered, could not possibly implicate either Shaw or Norman.

And the man whom they selected as their unsuspecting accomplice was a man who had booked a modest passage on the *S.S. Orion,* under the name of Nicholas Brande.

It was necessary for Shaw to return to his mission to wind up his affairs there before sailing—and so the actual details of getting the necklace into the possession of Nicholas Brande were left to Mr. Norman. For days Norman traced the activities of Mr. Brande, and finally, on the Tuesday before the *Orion* sailed, he accomplished his purpose.

The necklace of diamonds, with a heavy layer of synthetic amber coating to cover each precious stone, had been transformed into a quite ordinary string of beads. Only the glitter of the central core of diamonds could not be disguised, and gave to the necklace a sparkling beauty which Norman counted on to catch the eye of his prospective buyer. An ordinary street peddler of trinkets and souvenirs was stationed by Norman in front of the hotel where Brande was staying, and the peddler was carefully coached in his task. He was to offer the necklace to Brande, and only Brande—and he was to sell it for whatever his customer was willing to pay. Within a day, the sale was accomplished. The man known as Nicholas Brande, probably attracted by the curiously bright beauty of the amber beads, and prompted by some mysterious collector's instinct, had purchased the necklace for the sum of two dollars and twenty cents.

So far, so good.

The Reverend Shaw reached Shanghai a day or two later, and received a communication from his partner in the Biblical code which they had adopted years before. That message was the one which Timothy had deciphered earlier in the evening: *"Diamonds covered with amber planted with Brande. Watch until customs passed."*

This much of the story we learned from Mrs. Shaw. She, in turn, had learned it from a letter written by her husband, and found after his death. It was a letter addressed to the Foreign Missions Board of Shaw's church, and in it he made a full confession of his business career.

The confession was evidently written on the last evening of Shaw's life—but there was no indication that he knew he was to die that night, nor at any other specific time. His revelation was apparently prompted by another motive entirely—the motive of repentance, pure and simple. It seemed that Shaw had experienced one of those curious psychological shifts—a sort of reversal of personality. His conscience, so long dormant, had suddenly rebelled beneath the weight of guilt and deception. The Reverend Shaw, after twenty years of deception, had reverted to his youthful piety and righteousness, and, in the very hour of his death, he had made his final gesture of atonement. *He had tried to return the diamond necklace to*

*Mrs. Hertz.* But death had overtaken him before he could accomplish his sacrifice.

It was not, however, merely the thought of his dishonest fortune which had driven Shaw to such lengths of remorse. There was another and far heavier load that burdened his conscience to the breaking point. The Reverend Shaw was a murderer.

The story of this last and boldest deed was told in the final section of Shaw's confession. It seemed that on the same day when he arrived in Shanghai and received his partner's message that the diamond necklace was safely disguised and entrusted to the unknowing care of Nicholas Brande, Shaw had been summoned to a certain café in Shanghai by the barkeep. This man had, for years, been one of Shaw's contacts in the business of locating and purchasing valuable and stolen goods. But this time the barkeep had a very different sort of message for Shaw. It was a message of warning—a warning that Shaw's life was in grave danger. Through a conversation overheard at his bar between Samuel Norman and one of his cronies, the barkeep had learned that Norman was planning, coolly and deliberately, to murder his partner during the voyage to America—and to collect the full sum from the eventual sale of the diamond necklace for his own.

Shaw had been completely stunned by the amazing news of his partner's treachery, but he was persuaded beyond any doubt that the threat against his life was an actual fact. That left Shaw with three possible choices. Either he could fail to embark on the *Orion,* and leave his partner to negotiate the reclaiming and sale of the necklace—in which case Shaw would most certainly never receive his share of the ultimate profit—or Shaw could board the *Orion* and take his chances on protecting his life from

Norman's threatened plan. Or—the third possibility—
Shaw could beat his partner at his own game of treachery.
And after hours of wretched indecision, Shaw had chosen
the final and most desperate way out. He resolved to save
his life and his fortune by killing Samuel Norman *before
Norman had a chance to rob him of those two things.*

Once decided on his course of action, Shaw set himself to think out the details of his plan. It was during this
time, while Shaw sat alone in the cafe the next afternoon,
pondering his daring plot, that he fell into conversation
with young Ned Covell. And before they had talked for
half an hour, Shaw realized that this lad was the very person he must have to help him carry through the plant.
Unquestionably it was Shaw's intention to use Ned merely
as a tool. He needed someone to help him gain possession
of the necklace again—and, more important, Ned was to
supply an alibi in case Shaw were implicated in the death
of his partner. It must have been evident to Shaw, from
Ned's ready acceptance of his far-fetched story, that the
boy was completely inexperienced in the sort of business
he was contemplating—and furthermore, it was plain that
Ned would do practically anything in order to earn a few
hundred dollars. Both of which qualifications made him
quite ideal from Shaw's point of view. And so the new
partnership was formed.

Once on board the *Orion,* Shaw lost no time in going to
work. His one thought was to accomplish the deed quickly—before Norman had a chance to get ahead of him—
and before his own resolution should have time to falter.
Being thoroughly familiar with the habits of his longtime
partner, Shaw was certain that Norman would be in his
room resting between four and six in the afternoon—
and he laid his plans accordingly. At four-thirty on the

Saturday we sailed, Shaw made absolutely certain that his partner was in his stateroom alone. Shaw then went to his own room, fetched the ivory paper-knife he had selected as a weapon, and returned to Norman's cabin. Under the circumstances, it was quite natural that he should visit his partner, ostensibly to discuss the details of the business about the necklace. During the conversation, Shaw waited his chance—and at a moment when the unsuspecting Norman turned his back and bent over the desk—presumably to take his medicine—Shaw drew the ivory knife from his pocket, and brought the weighted handle down upon his partner's bent head with all the force of desperation. It was done, Shaw said, in his confession, before he had time to realize what was happening—and the next instant he found himself looking down at the body of Samuel Norman, lying crumpled and lifeless at his feet.

It was probably in that very instant that the tide of remorse began to rise in the consciousness of Asa Shaw. But he, as yet, was not aware of it. Coolly—deliberately, he set about to cover his tracks.

First, Shaw left his partner's room without disturbing or touching anything, and he made certain that the door was left unlatched. Next he found Ned Covell, and delivered to him the ivory knife, bearing two small blood-stains, and directed Ned to go to Norman's room promptly at five-thirty, supposedly for the purpose of locating the amber necklace.

With Ned out of the way, Shaw proceeded with his carefully thought out alibi. He had already made arrangements with Dr. Sloane to give him the insulin treatments, and he arranged it so that he should be with the doctor, *in the doctor's own office,* at just five-thirty when Ned Covell would discover Norman's death. For it never occurred to

Shaw that Ned would not send for Dr. Sloane the moment he discovered what had happened to Norman.

But it was at that point that Shaw's plan hit the first snag. Instead of broadcasting the news of Norman's death, Ned confided it to Nicholas Brande—quite as he had told Timothy. And Brand; far from giving an alarm, had insisted on leaving the matter to be discovered by someone else. And here Mr. Ezry, alias Brande, took up the thread of the story.

Mr. Ezry repeated the episode of meeting Ned in the corridor just as the lad was leaving Norman's room that evening. He said that when Ned blurted out the fact that he had just found a man murdered, he took pity on the boy simply because he was so obviously and badly frightened. After sending Ned down to the bar, Mr. Ezry went into Norman's room and had a look around. It was plain, of course, that the man had been murdered—but why, or by whom, Mr. Ezry had no idea. The thing that really puzzled him, however, was the fact that Ned had come out of Norman's room with the ivory knife in his hand. Mr. Ezry was perfectly certain that the heavy carved handle of that knife had smashed the dead man's skull, and yet he was *equally certain that Ned Covell never killed the man*. In which case, there was only one answer that he could see. Somehow, for some reason, someone was trying to implicate Ned Covell in the death of Norman. Mr. Ezry's original impulse, therefore, was to help the lad out of what looked like an extremely serious jam.

In looking about Norman's room, however, Mr. Ezry saw something which made him suddenly change his plans. It was a small penciled memorandum which lay on the desk next to the note Norman had written to Mrs. Hertz, asking her to have cocktails with him. The memorandum

was simply a number: *123-E*—but it was a number which
was strangely significant to Mr. Ezry. For it was the number of his stateroom. It happened furthermore that earlier
in the afternoon, Mr. Ezry had overheard a conversation
between Mrs. Hertz and Norman on the subject of amber
necklaces—and as he stood there in the dead man's room,
pondering those three apparently unrelated things: the
note from Norman to Mrs. Hertz, the memorandum of Mr.
Ezry's stateroom number, and the conversation about an
amber necklace, Mr. Ezry thought he saw the meaning of
it all. He believed that Norman had somehow discovered
that Nicholas Brande, in room 123-E, was actually J. T.
Ezry—and that he had, in his possession, a certain amber
necklace. If, as Mr. Ezry guessed, Norman and Mrs. Hertz
were a team of clever thieves, it was not unlikely that they
would suppose that anything which J. T. Ezry was bringing home from the Orient would be of considerable value.
Therefore it seemed quite clear to Mr. Ezry that Norman
and Mrs. Hertz were planning to steal his necklace—and
although Norman was dead, Mrs. Hertz was undoubtedly
still alive. And Mr. Ezry resolved then and there to elimi-
nate himself from any further participation—unwilling or
otherwise—in a plot which had already included a murder.

Time was short, but Mr. Ezry acted quickly. Knowing
the amber necklace to be nothing more than an artificial
product, and believing it to be of no particular value, it
was obviously the best plan to get rid of the necklace.
Therefore, Mr. Ezry fetched it from his room, placed the
oblong box on Norman's desk, and—as a finishing touch—
he copied the late Mr. Norman's handwriting and penned
a neat little note, giving the beads to Mrs. Hertz. That
done, he disposed of the memorandum noting his cabin number, took the original note inviting Mrs. Hertz to

have cocktails with Mr. Norman, and went to find Ned
in the bar. Mr. Ezry gave the sealed letter to Ned, with
directions to deliver it at Mrs. Hertz's door and a strict
warning to say nothing of what he had seen in Norman's
room—and that was that.

Mr. Ezry felt a trifle shaken, but, on the whole, distinctly pleased with himself. He had a cognac, and then
went upstairs to Captain Cobb's quarters to attend to the
final detail of his plan. And that was to warn his friend the
Captain—who was, of course, the only person on board
aware of his incognito—that if any rumors concerning the
true identity of Nicholas Brande were to get abroad, the
Captain was to spike them promptly by a flat denial that
J. T. Ezry was aboard. After which, Mr. Ezry had himself
another cognac and went to dinner, confident that he was
well out of the whole affair—and quite forgetting, in his
complacent reflection, that he had overlooked one thing.
The carved ivory paper knife was, at that very moment, re-
posing on the desk of Captain Cobb, where, while he had
talked with the Captain, Mr. Ezry had left it.

But that oversight was not discovered by anyone until Timothy picked up the knife from the Captain's desk
three days later. In the meantime, Mr. Ezry said, he simply
sat back and watched developments, and felt quite certain
that whatever happened would not involve him any further. And perhaps, with the necklace now out of his possession, Mr. Ezry might *not* have been involved again, if
he had not chosen to interfere himself.

It was on Tuesday, the night Shaw was found dead in
Mrs. Hertz's room, that Mr. Ezry went into action again.
Having heard the story of the two attempts which had
been made the night before to steal the amber necklace
from Mrs. Hertz's room, Mr. Ezry became increasingly

curious about the mysterious attraction of the beads—and
he decided to do a little further detective work of his own.
He planned to get the necklace from Mrs. Hertz's room
that night, simply for the purpose of examining it more
carefully. But he dared not enter her room without having
someone stand watch for him outside. Obviously the person to help him was Ned Covell—for whom Mr. Ezry had
already done a considerable favor. Accordingly, Ned was
consulted, and after being reminded of his indebtedness
by Mr. Ezry, the lad finally agreed to assist with the plan.

At the time appointed, a few minutes before midnight
Tuesday night, Mr. Ezry went to Mrs. Hertz's room. He
found the door unlocked, and entered. But once inside,
every thought of the necklace fled from his mind. For
there on the floor before him lay the Reverend Asa Shaw.
Mr. Ezry did not know whether Shaw was living or dead—
and he did not wait to find out. He did not know, either,
that Ned had told Shaw of Mr. Ezry's intention to get hold
of the necklace that night, nor was he aware that Mrs.
Hertz had already given the beads to Shaw as a gift for his
wife. And no one knew, until the moment when Mrs. Shaw
told us the final chapter of her husband's confession, that
Shaw went to Mrs. Hertz's room that night—*not* to steal
the necklace, which already his, but to return it to
Mrs. Hertz.

It was here that Timothy took up the story.

"You see," he said, "when Shaw found that the necklace
had been left to Mrs. Hertz—after Norman's death—he
realized that he must somehow get possession of it at once.
He tried first to buy it from Mrs. Hertz and he damned near
succeeded with that clever sob story about saving up twenty-
five dollars to purchase a gift for his wife. When that
failed, he resorted to more direct means, and on Monday

night he made two trips to Mrs. Hertz's room—having first taken the precaution of swiping Dr. Sloane's uniform coat as a disguise. The first time he failed to get the necklace because Mrs. Hertz screamed and made a grab at his arm; and the second time, when he came better prepared, and made certain no one would scream by landing a good stiff blow on the head which occupied Mrs. Hertz's pillow—" Timothy rubbed his forehead reminiscently, "it was still no go, because that time the necklace wasn't in the room. Shaw did do one thing, however. He took the opportunity to look through the stuff in Mrs. Hertz's desk—hoping, no doubt, to find that message that left the necklace to her. I expect Shaw was pretty keen to know who had interfered with his carefully laid plans, and gummed things up by forging the note that gave the beads to Mrs. Hertz.

"Anyway, having failed again to get the necklace, Shaw was resting on his oars the next day, probably looking up some new plan to get the beads. It was that evening that Mrs. Hertz came to Shaw and surprised him by handing over the beads, saying that she had reconsidered, and wanted him to accept them as a gift for his wife.

"Well—that ought to have settled the matter then and there. Shaw had the necklace, and no questions asked—but you never can tell about a missionary—" Timothy shook his head. "Whether it was the unsuspecting kindness of Mrs. Hertz that upset Shaw—or just a plain case of the jitters—"

"According to his own confession," said Captain Cobb, "it was the voice of God that spoke to Mr. Shaw—and warned him to repent before it was too late."

Timothy looked at the Captain. "Well—stranger things have happened," he said. "At any rate, whatever the provocation—he repented, and repented thoroughly. He must have spent a couple of hours in the writing-room, pouring out his life story for the Missions Board. And then, as his big gesture, he took the necklace and went to Mrs. Hertz's room—planning to return it to her. It must have been just as he got there that the acute illness overcame him. Dr. Sloane will tell you that's the way insulin acts in an overdose—a sudden attack, precisely like a heart attack, coming some hours after the dose has been injected—"

"Wait a minute, Mr. Fowler," Mr. Ezry leaned forward earnestly. "Mightn't it have been the fact that Shaw was anticipating his death which prompted his repentance? He may have been warned, perhaps . . ."

"I hardly think so, Mr. Ezry," Timothy answered slowly. "You see, the man that Shaw had reason to fear was dead. Dead two days before, by Shaw's own hand—"

"Norman was dead, yes," Mr. Ezry nodded. "But there must have been somebody else. The person who was responsible for the overdose of insulin—"

"There was no one else, Mr. Ezry," again Timothy spoke deliberately.

It took a moment for Timothy's meaning to register— then the Captain brought his fist sharply down on the desk. "Good God, Fowler—is it possible that you're saying that Samuel Norman was responsible for Shaw's death?"

"That's precisely what I'm saying, Captain. You remember that when the Shanghai barkeep warned Shaw that his partner was plotting to kill him, he didn't say how the thing was to be done. Shaw figured, quite naturally, that if he got to Norman *before* Norman had a chance to strike first—he was safe. And he would have been—but actually, at the moment when Shaw killed Samuel Norman, *Norman had already murdered Shaw* by substituting a fatal overdose of insulin for one of the regular ampoules in the package from which Shaw was getting his daily injections. And so you see, quickly as Shaw acted—he was still not quick enough, and the fate that Norman had planned for him overtook him just as surely as though Norman had still been alive. It just goes to show, I suppose, that the living can't always be safe from the dead."

There was a moment's pause, then Timothy got up and poured himself a drink. "I guess that finishes our story," he said, "except for two more points. First, if you don't mind, I'd like to know whose idea it was to tip me off that the late Samuel Norman was really J. T. Ezry?" He looked at the two men before him.

Mr. Ezry shook his head. "*I* didn't know a thing about it, Inspector."

"I see," said Timothy.

The Captain cleared his throat. "I—I think I ought to say, Mr. Fowler, that I didn't intend to deliberately mislead you. My intention was simply to—ah, put an end to the rumors that were circulating among the passengers. Then, too, I was making every effort to protect Mr. Ezry himself . . ."

"I see," said Timothy, a trifle more dryly this time. "Well—now that that point is explained, there's just one thing left. Mr. Ezry's visit to Mrs. Shaw's room tonight." He turned to Ezry. "When did the idea of that visit occur to you, Mr. Ezry?"

"Last night at dinner," said Mr. Ezry. "It was something your wife said that gave me the notion. She mentioned the subject of incense, and in the course of the conversation that followed, Mrs. Shaw said that her husband had a good deal of the stuff packed away in his luggage. I—well, it was doubtless very stupid of me, Inspector, but that was the first time it occurred to me that Shaw might have been in the smuggling business. I remembered hearing some years ago of a chap who used incense pellets as a way to conceal unset jewels—and the more I thought about it, the more curious I was to have a look at those packages of incense that Shaw had been taking home, I still didn't know where the amber necklace fitted into the picture—but I thought that if I could establish the fact that Shaw had been in some sort of a smuggling racket, it might give me a clue to the rest of the story.

"Well—I waited my chance, and tonight, while the concert was going on, seemed a good time to have a look. I never dreamed, of course, that Mrs. Shaw would decide to come back to her room before the concert was over—but she did, and there I was—" Mr. Ezry spread his hands expressively, "caught red-handed, so to speak, with the incense and jewels spread all around. Mrs. Shaw jumped at the conclusion that I was trying to rob her—and in an effort to explain my position, I was forced to tell her that it was her husband and not I who was the dishonest one. Then I asked her if she'd let me have one more look at her necklace—to see if I couldn't find out once and for all what the secret of its value might be—but that was the greatest mistake of all." Mr. Ezry shook his head ruefully. "Before I had time to stop her, or even to protest, she snatched up necklace, incense, jewels and all—and was out of the room like a flash. I got to the door just as she slammed it shut and locked me in from the outside. The only thing I heard Mrs. Shaw say, through the door, was that she would put those jewels away where no one should ever see them again . . ." Mr. Ezry shrugged. "And that was all, until you came to my rescue, Inspector."

Timothy finished his drink and put the glass down.

"I guess that's all for any of us," he said. "You've got no arrests to make, Captain—for your two murderers have already taken care of each other. As for the necklace— well, Mrs. Shaw was right. No one will ever see it again . . ." He paused as Mr. Ezry passed his hand across his eyes and sighed. "That's a tough break for you, Mr. Ezry," Timothy said, "but, after all, I suppose there are more necklaces where that one came from."

"Not many more like that one," Mr. Ezry shook his head wearily. "Mr. Shaw and Mr. Norman were quite right in staking as much as they did on it. Unless I'm mistaken, they had hold of the original Catherina necklace. It was one of the finest pieces among the Russian Crown jewels. It's been missing for years, even though it's known to collectors all over the world. I'd have given a good deal just to look at the thing—and to think that I actually owned it, and then *gave it away*— " Mr. Ezry broke off with a bitter laugh. "It's not so much the value of the necklace I mind losing, you know. Money's never meant anything special to me, just for its own sake— probably because I've always had too much of it. Luxury and comfort, and all the things that money means to most people are nothing to me. I understand it's very eccentric of me, but I've always preferred to live simply—almost frugally— " He stopped again and looked from Timothy to me with a curious twisted smile. "I don't need to tell you and Mrs. Fowler how simply I live," he said. "No doubt you found it very amusing that I prefer to do my own laundry, and press my clothes. Well—no matter about that now. No matter about anything, except that our story is ended, and the beautiful Catherina diamonds are gone forever."

"Gone forev—" Timothy tried to echo the words sympathetically, but a sudden yawn stopped him.

The Captain started to clear his throat, but he too was caught by an unexpected yawn. "Well—I expect the best thing for us all would be a bit of sleep," he said.

On the way down to our room, Timothy and I stepped out onto the deserted deck for a breath of air. A cool night wind was blowing, and I shivered a little as we walked over to the rail. Looking down at the water, I stood quite still for a moment, thinking of the strange ending to our strange story—and as I listened to the soft swish of waves against the side of the boat, I thought of the diamond necklace, somewhere, miles behind us, drifting down and down through the silence of black water.

# 20
## CONCLUSION

Our story was not, after all, quite ended.

On the morning when we landed in San Francisco I stood on the dock, surrounded by luggage, waiting my turn at the customs and listening to the oddly disjointed fragments of conversation all about me.

". . . certainly very pleasant meeting you and your good husband . . ."

". . . ever come to Minneapolis . . . fail to look us up . . ."

". . . camera . . ."

". . . sister's address on this card . . . if you should ever be passing through New York . . . she'll be delighted . . ."

". . . and good luck . . ."

". . . some of those snapshots . . . if they turn out . . ."

". . . well . . ."

". . . meet again sometime . . ."

". . . Mediterranean cruise next winter . . ."

". . . that tan suitcase . . . I told the steward expressly . . ."

". . . so nice knowing you . . . good-bye . . ."

". . . good-bye . . ."

Suddenly I was aware of a commotion over at one side of the dock. Several customs officials were gathered around, all talking at once—but I failed to see who it was that they

were addressing. While I hesitated, wondering whether I
dare leave the luggage to go and find out, someone tapped
my arm, and I turned to see Mrs. Hertz at my elbow.

"Oh, Joan," she said, "isn't it just too *awful* about the
necklace? I simply *can't* believe it—I mean, he seemed like
such a fine young man—and so clever, too—"

I stared blankly at Mrs. Hertz's flushed face.

"What *are* you talking about?" I asked. "Who seemed
like a fine young man?"

"Why, Joan—haven't you *heard?*" Mrs. Hertz's bosom
heaved with excitement. "They've found the necklace. He
was trying to smuggle it in, they say—but he found it just
in time—"

"Mrs. Hertz—who is *he?*"

"Ned. Ned Covell—"

"*Ned Covell*—trying to smuggle in the necklace—?"

"No, *no,* dear—it was Ned who *found* the necklace. Tod
Hutten was bringing it in. They say he had the beads all
unstrung and hidden inside some oranges. The customs
inspector would never have found them if Ned hadn't come
along and started to eat one of the oranges . . ."

"But, Mrs. Hertz—how *could* he? Mrs. Shaw threw that
necklace into the ocean five days ago . . ."

"No, dear, she *didn't,*" said Mrs. Hertz patiently. "She
just *thought* she did. She was all upset that night, you
know—almost hysterical, you might say—and she didn't
know *what* she was doing. She tried to throw the beads
in—but somehow or other, she must have dropped them
in that gutter on the deck, or something. Anyway, that
Tod Hutten found them—and, would you believe it, he
never said one word. Just hid them away, and then tried to
smuggle them into the country. Why—it's just the same as

stealing. Worse, in a way," Mrs. Hertz nodded indignantly. "And to think of his being a Yale man? It just goes to prove what Mr. Hertz is always saying about colleges . . ."

"Well—but how marvelous for Ned—" I said suddenly. "I mean—I suppose he gets a reward, doesn't he?"

"Oh, my goodness, yes," Mrs. Hertz nodded emphatically. "And do you know, Mr. Ezry stepped right up the minute he'd heard the necklace was found, and he took out a pen-knife and started scraping off the amber coating. *My*—you ought to see the diamonds that are inside, Joan. Why, they're as big as *that!* And Mr. Ezry was almost crying, he was so excited. Of course, the beads really belong to Mrs. Shaw—and he told her right there in front of everybody that he'd like to buy them from her. He said he wouldn't name a price, though, until the necklace had been valued. Now wasn't that sweet of him? You know, Joan, I think we kind of misjudged Mr. Ezry—or anyway, I think he's a lot nicer as himself than he was when we thought he was Mr. Brande. Well, anyway, I do think it's just lovely about Mrs. Shaw getting all that money—and Ned, too. It reminds me of what Mr. Hertz always says about life coming out even in the end. Mrs. Shaw didn't get such a good husband—but now she'll have all the money. I suppose that's probably why I was sort of fated to give the necklace to her, because goodness knows I've had a happier life than hers . . ." Mrs. Hertz paused, and a wistful look came over her plump face.

"It's a shame," I said warmly, "that you didn't get something from the necklace. After all, it *was* yours—"

"Oh, but I *did* get something," Mrs. Hertz brightened at once. "Mr. Ezry was terribly nice about that. He wanted to give me half what he paid Mrs. Shaw for it—but, of course, I wouldn't hear of it—and so he said he was going to send me an amber necklace—*real* amber this time—the most beautiful one he could find."

"Well—that *was* nice of him."

"Wasn't it, though?" Mrs. Hertz beamed at me. "Of course, I don't quite know what Mr. Hertz will think about it—but then," she sighed cheerfully, "I don't have to think of that until I get to Paterson. Well—good-bye, Joan dear, and don't forget you and Timothy have promised to come down and spend a Sunday with us the very first chance you have after you get home. I just know Mr. Hertz is going to love you two—"

When Timothy came back he found me sitting on a suitcase, gazing up at the bow of the *Orion* that loomed high and black beside the dock. I gathered from his expression that I must have looked slightly forlorn.

"Tired?" he said.

"Not exactly," I shook my head. "Only I was just thinking—I suppose I ought to be glad the crossing's over, after all the dreadful things that have happened, but I'm not. As a matter of fact, I feel a little sorry to be saying good-bye to the *Orion*—"

Timothy grinned down at me. "Do you know," he said, "I think you're going to like being a detective's wife after all. What do you think?"

I stood up and linked my arm in his. "You're wrong, Inspector," I said. "I don't like it—I love it! And if that makes a heartless brute of me—"

"Then I hope," Timothy finished it for me, "that you'll go right on being a heartless brute!"

He got his wish. I still love it.

COACHWHIP PUBLICATIONS
CoachwhipBooks.com

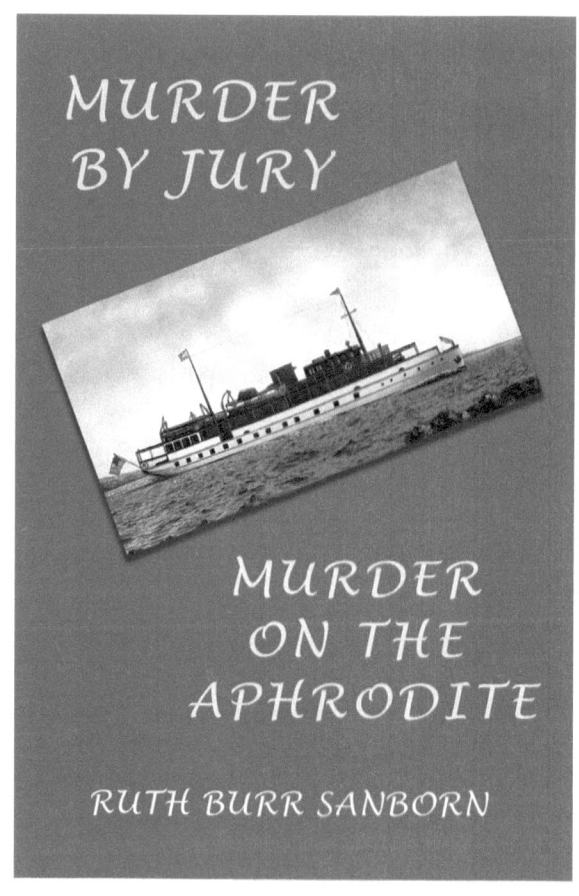

MURDER
BY JURY

MURDER
ON THE
APHRODITE

RUTH BURR SANBORN

# COACHWHIP PUBLICATIONS
## CoachwhipBooks.com

MURDER
À LA RICHELIEU
THE ADELAIDE ADAMS MYSTERIES
ANITA BLACKMON

COACHWHIP PUBLICATIONS
CoachwhipBooks.com

THE SERGEANT HARTY MYSTERIES

JOEL Y. DANE

MURDER CUM LAUDE

1

THE CABANA MURDERS

MURDER
A LA
MODE

*ELEANORE
KELLY
SELLARS*

*CLASSIC RED BADGE PRIZE MYSTERY*

COACHWHIP PUBLICATIONS
CoachwhipBooks.com

THE
RUMBLE
MURDERS

Henry Ware Eliot, Jr.

## COACHWHIP PUBLICATIONS
### CoachwhipBooks.com

THE
BEACON HILL
MURDERS

THE
BACK BAY
MURDERS

THE ROGER SCARLETT MYSTERIES
VOL. 1

# COACHWHIP PUBLICATIONS
## CoachwhipBooks.com

THE STRAWSTACK
MURDER CASE
KIRKE
MECHEM

COACHWHIP PUBLICATIONS

CoachwhipBooks.com

THE
WEEK-END
MYSTERY

ROBERT A. SIMON

**COACHWHIP PUBLICATIONS**
CoachwhipBooks.com

THE INVISIBLE
BULLET

& Other Strange Cases of
Magnum, Scientific Consultant

MAX RITTENBERG

www.ingramcontent.com/pod-product-compliance
Lightning Source LLC
Chambersburg PA
CBHW030239030726
47493CB00023B/177